About the Authors

Hewitt has worked a variety of different jobs, drama teacher to editorial assistant to youth ...er, but writing romance is the best one yet. She writes women's fiction and all her stories celebrate healing and redemptive power of love. Kate lives a tiny village in the English Cotswolds with her band, five children, and an overly affectionate Golden Retriever.

ate Carlisle writes for Mills & Boon Desire and is also the *New York Times* bestselling author of the Bibliophile Mystery series for NAL. Kate spent twenty ears in television production before enrolling in law hool, where she turned to writing fiction as a lawful ay to kill off her professors. She eventually left law hool, but the urge to write has never left her. Kate and r husband live near the beach in Southern California here she was born and raised.

2002 **Janice Maynard** left a career as a teacher to rsue writing full-time. Her first love is creating sexy, aracter-driven, contemporary romance. She has written for Kensington and NAL, and is very happy to be part of the Mills & Boon family – a lifelong dream. Janice and her husband live in the shadow of the Great moky Mountains. They love to hike and travel. Visit er at www.JaniceMaynard.com

Tropical Temptation

Tropical Temptation: Exotic Affairs

KATE HEWITT

KATE CARLISLE

JANICE MAYNARD

MILLS & BOON

First Published in Great Britain 2020
By Mills & Boon, an imprint of HarperCollins*Publishers*
1 London Bridge Street, London, SE1 9GF

TROPICAL TEMPTATION: EXOTIC AFFAIRS © 2020
Harlequin Books S.A.

The Darkest of Secrets © 2012 Kate Hewitt
An Innocent in Paradise © 2011 Kathleen Beaver
Impossible to Resist © 2012 Janice Maynard

ISBN: 978-0-263-28146-0

MIX
Paper from
responsible sources
FSC® C007454

FSC
www.fsc.org

Printed and bound in Spain
by CPI, Barcelona

THE DARKEST OF SECRETS

KATE HEWITT

CHAPTER ONE

'OPEN it up.'

It had taken the better part of two days to reach this moment. Khalis Tannous stood back as the two highly skilled engineers he'd employed to open his father's steel vault finally eased the door off its hinges. They had used all their knowledge and skill trying to unlock the thing, but his father was too paranoid and the security too advanced. In the end they'd had to use the newest laser technology to cut straight through the steel.

Khalis had no idea what lay inside this vault; he hadn't even known the vault had existed, on the lowest floor of the compound on his father's private island. He'd already been through the rest of the facility and found enough evidence to see his father put in prison for life, if he were still alive.

'It's dark,' one of the engineers said. They'd propped the sawn-off door against a wall and the opening to the vault was black and formless.

Khalis gave a grim smile. 'Somehow I doubt there are windows in there.' What *was* in there he couldn't even guess. Treasure or trouble? His father had had a penchant for both. 'Give me a torch,' he said, and one was passed into his hand.

He flicked it on, took a step towards the darkness. He

could feel his hand slick on the torch, his heart beating far too hard. He was scared, which annoyed him, but then he knew enough about his father to brace himself for yet another tragic testament to the man's power and cruelty.

Another step, and the darkness enveloped him like velvet. He felt a thick carpet under his feet, breathed in the surprising scents of wood and furniture polish, and felt a flicker of relief—and curiosity. He lifted the torch and shone it around the vault. It was a surprisingly large space and fashioned like a gentleman's study, with elegant sofas and chairs, even a drinks table.

Yet somehow Khalis didn't think his father came down to a sealed underground vault just to relax with a tumbler of his best single malt. He saw a switch on the wall and flicked it on, bathing the room in electric light. His torch lay forgotten in his hand as he slowly turned in a circle, gazing first at the furniture and then at the walls.

And what they held…frame after frame, canvas after canvas. Some he recognised, others he didn't but he could guess. Khalis gazed at them all, felt a heaviness settle on him like a shroud. Yet another complication. Another testament to his father's many illegal activities.

'Mr Tannous?' one of the engineers asked uneasily from the outside hallway. Khalis knew his silence had gone on too long.

'It's fine,' he called back, even though it wasn't fine at all. It was amazing…and terrible. He stepped further into the room and saw another wood-panelled door in the back. With a flicker of foreboding, he went to it. It opened easily and he entered another smaller room. Only two paintings were in this tiny chamber, two paintings that made Khalis squint and step closer. If they were what he thought they were…

'Khalis?' his assistant, Eric, called, and Khalis came

out of the little room and closed the door. He switched off the light and stepped out of the vault. The two engineers and Eric all waited, their expressions both curious and concerned.

'Leave it,' he told the engineers, who had propped the enormous steel door against the wall. He felt the beginnings of a headache and gave a brisk nod. 'I'll deal with all this later.'

No one asked any questions, which was good since he had no intention of spreading the news of what was in that vault. He didn't yet trust the skeleton staff left on the compound since his father's death, all of them now in his employ. Anyone who had worked for his father had to be either desperate or completely without scruples. Neither option inspired trust. He nodded towards the engineers. 'You can go now. The helicopter will take you to Taormina.'

They nodded, and after Khalis disarmed the security system everyone headed into the lift that led to the floors above ground. Khalis felt tension snap through his body, but then he'd been tense for a week, ever since he'd left San Francisco for this godforsaken island, when he'd learned his father and brother had both died in a helicopter crash.

He hadn't seen either of them in fifteen years, hadn't had anything to do with Tannous Enterprises, his father's dynastic business empire. It was huge, powerful and corrupt to its core...and it was now in Khalis's possession. Considering his father had disowned him quite publicly when he'd walked away from it all at the age of twenty-one, his inheritance had come as a bit of a surprise.

Back in his father's office, which he'd now taken for his own, he let out a long, slow breath and raked his hands through his hair as he considered that vault. He'd spent the last week trying to familiarise himself with his father's many assets, and then attempt to determine just how illegal they were. The vault and its contents was yet another complication in this sprawling mess.

Outside, the Mediterranean Sea sparkled jewel-bright under a lemon sun, but the island felt far from a paradise to Khalis. It had been his childhood home, but it now felt like a prison. It wasn't the high walls topped with barbed wire and broken glass that entrapped him, but his memories. The disillusionment and despair he'd felt corroding his own soul, forcing him to leave. If he closed his eyes, he could picture Jamilah on the beach, her dark hair whipping around her face as she watched him leave for the last time, her aching heart reflected in her dark eyes.

Don't leave me here, Khalis.

I'll come back. I'll come back and save you from this place, Jamilah. I promise.

He pushed the memory away, as he had been doing for the last fifteen years. *Don't look back. Don't regret or even remember.* He'd made the only choice he could; he just hadn't foreseen the consequences.

'Khalis?'

Eric shut the door and waited for instructions. In his board shorts and T-shirt, he looked every inch the California beach bum, even here on Alhaja. His relaxed outfit and attitude hid a razor-sharp mind and an expertise in computers that rivalled Khalis's own.

'We need to fly an art appraiser out here as soon as possible,' Khalis said. 'Only the best, preferably someone with a specialisation in Renaissance paintings.'

Eric raised his eyebrows, looking both intrigued and impressed. 'What are you saying? The vault had *paintings*?'

'Yes. A lot of paintings. Paintings I think could be worth millions.' He sank into the chair behind his father's desk, gazed unseeingly at the list of assets he'd been going through. Real estate, technology, finance, politics. Tannous Enterprises had a dirty finger in every pie. How, Khalis wondered, not for the first time, did you take the reins of a company that was more feared than revered, and turn it into something honest? Something good?

You couldn't. He didn't even want to.

'Khalis?' Eric prompted.

'Contact an appraiser, fly him out here. Discreetly.'

'No problem. What are you going to do with the paintings once they're appraised?'

Khalis smiled grimly. 'Get rid of them.' He didn't want anything of his father's, and certainly not some priceless artwork that was undoubtedly stolen. 'And inform the law once we know what we're dealing with,' he added. 'Before we have Interpol crawling all over this place.'

Eric whistled softly. 'This is one hell of a mess, isn't it?'

Khalis pulled a sheaf of papers towards him. 'That,' he told his assistant and best friend, 'is a complete understatement.'

'I'll get on to the appraiser.'

'Good. The sooner the better—that open vault presents too much risk.'

'You don't actually think someone is going to steal something?' Eric asked, eyebrows raised. 'Where would they go?'

Khalis shrugged. 'People can be sly and deceptive. And I don't trust anyone.'

Eric gazed at him for a moment, his blue eyes narrowed shrewdly. 'This place really did a number on you, didn't it?'

Khalis just shrugged again. 'It was home,' he said, and turned back to his work. A few seconds later he heard the door click shut.

* * *

'Special project for La Gioconda.'

'So amusing,' Grace Turner said dryly. She swivelled in her chair to glance at David Sparling, her colleague at Axis Art Insurers and one of the world's top experts on Picasso forgeries. 'What is it?' she asked as he dangled a piece of paper in front of her eyes. She refused to attempt to snatch it. She smiled coolly instead, eyebrows raised.

'Ah, there's the smile,' David said, grinning himself. Grace had been dubbed La Gioconda—the Mona Lisa—when she'd first started at Axis, both for her cool smile and her expertise in Renaissance art. 'Urgent request came in to appraise a private collection. They want a specialist in Renaissance.'

'Really?' Her curiosity was piqued in spite of her determination to remain unmoved, or at least appear so.

'Really,' David said. He dangled the paper a bit closer. 'Aren't you just a teeny bit curious, Grace?'

Grace swivelled back to her computer and stared at the appraisal she'd been working on for a client's seventeenth century copy of a Caravaggio. It was good, but not that good. It wouldn't sell for as much as he'd hoped. 'No.'

David chuckled. 'Even when I tell you they'll fly the appraiser out to some private island in the Mediterranean, all expenses paid?'

'Naturally.' Private collections couldn't be moved easily. And most people were very private about their art. She paused, her fingers hovering over the keys of her computer. 'Do you know the collector?' There were only a handful of people in the entire world who owned significant collections of Renaissance paintings of real value, and most of them were extremely discreet…so discreet they didn't want appraisers or insurers looking in and seeing just what kind of art they had on their walls.

David shook his head. 'Too top secret for me. The boss wants to see you about it ASAP.'

'Why didn't you tell me?' she asked, and David just grinned. Pressing her lips together, she grabbed the print-out he'd been teasing her with and strode towards the office of Michel Latour, the CEO of Axis Art Insurers, her father's oldest friend and one of the most powerful men in the art world.

'You wanted to see me?'

Michel turned from the window that overlooked the Rue St Honoré in the 1st arrondissement of Paris. 'Close the door.' Grace obeyed and waited. 'You received the message?'

'A private collection with significant art from the Renaissance period to be appraised.' She shook her head slowly. 'I can think of less than half a dozen collectors who fit that description.'

'This is different.'

'How?'

Michel gave her a thin-lipped smile. 'Tannous.'

'Tannous?' She stared at him, disbelieving, her jaw dropping before she thought to snap it shut. 'Balkri Tannous?' Immoral—or perhaps amoral—businessman, and thought to be an obsessive art collector. No one knew what his art collection contained, or if it even existed. No one had ever seen it or even spoke of it. And yet the rumours flew every time a museum experienced a theft: a Klimt disappeared from a gallery in Boston, a Monet from the Louvre. Shocking, inexplicable, and yet the name Tannous was always darkly whispered around such heists. 'Wait,' Grace said slowly. 'Isn't he dead?'

'He died last week in a helicopter crash,' Michel confirmed. 'Suspicious, apparently. His son is making the enquiry.'

'I thought his son died in the crash.'

'His other son.'

Grace was silent. She had not known there was another son. 'Do you think he wants to sell the collection?' she finally asked.

'I'm not sure what he wants.' Michel moved to his desk, where a file folder lay open. He flipped through a few papers; Grace saw some scrawled notes about various heists. Tannous suspected behind every one, though no one could prove it.

'If he wanted to sell on the black market, he wouldn't have come to us.' There were plenty of shady appraisers who dealt in stolen goods and Axis was most assuredly not one of them.

'No,' Michel agreed thoughtfully. 'I do not think he intends to sell the collection on the black market.'

'You think he's going to donate it?' Grace heard the disbelief in her voice. 'The whole collection could be worth millions. Maybe even a billion dollars.'

'I don't think he needs money.'

'It doesn't have to be about need.' Michel just cocked his head, his lips curving in a half-smile. 'Who is he? I didn't even know Tannous had a second son.'

'You wouldn't. He left the Tannous fold when he was only twenty-one, after graduating from Cambridge with a First in mathematics. Started his own IT business in the States, and never looked back.'

'And his business in the U.S.? It's legitimate?'

'It appears to be.' He paused. 'The request is fairly urgent. He wishes the collection to be dealt with as soon as possible.'

'Why?'

'I can certainly appreciate why an honest businessman

would want to legally off-load a whole lot of stolen art quite quickly.'

'If he is honest.'

Michel shook his head, although there was a flicker of sympathy in his shrewd grey eyes. 'Cynicism doesn't suit you, Grace.'

'Neither did innocence.' She turned away, her mind roiling from Michel's revelations.

'You know you want to see what's in that vault,' Michel said softly.

Grace didn't answer for a moment. She couldn't deny the fact that she was curious, but she'd experienced and suffered too much not to hesitate. Resist. Temptation came in too many forms. 'He could just turn it all over to the police.'

'He might do so, after it's been appraised.'

'If it's a large collection, an appraisal could take months.'

'A proper one,' Michel agreed. 'But I believe he simply wants an experienced eye cast over the collection. It will have to be moved eventually.'

She shook her head. 'I don't like it. You don't know anything about this man.'

'I trust him,' Michel said simply. 'And I trust the fact that he went to the most legitimate source he could for appraisal.'

Grace said nothing. She didn't trust this Tannous man; of course she didn't. She didn't trust men full stop, and especially not wealthy and possibly corrupt tycoons. 'In any case,' Michel continued in that same mild tone, 'he wants the appraiser to fly to Alhaja Island—tonight.'

'Tonight?' Grace stared at her boss, mentor and one-time saviour. 'Why the rush?'

'Why not? I told you, holding onto all that art has to be an unappealing prospect. People are easily tempted.'

'I know,' Grace said softly, and regret flashed briefly in Michel's eyes.

'I didn't mean—'

'I know,' she said again, then shook her head. That brief flare of curiosity died out by decision. 'It's not something I can be involved with, Michel.' She took a deep breath, felt it sear her lungs. 'You know how careful I have to be.'

His eyes narrowed, mouth thinning. 'How long are you going to live your life enslaved to that—?'

'As long as I have to.' She turned away, not wanting Michel to see her expression, the pain she still couldn't hide, not even after four years. She was known by her colleagues to be cool, emotionless even, but it was no more than a carefully managed mask. Just thinking about Katerina made tears rise to her eyes and her soul twist inside her.

'Oh, *chérie*.' Michel sighed and glanced again at the file. 'I think this could be good for you.'

'*Good* for me—'

'Yes. You've been living your life like a church mouse, or a nun, I don't know which. Perhaps both.'

'Interesting analogies,' Grace said with a small smile. 'But I need to live a quiet life. You know that.'

'I know that you are my most experienced appraiser of Renaissance art, and I need you to fly to Alhaja Island—tonight.'

She turned to stare at him, saw the iron in his eyes. He wasn't going to back down. 'I can't—'

'You can, and you will. I might have been your father's oldest friend, but I am also your employer. I don't do favours, Grace. Not for you. Not for anyone.'

She knew that wasn't true. He'd done her a huge favour four years ago, when she'd been desperate and dying inside. When he'd offered her a job at Axis he had, in his own way, given her life again—or as much life as she could have, given her circumstances. 'You could go yourself,' she pointed out.

'I don't have the knowledge of that period that you do.'

'Michel—'

'I mean it, Grace.'

She swallowed. She could feel her heart beating inside her far too hard. 'If Loukas finds out—'

'What? You're just doing your job. Even he allows you that.'

'Still.' Nervously, she pleated her fingers together. She knew how high-octane the art world could be. Dealing with some of the finest and most expensive art in the world ignited people's passions—and possessiveness. She'd seen how a beautiful picture could poison desire, turn love into hate and beauty into ugliness. She'd lived it, and never wanted to again.

'It will all be very discreet, very safe. There's no reason for anyone even to know you are there.'

Alone on an island with the forgotten son of a corrupt and hated business tycoon? She didn't know much about Balkri Tannous, but she knew his type. She knew how ruthless, cruel and downright dangerous such a man could be. And she had no reason—yet—to believe his son would be any different.

'There will be a staff,' Michel reminded her. 'It's not as if you'd be completely alone.'

'I know that.' She took a deep breath and let it out slowly. 'How long would it take?'

'A week? It depends on what is required.'

'A *week*—'

'Enough.' Michel held up one hand. 'Enough. You will go. I insist on it, Grace. Your plane leaves in three hours.'

'Three hours? But I haven't even packed—'

'You have time.' He smiled, although his expression remained iron-like and shrewd. 'Don't forget a swimming costume. I hear the Mediterranean's nice this time of year. Khalis Tannous might give you some time off to swim.'

Khalis Tannous. The name sent a shiver of something—curiosity? Fear?—through her. What kind of man was he, the son of an undoubtedly unscrupulous or even evil man, yet who had chosen—either out of defiance or desperation—to go his own way at only twenty-one years old? And now that he was back, in control of an empire, what kind of man would he become?

'I don't intend to swim,' she said shortly. 'I intend to do the job as quickly as possible.'

'Well,' Michel said, smiling, 'you could try to enjoy yourself—for once.'

Grace just shook her head. She knew where that led, and she had no intention of *enjoying herself* ever again.

CHAPTER TWO

'THERE it is.'

Grace craned her neck to look out of the window of the helicopter that had picked her up in Sicily and was now taking her to Alhaja Island, no more than a rocky crescent-shaped speck in the distance, off the coast of Tunisia. She swallowed, discreetly wiped her hands along the sides of her beige silk trench coat and tried to staunch the flutter of nerves in her middle.

'Another ten minutes,' the pilot told her, and Grace leaned back in her seat, the whine of the propeller blades loud in her ears. She was uncomfortably aware that two of Khalis Tannous's family members had died in a helicopter crash just a little over a week ago, over these very waters. She did not wish to experience the same fate.

The pilot must have sensed something of her disquiet, for he glanced over at her and gave her what Grace supposed was meant to be a reassuring smile. 'Don't worry. It is very safe.'

'Right.' Grace closed her eyes as she felt the helicopter start to dip down. She might be one of the foremost appraisers of Renaissance art in Europe, but this was still far out of her professional experience. She mostly dealt with museums, inspecting and insuring paintings that hung on revered walls around the world. Her job took her to quiet back rooms and sterile laboratories, out of the public eye and away from scandal. Michel himself handled many private collections, dealt with the tricky and often tempestuous personalities that accompanied so much priceless art.

Yet this time he'd sent her. She opened her eyes, saw the ground seeming to swoop towards them. A strip of white sand beach, a rocky cove, a tangle of trees and, most noticeably of all, a high chain-link fence topped with two spiky strands of barbed wire and bits of broken glass. And Grace suspected that was the least of Tannous's security.

The helicopter touched down on the landing pad, where a black Jeep was already waiting. Her heart still thudding, Grace stepped out onto the tarmac. A slim man in a tie-dyed T-shirt and cut-off jeans stood there, his fair hair blowing in the sea breeze.

'Ms Turner? I'm Eric Poulson, assistant to Khalis Tannous. Welcome to Alhaja.'

Grace just nodded. He didn't look like what she'd expected, although she hadn't really thought of what a Tannous employee would look like. Certainly not a beach bum. He led her to the waiting Jeep, tossing her case in the back.

'Mr Tannous is expecting me?'

'Yes, you can refresh yourself and relax for a bit and he'll join you shortly.'

She prickled instinctively. She hated being told what to do. 'I thought this was urgent.'

He gave her a laughing glance. 'We're on a Mediterranean island, Ms Turner. What does urgent even mean?'

Grace frowned and said nothing. She didn't like the man's attitude. It was far from professional, and that was what she needed to be—always. Professional. Discreet.

Eric drove the Jeep down a pebbly road to the compound's main gates, a pair of armoured doors that looked incredibly forbidding. They opened seamlessly and silently and swung just as quietly shut behind the Jeep, yet Grace still felt them clang through her. Eric seemed relaxed, but then he obviously knew the security codes to those gates. She didn't. She had just become a prisoner. *Again.* Her heart raced and her palms dampened as nausea churned along with the memories inside her. Memories of feeling like a prisoner. *Being* a prisoner.

Why had she agreed to this?

Not just because Michel had insisted, she knew. Despite his tough talk, she could have refused. She didn't think Michel would actually fire her. No, she'd agreed because the desire to see Tannous's art collection—and see it, God willing, restored to museums—had been too strong to ignore. A temptation too great to resist.

And temptation was, unfortunately, something she knew all about.

As Grace slid out of the Jeep, she looked around slowly. The compound was an ugly thing of concrete, like a huge bunker, but the gardens surrounding it were lovely and lush, and she inhaled the scent of bougainvillea on the balmy air.

Eric led her towards the front doors of the building and disarmed yet another fingerprint-activated security system. Grace followed him into a huge foyer tiled in terracotta, a soaring skylight above, and then into a living room decorated with casual elegance, sofas and chairs in soothing neutral shades, a few well placed antiques and a view through the one-way window of the startling sweep of sea.

'May I offer you something to drink?' Eric asked, his hands dug into the pockets of his cut-off jeans. 'Juice, wine, a pina colada?'

Grace wondered if he was amused by her buttoned-up attitude. Well, she had no intention of relaxing. 'A glass of sparkling water, please.'

'Sure thing.' He left her alone, and Grace slowly circled the room. She summed up the antiques and artwork with a practised eye: all good copies, but essentially fakes. Eric returned with her water and withdrew again, promising that Tannous would be with her in a few minutes and she could just 'go ahead and relax'. *No, thanks.* Grace took a sip, frowning as the minutes ticked on. If Tannous's request really was urgent, why was he keeping her waiting like this? Was it on purpose?

She didn't like it, but then she didn't like anything about being here. Not the walls, not the armoured gates, not the man she was meant to meet. All of it brought back too many painful memories, like knives digging into her skull. What didn't kill you was meant to make you stronger, wasn't it? Grace smiled grimly. Then she must be awfully strong. Except she didn't feel strong right now. She felt vulnerable and even exposed, and that made her tense. She worked hard to cultivate a cool, professional demeanour, and just the nature of this place was causing it to crack.

She could not allow that to happen. Quickly she went to the door and tried the handle. With a shuddering rush of relief she felt it open easily. Clearly she was acting a little paranoid. She stepped out into the empty entry hall and saw a pair of French windows at the back that led to an enclosed courtyard, and an infinity pool shaded by palms shimmering in the dusky light.

Grace slipped outside, breathing in the scents of lavender and rosemary as a dry breeze rustled the hair at the nape of her neck. She brushed a tendril away from her face, tucking it back into her professional chignon, and headed towards the pool, her heels clicking on the tiles. She could hear the water in the pool slapping against the sides, the steady sound of limbs cutting through water. Someone was swimming out here in the twilight, and she thought she knew who it was.

She came around a palm tree into the pool area and saw a man cutting through the water with sinuous ease. Even swimming he looked assured. Arrogant and utterly confident in his domain.

Khalis Tannous.

A dart of irritation—no, anger—shot through her. While she was cooling her heels, anxious and tense, he was *swimming*? It felt like the most obvious kind of power play. Deliberately Grace walked to the chaise where a towel had been tossed. She picked it up, then crossed over to where Khalis Tannous was finishing his lap, her four-inch heels surely in his line of vision.

He came to the edge, long lean fingers curling around the slick tile as he glanced upwards. Grace was not prepared for the jolt of—what? Alarm? Awareness? She could not even say, but something in her sizzled to life as she gazed down into those grey-green eyes, long dark lashes spiky with water. It terrified her, and she instantly suppressed it as she coolly handed him the towel.

'Mr Tannous?'

His mouth twisted in bemusement but she took in the narrowing of his eyes, the flickering of suspicion. He was on his guard, just as she was. He hoisted himself up onto the tiles in one fluid movement and took the towel from her. 'Thank you.' He dried himself off with deliberate ease, and Grace could not keep her gaze from flicking downwards to the lean chest and lithe torso, muscled yet trim, his golden-brown skin now flecked with droplets of water. Tannous had a Tunisian father and a French mother, Grace knew, and his mixed ethnicity was evident in his unique colouring. He was beautiful, all burnished skin and sleek, powerful muscle. He gave off an aura of power, not from size, although he was tall, but from the whipcord strength and energy he exuded in every easy yet precise movement.

'And you are?' he finally said, and Grace jerked her gaze upwards.

'Grace Turner of Axis Art Insurers.' She reached in the pocket of her coat for her business card and handed it to him. He took it without looking. 'I believe you were expecting me.'

'So I was.' He slung the towel around his hips, his shrewd gaze flicking over her in one quick yet thorough assessment.

'I thought,' Grace said, keeping her voice professionally level, 'this appraisal was urgent?'

'Fairly urgent,' Tannous agreed. She said nothing, but something of her censure must have been evident for he smiled and said, 'I must apologise for what appears to have been discourtesy. I assumed the appraiser would wish to refresh himself before meeting me, and I would have time to finish my swim.'

'Herself,' Grace corrected coolly, 'and, I assure you, I am ready to work.'

'Glad to hear it, Miss—' he glanced down at her card, his eyebrows arching as he corrected himself '—*Ms* Turner.' He looked up, his gaze assessing once more, although whether he was measuring her as a woman or a professional Grace couldn't tell. She kept her gaze level. 'If you care to follow me, I'll take you to my office and we can discuss what you've come here for.'

Nodding her acceptance, Grace followed him through the pool area to a discreet door in the corner. They walked down another long hallway, the windows' shutters open to the fading sunlight still bathing the courtyard in gold, and then into a large masculine office with tinted windows overlooking the landscaped gardens on the other side of the compound.

Unthinkingly Grace walked to the window, pressed one hand against the cool glass as she gazed at all that managed beauty kept behind those high walls, the jagged bits of glass on top glinting in the last of the sun's rays. The feeling of being trapped clutched at her, made her throat close up. She forced herself to breathe evenly.

Khalis Tannous came to stand behind her and she was uncomfortably aware of his presence, and the fact that all he wore was a pair of swimming trunks and a towel. She could hear the soft sound of his breathing, feel the heat of him, and she tensed, every nerve on high alert and singing with an awareness she definitely did not want to feel.

'Very beautiful, don't you think?' he murmured and Grace forced herself not to move, not to respond in any way to his nearness.

'I find the wall quite ruins the view,' she replied and turned away from the window. Her shoulder brushed against his chest, a few water droplets clinging to the silk of her blouse. Tension twanged through her again so she felt as if she might snap. She could not deny the physical response she had to this man, but she could suppress it. Completely. Her body stiff, her head held high, she moved past him into the centre of the room.

Tannous gazed at her, his expression turning thoughtful. 'I quite agree with your assessment,' he said softly. She did not reply. 'I'll just get dressed,' he told her, and disappeared through another door tucked in the corner of the room.

Grace took a deep breath and let it out slowly. She could handle this. She was a professional. She'd concentrate on her job and forget about the man, the memories. For being in this glorified prison certainly brought back the memories of another island, another wall. And all the heartbreak that had followed—of her own making.

'Ms Turner.'

Grace turned and saw Tannous standing in the doorway. He had changed into a pewter-grey silk shirt, open at the throat, and a pair of black trousers. He'd looked amazing in nothing but a towel, but he looked even better in these casually elegant clothes, his lean strength powerfully apparent in every restrained movement, the silk rippling over his muscled body. She took a slight step backwards.

'Mr Tannous.'

'Please, call me Khalis.' Grace said nothing. He smiled faintly. 'Tell me about yourself, Ms Turner. You are, I take it, experienced in the appraisal of Renaissance art?'

'It is my speciality, Mr Tannous.'

'Khalis.' He sat behind the huge oak desk, steepling his fingers under his chin, clearly waiting for her to continue.

'I have a PhD in seventeenth century da Vinci copies.'

'Forgeries.'

'Yes.'

'I don't think you will be dealing with forgeries here.'

A leap of excitement pulsed through her. Despite her alarm and anxiety about being in this place, she really did want to see what was in that vault. 'If you'd like to show me what you wish to be appraised—'

'How long have you been with Axis Art Insurers?'

'Four years.'

'You are, I must confess, very young to be so experienced.'

Grace stifled a surge of annoyance. She was, unfortunately, used to clients—mainly men—casting doubt upon her abilities. Clearly Khalis Tannous was no different. 'Monsieur Latour can vouch for my abilities, Mr Tannous—'

'Khalis,' he said softly.

Awareness rippled over her in a shiver, like droplets of water on bare skin. She didn't want to call him by his first name, as ridiculous as that seemed. Keeping formal would be one way of maintaining a necessary and professional distance. 'If you'd prefer another appraiser, please simply say so. I will be happy to oblige you.' Leaving this island—and all the memories it churned up—would be a personal relief, if a professional disappointment.

He smiled, seeming so very relaxed. 'Not at all, Ms Turner. I was simply making an observation.'

'I see.' She waited, wary, tense, trying to look as unconcerned as he did. He didn't speak, and impatience bit at her. 'So the collection…?' she finally prompted.

'Ah, yes. The collection.' He turned to stare out of the window, his easy expression suddenly turning guarded, hooded. He seemed so urbane and assured, yet for just a moment he looked like a man in the grip of some terrible force, in the cast of an awful shadow. Then his face cleared and he turned back to her with a small smile. 'My father had a private collection of art in the basement of this compound. A collection I knew nothing about.' Grace refrained from comment. Tannous arched one eyebrow in gentle mockery. 'You doubt me.'

Of course she did. 'I am not here to make judgements, Mr Tannous.'

'Are you ever,' he mused, 'going to call me Khalis?'

Not if she could help it. 'I prefer work relationships to remain professional.'

'And calling me by my first name is too intimate?' There was a soft, seductive lilt to his voice that made that alarming awareness creep along Grace's spine and curl her toes. The effect this man had on her—his voice, his smile, his body—was annoying. Unwanted. She smiled tightly.

'*Intimate* is not the word I would use. But if you feel as strongly about it as you seem to, then I'm happy to oblige you and call you Khalis.' Her tongue seemed to tangle itself on his name, and her voice turned breathy. Grace inwardly flinched. She was making a fool of herself and yet, even so, she'd seen something flare in his eyes, like silver fire, when she said his name. Whatever she was feeling—this attraction, this magnetism—he felt it, too.

Not that it mattered. Attraction, to her, was as suicidal as a moth to a flame. 'May I see the paintings?' she asked.

'Of course. Perhaps that will explain things.'

In one fluid movement Khalis rose from the desk and walked out of the study, clearly expecting Grace to follow him. She suppressed the bite of irritation she felt at his arrogant attitude—he didn't even look back—only to skid to a surprised halt when she saw him holding the door open for her.

He smiled down at her, and Grace had the uncomfortable feeling that he knew exactly what she'd been feeling. 'After you,' he murmured and, fighting a flush, she walked past him down the same corridor they had used earlier. 'Where am I going?' she asked tersely. She could *feel* Khalis walking behind her, heard the whisper of his clothes as he moved. Everything about him was elegant, graceful and sinuous. Sexy.

No. She could not—would not—think that way. She hadn't looked at a man in a sexual or romantic way in four years. She'd trained herself not to, suppressed those longings because she'd had to. One misstep would cost her if not her life, then her very soul. It was insane to feel anything now—and especially for a man like Khalis Tannous, a man who was now the CEO of a terrible and corrupt empire, a man she could never trust.

Instinctively she walked a little faster, as if she could distance herself from him, but he kept pace with ease.

'Turn right,' he murmured, and she heard humour in his voice. 'You are amazingly adept in those very high heels, Ms Turner. But it's not a race.'

Grace didn't answer, but she forced herself to slow down. A little. She turned and walked down another long corridor, the shutters open to a different side of the villa's interior courtyard.

'And now left,' he said, his voice a soft caress, raising the tiny hairs on the back of Grace's neck. He'd come close again, too close. She turned left and came to a forbidding-looking lift with steel doors and a complex security pad.

Khalis activated the security with a fingerprint and a numbered code while Grace averted her eyes. 'I'll have to give you access,' he said, 'as all the art will need to stay on the basement level.'

'To be honest, Mr Tannous—'

'Khalis.'

'I'm not sure how much can be accomplished here,' Grace continued, undeterred. 'Most appraisals need to be done in a laboratory, with the proper equipment—'

Khalis flashed her a quick and rather grim smile. 'It appears my father had the same concerns you do, Ms Turner. I think you will find all the equipment and tools you need.'

The lift doors opened and Khalis ushered her inside before stepping into the lift himself. The doors swooshed closed, and Grace fought a sudden sense of claustrophobia. The lift was spacious enough, and there were only two of them in there, but she still felt as if she couldn't breathe. Couldn't think. She was conscious of Khalis next to her, seeming so loose-limbed and relaxed, and the lift plunging downwards, deep below the earth, to the evil heart of this awful compound. She felt both trapped and tempted—two things she hated feeling.

'Just a few more seconds,' Khalis said softly, and she knew he was aware of how she felt. She was used to hiding her emotions, and being good at it, and it amazed and alarmed her that this stranger seemed to read her so quickly and easily. No one else ever had.

The doors opened and he swept out one arm, indicating she could go first. Cautiously Grace stepped out into a nondescript hallway, the concrete floor and walls the same as those in any basement. To the right she saw a thick steel door, sawn off its hinges and now propped to the side. Balkri Tannous's vault. Her heart began to beat with heavy thuds of anticipation and a little fear.

'Here we are.' Khalis moved past her to switch on the light. Grace saw the interior of the vault was fashioned like a living room or study and, with her heart still beating hard, she stepped into that secret room.

It was almost too much to take in at once. Paintings jostled for space on every wall, frames nearly touching each other. She recognised at least a dozen stolen paintings right off the bat—Klimt, Monet, Picasso. Millions and millions of dollars' worth of stolen art.

Her breath came out in a shudder and Khalis laughed softly, the sound somehow bleak. 'I'm no expert, but even I could tell this was something else.'

She stopped in front of a Picasso that hadn't been seen in a museum in over twenty years. She wasn't that experienced with contemporary art, but she doubted it was a forgery. 'Why,' she asked, studying the painting's clean geometric shape and different shades of blue, 'did you ask for a Renaissance expert? There's art from every period here.'

'True,' Khalis said. He came to stand by her shoulder, gazing at the Picasso as well. 'Although, frankly, that looks like something my five-year-old god-daughter might paint in Nursery.'

'That's enough to make Picasso roll in his grave.'

'Well, she is very clever.'

Grace gave a little laugh, surprising herself. She rarely laughed. She rarely let a man make her laugh. 'Is your god-daughter in California?'

'Yes, she's the daughter of one of my shareholders.'

Grace gazed at the painting. 'Clever she may be, but most art historians would shudder to compare Picasso with a child and a box of finger paints.'

'Oh, she has a paintbrush.'

Grace laughed again, softly, a little breath of sound. 'Maybe she'll be famous one day.' She half-turned and, with a somersault of her heart, realised just how close he had come. His face—his *lips*—were mere inches away. She could see their mobile fullness, amazed at how such a masculine man could have such lush, kissable, *sexy* lips. She felt a shaft of longing pierce her and quickly she moved onto the next painting. 'So why me? Why a Renaissance specialist?'

'Because of these.'

He took her hand in his own and shock jolted through her with the force of an electric current, short-circuiting her senses. Grace jerked her hand away from his too hard, her breath coming out in an outraged gasp.

Khalis stopped, an eyebrow arched. Grace knew her reaction had been ridiculously extreme. How could she explain it? She could not, not easily at any rate. She decided to ignore the whole sorry little episode and raised her chin a notch. 'Show me, please.'

'Very well.' With one last considering look he led her

to a door she hadn't noticed in the back of the room. He opened it and switched on an electric light before ushering her inside.

The room was small and round, and it felt like being inside a tower, or perhaps a shrine. Grace saw only two artworks on the walls, and they stole the breath right from her lungs.

'What—' She stepped closer, stared hard at the wood panels with their thick brushstrokes of oil paint. 'Do you know what these are?' she whispered.

'Not precisely,' Khalis told her, 'but they definitely aren't something my god-daughter could paint.'

Grace smiled and shook her head. 'No, indeed.' She stepped closer, her gaze roving over the painted wood panels. 'Leonardo da Vinci.'

'Yes, he's quite famous, isn't he?'

Her smile widened, to her own amazement. She hadn't expected Khalis Tannous to *amuse* her. 'He is, rather. But they could be forgeries, you know.'

'I doubt they are,' Khalis answered. 'Simply by the fact they're in their own little room.' He paused, his tone turning grim. 'And I know my father. He didn't like to be tricked.'

'Forgeries can be of exceptional quality,' Grace told him. 'And they even have their own value—'

'My father—' Khalis cut her off '—liked the best.'

She turned back to the paintings, drinking them in. If these were real…how many people had seen these *ever*? 'How on earth did he find them?'

'I have no idea. I don't really want to know.'

'They weren't stolen, at least not from a museum.'

'No?'

'These have never been in a museum.'

'Then they are rather special, aren't they?'

She gave a little laugh. 'You could say that.' She shook her head slowly, still trying to take it in. Two original Leonardo paintings never seen in a museum. Never known to exist, beyond rumours. 'If these are real, they would comprise the most significant find of the art world in the last century.'

Khalis sighed heavily, almost as if he were disappointed by such news. 'I suspected as much,' he said, and flicked out the lights. 'You can examine them at length later. But right now I think we both deserve some refreshment.'

Her mind still spinning, Grace barely took in his words. 'Refreshment?'

'Dinner, Ms Turner. I'm starving.' And with an almost wolfish smile he led her out of the vault.

CHAPTER THREE

GRACE paced the sumptuous bedroom Eric had shown her to, her mind still racing from the revelations found in that vault. She longed to ring Michel, but she'd discovered her mobile phone didn't get reception on this godforsaken island. She wondered if that was intentional; somehow she didn't think Balkri Tannous wanted his guests having free contact with the outside world. But what about Khalis?

It occurred to her, not for the first time but with more force, that she really knew nothing about this man. Michel had given her the barest details: he was Balkri Tannous's younger son; he'd gone to Cambridge; he'd left his family at twenty-one and made his own way in America. But beyond that?

She knew he was handsome and charismatic and arrogantly assured. She knew his closeness made her heart skip a beat. She knew the scent and heat of him had made her dizzy. He'd made her laugh.

Appalled by the nature of her thoughts, Grace shook her head as if the mere action could erase her thinking. She could not be attracted to this man. And even if her body insisted on betraying her, her mind wouldn't. Her heart wouldn't.

Not again.

She took a deep, shuddering breath and strove for calm.

Control. What she didn't know about Khalis Tannous was whether the reality of a huge billion dollar empire would make him power hungry. Whether the sight of millions of dollars' worth of art made him greedy. Whether he could be trusted.

She'd seen how wealth and power had turned a man into someone she barely recognised. Charming on the outside—and Khalis *was* charming—but also selfish and cruel. Would Khalis be like that? Like her ex-husband?

And why, Grace wondered with a lurch of panic, was she thinking about Khalis and her ex-husband in the same breath? Khalis was her client, no more. Her client with a great deal of expensive art.

Another breath. She needed to think rationally rather than react with emotion, with her memories and fears. This was a different island, a different man. And she was different now, too. Stronger. Harder. Wiser. She had no intention of getting involved with anyone…even if she could.

Deliberately she sat down and pulled a pad of paper towards her. She'd make notes, handle this like any other assignment. She wouldn't think of the way Khalis looked in his swimming trunks, the clean, sculpted lines of his chest and shoulders. She wouldn't remember how he'd made her smile, lightened her heart—something that hardly seemed possible. And she certainly wouldn't wonder if he might end up like his father—or her ex-husband. Corrupted by power, ruined with wealth. It didn't matter. In a few days she would be leaving this wretched island, as well as its owner.

Grace Turner. Khalis stared at the small white card she'd given him. It listed only her qualifications, the name of her company and her phone number. He balanced the card on his knuckles, turning his hand quickly to catch it before he brought it unthinkingly to his lips, almost as if he could catch the scent of her from that little bit of paper.

Grace Turner intrigued him, on many levels. Of course he'd first been struck by her looks; she was an uncommonly beautiful woman. A bit unconventional, perhaps, with her honey-blond hair and chocolate eyes, an unusual and yet beguiling combination. Her lashes were thick and sooty, sweeping down all too often to hide the emotions he thought he saw in her eyes.

And her figure…generous curves and endless legs, all showcased in business attire that was no doubt meant to look professional but managed to be ridiculously alluring. Khalis had never seen a white silk blouse and houndstooth pencil skirt look so sexy. Yet, despite the skyscraper heels, he doubted she intended to look sexy. She was as prickly as a sea urchin, and might as well have had *do not touch* emblazoned on her forehead.

Yet he *did* want to touch her, had wanted it from the moment those gorgeous legs had entered his vision when he'd completed his lap in the pool. He hadn't been able to resist when they'd been in the vault, and her reaction to his taking her hand had surprised, he thought, both of them.

She was certainly a woman of secrets. He sensed her coiled tension, even her fear. Something about this island—about him—made her nervous. Of course, on the most basic level he could hardly blame her. From the outside, Alhaja Island looked like a prison. And he was a stranger, the son of a man whose ruthless exploits had been whispered about if not proved. Even so, he didn't think her fear was directed simply at him, but something greater. Something, Khalis suspected, that had held her in its thrall for a while.

Or was he simply projecting his own emotions onto this mysterious and intriguing woman? For he recognised his own fear. He hated being back on Alhaja, hated the memories that rose to the forefront of his mind like scum on the surface of a pond.

Get used to it, Khalis. This is how it is done.

Don't leave me here, Khalis.

I'll come back...I promise.

Abruptly he rose from his chair, prowled the length of his study with an edgy restlessness. He'd resolutely banished those voices for fifteen years, yet they'd all come rushing back, taunting and tormenting him from the moment he'd stepped on this wretched shore. Despite Eric's tactful suggestion that he set up a base of operations in any number of cities where his father had had offices, Khalis had refused.

He'd run from this island once. He wasn't going to do it again.

And at least the enigmatic and attractive Grace Turner provided a welcome distraction from the agony of his own thoughts.

'Khalis?' He glanced up and saw Eric standing in the doorway. 'Dinner is served.'

'Thank you.' Khalis slid Grace's business card into the inside pocket of the dark grey blazer he'd put on. He felt a pleasurable tingle of anticipation at the thought of seeing the all too fascinating Ms Turner again, and firmly pushed away his dark thoughts once and for all. There was, he'd long ago decided, never any point in looking back.

He'd ordered dinner to be served on a private terrace of the compound's interior courtyard, and the intimate space flickered with torchlight as Khalis strolled up to the table. Grace had not yet arrived and he took the liberty of pouring a glass of wine for each of them. He'd just finished when he heard the click of her heels, felt a prickle of awareness at her nearness. Smiling, he turned.

'Ms Turner.'

'If you insist on my calling you Khalis, then you must call me Grace.'

He inclined his head, more gratified than he should be at her concession. 'Thank you…Grace.'

She stepped into the courtyard, the torchlight casting her into flickering light and wraith-like shadow. She looked magnificent. She'd kept her hair up in its businesslike coil, but had exchanged her work day attire for a simple sheath dress in chocolate-brown silk. On another woman the dress might have looked like a paper sack but on Grace it clung to her curves and shimmered when she moved. He suspected she'd chosen the dress for its supposed modesty, and the fact that she had little idea how stunning she looked only added to her allure. He realised he was staring and reached for one of the glasses on the table. 'Wine?'

A hesitation, her body tensing for a fraction of a second before she held out one slender arm. 'Thank you.'

They sipped the wine in silence for a moment, the night soft all around them. In the distance Khalis heard the whisper of the waves, the wind rustling the palm trees overhead. 'I'd offer a toast, but the occasion doesn't seem quite appropriate.'

'No.' Grace lowered her glass, her slim fingers wrapped tightly around the fragile stem. 'You must realise, Mr Tannous—'

'Khalis.'

She laughed softly, no more than a breath of sound. She did not seem like a woman used to laughing. 'I keep forgetting.'

'I think you want to forget.'

She didn't deny it. 'I told you before, I prefer to keep things professional.'

'It's the twenty-first century, Grace. Calling someone by a first name is hardly inviting untoward intimacies.' Even if such a prospect attracted him all too much.

She lifted her gaze to his, her dark eyes wide and clear with a sudden sobriety. 'In most circles,' she allowed, intriguing him further. 'In any case, what I meant to tell you was that I'm sure you realise most of the art in that vault downstairs has been stolen from various museums around the world.'

'I do realise,' he answered, 'which is why I wished to have it assessed, and assured there are no forgeries.'

'And then?'

He took a sip of wine, giving her a deliberately amused look over the rim of his glass. 'Then I intend to sell it on the black market, of course. And quietly get rid of you.'

Her eyes narrowed, lips compressed. 'If that is a joke, it is a poor one.'

'If?' He stared at her, saw her slender body nearly vibrating with tension. 'My God, do you actually think there is any possibility of such a thing? What kind of man do you think I am?'

A faint blush touched her pale cheeks with pink. 'I don't know you, Mr Tannous. All I know is what I've heard of your father—'

'I am nothing like my father.' He hated the implication she was making, the accusation. He'd been trying to prove he was different his whole life, had made every choice deliberately as a way to prove he was not like his father in the smallest degree. The price he'd paid was high, maybe even too high, but he'd paid it and he wouldn't look back. And he wouldn't defend himself to this slip of a woman either. He forced himself to smile. 'Trust me, such a thing is not in the remotest realm of possibility.'

'I didn't think it was,' she answered sharply. 'But it is something, perhaps, your father might have done.'

Something snapped to life inside him, but Khalis could not say what it was. Anger? Regret? *Guilt?* 'My father was not a murderer,' he said levelly, 'as far as I am aware.'

'But he was a thief,' Grace said quietly. 'A thief many times over.'

'And he is dead. He cannot pay for his crimes, alas, but I can set things to rights.'

'Is that what you are doing with Tannous Enterprises?'

Tension tautened through his body. 'Attempting. It is, I fear, a Herculean task.'

'Why did he leave it to you?'

'It is a question I have asked myself many times already,' he said lightly, 'and one for which I have yet to find an answer. My older brother should have inherited, but he died in the crash.'

'And what about the other shareholders?'

'There are very few, and they hold a relatively small percentage of the shares. They're not best pleased, though, that my father left control of the company to me.'

'What do you think they'll do?'

He shrugged. 'What can they do? They're waiting now, to see which way I turn.'

'Whether you'll be like your father.' This time she did not speak with accusation, but something that sounded surprisingly like sympathy.

'I won't.'

'A fortune such as the one contained in that vault has tempted a lesser man, Mr...Khalis.' She spoke softly, almost as if she had some kind of personal experience of such temptation. His name on her lips sent a sudden thrill through him. Perhaps using first names did invite an intimacy...or at least create one.

'I have my own fortune, Grace. But I thank you for the compliment.'

'It wasn't meant to be one,' she said quietly. 'Just an observation, really.' She turned away and he watched her cross to the edge of the private alcove as if looking for exits. The little nook was enclosed by thick foliage on every side but one that led back into the villa. Did she feel trapped?

'You seem a bit tense,' he told her mildly. 'Granted, this island has a similar effect on me, but I wish I could put you at ease in regard to my intentions.'

'Why didn't you simply hand the collection over to the police?'

He gave a short laugh. 'In this part of the world? My father may have been corrupt, but he wasn't alone. Half of the local police force were in his pocket already.'

She nodded, her back still to him, though he saw the tension radiating along her spine, her slender back taut with it. 'Of course,' she murmured.

'Let me be plain about my intentions, Grace. After you've assessed the art—the da Vincis, mainly—and assured me they are not forgeries, I intend to hand the entire collection over to Axis to see it disposed of properly, whether that is the Louvre, the Met, or a poky little museum in Oklahoma. I don't care.'

'There are legal procedures—'

He waved a hand in dismissal. 'I'm sure of it. And I'm sure your company can handle such things and make sure each masterpiece gets back to its proper museum.'

She turned suddenly, looking at him over her shoulder, her eyes wide and dark, her lips parted. It was an incredibly alluring pose, though he doubted she realised it. Or perhaps he'd just been too long without a lover. Either way, Grace Turner fascinated and attracted him more than any woman had in a long time. He wanted to kiss those soft parted lips as much as he wanted to see them smile, and the realisation jarred him. He felt more for this woman than mere physical attraction. 'I told you before,' she said, 'those Leonardos have never been in a museum.'

He pushed away that unwanted realisation with relief. 'Why not?'

'No one has ever been sure they even existed.'

'What do you mean?'

'Did you recognise the subject of the paintings?'

'Something in Greek mythology, I thought.' He racked his brain for a moment. 'Leda and the Swan, wasn't it?'

'Yes. Do you know the story?'

'Vaguely. The Swan was Zeus, wasn't it? And he had his way with Leda.'

'Yes, he raped her. It was a popular subject of paintings during the Renaissance, and depicted quite erotically.' She'd turned to face him and in the flickering torchlight her face looked pale and sorrowful. 'Leonardo da Vinci was known to have done the first painting downstairs, of Leda and the Swan. A romantic depiction, similar in style to others of the period, yet of course by a master.'

'And yet this painting was never in a museum?'

'No, it was last seen at Fontainebleau in 1625. Historians think it was deliberately destroyed. It was definitely known to be damaged, so if it is genuine your father or a previous owner must have had it restored.'

'If it hasn't been seen in four hundred years, how does anyone even know what it looked like?'

'Copies, all based on the first copy done by one of Leonardo's students. You could probably buy a poster of it on the street for ten pounds.'

'That's no poster downstairs.'

'No.' She met his gaze frankly, her eyes wide and a soft,

deep brown. Pansy eyes, Khalis thought, alarmed again at how sentimental he was being. *Feeling*. The guarded sorrow in her eyes aroused a protective instinct in him he hadn't felt in years. Hadn't wanted to feel. Yet one look from Grace and it came rushing back, overwhelming him. He wanted, inexplicably, to take care of this woman. 'In fact,' Grace continued, 'I would have assumed the painting downstairs is a copy, except for the second painting.'

'The second painting,' Khalis repeated. He was having trouble keeping track of the conversation, due to the rush of his own emotions and the effect Grace was having on him. A faint flush now coloured her cheekbones, making her look more beautiful and alluring than ever. He felt his libido stir insistently to life and took a sip of wine to distract himself. What was it about this woman that affected him so much—in so many ways?

'Yes, you see the second painting is one art historians thought Leonardo never completed. It's been no more than a rumour or even a dream.' She shook her head slowly, as if she couldn't believe what she'd seen with her own eyes. 'Leda not with her lover the Swan, but with her children of that tragic union. Helen and Polydeuces, Castor and Clytemnestra.' Abruptly she turned away from him, and with the sudden sweep of those sooty lashes Khalis knew she was hiding some deep and powerful emotion.

'If he never completed it,' he asked after a moment, 'how do art historians even know about its possibility?'

'He did several studies. He was fascinated by the myth of Leda.' Her back was still to him, radiating tension once more. Khalis fought the urge to put his hand on her shoulders, draw her to him, although for a kiss or a hug of comfort he wasn't even sure. He felt a powerful desire to do both. 'He's one of the few artists ever to have thought of painting Leda that way. As a mother, rather than a lover.'

'You seem rather moved by the idea,' he said quietly, and he felt the increase of tension in her lithe body like a jolt of electricity that wired them both.

She drew in a breath that sounded only a little ragged and after a second's pause, turned to him with a cool smile. 'Of course I am. As I told you before, this is a major discovery.'

Khalis said nothing, merely observed her. Her gaze was level, her face carefully expressionless. It was a look, he imagined, she cultivated often. A mask to hide the turbulent emotions seething beneath that placid surface. He recognised it because he had a similar technique himself. Except his mask went deeper than Grace's, soul-deep. He felt nothing while her emotions remained close to the surface, reflected in her eyes, visible in the soft, trembling line of her mouth.

'I didn't mean the discovery,' he said, 'but rather the painting itself. This Leda.'

'I can't help but feel sorry for her, I suppose.' She shrugged, one slender shoulder lifting, and Khalis's gaze was irresistibly drawn to the movement, the shimmery fabric of her dress clinging lovingly to the swell of her breast. She noticed the direction of his gaze and, her eyes narrowed and mouth compressed, pushed past him. 'You mentioned earlier you were starving. Shall we eat?'

'Of course.' He moved to the table and pulled out her chair. Grace hesitated, then walked swiftly towards him and sat down. Khalis inhaled the scent of her perfume or perhaps her shampoo; it smelled sweet and clean, like almonds. He gently pushed her chair in and moved to the other side of the table. Nothing Grace had said or done so far had deterred him or dampened his attraction; in fact, he found the enigmatic mix of strength and vulnerability she showed all the more intriguing—and alluring. And as for the emotions she stirred up in him… Khalis pushed these aside. The events of the last week had left him a little raw, that was all. It should come as no surprise that he was feeling a bit stupidly emotional. It would pass…even as his attraction to Grace Turner became stronger.

Grace laid her napkin in her lap with trembling fingers. She could not believe how unnerved she was. She didn't know if it was being on this wretched island, seeing those amazing paintings, or the proximity to Khalis Tannous. Probably—and unfortunately—all three.

She could not deny this man played havoc with her peace of mind by the way he seemed to sense what she was thinking and feeling. The way his gaze lingered made her achingly aware of her own body, created a response in her she didn't want or like.

Desire. *Need.*

She'd schooled herself not to feel either for so long. How could this one man shatter her defences so quickly and completely? How could she let him? She knew what happened when you let a man close. When you trusted him. Despair. Heartbreak. *Betrayal.*

'So tell me about yourself, Grace Turner,' Khalis said, his voice low and lazy. It slid over her like silk, made her want to luxuriate in its soft, seductive promise. He poured her more wine, which Grace knew she should refuse. The few sips she'd taken had already gone to her head—or was that just the effect Khalis was having on her?

'What do you want to know?' she asked.

'Everything.' He sat back, smiling, the glass of wine cradled between his long brown fingers. Grace could not keep her gaze from wandering over him. Wavy ink-black hair, left just a little long, and those surprising grey-green eyes, the colour of agate. He lifted his brows, clearly waiting, and, startled from her humiliatingly obvious perusal of his attractions, Grace reached for her wine.

'That's rather comprehensive. I told you I did my PhD in—'

'I'm not referring to your professional qualifications.' Grace said nothing. She wanted—had to—keep this professional. 'Where are you from?' he asked mildly, and she let out the breath she hadn't realised she'd been holding.

'Cambridge.'

'And you went to Cambridge for your doctorate?'

'Yes, and undergraduate.'

'You must have done one after the other,' he mused. 'You can't be more than thirty.'

'I'm thirty-two,' Grace told him. 'And, as a matter of fact, yes, I did do one after the other.'

'You know I went to Cambridge?' She inclined her head in acknowledgement; she'd read the file Michel had compiled on him on the plane. 'We almost overlapped. I'm a few years older than you, but it's possible.'

'An amazing coincidence.'

'You don't seem particularly amazed.'

She just shrugged. She had a feeling that if Khalis Tannous had been within fifty miles of her she would have known it. Or maybe she wouldn't have, because then she'd been dazzled by another Cambridge student—her ex-husband. Dazzled and blinded. She felt a sudden cold steal inside her at the thought that Khalis and Loukas might have been acquaintances, or even friends. What if Loukas found out she was here? Even though this trip was business, Grace knew how her ex-husband thought. He'd be suspicious, and he might deny her access to Katerina. *Why* had she let Michel bully her into coming?

'Grace?' She refocused, saw him looking at with obvious concern. 'You've gone deathly white in the space of about six seconds.'

'Sorry.' She fumbled for an excuse. 'I'm a bit tired from the flight, and I haven't eaten since breakfast.'

'Then let me serve you,' Khalis said and, as if on cue, a young woman came in with a platter of food.

Grace watched as Khalis ladled couscous, stewed lamb and a cucumber yogurt salad onto her plate. She told herself it was unlikely Khalis knew Loukas; he'd been living in the States, after all. And, even if he did, he'd surely be discreet about his father's art collection. She was, as usual, being paranoid. Yet she *had* to be paranoid, on her guard always, because access to her daughter was so limited and so precious…and in her ex-husband's complete control.

'Bon appétit,' Khalis said, and Grace forced a smile. 'It looks delicious.'

'Really? Because you're looking at your plate as if it's your last meal.'

Grace pressed two fingers to her forehead; she felt the beginnings of one of her headaches. 'A delicious last meal, in any case.' She tried to smile. 'I'm sorry. I'm just tired, really.'

'Would you prefer to eat in your room?'

Grace shook her head, not wanting to admit to such weakness. 'I'm fine,' she said firmly, as if she could make it so. 'And this really does look delicious.' She took a bite of couscous and somehow managed to choke it down. She could feel Khalis's gaze on her, heavy and speculative. Knowing.

'You grew up in Cambridge, you said?' he finally asked, and Grace felt relief that he wasn't going to press.

'Yes, my father was a fellow at Trinity College.'

'Was?'

'He died six years ago.'

'I'm sorry.'

'And I should say the same to you. I'm sorry for the loss of your father and brother.'

'Thank you, although it's hardly necessary.'

Grace paused, her fork in mid-air. 'Even if you were estranged from them, it's surely a loss.'

'I left my family fifteen years ago, Grace. They were dead to me. I did my grieving then.' He spoke neutrally enough, yet underneath that easy affability Grace sensed an icy hardness. There would be no second chances with a man like Khalis.

'Didn't you miss them? At the time?'

'No.' He spoke flatly, the one word discouraging any more questions.

'Do you enjoy living in the States?' she tried instead, keeping her tone light.

'I do.'

'What made you choose to live there?'

'It was far away.'

It seemed no question was innocuous. They ate in silence for a few moments, the only sound the whisper of the waves and wind. When she couldn't see those high walls she could almost appreciate the beauty of this island paradise in the middle of the Mediterranean. Yet she could still *feel* them, knew that the only way out of here was by another person's say-so. At this thought another bolt of pain lanced through her skull and her hand clenched around her fork. Khalis noticed.

'Grace?'

'Did you grow up here?' she asked abruptly. 'Behind these walls?'

He didn't answer for a moment, and his narrowed gaze rested on her thoughtfully. 'Holidays mostly,' he finally said. 'I went to boarding school when I was seven, in England.'

'Seven,' she murmured. 'That must have been hard.'

Khalis just shrugged. 'I suppose I missed my parents, but then I didn't know as much about them as I should have, being only a child.'

'What do you mean?'

'You are most certainly aware that my father was not the most admirable of men.'

'I'm aware.'

'As a child, I did not realise that. And so I missed him.' He said it simply, bluntly, as if it were no more than an obvious fact. Yet Grace was both curious and saddened by his statement. When, she wondered, had Khalis become disillusioned with his father? When he left university? And did learning of a loved one's flaws make you stop loving them? In Khalis's view, it certainly seemed so.

'What about your mother?'

'She died when I was ten,' Khalis told her. 'I don't remember much about her.'

'You don't?' Grace didn't hide her surprise. 'My mother died when I was thirteen, and I remember so much.' The scent of her hand lotion, the softness of her hair, the lullabies she used to sing. She also remembered how dusty and empty their house on Grange Road had seemed after her death, with her father immersed in his books and antiques.

'It was a long time ago,' Khalis said, and although his tone was pleasant enough Grace could still tell the topic of conversation was closed. It almost sounded as if he didn't *want* to remember his mother…or anyone in his past.

She felt an entirely unreasonable flash of curiosity to *know* this man, for she felt with a deep and surprising certainty that he hid secrets. Sorrow. Despite his often light tone, the easy smile, Grace knew there was a darkness and a hardness in him that both repelled and attracted her. She had no business being attracted to any man, much less a man like Khalis. Yet here she was, seeing the sleepy, veiled look in his grey-green eyes, feeling that slow spiral of honeyed desire uncurl in the pit of her belly, even as pain continued to lance her skull. How appropriate. Pain and pleasure. Temptation and torture. They always went together, didn't they?

With effort she returned the conversation to work. 'Tomorrow morning I should like to see the equipment you mentioned,' she told him, keeping her voice brisk. 'The sooner I am able to assess whether the Leonardos are genuine, the better.'

'Do you really doubt it?'

'My job is to doubt it,' Grace told him. 'I need to prove they're real rather than prove they're forgeries.'

'Fascinating,' Khalis murmured. 'A quest for truth. What drew you to such a profession?'

'My father was a professor of ancient history. I grew up around antiques, spent most of my childhood in museums, except for a brief horse-mad phase when all I wanted to do was ride.' She gave him a small smile. 'The Fitzwilliam in Cambridge was practically a second home.'

'Like father like daughter?'

'Sometimes,' Grace said, her gaze locking with his, 'you are your father's child in more than just blood.'

His grey-green gaze felt like a vice on her soul, for she could not look away. It called to something deep within her, something she had suppressed for so long she barely remembered she still possessed it. The longing to be understood, the desire to be known or even revealed. And reflected back in those agate eyes she saw a strange and surprising torment of emotions: sorrow, anger, maybe even despair. Or was she simply looking into a mirror? Her head pounded with the knowledge of what she'd seen and felt, the ache increasing so she longed to close her eyes. Then he broke their gaze, averting his face, his mouth hardening as he looked out at the gardens now cloaked in darkness.

'You must have some dessert,' he finally said, and his voice was as light as ever. 'A Tunisian speciality, almond sesame pastries.' The young woman entered with a plate of pastries as well as a silver tray with a coffee pot and porcelain cups.

Grace took a bite of the sticky sweet pastry, but she could not manage the coffee. Her head ached unbearably now, and she knew if she did not lie down in the dark she would be incapacitated for hours or even days. She'd had these migraines with depressing regularity, ever since her divorce. With an unsteady clatter she returned her coffee cup to its saucer. 'I'm sorry, but I am very tired. I think I'll go to bed.'

Khalis rose from the table, concern darkening his eyes. 'Of course. You look unwell. Do you have a headache?'

Tightly Grace nodded. Spots swam in her vision and she rose from the table carefully, as if she might break. Every movement sent shafts of lightning pain through her skull.

'Come.' Khalis took her by the hand, draping his other arm around her shoulder as he led her from the table.

'I'm sorry,' she murmured, but he brushed aside her apologies.

'You should have told me.'

'It came on suddenly.'

'What do you need?'

'To lie down…in the dark…'

'Of course.'

Then, to Grace's surprise, he pulled her up into his

arms, cradling her easily. 'I apologise for the familiarity, but it is simpler and quicker this way.' Grace said nothing, shock as well as pain rendering her speechless. In her weakened state she didn't have the strength to draw away, nor, she realised, the will. It felt far too good to be held, her cheek pressed against the warm strength of his chest. It had been so very long since she'd been this physically close to someone, since she'd felt taken care of. And even though she knew better than to want it, knew where letting someone take care of you led, she did not even attempt to draw away. Worse, she instinctively, irresistibly nestled closer, her head tucked in the curve of his shoulder. 'You should have told me sooner,' he murmured, brushing a tendril of hair from her cheek, and Grace just closed her eyes. The pain in her head overwhelmed her now, making speech or even thought impossible.

Eventually she heard a door open, felt Khalis lay her gently on a silk duvet. He left, making her feel suddenly, ridiculously bereft, only to return moments later with a cool damp cloth he laid over her forehead. Grace could not keep from groaning in relief.

'Can you manage these?' he said, pressing two tablets in her hand.

She gave the barest of nods. 'What are they?'

'Just paracetamol, I'm afraid. I don't have anything stronger.' He handed her a glass of water and, despite the dagger points of pain thrusting into her skull, she managed to choke the tablets down. She lay back on the bed, utterly spent, in too much pain even to feel humiliated that Khalis was seeing her so weak and vulnerable, and on her very first day.

She felt him slip off her heels, and then he took her feet in his hands and began massaging her soles with his thumbs. Grace lay on the bed in supine surrender as he ministered to her, rubbing his thumbs in deep, slow circles. It felt unbelievably, unbearably good and she felt her headache start to recede, her body relax. She would not have moved even if she possessed the strength to do so.

She must have fallen asleep, for the last thing she remembered until morning was Khalis still rubbing her feet, his touch sure, knowing and so achingly gentle.

CHAPTER FOUR

GRACE woke to sunlight streaming through the crack in the curtains and her head feeling much better. She opened her eyes and stretched, felt a surge of relief mingled with an absurd disappointment that Khalis was gone.

Of course he was gone, she told herself. It was morning. She *wanted* him to be gone. The thought that he might have spent the entire night in her bedroom made her squirm with humiliation. And yet he'd seen enough; she still recalled the gentle way he'd rubbed her feet, how tenderly he'd cared for her. She squirmed some more. She hated feeling weak or vulnerable. Hated the thought of Khalis seeing that and using it to his advantage somehow, even if last night he'd made her feel cherished and cared for.

Forget it, she told herself. *Forget Khalis, forget how he made you feel.* Quickly she rose from the bed, even though it made her head swim a bit. She took a deep breath and staggered to the shower, determined to forget the events of last night and put today on an even and professional keel. She felt better when she'd showered and dressed in work clothes, a pair of slim black trousers and a fitted white T-shirt. She applied the minimum of neutral make-up, pulled her hair back into a ponytail and reached for her attaché case, her professional armour now firmly in place. This was how she needed to be with Khalis, with any man. Professional, strong and completely in control. Not weak or needy. Not wanting.

Khalis's assistant Eric met her at the bottom of the main staircase. He wore a pair of board shorts and a T-shirt with a logo that read 'I work at Silicon Valley. But if I told you more I'd have to kill you'.

Grace thought of her admonition last night. *If that is a joke...* She must have seemed completely ridiculous.

'Ms Turner,' Eric greeted her with an easy smile, 'may I show you to the breakfast room?'

'Thank you.' He led her down a tiled hallway and, curious, she asked, 'Did you meet Mr Tannous in California?'

He turned back to give her a smiling glance. 'How did you know?'

'Oh, I don't know, maybe the hair,' she replied with a small smile. He had light blond hair, bleached by the sun in rather artful streaks. 'Have you known him long?'

'Since he moved out there fifteen years ago. I've been with his gig from the start. He had big ideas and, while I don't have any of those, I'm pretty decent with the admin side.'

'Did you know about his family?'

Eric hesitated for only a second. 'Everyone in California is starting over, more or less,' he said and, although his tone was relaxed, it was also final. He had the same kind of affability Khalis possessed, Grace thought wryly, although rather less of the unyielding hardness she sensed underneath. 'Here you go,' he said, and ushered her into a pleasant room at the back of the building. Khalis was already seated at the table, drinking coffee and reading the newspaper on his tablet computer. He glanced up as she entered, his easy and rather familiar smile making her flush and remember how he'd held her last night. How she'd pressed her cheek against his chest, how he'd rubbed her feet. How much she'd savoured it all. Judging by that smile, he'd probably been able to tell.

'You look like you're feeling better.'

She sat down and poured herself coffee, her gaze firmly on the cup. 'Yes, thank you. I apologise for last night.'

'What is there to be sorry for?'

She added milk. 'I was incapacitated—'

'You were in pain.'

He spoke so quietly and firmly that Grace was startled into looking up, her gaze locking on his green-grey one that was full of far too much understanding. It almost made her want to tell him things. She stirred her coffee and took a sip. 'Still, I am here to perform a set task—'

'And I'm sure you will perform it admirably today. What exactly is on the agenda?'

Relief surged through her as she realised he was going to graciously drop the subject of last night. Today she could talk about. 'First I'll need to catalogue all the works in the vault and check them against the Art Loss Register. Those that appear to have been stolen can be, for the moment, set to one side. Experts from the museums concerned will need to be contacted along with—'

'I'd prefer,' Khalis said, 'not to contact anyone until we know just what we're dealing with.'

Unease crept along her spine with cold fingers. Ridiculous it might be, but she couldn't keep from feeling it. She didn't think Khalis intended to keep the art for himself, but she still didn't trust him. Not on either a professional or personal level. 'And why is that?'

'Because the media storm that will erupt when it is discovered my father had however many stolen paintings in his possession is one I want to control, at least somewhat,' he replied mildly. 'I don't particularly like publicity.'

'Nor do I.'

'And yet,' he said musingly, 'you will certainly be mentioned in any of the articles that will undoubtedly appear.'

'Axis Art Insurers will,' Grace replied swiftly. 'My name will be kept out of it. That has always been our agreement.'

He gazed at her over the rim of his coffee cup. 'You really don't like publicity.'

'No.'

'Then my decision to wait to contact any outside source should meet with your approval.'

'I don't like being managed,' Grace said flatly.

Khalis arched an eyebrow. 'I'd hardly call a request to wait on calling the police being *managed*.'

'It potentially compromises my position.'

'You have a moral objection?'

She bit her lip. She didn't, not really, not if she trusted him to inform the proper legal authority and dispose of the art as necessary. And, logically, she knew she should. She had no real reason to think otherwise, and yet…

And yet she'd once believed a man's assurances. Trusted his promises. Let herself be led into captivity and despair. Every muscle coiled and tightened at the memory. Pain snapped at the edges of her mind, the remnants of her migraine mocking her. *Khalis Tannous is not your ex-husband. Not even close. All you have is a professional relationship.*

'You still don't trust me,' Khalis said quietly. 'Do you? To handle my father's collection properly.'

Grace was not about to admit this wasn't really about the art. It went deeper, darker, and she didn't even understand why. She barely knew this man. She met his gaze as levelly as she could. 'I don't even know you.'

'And yet,' Khalis observed, 'if I intended to keep the paintings or sell them on the black market, contacting your company would be just about the most idiotic thing I could do. Your lack of trust borders on ridiculous, Grace.'

She knew that. She knew his intentions towards the art had to be legitimate. And yet she couldn't keep her frightened instinct from kicking in, from remembering how it felt to be like one of those paintings in that vault, adored and hidden away, for no one else to see. It had been a miserable life for her, just as it was for Leda. And it coloured her response to this man, in shades too dark for her to admit.

And as for what was ridiculous… When he said her name, in really, a completely normal tone of voice…why did it make her insides unfurl, like a seedling seeking sunlight? *That* was absurd. 'It might seem ridiculous to you,' she said stiffly, 'but I've experienced enough to be justified in my lack of trust.'

'Experienced professionally? Or personally?'

'Both,' she said flatly, and began to butter her toast. Khalis was silent for a long moment, but she could still feel his speculation as he sipped his coffee. She'd said too much. Just one word, but it had been too much. Not that it mattered. All it would take was one internet search for Khalis to learn her history, or at least some of it. Not the most painful parts, but still enough to hurt. Perhaps he'd learned it already, although his air of unconcern suggested otherwise.

'So,' he finally said, 'what will you do after you catalogue the paintings and check them against this register?'

'Run preliminary tests on the ones that do not appear to come from any museum. I don't suppose your father kept any files on his artwork?'

'I don't think so.'

'Most paintings of any real value have certificates of

authentication. It's virtually impossible to sell a valuable painting without one.'

'You're saying my father should have these certificates?'

'Of the ones that are not stolen, yes. Obviously the stolen works' certificates would remain with the museums they were taken from. Really, some legal authority should be contacted. Interpol, or the FBI's Art Crimes department—'

'No.' He still spoke evenly enough, but his voice made Grace go cold. It reminded her of Loukas's implacable tone when she'd asked to go to Athens for a shopping trip. One miserable little shopping trip, for things for Katerina. She'd said nothing then, and she said nothing now. Perhaps she hadn't changed as much as she'd hoped. 'I'm not ready to have law enforcement of any kind swarming over this compound and investigating everything.'

'You're hiding something,' she said, the words seeming to scrape her throat.

'My father hid plenty of things,' he corrected. 'And I intend to find out what they all were before I invite the law in.'

'So you can decide which ones to reveal and which ones to keep hiding?'

Ice flashed in his eyes and he leaned forward, his hand encircling her wrist, his movements precise and controlled, yet radiating a leashed and lethal power. 'Let me be very clear. I am not corrupt. I am not a criminal. I do not intend to allow Tannous Enterprises to continue to engage in any illegal activity. But neither do I intend to hand the reins over to a bunch of bureaucratic, bumbling policemen who might be as interested in lining their pockets as my father was. Understood?'

'Let go of my wrist,' she said coldly, and Khalis looked

down as if surprised he was touching her. He hadn't grabbed her, hadn't hurt her at all, yet she felt as if he had.

'I'm sorry.' He released her, then let out a gusty sigh as he raked a hand through his hair. 'I'm sorry if I scared you.' Grace said nothing. She wasn't about to explain that she had been scared, or why. Khalis gave her a thoughtful look from under his lashes, his mouth pursed. 'You've been hurt, haven't you? By a man.'

Shock caused her to freeze, her nerveless fingers almost dropping her coffee cup before she replaced it on its saucer. 'That,' she said, 'is none of your business.'

'You're right. Again, I apologise.' He looked away; the silence in the room felt electric. 'So these preliminary tests. What are they?'

'I need to see what facilities are in the basement. Artwork, especially older artwork, needs to be handled very carefully. A few minutes' exposure to sunlight can cause irreparable damage. But I would expect to analyse the pigments used, as well as use infrared photography to determine what preliminary sketches are underneath the paintings. If I have the right equipment, I can test for the age of the wood of the panels used. This is an especially good way of dating European masters, since they almost always painted on wood.'

'The two in the back room are on wood.'

'Yes.'

'Interesting.' He shook his head slowly. 'Really quite fascinating.'

'I certainly think so.'

He shot her a quick smile and she realised how invigorating it was to have a man actually interested in her work. During their marriage, Loukas had preferred for her never to discuss it, much less practise her chosen profession.

She'd gone along for the sake of marital accord, but it had tried her terribly. Too terribly.

'I'd better let you get to it,' Khalis said, and Grace nodded, pushing away her plate. She'd only eaten half a piece of toast, but she had little appetite.

'Eric will escort you to the basement. Let me know if there is anything you require.' And, with another parting smile, Khalis took his computer and left the room. Grace watched him go, hating that she suddenly felt so lonely.

The rest of the day was spent in the laborious yet ultimately rewarding work of checking all the artworks against the international Art Loss Register. The results were dispiriting. Many of the paintings, as Grace had suspected, were stolen. It made her job of authentication and appraisal easier, yet it saddened her to think of how many paintings had been lost to the public, in some cases for generations.

At noon the young woman who had served her meals earlier brought down a plate of sandwiches and a carafe of coffee. 'Mr Tannous said you needed to eat,' she murmured in hesitant English, and Grace felt a curious mingling of gratitude for his thoughtfulness and disappointment that she wouldn't see him.

Stupid. She hadn't really expected to share another meal with him, had she? Last night had been both an introduction and an aberration. Even so, she could not deny the little sinking feeling she had at the thought of an afternoon working alone. It had never bothered her before; she was certainly used to solitude. It wouldn't bother her now. Frowning, she turned back to her laptop with grim concentration.

Immersed in her work, she wasn't really aware of time passing until she heard a light tap-tap at the door of the lab across from the vault where she'd set up her temporary office. She looked up to see Khalis standing in the doorway. He had changed from his dark trousers and silk shirt of this morning into board shorts and a T-shirt that hugged the lean sculpted muscles of his chest. His hair was a little rumpled.

'You've been at it for eight hours.'

She blinked, surprised even as she felt the muscles in her neck cramp. 'I have?'

'Yes. It's six o'clock in the evening.'

She shook her head, smiling a little, unable to staunch the ripple of pleasure she felt at seeing him. 'I was completely absorbed.'

He smiled back. 'So it would appear. I didn't realise art appraisal was *that* fascinating.'

'I've checked all the works against—'

'No, no talk about art and theft or work. It's time to relax.'

'Relax?' she repeated warily. Both Eric and Khalis seemed big on relaxing, yet she had no intention of letting down her guard, and especially not with this man. Last night's headache episode had been bad enough. She didn't intend to give him another chance to get close, to *affect* her.

'Yes, relax,' Khalis said. 'The sun will set in another hour, and before it does I want to go for a swim.'

'Please, don't let me stop you.'

His mouth quirked in another smile. 'I want you to go with me.'

Her heart seemed to fling itself against her ribs at the thought. 'I don't—'

'Swim? I could teach you. We'll start with the dog paddle.' He mimed a child's paddling stroke and Grace found herself smiling. Again.

'I think I can manage to keep myself afloat, thanks very

much.' Strange, how light he made her feel. How *happy.* It was as dangerous and addictive as the physical response her body had to him. She shook her head. 'I really should get this done—'

Khalis dropped his arms to his sides. 'It's not good to work without taking a break, especially considering the strength of your migraine last night. I let you work through lunch, but you really need to take some time off.'

'Most employers don't insist on their staff taking time off.'

'I'm not most employers. Besides, you're not actually my employee. I'm your client.'

'Still—'

'Anyone with sense knows that people work more effectively when they're rested and relaxed. At least they know that in California.' He held out one hand, his long lean fingers stretching so enticingly towards her. 'Come on.'

She absolutely shouldn't take his hand. *Touch* him. And she shouldn't go for a swim. She shouldn't even *want* to go for a swim, because she didn't want to want anyone ever again. As for love, trust, desire...? Forget it. Forget them all.

And yet... And yet she remained motionless, hesitating, suspended with suppressed longing, because no matter what her brain told her about staying safe, strong and in control, her body and maybe even her heart said differently. They said, *Yes. Please.*

'Do you have a swimming costume?'

Reluctantly she nodded. She had brought one, despite what she'd told Michel.

'Well, then? What's stopping you?'

You. Me. The physical temptation that the very idea of

a swim with Khalis presented. The two of them, in the water and wearing very little.

And then there was the far more alarming emotional temptation…to draw closer to this man, to care about him when she couldn't care about anyone. Never mind what restrictions her ex-husband had placed on her, her heart had far more stringent ones.

'Grace.' He said her name not as a question or a command, but as a statement. As if he knew her. And when he did that Grace felt as though she had no choice, and it both aggravated and amazed her. How could she fight this?

She reached out and took his hand. His fingers closed around hers with both strength and gentleness, and he glanced at her carefully, as if he needed to check she was OK. And, after the way she had yanked her hand away from his last night, he probably did.

Taking a breath, Grace met his questioning gaze—and nodded her assent.

Khalis felt an entirely triumphant thrill as he led her from the basement, up into the sunshine and fresh air. He felt as if he'd won a major victory, not against her, but for her. Something about Grace's hidden vulnerability called out to him, made him want to offer her both protection and pleasure. He'd spent the better part of the day thinking about her, wondering what she was doing, thinking, feeling. Wondering about the man who had hurt her and how soft her lips would be if—*when*—he kissed her.

It had been a long time since he'd been in a relationship, even longer since a woman had aroused these kinds of protective feelings in him. Never before, if he were honest, at least not on a romantic, sexual level. The last woman who he'd been emotionally close to had been his sister. Jamilah.

And look what happened then.

Khalis resolutely pushed the thought away. It was just this island, these memories that were temporarily awakening his emotions.

This woman.

It would pass, Khalis told himself. He'd leave Alhaja and get back to his normal life soon enough. And in the meantime Grace provided a welcome distraction.

Except to think of her as a distraction was to think of her dismissively, as something disposable, and he knew he didn't. Couldn't. Already it had become something more, and he didn't know whether to be alarmed, annoyed or amazed. Perhaps he was all three. But, for right now, all he wanted was a simple swim.

Up in the foyer, she stopped, pulled her hand away from his with firm purpose. 'I need to change.'

'Why don't I meet you at the pool?'

'All right.'

Fifteen minutes later a stiff and self-conscious Grace approached the pool area. He was sitting on the edge of the pool waiting for her, dangling his legs in the water, enjoying the last golden rays of sunshine. He took in her appearance in one swift and silent glance. Her swimming costume was appalling. Well, appalling might be too strong a word. It fitted, at least. But it was black and very modest, with a high neckline and a little skirt that covered her thighs. She looked like a grandmother. A very sexy grandmother, but still. Clearly she meant to hide her attractions. He smiled. Even a ridiculous swimming costume couldn't make Grace Turner unattractive. Her long, slim legs remained on elegant display, and a swimming costume was, after all, a swimming costume. Her generous curves were also on enticing view.

She stiffened under his rather thorough inspection and then tilted her chin in that proud, defensive way he was coming to know so well. He stretched out his hand, which she ignored, instead moving gingerly to the steps that led into the shallow end.

'The water's warm,' he offered.

'Lovely.' She dipped a toe in, then stood on the first step, up to her ankles, looking as if she were being tortured.

'Lovely, you said?' he teased, his voice rich with amusement, and she looked startled before giving him a very small smile.

'I'm sorry. I'm not used to this.'

'And here you told me you could swim.'

Impatiently, she shook her head, gesturing between them with one hand. *'This.'*

And he knew—of course he knew—that she felt it, too. This connection, this energy between them. And, while it alarmed him, he had a feeling it *terrified* her. He saw that, felt it and, without thinking too much about what he was doing—or why—he slipped waist-deep into the water and strode towards her. She watched him approach with wide, wary eyes. He stopped a few feet away and gave her a little splash. She blinked, bewildered.

'What are you doing?'

'Having fun?' Her mouth tightened and she looked quickly away. Intrigued, he asked softly, 'Is there something wrong with that?'

'No,' she said, but she didn't sound convinced. He splashed her again, gently, and to his relief he got a little smile, a sudden flash of fire in her eyes.

'You're asking for it, aren't you?'

Desperately. He waited, watched as she trailed her fingers in the water. She had beautiful fingers, long and slim with elegant rounded nails. His gaze was still fixed on them when she suddenly lifted her hand and hit the water hard with the flat of her palm, sending a wave of water crashing over him, leaving him blinking and spluttering. And laughing, because it was just about the last thing he'd expected.

He sluiced the water from his face and grinned at her. She smiled back, almost tremulously, as if her lips weren't used to it. 'Got you.'

'Yes,' he said, and his voice came out in a husky murmur. 'You did.' Even in that awful swimming costume, she was incredibly, infinitely desirable. And when she smiled he was lost. He felt his fears fall away when he looked at her, any alarm that this was all going too fast and too deep seemed ridiculous. He wanted this. He wanted her. He took a step towards her and she stilled, and then another step so he was close enough to feel her breath feather his face, see the pulse beating in her throat. Then he leaned down and kissed her.

It was the gentlest kind of kiss, his mouth barely brushing over hers. She didn't move away, but she trembled. Her lips parted, but it didn't feel like surrender. It felt like surprise. He reached with one hand to cradle her face, his palm cupping the curve of her cheek, revelling in the satiny softness of her skin. It didn't last more than a few seconds, but it felt endless and yet no time at all. And then it was over.

With a ragged gasp she tore away, stared at him with eyes wide with shock and even anger.

'Grace—'

He didn't get the chance to say any more. As if she had the devil himself on her heels, she scrambled out of the pool, slipping on the wet tiles and landing hard on one knee before lurching upright and running back into the villa.

CHAPTER FIVE

STUPID. Stupid, stupid, stupid idiot—

The litany of self-recrimination echoed remorselessly through her as Grace ran through the villa, pounded up the stairs and then into her room, slamming and locking the door behind her as if Khalis were actually chasing her.

She let out a shuddering breath and then turned from the door, tearing the swimming costume from her body before she went to the en suite bathroom and started the shower.

What had possessed her to go swimming? To splash him? *Flirt?* When he'd moved closer to her in the water she'd known—of course she'd known—what he intended to do. In that moment she'd wanted him to kiss her. And the feel of his lips on hers, his hand on her cheek, had been so unbearably, achingly wonderful—until realisation slammed into her and Katerina's face swam in her vision, reminding her just how much she had to lose.

And not just Katerina, Grace thought with a surge of self-recrimination. What about herself? Her freedom? Her *soul*? Marriage to Loukas had nearly destroyed her. He'd levelled her identity, his words and actions a veritable emotional earthquake, and for years afterwards she'd felt blank, a cipher of a person. Working at Axis had helped restore some of her sense of self, yet she still felt as if she drifted through parts of life, had empty spaces and yawning silences where other people had companionship and joy. And perhaps she always would feel that way, as long as she didn't have her daughter. But she'd at least keep herself, Grace thought fiercely. She'd keep her identity, her independence, her strength. She wouldn't give those away to the first man who kissed her, even if his gentleness nearly undid her.

Grace stepped into the shower and let the hot water rush over her, wash away the memory of Khalis's gentle touch. She felt that endless ache of loneliness deep inside, a well of emptiness she'd convinced herself she'd got used to. Preferred, even. Yet it had only taken one man—one touch—for her to realise just how lonely she really was. She might be strong and safe and independent, but a single kiss had made her achingly aware of the depths of her own unhappiness.

Swallowing hard, she turned off the taps and stepped out of the shower. Work. Work would help. It always did. Quickly she dressed, pulled her damp hair into another serviceable ponytail and then headed downstairs.

Eric had given her a temporary password for the lift's security system and Grace used it, glancing around quickly in search of Khalis. He was nowhere to be found.

Squaring her shoulders, she entered the laboratory that Balkri Tannous had had built to verify the authenticity of the artworks, stolen or otherwise, he acquired on the black market. Grace had been reluctantly impressed by his thoroughness; the laboratory held all the necessary equipment for infrared photography, pigment analysis, dendrochronology and many of the other tests necessary to authenticate a work of art.

She opened her laptop, stared blankly at the catalogue she'd made of the vault's inventory; she'd already checked most of it against the Art Loss Register. It would take another hour or two to finish, yet now she couldn't summon the energy to do it. Instead she slipped off her stool and went back into the vault, past all the canvases in the main room, to the tiny little shrine in the back. She flicked on the lights and sat on the room's one chair; clearly this room had been meant only for Balkri Tannous. She let out a shuddering breath as she stared at the painted wood panels.

The first one, of Leda and the Swan, she'd seen many times before. Not the original, of course, but very good copies. The original, for she didn't really doubt this was the original, had been painted on three wooden panels. The panels had split apart—that had been documented four hundred years ago—but someone had very carefully repaired them. The damaged sections of the painting had been restored, although Grace could still see where the damage had occurred. Still, the painting was incredibly arresting. Leda stood naked and voluptuous, yet with her head bowed in virginal modesty. Her face was turned away as if she were resisting the advances of the sinuous swan, but she had a sensual little half-smile on her face, reminiscent of the Mona Lisa. Did she welcome Zeus's attentions? Had she any idea of the heartbreak that lay ahead of her?

'There you are.'

Grace tensed, even though she wasn't really surprised that Khalis had found her. The overwhelming emotional response she'd felt when he kissed her had receded to a weary resignation that felt far more familiar. Safer, too. 'Do you think she looks happy?' she asked, nodding towards Leda.

Khalis studied the painting. 'I think she's not sure what she feels, or what she wants.'

Grace's gaze remained fixed on Leda's little half-smile, her face turned away from the swan. 'I can't become involved with you, in any way,' she said quietly. 'Not even a kiss.'

Khalis propped one shoulder against the doorway to the little room. 'Can't,' he asked, 'or won't?'

'Both.'

'Why not?'

Another deep breath. 'It's unprofessional to be involved with a client—'

'You didn't sprint from the pool because it was unprofessional.' Khalis cut her off affably enough, although she sensed the steel underneath. 'How's your knee?'

It ached abominably, but Grace had no intention of saying that, or explaining any more. 'There's no point in pressing the matter.'

'You're attracted to me, Grace.'

'It doesn't matter.'

'Do you still not trust me?' he asked quietly. 'Is that it? Are you afraid—of me?'

She let out a little sigh and turned to face him. He looked so achingly beautiful just standing there, wearing faded jeans and a grey T-shirt that hugged the sculpted muscles of his chest. His ink-black hair was rumpled, his eyes narrowed even though he was smiling, a half-smile like Leda's.

'I'm not afraid of you,' she said, and meant it. She might not trust him, but she didn't fear him, either. She simply didn't want to let him have the kind of power opening your body or heart to someone would give. And then, of course, there was Katerina. So many reasons not to get involved.

'What, then?' She just shook her head. 'I know you've been hurt,' he said quietly and she let out a sad little laugh. He was painting his own picture of her, she knew then, a happy little painting like one his god-daughter might make. Too bad he had the wrong paintbox.

'And how do you know that?' she asked.

'It's evident in everything you do and say—'

'No, it isn't.' She rose from the chair, half-inclined to disabuse him of his fanciful notion that she'd been hurt. She *had* been hurt, but not the way he thought. She'd never been an innocent victim, as much as she wished things could be that simple. And she knew, to her own shame and weakness, that she wouldn't say anything. She didn't want him to look at her differently. With judgement rather than compassion, scorn instead of sympathy.

'Why can't you get involved then, Grace?' Khalis asked. 'It was just a kiss, after all.' He'd moved to block the doorway, even though Grace hadn't yet attempted to leave. His face looked harsh now, all hard angles and narrowed eyes, even though his body remained relaxed. A man of contradictions—or was it simply deception? Which was the real man, Grace wondered—the smiling man who'd rubbed her feet so gently, or the angry son who refused to grieve for the family he'd just lost? Or was he both, showing one face to the world and hiding another, just as she was?

It didn't matter. She could not have anything more to do with Khalis Tannous except the barest of professional acquaintances. 'It's complicated, and I don't feel like explaining it to you,' she said shortly. 'But if you've done any digging on the internet, you'll be aware of the details.'

'Is that an invitation?'

She shrugged. 'Just a fact.'

'I'm not some internet stalker,' Khalis told her flatly. 'I'd prefer to hear the truth from you, rather than some gossip website.' She said nothing and he sighed, raking a hand through his hair. Grace nodded towards the exit he was still blocking.

'I should get back to work.'

'It's after seven.'

'Still. If I start running the preliminary tests now, you should have enough information to contact a legal authority in a day or two.'

'Is that what you want?' He gazed at her almost fiercely, and she felt a spasm of longing to walk into his arms, to tell him everything. To feel safe and desired all at once.

Ridiculous. *Dangerous.* To do such a thing would be to open herself up to all kinds of shame and pain, and it would certainly put an end to feeling safe or desired.

'Of course it is,' she said and made to walk past him. He didn't move, so she had to squeeze past in the narrow doorway, her breasts brushing his chest, every point of contact seeming to sizzle and snap her nerve endings to life. She looked up at him, which was a mistake. His eyes blazed need and for an endless charged moment she thought he would kiss her again. He'd grab her and take her right there, with Leda watching with her half-smile. She wouldn't resist, not in that moment. She wouldn't be able to. But instead he stepped back and as she moved past he let out a shuddering breath. She kept walking.

Half an hour later he sent a dinner tray down to the lab. He'd included a snowy-white linen napkin, sterling silver cutlery, and even a carafe of wine and a crystal wine glass. His thoughtfulness made her ache. Did he realise how he was taking apart her defences with these little gestures? Could he possibly know how much they hurt, because they made her afraid and needy all at once?

She picked at the meal, alone in the sterile, window-less lab, feeling lonelier than ever and hating that she did.

Then she determinedly pushed the tray away and turned back to her work.

She didn't see him all the next day, although she felt his presence. At breakfast he'd left a newspaper by her plate, already turned to the Arts section. He'd even written a funny little comment next to one of the editorials, making her smile. She pushed the paper away and drank her coffee and ate her toast alone before heading back downstairs.

Work kept her from thinking too much about him, although he remained on the fringes of her mind, haunting her thoughts like a gentle ghost. She'd had Eric help her move the panels into the lab, and she started running a basic dendrochronology test on the wood. At noon the young woman—her name, Grace had learned, was Shayma—brought her sandwiches and coffee. The tray also held a narrow vase with a single calla lily. After Shayma had left Grace reached for the lily and brushed the fragrant petals against her lips. She closed her eyes, remembering how Loukas had sent her roses. She'd been so touched at the time, grieving her father's death, needing someone's attention and love. Only later did she wonder if the flowers had been a genuine expression of his affection, or just a rote seduction. Did it even matter when things had broken down, or what had been real? She'd learned her lesson. She'd learned it the hard way, which was why this had to stop.

She shoved the tray away and turned back to her work. She worked the rest of the day, through dinner, and went directly up to her room. Both exhausted and restless, she fell into an uneasy sleep.

The next day followed the same pattern. She analysed the pigments used in both the Leonardos, and ate from trays brought down by Shayma. And thought about Khalis.

She could feel his presence in every thoughtful touch, from the different flowers on her tray to the newspaper left on the breakfast table, to the subtle changes in the lab: better lighting, a more comfortable chair. How did he even know? She didn't see him at all, though, and she realised she missed him.

An emotion, she knew, she didn't want and couldn't afford to feel. Over the last four years loneliness was a price she'd always been willing to pay for her freedom. Yet in just the space of a few days Khalis had opened up a sweet yearning inside her, a longing for a closeness she'd denied herself and half-forgotten. A longing that terrified her on so many levels.

That night she left the lab craving fresh air, and slipped out of the doors in the back of the entrance hall that led to the interior courtyard of the villa. She stopped by the pool, now still and empty, and realised by the flash of disappointment she felt that she'd been hoping to see him there. Amazing, how deceptive her own heart could be. She'd convinced herself she simply wanted some air but, really, she wanted Khalis.

She pressed her hands to her temples, as if she could will the want away. *Think what you have to lose. Your daughter. The precious moments you have with her. One Saturday a month. Just twelve days a year.*

She started walking down one of the twisting garden paths as fast as she could, as if she could outrun her thoughts. But they chased her, relentless in their power. *Let a man close and not only will you lose your daughter, you'll lose yourself. Khalis can't be that different. And, even if he is...you aren't.*

Yet right now she wanted to be different. She craved the possibility of a loving, generous, equal relationship.

Impossible. Even if it existed, she couldn't have it. She

couldn't risk it, and yet, for the sake of one man, one unbearably kind and gentle man, she was tempted to try. To throw it all away—and for what? A kiss? An affair? She could not believe she could be so weak…again.

Suddenly a pair of strong hands clamped around her shoulders and she let out a shocked yelp.

'It's just me.' Khalis loomed in front of her, his smile gleaming in the moonlight. She could feel the heat radiating from his lithe body.

'You startled me.'

'So I see.' He released her and stepped back. 'I was out here walking as well, and you almost crashed into me.'

'I'm sorry.'

'It's OK.'

They stood there, a foot or so separating them, yet, considering the nature of her recent thoughts, it felt like an endless chasm. She wanted to walk into his arms and run away both at the same time. She was, Grace thought, an emotional schizophrenic. The sooner she got off this island the better.

'Do you want to walk with me?' Khalis asked and, after a charged pause, she nodded. *Compromise.* There was not room on the narrow little paths to walk side by side, so Khalis let her go first, wending her way among the fragrant foliage, the silver swathe the moon cut through the gardens their only guide.

'Did you play out here?' Grace asked. 'When you were a child?'

Khalis shrugged. 'Sometimes.'

'With your brother?'

'Not really. With my…' A second's pause. 'With my sister.'

'I didn't realise you had a sister.'

'She died.'

'Oh!' Grace turned around. Even in the darkness she saw how hooded his expression seemed. 'So your whole family has died,' she said quietly. 'I'm sorry.'

'So has yours.'

'Yes…' She felt a shudder run through her. 'But it must be harder for you, to lose siblings—'

'I do miss my sister,' Khalis said, the words seeming to be drawn reluctantly from him, although he spoke with a quiet evenness. 'I never had a chance to say goodbye to her.'

'How did she die?'

'A boating accident, right off the coast here. She was nineteen.' He sighed, digging his hands into his pockets. 'She was about to be married. My father had arranged it, but she didn't like the chosen groom.'

Grace frowned, connecting the pieces, threaded together by the darkness of Khalis's tone. 'Do you think it…it wasn't an accident?'

He didn't answer for a long moment. 'I don't know. I hate to think that, but she was determined in her own way, and it would have been a way to escape the marriage.'

'A terrible way.'

'Sometimes life is terrible,' Khalis said, and his voice was bleak. 'Sometimes there are only terrible choices.'

'Yes,' Grace said quietly. 'I think that's true.'

He gave her a wryly sorrowful smile, his teeth gleaming in the darkness. 'I never speak of my sister. Not to anyone. What is it about you, Grace, that makes me say things I wouldn't say to another soul? And *want* to say them?'

She shook her head, her heart thudding treacherously. 'I don't know.'

'Do you feel it?' he asked in a low voice, and in the soft darkness of the garden she couldn't deny or pretend.

'Yes,' she said, the word no more than a thread of sound.

'It scares you.'

Of course it does. She took a deep breath. 'I told you before, I can't—'

'Don't give me that,' Khalis said almost roughly. 'You think this is easy for me and hard for you?'

'No—' Yet she realised she had thought that. He seemed so relaxed and assured, so comfortable with what stretched and strengthened between them, and she was the only one quaking with nerves and memories and fear. She let out a wobbly laugh. 'Maybe it's just the island.'

'The island?'

She gestured to the dense fragrant foliage around them. 'It's like a place and time apart, separate from reality. We can say what we want here. Feel what we want.'

'Except,' Khalis said quietly, 'I don't think you know what you want to feel.'

She felt a sudden spark of anger. 'Don't patronise me.'

'Am I wrong?'

She swallowed and looked away. 'I already explained to you—'

'You didn't explain anything,' Khalis said, cutting her off. He sighed, stepping towards her, his hand resting on her shoulder. 'Life hasn't been very fair to you, has it, Grace?'

She tensed under his touch, as well as his assumption. 'Life isn't very fair,' she said in a low voice.

'No,' Khalis agreed. His hand was warm and heavy on her shoulder, a comforting weight she longed to lean into. 'Life isn't very fair at all. I think we've both learned that the hard way.'

Her whole body tensed, fighting the desire to lean into him. It was like trying to resist a magnetic force. 'Maybe,' she said, the word half-strangled.

'And here we are,' he mused softly, 'two people completely alone in this world.'

Her throat tightened with emotion. This man made her feel so much. 'I feel alone,' she whispered, the words drawn from her painfully. She almost choked on them. 'I feel alone all the time.'

His hand still rested on one shoulder, and he laid his other hand on her shoulder and drew her gently to him. 'I know you do,' he said quietly. 'So do I.' She rested in the circle of his arms for a moment, savouring the closeness as she breathed in the woodsy scent of his aftershave, felt the comforting heat of his body. It felt so good, so safe, and it would be so easy to stay here, or even to tilt her head up for him to kiss her. So easy, and so dangerous.

Think what you have to lose.

Resolutely she turned away from him, jerking away from his grasp, not wanting him to see the storm of unwilling need she knew would be apparent on her face. She plunged down the twisting path, only to stop abruptly when it ended against a stone wall. The wall that surrounded the villa, the moon illuminating the evil shards of broken glass on its top, reminding her that she was a prisoner. Always a prisoner.

In a sudden burst of fury, Grace slapped her hands against the stone, her palms stinging, as if she could topple it over. 'I hate walls,' she cried in frustration, knowing it was a ridiculous thing to say, to *think*, yet feeling it with every breath and bone.

'Then let's leave them behind,' Khalis said and reached for her hand. Too surprised to resist, she let him lead her away from the wall and down another dark path.

Khalis kept hold of her hand as he guided her down several paths and then finally to a door. The high, forbidding wall had a door, and Khalis possessed the key. Grace watched as he activated the security system, first with his fingerprint and then a number code, before swinging the door open and leading her out to freedom.

The air felt cooler, fresher and more pure without the walls. Khalis led her away from the compound and down a rocky little path towards the shore.

He still held her hand, his fingers wrapped warm and sure around hers as he guided her down the path to the silky sweep of sand. She heard the roar of the waves crashing onto the shore and saw the beach nestled in a rocky cove, now washed in silver.

'This feels better,' she said, as if she'd just had a little dizzy spell.

'Why do you hate walls so much?'

She tugged her hand out of his. 'Who likes them?'

'Nobody really, I suppose, but it seems personal to you.'

Grace kept her gaze on the silvered sea. 'It is. I used to live on an island like this. Private, remote, with high walls. I didn't like it.'

'Couldn't you leave?'

'Not easily.'

She could feel him staring at her, trying to figure her out, even though her back was to him. 'Are you saying,' he asked finally, 'you were some kind of prisoner?'

She sighed. 'Not really. Not literally. But other things can imprison you besides walls.' She turned so she was half-facing him. 'Hopes. Fears.' She paused, her gaze sliding to and then locking with his. 'Mistakes. Memories.'

She felt tension snake through him, even though he kept his voice light. 'That sounds like psychobabble.'

'It probably is,' she admitted with a shrug. 'But can you really deny this island has an effect on you?'

Khalis didn't answer for a moment. 'No,' he said finally, 'I can't.'

Neither of them spoke for a moment, the truth of what he'd said seeming to reverberate through them. 'What will you do with this place?' Grace asked eventually. 'Will you live here?'

He gave a harsh laugh. 'After what you just observed? No, never. Once I've finished going through my father's assets, I'll sell it.'

'Will you manage Tannous Enterprises from the States, then?'

'I don't intend to manage Tannous Enterprises at all. I'm going to dismantle it and sell it off piece by piece, so no one has that kind of power again.'

'Sell it?' Even in the moonlit darkness she could make out the hard set of his jaw, the flintiness in his eyes. 'I thought you were going to turn it around. Redeem it.'

He looked away from her, out to the sea. 'Some things can't be redeemed.'

'Do you really think so?' She felt a sudden sorrowful twist of disappointment inside her. 'I like to think they can. I like to think any…mistake can be forgiven, if not rectified.'

'My father is not alive for me to forgive him,' Khalis said flatly. 'If I even wanted to.'

'You don't?'

'Why should I? Do you know what kind of man my father was?'

'Sort of, but—'

'Shh.' Smiling now, Khalis drew her to him and pressed one finger to her lips. His touch was soft and yet electric, the press of his skin against her lips making the bottom of her stomach seem to drop right out. 'I didn't bring you to this moonlit cove to talk about my father.'

'I could tell you about what I've discovered about the panels—' Grace began. Her heart beat hard in her chest for she could not mistake the look of intent in Khalis's eyes. Or the answering pulse of longing she felt in herself.

He laughed softly. 'I didn't bring you here for that, either.'

Her heart thudded harder. 'Why, then?'

'To have you kiss me.'

Shock made her mouth drop right open and he traced the curve of her parted lips with the tip of his finger. A soft sigh escaped her before she could suppress it. 'Kiss you—'

'The reaction when I kissed you was not quite what I was hoping for,' Khalis explained, a hint of humour in his voice although his gaze blazed into hers. 'So I thought perhaps we'd try it the other way.'

His finger still rested on her mouth, making her dizzy. 'How do you know I even want to kiss you?' she challenged.

'Do you?'

How could she lie? His gaze was hungry and open; he hid nothing. And she hid so much. From him, and even from herself. For even if she didn't want to want him, she knew she did. And she wouldn't hide it. 'Yes,' she whispered, and Khalis waited.

Grace took a shuddering breath. Just one kiss. One kiss no one would ever know about. And then she'd walk away, go back to being safe and strong and independent. Slowly she reached out and touched his cheek, his own hand falling away from her mouth. She took a step towards him so her breasts brushed his chest. He gazed down at her, still, steady. Trustworthy.

Her palm cradled his cheek, the tips of her fingers brushing the softness of his hair. She leaned closer, so her body pressed fully against his and she could feel the hard thrust of his arousal. And then she kissed him.

CHAPTER SIX

Her lips barely brushed his, but Khalis held himself still, and Grace knew he was purposely letting her control the kiss. She closed her eyes, luxuriating in the feel and taste of him. He tasted like mint and whisky, a sensual combination. His lips were soft and yet his yielding touch was firm, so that even though she was in charge she knew it was only because he allowed it. And somehow that made her feel safe rather than threatened or repressed.

Gently she touched her tongue to his lips, exploring the seam of his mouth, the caress a question. She felt a shudder go through him but he didn't move. She pulled away, blinking up at him with a new shyness. She saw his eyes were closed, his body rigid. He looked almost as if he were in pain, but surely he couldn't be…unless it was costing him to remain so still.

'A kiss involves a bit of give and take, you know,' she told him.

He opened his eyes, giving her a wry smile. 'I didn't want to scare you off.'

'I don't scare quite that easily.' At least she hoped she didn't.

'No?' His arms came around her, gently, slowly, giving her time to pull away. She didn't. She'd allow herself this one moment, that was all. In a minute she'd step away.

'Good,' Khalis murmured, and Grace slid her hands up along the hard wall of his chest, lacing her fingers around his neck as she pulled his mouth down towards her. And then she kissed him again, deeply this time, a plunging sensation in her stomach as he responded in kind, their tongues tangling in a blaze of exquisite sensation. When had she last kissed like this? Felt like this?

You know when.

A shudder ran through her, a shudder of both longing and loss. It felt so wonderful and it had been so long, and yet just the memory of a man holding her made the memories rise up, the shame rushing through her in a hot, fast river, along with the desire and the hope. She closed her eyes and kissed Khalis more deeply, pressing herself against him, wanting desperately to banish the memories that taunted her even now.

You kissed a man like this. You wanted a man like this. And it cost you your daughter.

She felt Khalis's hands span her waist, then slide under her T-shirt. The warmth of his palm against her skin made her shudder again and he stilled, waiting. He was so careful, so *caring*, yet she could not halt the relentless encroaching of her memories and that cold hard logic that swamped even her desire, and she knew he felt it, too.

'Grace...?'

She pulled away from him, her head bowed, her hair falling in front of her face. 'I'm sorry.'

'No need to be sorry.' He took her chin in his hand so he could study her face. See her blush. 'We don't need to rush this, do we?'

Yes, she wanted to say, *we do. Because this is all we have.*

'I shouldn't have kissed you.'

'It's a little late for regrets,' he said wryly and Grace jerked her chin from his hand.

'I know that.'

'Why shouldn't you have kissed me, Grace?'

'Because—' Her breath came out in a rush. *Because I'm scared. Of so many things. Of losing myself in you, and losing my daughter as well.* How could she explain all that? She couldn't, didn't want to, because to explain was to open herself up to all kinds of vulnerability and pain. She just shook her head.

Khalis let out a slow breath, the sound of controlled impatience. 'Are you married or something?'

She forced herself to meet his gaze levelly. 'No. But I was.'

He stilled, his eyes narrowing. 'You're divorced?'

'Yes.'

'I still don't understand.'

'It's…complicated.'

'That much I could guess.'

She turned away, wrapping her arms around herself. Now the wind felt cold. 'I just can't be involved with you,' she said quietly. 'My marriage wasn't… It wasn't happy. And I'm not…' She let out a little weary sigh. 'I can't…' She stopped again, her throat too tight for any more words.

'What,' he asked, 'would it take for you to trust me?'

Grace turned back to him, and she saw a man who had only been gentle and patient and kind. 'I don't know,' she whispered. 'But it doesn't matter, Khalis. I wish it did matter, in a way. But, even if I wanted to, I couldn't be in a relationship with you.' Belatedly she realised he'd never actually said that word. *Relationship.* It implied not just intimacy, but commitment. 'Or anything,' she added hurriedly. 'There can't be anything between us.' And, before he could answer, she walked quickly down the beach, back towards the door and that high, high wall.

That night she slept terribly. Memories came in fragments, as dreams, bizarre and yet making too much sense. Khalis kissing her. Her kissing Khalis. The sweet yearning of it, suddenly obliterated by the shame and guilt as she stared into Loukas's face so taut with anger, his lips compressed into an accusing line.

How could you do this to me, Grace? How could you betray me so?

With a cry she sat up in bed, the memory roiling through her mind, racking her body with shudders. Knowing she would not be able to get back to sleep, she rose from the bed and pulled on a pair of jeans and a light cotton jumper. She piled her hair up with a clip and slipped out of her room, along the cool, dark corridors and downstairs.

The basement felt eerily still in the middle of the night, even though Grace knew it should make no difference. The place had no windows. She switched on the lights and gazed down at the panels laid out on a stainless steel table.

She'd spent most of her time so far authenticating the first painting of Leda and the Swan, but now she let her gaze turn to the second painting, the one that caused a fresh shaft of pain to lance through her. Leda and her children.

Over the centuries there had been speculation about this painting; Leonardo had done several studies, a few sketches of Leda sitting, her face downcast, her children by her side. Yet the reality of the actual painting was far more powerful than any sketch. Unlike the other painting, in this one Leda was seated and clothed, the voluptuous temptress hidden or perhaps forgotten. Two children, Castor and Polydeuces, stood behind her, sturdy toddlers, their hands on her shoulders as if they were anchoring themselves, or perhaps protecting their mother. Clytemnestra and Helen were rotund babies, lolling in Leda's lap, their angelic faces upturned towards their mother.

And Leda… What was the expression on her face? Was it sorrow, or wistfulness, or even a wary joy? Was there knowledge in those lowered eyes, knowledge of the terrible things to come? Helen would start a war. Castor would die in it. And Clytemnestra would lose a daughter.

Abruptly Grace turned away from the painting. If she worked for a few hours, she could present Khalis with a file of her findings tomorrow, enough for him to go on with, and for her to leave Alhaja. Leave Khalis. And they could both get on with their lives.

Khalis watched as a wan and fragile-looking Grace entered the breakfast room the next morning. She looked as if she'd barely slept, although her pale face was composed and as lovely as ever. She was dressed in a slim-fitting black skirt and white silk blouse and carried a file, and Khalis knew exactly what she was about. After last night's frustrating and half-finished kiss, he'd expected something like this. He sat back in his chair and sipped his coffee, waiting for her to begin.

'I've completed most of the preliminary tests on the Leonardos.'

'You have?'

She placed the file on the table, her lips pressed together in determination. 'Yes. The analyses of the pigments and the wood panels are consistent with the time period that he would have completed these paintings. There are also several—'

'Grace.'

She stopped, startled, and Khalis smiled at her. 'You don't need to give me a lecture. I'll read the file.'

Her lips thinned even more. 'All right, then.'

Khalis took a sip of his coffee. 'So you feel you've finished?'

'I've done all that I can do on my own. You really need to call a legal authority to—'

'Yes, I'll take care of that.'

She stopped, her eyes narrowing, and Khalis felt a sliver of hurt needle his soul. Did she *still* not trust him about the damn art? Then slowly, resolutely, she nodded. Acceptance, and he felt a blaze of gratified triumph.

'Very well.' She straightened, pressed her hands down the sides of her skirt. 'Then my work here is done. If you could arrange—'

'Done? Good.' Khalis smiled, saw the flash of hurt in her chocolate eyes that was quickly veiled. Suppressed, but he'd seen it and it gave fire to his purpose. No matter what she'd said last night, no matter how her ex-husband had hurt her so badly she trembled at the thought of a kiss, she still wanted to be with him. 'Then you can take the day off.'

'What…what do you mean?'

'A day of leisure, to enjoy yourself. With me.'

'I don't—'

'Your work was expected to take a week. It's been three days. I think you can take a day off.'

'I told you before—'

'One day. That's all. Surely you can allow yourself that?'

She hesitated, and he saw the longing in her eyes. What, he wondered yet again, kept her from enjoying herself? From *living*? 'You want to.' He leaned forward, not bothering to hide the need he was sure she could see in his eyes. The need he was sure she felt, too. '*I* want to. Please, Grace.'

Still she hesitated. Khalis waited. 'All right,' she said at last. She offered him a rather tentative smile. 'All right.'

Khalis couldn't keep himself from grinning. 'Wonderful. You'd better change into something a bit more serviceable, and I'll meet you in the foyer in five minutes.'

'That's rather quick.'

'I want to take advantage of every moment with you.'

A flush tinted her cheeks rose-pink and she turned away. 'One day,' she murmured, and he couldn't tell if she was warning him—or herself.

Grace hadn't brought too many serviceable clothes with her, at least not the kind she thought Khalis had in mind. While working she dressed with discreet professionalism, clothes that were flattering without being obvious. After a few moments' consideration she chose the slim black trousers and white fitted T-shirt she'd worn earlier in the week, and threw a cardigan in charcoal-grey cashmere over her shoulders, in case the breeze from the sea was strong.

Where could he be taking her? Alhaja Island hadn't looked that large from the air. Besides the enclosed compound, there were only a few stretches of beach and a tangle of trees. Yet Grace knew it didn't even matter where he might be taking her, because she simply wanted to be with him—for one day. One day that posed no risk to her heart or her time with Katerina. One day out of time and reality, a memory she would carry with her in all the lonely days and nights ahead.

Khalis was already waiting in the foyer when she came down the stairs, wearing jeans and a white button-down shirt, open at the throat, so Grace's gaze was inexorably drawn to that column of golden-brown skin, the pulse beating strongly. She jerked her gaze upwards and gave him a tentative smile.

'Where are we going?'

'Just to the beach,' he said, but there was a glint in his eye that told her he had something planned. Grace followed him outside to an open-topped Jeep waiting in the drive. She climbed in and fastened her seat belt as Khalis drove through the forbidding-looking gates and then out along a rutted dirt road that looked to circumnavigate the island.

Grace pushed her hair from her face and shaded her eyes as she glanced at the rocky outcrops and the stretch of golden beach, the sea jewel-bright and winking under the sun in every direction. 'This island's not very big, is it?'

'Two miles long and half a mile wide. Not large at all.'

'Did you ever feel…trapped? Living here?'

Khalis slid her a speculative glance and Grace pretended not to notice. 'Yes,' he answered after a moment, his hands tightening reflexively on the steering wheel, 'but not because of the island's size.'

'Why, then?'

His mouth curved grimly. 'Because of the island's inhabitants.'

'Your father?'

'Mainly. My brother and I didn't get along very well, either.'

'Why not?'

He shrugged. 'Ammar was my father's heir, and my father poured everything into him. He was tough with him, too tough, and I suppose Ammar needed to take it out on someone.'

'He was a bully? Your brother?'

Khalis just shrugged again. 'Boarding school was a bit of a relief.'

'What about your sister?'

He didn't answer for a moment, and Grace felt the tension in his body. 'I missed her,' he finally said. 'I'm sure she felt more trapped here than I did. My father didn't believe in educating daughters. He employed a useless governess for a while, but Jamilah never had the opportunities Ammar and I did. Opportunities she would have had if—' He stopped suddenly, shaking his head. His expression, Grace saw, had become shuttered. Closed. 'Old memories,' he said finally. 'Pointless.'

'Do you think,' she asked after a moment, 'the helicopter crash was an accident?'

'It's not outside the realm of possibility that one of his enemies—or even his allies—tinkered with the engine. I don't know what they would have hoped to gain. Perhaps it was an act of revenge—my father did business with the dregs of every society. People like that tend not to die in their beds.'

Grace felt a chill of trepidation at how indifferent Khalis sounded, as if the way his father and brother had died was a matter of little concern. His attitude towards his family was so different from the affable man she'd come to know and even to trust. Again she glimpsed a core of hard, unyielding iron underneath all that easygoing friendliness. 'You sound rather heartless,' she told him quietly.

'*I* sound heartless?' Khalis gave a short laugh. 'Good thing you never met my father.'

Grace knew she could not explain to Khalis why his opinion of his father disquieted her so much. She had heard rumours of Balkri Tannous, the bribes he took, the kind of shady business he conducted. Why was she, in her own twisted way, trying to defend him?

Because you still feel guilty. In need of forgiveness. Just like him.

'How did you find out?' she asked and Khalis did not pretend to misunderstand.

'I was sixteen,' he said quietly. 'Home from school for the summer holidays. I went looking for my father, to tell him I'd won the mathematics prize that year.' He lapsed into a silence and Grace knew he was remembering, saw the pain of that memory in the tautness of his face. 'I found him in his study. He was on the telephone, and he waved for me to sit down. I couldn't help but overhear him—not that he was trying to hide it. At first I didn't understand. He said something about money, and asking for more, and I thought he was just talking about business. Then he said, "You know what to do if he resists. Make sure he feels it this time." It sounded like something a school bully would say. I'd certainly heard such talk at school. But coming from my father—I couldn't credit it. So much so that when he got off the telephone I asked him about it, almost as if it were a joke. "Papa," I said, "it almost sounded like you were ordering someone to be beaten up!" My father gave me one hard look and then he said, "I was."'

Khalis said nothing more. He'd pulled the Jeep onto a flat stretch of beach and killed the engine, so the only sound was the crash of waves onto the shore and the distant raucous cry of gulls. 'And what then?' Grace asked, for she knew there was more.

He lifted one shoulder in something close to a shrug. 'I was shocked, of course. I don't remember what I said—something stupid about it being wrong. My father came over to me and slapped my face. Hard.' With a small smile he gestured to a tiny white scar on the corner of his mouth. 'His ring.'

'That's terrible,' Grace said quietly.

'Oh, it's not that terrible. I was sixteen, after all, almost a man. And he didn't hit me again. But it was shocking to me because he'd never hit me before. I'd adored him, and he loved to be adored. Ammar had it much worse. My father didn't pay much attention to me, although I always wanted him to. Until that day, when I realised just what kind of man he was.'

'But you didn't leave until you were twenty-one.'

Khalis's mouth tightened before he gave a hard smile. 'No. I made justifications for his activities, you see. Excuses. It was only the one time. The person he was dealing with was difficult or corrupt. So many absurd excuses because I didn't have the courage to just leave.'

'You were young,' Grace said softly. 'And that's easy to do.'

'For a while, perhaps, but then it's just wilful blindness. Even when I didn't want to, I started noticing things. The way the servants shrank from him, the telephone conversations he had. And then I started doing a bit of digging—I went through his desk once when he was away on business. He hadn't even locked his office—too arrogant to think his family would nose about. I probably saw enough in that one afternoon to put him in prison.' He shook his head. 'He helped rig an election in an island country that was desperately poor. My father lined his pockets and the people got poorer.'

'What did you do then?'

'Nothing.' Khalis practically spat the word. 'I was nineteen, about to start Cambridge, and I knew I couldn't manage on my own. So I just put it all back and tried to forget about it—for a little while at least. But I couldn't forget. I'll never forget.' Khalis shook his head, his eyes narrowed against the harsh glare of the sun, or perhaps just in memory.

Grace swallowed. 'And so you left.'

'Finally.' The one word was harsh with self-recrimination. 'I took his money to go to university first. I didn't work up the courage to leave until I knew I could make a go of it on my own.' His mouth twisted in condemnation of his own actions. 'So I wasn't really much better than he was.'

'That's rather harsh,' Grace protested. 'You weren't responsible for your father's actions.'

'No. But doing nothing can be as damaging as the action itself.'

'You were young—'

'Not that young.' He turned to her with a quick smile, his expression clearing although Grace still saw the storm clouds lurking in the depths of his agate eyes. 'You're very forgiving, much more forgiving than I am.' Grace looked away. Yes, she tried to be forgiving because she knew how easy it was to fall. The only person she couldn't forgive was herself. 'We've talked about this enough,' Khalis said. 'I didn't intend to spend the day with you raking up bitter memories. What is done, is done.'

'Is it?' Grace asked, her voice hoarse as she stared out to sea. 'Or does it just go on and on?'

Khalis gazed at her for a moment. 'It is done,' he said quietly. 'Whatever it is, Grace, it is done.'

She knew he didn't know what he was talking about, what secrets she still hid, and yet even so she wanted to believe him. She wanted to believe that things could really be finished, sins truly forgiven. His father's…and hers. She wanted to believe in a second chance even if she never got one. Silently she took his hand and let him lead her out of the Jeep.

They walked down the beach, Khalis's hand still loosely linked with her own, until they came to a sheltered spot, the rocks providing protection from the relentless wind.

Grace stopped in surprise at the sight of two gorgeous horses, a bay mare and a chestnut stallion, saddled and waiting, a groom holding their reins.

'What—?'

'I thought you might like to go riding.'

She shot him a sideways glance. 'How do you even know if I ride?'

'You mentioned a horse-mad phase,' Khalis said with a smile. 'That first night.'

'So I did.' She'd forgotten. She'd almost forgotten how to ride. She stared at the horses, reached out to stroke the bay's satiny coat. 'And I suppose you've been riding since the day you were born?'

'Only since I was two. But it's been a while.'

'For me, too.'

'We can take it slowly.'

Were they talking about riding, Grace wondered, or something else? It didn't really matter. She was touched Khalis had thought of this, had remembered her offhand comment. And she wanted to ride. With a smiling nod she let the groom help her to mount. She was glad Khalis had told her to wear serviceable clothing.

Khalis mounted his own horse and smiled at Grace. 'Ready?'

She nodded again, surprised and gratified by how much she enjoyed the feel of riding again, the wind at her back, the sun shining down. She nudged the horse into a canter and Khalis followed suit, the horses happy to trot down the length of the beach.

The breeze ruffled her hair and gulls cried raucously overhead. Grace felt a grin bloom all over her face. She'd forgotten how free she felt when she rode, how everything seemed to shrink to a point of a pin, the cares and fears and even the memories. Nothing mattered but this moment. Without even realising she was doing so, she urged her mount into a gallop. She heard Khalis laugh as he matched her pace.

'Are we racing?' he shouted to her, his words torn away on the wind.

'I think we are,' she called back and leaned low over her horse, her heart singing. It felt so good to be free.

The horses' hooves churned up damp sand and her hair streamed out behind her as they raced down the beach. Grace saw a rocky inlet ahead and knew instinctively that it would be their finish line. Khalis pulled ahead and she urged her own mount onwards so they were neck and neck, both of them laughing. In the last moment Grace pulled ahead by half a length and the mare jumped neatly over the scattering of rocks that had comprised their impromptu finish line.

Laughing, she wheeled her mount around and brushed her hair from her eyes. 'I hope you didn't let me win.'

'Never.'

Khalis looked so utterly at ease on his mount, his eyes flashing humour, his skin like burnished gold in the sunlight, that Grace suddenly felt quite dizzy with longing. She knew there was no way she'd won on her own merit, not when she hadn't ridden in over a decade, and Khalis probably having grown up on a horse. Again it didn't matter. Nothing mattered but this day, this one perfect golden day Khalis was giving her, a gift. 'Liar,' she said, smiling, and slipped off the horse. 'But I'll still take the victory. It felt so good to race like that. I'd forgotten how much I like riding.'

'I'm glad you rediscovered it,' Khalis said. He smiled as he brushed a tendril of hair away from her face and her stomach dipped in response to that casual touch. She stood there, blinking up at him, unable to move away. She might as well ask him out loud to touch her again. To kiss her.

He didn't, though, just led their horses up the beach to where the groom was waiting; he must have driven there to meet them. The groom took control of the horses and Khalis reached for Grace's hand. She let him lace his fingers with hers, reminded herself that just for today it was allowed. Today was separate from the rest of her life, alone on this island with a man she could so easily fall in love with.

The thought jolted her, made her hand tense in Khalis's. She couldn't fall in love, not with Khalis, not with anyone. She'd half-convinced herself that she could have this day—just one day—and she would walk away with no one the wiser, her heart intact. But to fall in love? That surely could only mean heartbreak…and discovery.

'Come,' Khalis said. 'Our picnic is waiting.'

He led her to a secluded little cove surrounded by rocks, a blanket already spread across the sand and a basket waiting. Grace gave a soft laugh. 'This took some planning.'

'A little,' he allowed. 'It's easy when you have staff.'

'I can only imagine.'

He drew her down to the blanket and Grace tucked her legs underneath her. Khalis opened the basket and withdrew a bottle of champagne and two glasses. 'A toast,' he said, and popped the cork.

Grace accepted the glass, pushing away the reservations and regrets that still crouched in the corners of her mind. She wasn't falling in love; she was stronger than that. She just wanted to enjoy this moment. This brief and fragile happiness.

'What are we toasting?' she asked.

'To a perfect day,' Khalis suggested.

'To a perfect day,' she echoed, and drank. As she lowered her glass she felt Khalis's gaze rest heavily upon her. 'One perfect day,' she said, and she knew she was reminding herself as well as him.

Khalis watched Grace drink, enjoyed the sight of her looking happy and relaxed, her hair tousled and free, her face flushed with pleasure. He still saw the fear and sadness lurking in her eyes, and he longed to banish those shadows—not just for one day, but for ever. The fervent nature of his own thoughts didn't alarm him any more, which surprised him. He was ready for this. Over the years he'd had a couple of serious relationships, yet he'd never found a woman who really reached him before. Who touched him and made him say and feel things he hadn't to anyone else. Not until Grace.

From the moment he'd met her he'd been intrigued by her. But he felt more for her than a mere fascination... He admired her dedication to her career, her strength of purpose. He sensed, like him, she was a survivor. And he ached not just to touch her—although he certainly felt that—but to see her smile and hear her laugh.

Smiling, he reached over and plucked the glass from her fingers. 'Ready to eat?'

'OK.'

He fed her strawberries and slices of succulent melon, ripe juicy figs and the softest bread dipped in nutty olive oil. He loved watching her eat, loved to see her finally enjoying herself, the lines of strain around her mouth and eyes relaxing at last. He loved the sensuality of feeding her, of watching her lips part, her eyes widen, her pupils dilate. It felt quite unbearably erotic.

She finally shook her head, refusing the last lone strawberry, her lips still red from the juice. 'You're spoiling me.'

'You deserve to be spoiled.'

The very air around them seemed to tense, freeze. Grace shook her head, her gaze sliding from his. 'No, I don't.'

Khalis had stretched out beside her on the blanket, one arm pillowing his head, and with the other he wound a tendril of soft blond hair around his finger. 'Why do you say that?' he asked quietly.

She shook her head, hard enough for that silky tendril to slip from his finger. 'It doesn't matter.'

He wanted to tell her that it did matter, that everything about her mattered to him, but he swallowed down the words. She wasn't ready to hear them, and perhaps he wasn't ready to say them. Whatever existed between them now was too new and fragile to test it with brash proclamations. Like her, he wanted to enjoy this day. They had plenty of time to learn about each other—learn to trust and maybe even to love—after today. Today—this perfect day—was just the beginning.

Grace watched as Khalis reached for her hair again, winding one silky strand around his finger. He did it almost without thinking, the gesture so relaxed and sure, and yet that simple little touch rocked her to her very core. She shouldn't even feel it—hair, after all, was made up of dead cells, with no nerves. Yet while the scientific part of her brain was reciting these dusty facts, her body blazed to life.

She felt it. Forget science, forget reality, she felt it. She gazed up at him, her eyes wide as she drank him in, his bronzed skin and grey-green eyes now crinkled at the corners as his sensual mouth curled into a knowing smile. Grace's whole body tingled as awareness stole through her, a certain and lovely knowledge that he was going to kiss her.

He lowered his lips to hers slowly, one hand still fisted in her hair as his mouth came down on hers. Her hands slid along his sun-warmed shoulders to clench in the softness of his hair. He lifted his mouth from hers a fraction and his smile deepened; she could *feel* that smile. 'You taste like strawberries.'

She smiled back. 'So do you.'

He let out a little huff of laughter and lowered his head so his mouth claimed hers once more. Grace revelled in that kiss, in this moment, for surely nothing had never been so pure or perfect. Khalis kissed his way slowly along her jawline to the nape of her neck; she let out a sound that was something between a shudder and a laugh as his lips tickled that sensitive spot. He moved lower, to the neckline of her T-shirt, his tongue flicking along her skin, and he tugged it down to press a kiss against the vee between her breasts. Grace arched upwards, her body unfurling like a flower in the sun.

Khalis slid a hand along her waist, his seeking fingers lifting the hem of her T-shirt to touch the sensitized skin beneath. He kissed her again, deeply, and Grace pressed against him. Her own hands sought his skin, tugged up his shirt, slid along the warm, silky stretch of his bare back. She felt his hand slide down along her middle, his palm caressing the tender skin of her tummy.

Behind them a bird suddenly cawed raucously and Grace lurched upright, panic replacing desire. With her clothes in disarray, her hair mussed and her mouth swollen, she felt as if she'd been caught out. Trapped and shamed.

Khalis still reclined on one elbow, looking relaxed. He'd obviously noticed her overreaction, though he said nothing, just let his gaze sweep lazily over her.

'I'm sorry—' she began.

'There's no need to be sorry.'

She let out a shuddering breath. 'I'm not...I haven't...'

'I know.'

He sounded so *sure*, and it made Grace flinch. He didn't know. The assumptions he was making so easily and arrogantly were wrong. Completely, utterly wrong. 'Actually,' she told him, her voice low, 'you don't know.'

'Then tell me.'

No. She tried for a smile. 'We've spent enough time today talking about old memories.'

'That's a brush-off if I've ever heard one.' He didn't sound annoyed, just accepting or perhaps amused. He rolled to a sitting position and began packing the remains of their picnic. Was their perfect day over already?

'We don't have to go yet—'

He touched her heated cheek. 'You're getting sunburn. We're very close to the coast of Africa, you know. The sun is incredibly hot.'

Silently Grace helped him pack up their things. She felt a confused welter of emotions: frustration that the afternoon had ended, as well as relief that it hadn't gone too far. And over it all like a smothering blanket whose weight she'd become so unbearably used to, guilt. Always the guilt.

'Cheer up.' Chuckling softly, Khalis touched her cheek again, his fingers lingering on her skin. 'Don't look so disappointed, Grace. It's only one day.'

Exactly, she wanted to say. Shout. One day—that was all she had. All she'd allow herself, and Khalis knew that. He'd said so himself—hadn't he? Doubt suddenly pricked her. Had she assumed he understood because it was easier to do so? Easier to be blinded by your own desires, to justify and excuse and ignore. But if he didn't understand… if he hadn't accepted her silent, implied terms that today was all they would ever share…what did he want? What did he expect?

Whatever it was, she couldn't give it to him, and a poignant sorrow swept over her as she realised for the first time she wanted to.

CHAPTER SEVEN

WHEN Grace returned to her room she was surprised to find Shayma in attendance, along with an impressive array of clothes and beauty products. Grace stared at a tray of make-up and nail varnish in bewilderment.

'What is all this…?'

Shayma smiled shyly. 'Mr Tannous, he wishes me to help you prepare.'

'Prepare?' Grace turned to gaze at the half-dozen gowns spread out on the bed in bewilderment. 'For what?'

'He is taking you somewhere, I think?'

'Taking me…' Where on earth could he take her to? Not that it mattered; she couldn't go anywhere. She couldn't be seen in public with Khalis, or with any man. Not on a proper date, at least.

'Are they not beautiful?' Shayma said, lifting one of the gowns from the bed. Grace swallowed as she looked at it.

'Gorgeous,' she admitted. The dress was a body-hugging sheath in ivory silk, encrusted with seed pearls. It looked like a very sexy wedding gown.

'And this one as well.' Shayma lifted a dress in a blue so deep it looked black, the satin shimmering like moonlight on water.

'Amazing.' The dresses were all incredible, and she

could not suppress the purely feminine longing to wear one. To have Khalis see her in one.

'And shoes and jewels to match each one,' Shayma told her happily.

Grace shook her head helplessly. She could not believe the trouble and expense Khalis had gone to. She could not believe how much she wanted to wear one of the gowns, and go on a date—a proper date—with him.

See how it happens? her conscience mocked her. *Temptation creeps in, slithers and stalks. And before you know it you're doing things you never, ever thought you'd do. And telling yourself it's OK.*

She knew the rules of her agreement with Loukas. No inappropriate behaviour. No dating. No men. It wasn't fair or really even legal, but in the four years since her divorce she hadn't really cared about the restrictions Loukas had placed upon her. Her heart had its own restrictions. Don't trust. Don't love. *Don't lose yourself.* She hadn't wanted any of it—until Khalis. Khalis made her long to feel close to someone again, to feel the fire of physical desire and the sweetness of shared joy. For the first time in four years she was tempted to let someone in. To trust him with her secrets.

Grace turned away from the sight of those tempting dresses. It was impossible, she reminded herself. Even if her contrary heart had changed, the conditions of her custody arrangement had not.

'Miss…?' Shayma asked hesitantly, and Grace turned back with an apologetic smile.

'I'm sorry, Shayma. I can't wear any of these dresses.'

Shayma stared at her in confused dismay. 'You do not like them?'

'No, I love them all. But I'm not… I can't go out with Mr Tannous.' Shayma looked more confused, and even worried. Grace patted her hand. 'Don't worry. I'll explain to him myself.'

She took a moment to brush her hair and steel herself before heading towards the part of the compound that housed Khalis's study.

Khalis sat behind his desk, and he smiled as she came in. 'I need to tell you—'

He held up one hand. 'You'd like to thank me for the dresses, but you won't go out with me tonight.'

Grace stopped short. 'How did you know?'

'I'd expect nothing less from you, Grace. Nothing about you is easy.'

She bristled; she couldn't help it. 'I'm not sure why you bother, then.'

'I think you do. We share something unusual, something profound—don't we?' He didn't sound remotely uncertain. Grace said nothing, but her silence didn't seem to faze Khalis in the least. 'I've never felt that before with any woman, Grace. And I don't think you've felt it with any man.' He paused, his gaze intent and serious. 'Not even your ex-husband.'

She swallowed. Audibly. And still didn't speak.

'You fascinate me, Grace. You make me feel alive and open and *happy*.'

Grace shook her head slowly. Did he know what his heartfelt confessions did to her? How hungry and heartbroken they made her feel? 'I'm really not that fascinating.'

He smiled wryly. 'Perhaps I'm easily fascinated, then.'

'Perhaps you're easily misguided.'

He arched an eyebrow, clearly surprised by this turn in the conversation. 'Misguided? How?'

Her throat tightened around the words she couldn't say. 'You don't really know me,' she said softly.

'I'm getting to know you. I want to know you.' She shook her head again, unwilling to explain that she didn't want him to get to know her. She didn't want him to know. 'Why won't you go out with me tonight?'

'As I've told you before, I can't.'

'Can't,' Khalis repeated musingly. His body remained relaxed, but his gaze was hard now, unyielding, and Grace knew she would bend beneath that assessing stare. She would break. 'Are you afraid of your ex-husband?'

'Not exactly.'

'Stop talking in riddles.'

Grace knew she'd prevaricated long enough. Khalis had been gentle, patient, kind. He deserved a little honesty. Just a little.

'I have a daughter,' she said quietly. 'Katerina. She's five years old.'

Khalis's expression didn't change, not really, beyond the slight flare of realisation in his eyes, turning them darker, more grey than green, like the ice that covered a lake. You had no idea how hard or thick it was until you stepped on it, let it take your full weight. And then heard the resounding crack in the air as it broke beneath you.

'And?' he finally asked softly.

'My ex-husband has custody of her. I get to see her once a month.'

She could almost hear the creak of the ice, the cracks like spiderwebs splintering the solid ground beneath them. What Khalis had *thought* was solid ground. 'Why is that?' he asked, his tone carefully neutral.

She swallowed, words sticking in her throat, jagged shards of truth she could not dislodge. 'It's complicated,' she whispered.

'How complicated?'

'He's a very powerful and wealthy man,' she explained,

choosing each word with agonised care. 'Our marriage was…troubled and…and our divorce acrimonious. He used his influence to win complete custody.' Her throat closed up over those unsaid jagged shards so they cut her up inside, although surely they'd already done all their damage? She'd lived with the loss of her daughter and her own painful part in it for four years already. Yet it hurt more to tell Khalis now because she never spoke of it. Never to anyone she cared about. And she cared about Khalis. She'd tried not to, still wished she didn't, but she couldn't deny the truth he'd spoken. They did share something. She felt her mouth wobble and tried to look away.

Khalis walked towards her, his expression softening, a sad smile tipping the corners of his mouth. 'Oh, Grace.' She closed her eyes, not wanting to see the undeserved compassion in his gaze. He put his arms around her though she didn't lean into his embrace as she longed to. 'I'm sorry.'

'It was my fault…partly…' A big part.

Khalis brushed this aside, his arms tightening around her. 'Why didn't you fight the custody arrangement? Most judges are inclined favourably towards the mother—'

Except when the mother was thought to be unfit. 'I… couldn't,' she said. At least that was true. She hadn't possessed the strength or courage to fight a judgement her heart had felt was what she deserved.

Khalis tipped her chin up so she had to face him. He looked so tender it made her want to cry. To blurt out the truth—that she didn't deserve his compassion or his trust, and certainly not his love. 'What does this have to do with you and me?'

You and me. How she wanted to believe in that idea. 'Loukas—my ex-husband monitors my behaviour. He's made it a requirement that I don't become…romantically involved with any man. If I do, I lose that month's visit with Katerina.'

Khalis drew back and stared at her in complete bafflement. 'But that…that has to be completely illegal. And outrageous. How can he control your behaviour to such an absurd degree?'

'He has the trump card,' Grace said. 'My daughter.'

'Grace, surely you could fight this. With a *pro bono* solicitor if money is an issue. There's no way he should be able to—'

'No.' She spoke flatly, although her heart raced and her stomach churned. What on earth had possessed her to tell him so much—and yet so little? Now he'd paint her as even more of a victim. 'No, don't, please, Khalis. Leave it. Let's not discuss this any more.'

He frowned, shaking his head. 'I don't understand—'

'Please.' She laid a hand on his arm, felt the corded muscles leap beneath her fingers. 'Please,' she said again, her voice wobbling, and his frown deepened. She thought he'd resist, keep arguing and insisting she fight a battle she knew she'd already lost, but then he sighed and nodded.

'All right. But I'd still like you to go out with me.'

'After what I just told you?'

Smiling, although his eyes still looked dark and troubled, he reached for her hand and kissed her fingers. 'I understand you can't be seen in public with me—yet. But we can still go out.'

She felt the brush of his lips against her fingers like an electric current, jolting right through her and short-circuiting her resolve. She longed to open her hand and press it against his mouth, feel the warmth of his breath against her flattened palm. Step closer so her breasts brushed his chest. With the last vestiges of her willpower she drew her hand back and dredged up a response. 'Go out where?'

'Out there.' He gestured towards the window, the wall. 'Away from this wretched compound.'

'But where—?'

'Grace.' He cut her off, stepping closer so she could feel the intoxicating heat of his nearness and knew her resolve was melting clean away. 'Do you trust me,' he asked, 'to take you somewhere your ex-husband could never discover? A place where you'll be completely safe—with me?'

She stared at him, fear and longing clutching at her chest. One day. One date. It had been four long years and she'd never, *never* known a man like Khalis—a man so gentle he made her ache, so kind he made her cry. A man who made her burn with need. She nodded slowly. 'All right. Yes. I trust you.'

His mouth curled in a smile of sensual triumph and he reached for her hand, kissed her fingers again. 'Good. Because I really would like to take you out to dinner. I'd like to see you in one of those dresses, and I'd like to peel it slowly from your body as I make love to you tonight.' He gave her a wry smile even as his gaze seared straight into her soul. 'But I'll settle for dinner.'

The images he'd conjured brought her whole body tingling to life. 'I can't imagine a place where we can go to dinner that's not—'

'Leave that to me.' He released her hand. 'You can spend some time being spoiled by Shayma.' He pressed a quick, firm kiss against her mouth. 'We'll have a wonderful evening. I'm looking forward to seeing which gown you pick.'

Two hours later, having been massaged and made-up and completely pampered, Grace was dressed in the dress of deep blue satin. She'd wanted to wear the ivory gown, but it had looked too bridal for her to feel comfortable wearing it. She wasn't innocent enough for that dress.

In any case, the blue satin was stunning, with its halter top and figure-hugging silhouette before it flared out in a spray of paler blue at her ankles. Shayma had fastened a diamond-encrusted sapphire pendant around her neck and given her matching earrings as well. She felt like a movie star.

'You look beautiful, miss,' Shayma whispered as she handed Grace her gauzy wrap and Grace smiled her thanks.

'You've been wonderful to me, Shayma. It's been one of the most relaxing afternoons I've had in a long time.'

Khalis was waiting for her at the bottom of the staircase, and he blinked up at her for a moment before he gave her a wide, slow smile of pure masculine appreciation. 'You look,' he told her, reaching for her hand, 'utterly amazing.'

'You look rather nice yourself.' He wore a suit in charcoal-grey silk, but Grace knew he'd look magnificent in anything. He was, simply and utterly, an incredibly attractive man. The suit emphasised the lean, whipcord strength of his body, its restrained power. 'So where are we going?'

'You'll see.'

He led her by the hand out of the compound, through the forbidding gates and then towards the beach. Night was already settling softly on the island, leaving deep violet shadows and turning the placid surface of the sea to an inky stretch of darkness.

Khalis led her to a launch where an elegant speedboat bobbed gracefully in the water. 'We're going by boat?' Grace asked a bit doubtfully, glancing down at her floor-length evening gown. 'I hate to tell you, but I'm feeling a bit overdressed.'

'Well, you look magnificent.' He helped her into the boat, taking care to keep the hem of her gown from trailing in the water. 'I will confess, I had an elegant little hotel in Taormina in mind when I originally had those gowns brought over. But it doesn't really matter where we go, does it? I just want to be with you.' He smiled at her, and Grace's heart twisted.

You're saying all the right things, she wanted to cry. *All the sweet, lovely things any woman wants to hear, and the worst part is I think you mean them.* That was what hurt.

'I am curious,' she murmured, 'where this secret place of yours is.' And nervous. And even afraid. In the four years since her divorce, she'd lost her monthly visits with Katerina twice. Once for going out for a coffee with a colleague, and another time for being asked to dance at a charity function she'd attended for work. She'd refused, but it hadn't mattered. Loukas just liked to punish her.

Khalis headed towards the helm and within a few minutes he was guiding the boat through the sea, the engine purring to life and thrumming beneath them. Grace sat behind a Plexiglas shield, but even so her careful chignon began to fall into unruly tendrils, whipped by the wind.

'Oh, dear.' She held her hands up to her hair, but Khalis just grinned.

'I like seeing you with your hair down.'

She arched her eyebrows. 'Is that a euphemism?'

His grin turned wicked. 'Maybe.'

Laughing a little, feeling far too reckless, she took the remaining pins out of her hair and tossed them aside. Her hair streamed out behind her in a windblown tangle. She probably looked a fright but she didn't care. It felt good. She felt free.

'Excellent,' Khalis said, and the boat shot forward as he accelerated.

Grace still had no idea where they could be going. All around them was an endless stretch of sea, and as far as she knew there were no islands between Alhaja and Sicily. And he couldn't be taking her to Sicily, could he? He'd said somewhere private; he'd asked her to trust him. And she did, even if her stomach still churned with nerves.

'Don't worry,' Khalis told her. 'Where we're going is completely private. And it won't take long to get there.'

'How,' she asked ruefully, 'do you always seem to know what I'm thinking?'

He paused, considering. 'I'd say your every emotion is reflected in your face, but it isn't. It just feels that way.'

Her heart seemed to turn right over. She knew what he meant. Even at his most carefully expressionless, she felt as if she knew what Khalis was feeling, as if she could feel it, too, as if they were somehow joined. Yet they weren't, and in twenty-four hours it would be over. The connection would be severed.

Unless...

For a brief blissful moment she imagined how it could go on. How she'd tell Khalis everything and somehow they'd find a way to fight the custody arrangement. Was this connection they shared strong enough for that?

She glanced at Khalis, her gaze taking in his narrowed eyes, the hard line of his cheek and jaw as he steered the boat. She thought of how he refused to grieve for his family. Forgive his father. Under all the grace and kindness he'd shown her she knew there was an inflexible hardness that had carried him as far as he'd got. A man like that might love, but he wouldn't forgive.

She swallowed, those brief hopes blown away on the breeze like so much ash. They'd been silly dreams, of course. Happy endings. Fairy tales.

'You look rather deep in thought,' Khalis said. He'd

throttled back so the noise of the engine was no more than a steady purr, and Grace could hear the sound of the waves slapping against the sides of the boat.

'Just thinking how beautiful the sea is.' *And how, now that I want to live and love again, I can't.* Khalis had been right. Life wasn't fair, and it was her own fault.

'It is, isn't it?' Khalis agreed, but Grace had the distinct feeling that she hadn't fooled him, and he knew she'd been thinking about something else. About him.

'So are we almost there yet?' she asked, peering out into the unrelieved darkness. A sudden thought occurred to her. 'Are we…are we going to stay on the boat?'

Khalis chuckled. 'You think that's my big surprise? Sausages over a propane stove on a motorboat? I'm almost offended.'

'Well, it is a rather nice boat,' Grace offered.

'Not that nice. And I don't fancy eating my dinner on my lap, bobbing in the water. Come on.' He held out his hand and, surprised, Grace took it. She couldn't see much in the darkness, the only light from the moon cutting a pale swathe of silver across the water. She had no idea where Khalis might be taking her.

He led her to the front of the boat and, even more surprised, Grace realised they had come up next to a small and seemingly deserted island. A slender curve of pale beach nestled against a tangle of foliage, palm fronds drooping low into the water.

'What is this place?'

'A very small, very secluded island my father happened to own. It's not very big at all—a couple of hundred metres across. But my father valued his privacy, and so he bought all the land near Alhaja, even if it wasn't much bigger than a postage stamp.' He vaulted out of the boat easily and then held out his hand to her. 'Come on.'

Grace reached for his hand, teetering a bit in her high heels and long dress, until Khalis put both of his hands firmly on her waist and swung her down off the boat onto the beach. Her heels sunk a good two inches into the damp sand and, ruefully, she slipped them off.

'I think these are designer. I don't want to get them ruined.'

'Much more sensible,' Khalis agreed and kicked his own shoes off. Grace looked at the empty stretch of dark, silent beach, the jungle dense and impenetrable behind it. Everything was very still, and it almost felt as if they were the only two people in the entire world, or at least the Mediterranean.

She turned to Khalis with a little laugh. 'Now I really feel overdressed.'

'Feel free to take your clothes off if you'd be more comfortable.'

Her heart rate skittered. 'Maybe later.'

'Is that a promise?'

Grace gave a little smile. She couldn't believe she was actually *flirting.* And it felt good. 'Definitely not.'

She picked up her dress and held it about her knees as she picked her way across the sand. She hadn't felt so relaxed and even happy in a long, long time. 'So we're not having sausages on the boat. A barbecue on the beach?'

'Wrong again, Ms Turner.' Grinning, Khalis reached for her hand. 'Come this way.' He led her down the darkened beach, towards a sheltered inlet. Grace stopped in surprise at the sight that awaited her there. A tent, its sides rippling in the breeze, had been set up, its elegant interior flickering with torchlight.

It was a tent, but it was as far from propane stoves and camping gear as could be possible. With the teakwood table, silken pillows and elegant china and crystal, it looked like something out of an *Arabian Nights* fantasy.

'How,' Grace asked, 'did you arrange this in the space of a few hours?'

'It was easy.'

'Not that easy.'

'It did take some doing,' Khalis allowed as he reached for the bottle of white wine chilling in a silver bucket. 'But it was worth it.'

Grace accepted a glass of wine and glanced around at the darkness stretching endlessly all about them, cocooned as they were in the tent with the flickering light casting friendly shadows. Safe. She was safe. And Khalis had made it happen. 'Thank you,' she said softly.

Khalis gazed at her over the rim of his wine glass, his gaze heavy-lidded with sensual intent and yet also so very sincere. 'Thank you,' he said, 'for trusting me.'

'Finally,' she said, and he smiled.

'It didn't take as long as all that.' He started to serve them both hummus and triangles of pitta bread. 'So you must live a very quiet life, with these restrictions your ex-husband has placed on you.'

'Fairly quiet. I don't mind.'

He gave her a swift, searching glance. 'Don't you? I would.'

'You can get used to things.' She'd rather talk about anything else. 'And sometimes,' she half-joked, 'I think I prefer paintings to people.'

'I suppose paintings never let you down.'

'Oh, I don't know,' she said lightly, 'a few paintings have let me down. I once found what I thought was a genuine Giotto in someone's attic, only to discover it was a very good forgery.'

'Isn't it interesting,' Khalis mused, 'how a painting that

looks exactly like the original is worth so much less? Both are beautiful, yet only one has value.'

'I suppose it depends on what you value. The painter or the painting.'

'Truth or beauty.'

Truth. It always came back to truth. The weight of what she wasn't telling him felt as if it would flatten her. Grace took a sip of her wine, tried to swallow it all down. 'Some forgeries,' she said after a moment, 'are worth a fair amount.'

'But nothing like the original.'

'No.'

She felt her heart race, her palms slick, even though they were having an innocuous conversation about art. Except it didn't feel innocuous because what Khalis didn't know—or maybe he already suspected—was that Grace herself was the most worthless forgery of all.

An innocent woman. A maligned wife. Both false, no matter what he thought or how she appeared. No matter what he seemed determined to believe.

'Come and eat,' he said, gesturing to the seat across from him, and Grace went forward with relief. Perhaps now they could talk about something else.

'Had you ever been to this island before?' she asked, dipping a triangle of pitta bread into the creamy hummus. 'As a boy?'

'My brother and I sailed out here once.'

'Once?'

He shrugged. 'We didn't do much together. Everything was a competition to Ammar, one he had to win. And I started not to like losing.' He smiled wryly, but there was something hard about the twist of his lips, a darker emotion that hinted at more than the average sibling rivalry.

'Do you miss him?' Grace asked quietly. 'Your brother, at least, if not your father?'

Khalis's face tensed, his body stilling. 'I already told you I don't.'

'I just find it hard to understand.' Why she felt the need to press, she couldn't say. It was the same kind of compulsion as picking a scab or probing a sore tooth. To see how much it hurt, how much pain you could endure. 'I miss my parents even now—'

'My family was very different from yours.'

'What about your sister? You must miss her.'

'Yes,' Khalis said after a moment. 'I do. But there's no point in going on about it. She's been dead fourteen years.'

He spoke so flatly, so coldly, that Grace could not keep from blurting out, 'How can you… How can you just draw a line across your whole family?'

For a second Khalis's face hardened, his eyes narrowing, lips thinning, and Grace had to look away. This was the man of unrelenting, iron control. The man who never looked back. Never forgave.

'I haven't drawn a line, as you say,' he said evenly, 'across my whole family. I simply see no point in endlessly looking back. They're dead. I've moved on. From mourning them and from this conversation.' He leaned forward, his tone softening. 'My father and brother don't deserve your consideration. You are innocent, Grace, but if you knew the kinds of things they'd done—'

'I'm not as innocent as you seem to think I am.'

'I'm sorry, I don't mean to sound patronising. And I did not intend to talk about my family tonight. Surely there are better ways for us to spend our time.'

'I'm sure there are,' Grace agreed quietly. Why had she pressed Khalis when she had not wanted to talk about her own past? She'd wanted to enjoy herself tonight, and losing themselves in dark memories was not the way to do it.

Khalis served her the next course and she watched the firelight flicker over his golden skin, saw the strength of the corded muscles in his wrist as he ladled fragrant pieces of chicken and cardamom onto her plate. Suddenly the memory of this afternoon, of Khalis's lingering kiss, his hand sliding along her skin, rose up so Grace's whole body broke out into a prickly heat, every muscle and nerve and sinew remembering how heartbreakingly wonderful it had felt when he'd touched her.

She felt her face heat and she reached for her glass. Khalis smiled, his eyes glinting knowingly. 'I think we are both thinking of one way in particular we could spend our time.'

'Probably,' Grace managed, nearly choking on her wine. She could imagine it all too well.

'Let us eat.' The food was delicious, the evening air warm and sultry, the only sound the whisper of the waves against the sand and the rattle of the wind in the palms. Khalis moved the conversation to more innocuous subjects, and Grace enjoyed hearing about how he had built up his business, his life in San Francisco. Khalis asked her about her own life, too, and she was happy to describe her job and some of her more interesting projects. It felt wondrously simple to sit and chat and laugh, to enjoy herself without worry or fear. She'd been living too long under a cloud, Grace thought. She'd needed this brief foray into the light.

All too soon they'd finished their main course and were lingering over thick Turkish-style coffee Khalis had boiled in a brass pot and dessert—a sinful tiramisu—as the stars winked above them and were reflected below upon a placid sea. Grace didn't want the night to end, the magic to stop, for it surely felt like a fantasy, wearing this gown, gazing at the sea, being with Khalis on this enchanted island.

Yet it didn't have to end…not yet, anyway. Her body both tingled in anticipation and shivered with trepidation as she imagined how this magical night could continue. How Khalis could fulfil his promise and slip this gown from her shoulders. Make love to her…as she wanted him to.

Her fingers trembled and she returned her coffee cup to its saucer with a clatter. It had been so long since she'd been with a man. So long since she'd allowed herself the intimacy and vulnerability of being desired. Loved. It scared her still, but she also wanted it. More than she ever had before.

'Why do you look afraid?' Khalis asked quietly. 'We're safe here.' Grace heard both tender amusement and gentle concern in his voice and he reached over to cover her hand with his own.

'I'm not afraid.' She lifted her head to meet his gaze directly, even boldly. She was not afraid, not of him anyway, and not even of Loukas. There was no way he could discover her here. No, she was afraid of herself, and this intense longing that had seized her body and mind and maybe even her heart. Tomorrow she would have to walk away from it.

'Do you wish to return to Alhaja now?'

'Not unless we have to.' She smiled, her eyebrows arched even as her heart thudded. 'Do we?'

'No,' Khalis said in a low thrum of a voice. 'We could stay here.'

Grace didn't know if he meant a little longer or all night. She glanced at a large pillow of crimson and cream striped silk, the torchlight shimmering off the rich material. It looked incredibly soft and inviting, and she could imagine sleeping on it. She could also imagine *not* sleeping on it.

'More coffee?'

She shook her head. 'No, thank you.' Impulsively she leaned forward. 'Let's dance.'

Khalis raised his eyebrows. 'Dance?'

'Yes, dance. On the beach.' The idea had come to her suddenly; this was a date, the only date she'd ever have, and she wanted to enjoy it. She wanted to do all the things she was never able to do because of Loukas and his restrictions. She wanted to dance with Khalis.

A small smile quirked the corner of Khalis's mouth. 'But there's no music.'

Grace held out her arms, gesturing to the rich blue satin of her dress. 'I'm wearing an evening gown on a deserted island. Do we really need music?' She smiled, longing to grab this fragile happiness with both hands. 'Does it really matter?' she echoed his own words back to him.

'Not at all.' In one swift movement Khalis rose from the table and led her out to the beach. The sand was cool and silky beneath her bare feet and the darkness swirled around them, the moon shimmering on the surface of the sea, giving it a fine pearl-like sheen. Khalis turned to her. 'Since there's no music, we can pick the kind we like.'

Grace could hardly see him out here on the dark beach, but she felt the heat and intensity of him, the desire pulsing between them, a sustaining and life-giving force. Impossible to resist. Necessary for life. 'Which kind?' she asked in a voice that sounded a little hoarse.

'Something slow and lazy,' Khalis said. He reached out and pulled her towards him so her hips collided gently with his and heat pooled in her pelvis. She let her hands slide up his shoulders, lace around his neck as he started to sway. 'A saxophone, maybe. Do you like sax?'

'Sax,' Grace repeated dazedly. Khalis had slid his hands from her shoulders to her waist to her hips, and now his fingers were splayed along her bottom as he pulled her even closer, against the full thrust of his arousal. 'I... Yes, I think so.'

'Good,' he murmured, and they swayed silently together. Grace could have sworn she heard music, the lonely wail of a saxophone as they danced on the empty beach, their bare feet leaving damp footprints in the sand.

Above them the sky was scattered with stars, a hundred thousand glittering pin-pricks in an inky, endless sky. Grace laid her head on Khalis's shoulder, felt the steady thud of his heart against her own chest. After a moment she lifted her head and tilted back so she could look up into his eyes. His lips were a whisper away. The sleepy sensuality of the dance was replaced by something far more primal and urgent, something whose force was overwhelming and irresistible.

'Grace,' Khalis said and it almost sounded like a warning.

But Grace didn't want warnings. She didn't want memories or guilt or fear. She just wanted this. 'Khalis,' she whispered and his fingers brushed her cheek.

'I love it when you say my name.'

'I was amazingly resistant to saying it.' She turned her head so her lips brushed his fingers. She felt carefree to the point of wantonness, and after four years of being completely buttoned-up it felt good. Khalis let out a little shudder as her tongue darted out and touched his fingers, tasted the salt of his skin. He took her chin in his hand and gazed down at her with a ferocity that would have frightened her if she hadn't felt it herself.

Then he kissed her hard, so different from the gentle caresses of this afternoon, and yet so right. The very air seemed to ignite around them, the stars exploded in the sky as Grace kissed him back and Khalis pulled her even closer, his mouth moving from her lips to her jaw to her throat and she heard the primal sound of her own desperate moan of longing.

He pressed another kiss in the curve of her neck and she tilted her head back, allowing him access. The feel of his lips against her skin gave her a plunging sensation deep inside, turned her mind into a whirlpool of need.

'This dress is going to get very sandy,' Khalis murmured against her throat and Grace gave a shaky laugh.

'I don't care. Although I suppose you might.' She had to find the words from somewhere deep inside her, for thought of any kind was proving virtually impossible. Khalis had undone the halter top of the dress and was slowly peeling it away from her, just as he'd promised.

'I find,' he murmured as he slid the gown down her body, 'I don't care about this dress at all.'

'It is beautiful,' Grace gasped as he finished removing it and tossed it onto the sand. 'Was,' she amended, and Khalis let out a hoarse laugh as his gaze roved over her.

'Grace, *you* are beautiful. Utterly and shockingly beautiful.'

She should have felt embarrassed, standing in her knickers in the middle of a beach, but she didn't. She wasn't even wearing a bra because she hadn't brought one that fitted the halter-style top of the dress. The cool breeze puckered her bare skin into gooseflesh.

'Shockingly?' she repeated. 'That sounds rather alarming.'

'It is alarming,' Khalis told her. He stepped closer to her, ran his hands lightly over her shoulders before cupping her breasts. His palms were warm and dry and still

Grace shivered under his touch. 'It's alarming to me, what I feel for you,' he said in a low voice.

Grace's heart lurched. Yes, it was alarming to her, too. Terrifying and wonderful at the same time. 'Kiss me,' she murmured, and as Khalis brushed his lips against her own she closed her eyes.

He deepened the kiss, but only for a moment, pulling away from her to brush her lids with his fingers. 'Open your eyes.'

'Wh-what?' Her eyes fluttered open and she stared at him, the mobile curve of his mouth hardening just a little bit as he gazed back at her.

'Don't turn your mind off, Grace. I'm making love to you, body and mind and soul.'

'You don't ask for much, do you?'

'Just everything.' And then he claimed her mouth in a kiss that was as hard and unrelenting as she knew the core of him to be, reminding her that no matter how gentle this man was, how tender and even loving, he was still a dangerous proposition. 'Kiss me back,' he muttered against her mouth, and she did, returning the demand, answering it.

He pulled her closer, her breasts crushed against his chest as his hands slid down the bare expanse of her back and tugged off her knickers. Then, his gaze still locked on hers, he stepped back and reached for the buttons of his own shirt. Mesmerised, Grace watched as he began to undress, her own nakedness almost forgotten as he slid his shirt off and revealed the lean, muscled chest underneath. His skin was golden with a satiny sheen, a light sprinkling of hair veeing down to his waistband. Her breath hitched. Khalis undid his belt.

Seconds later, they were both naked. Grace tried not to shiver. Khalis's heated gaze was enough to fire her body, yet she could not shake the feeling of vulnerability that stole over her and made her cold. She'd forgotten how *intimate* this all was. How revealing. She'd been on her own for so long, buttoned-up and barricaded, protected. Now there was nothing. Now she was bare.

At least physically. Emotionally, Grace knew, she was still as guarded as ever. And now more than ever, as Khalis led her back to the tent and drew her down to the pillows' opulent softness, she wanted to tell the last of her secrets. She wanted to bare her soul. She wanted, Grace knew, to be understood and accepted. Forgiven. *Loved.*

Yet she didn't know how to begin. Her thoughts were a ferment of uncertainty, even as pleasure began to take over.

Khalis trailed kisses from her throat to her tummy and desire dazed her senses, scattering her thoughts. His mouth moved lower, his tongue flicking against her skin, and then, thankfully, she had no more thoughts at all.

Something was missing. Even as he heard Grace's little gasps and mews, even as his own libido ran rampant, Khalis knew it wasn't enough. He wanted more from Grace, more than this physical response, overwhelming as it was. He wanted to destroy the defences she'd put around herself. He wanted her completely open to him, body and mind, heart and soul.

You don't ask for much, do you?

He'd never wanted so much from a woman before, but then he'd never felt so much for a woman before. And yet, even as her body lay naked to him, even as she parted her legs and arched up towards his caress, Khalis knew she was closing off her mind. Her heart.

'Look at me, Grace.'

Her eyes fluttered open, unfocused and dazed with passion. 'What—' He braced himself on his elbows, poised over her as her breath came in little pants. *'Please—'*

He knew what she wanted. God knew he wanted it, too. In one stroke he could be embedded deep inside her and satisfy them both. He stayed still. 'Say my name.'

Confusion clouded her eyes. Her lips parted. 'Why—?'

'Say my name.'

It wasn't much, but it was, at least, a beginning. She would acknowledge him, own this connection between them. He wouldn't let her memories or fears crowd him out. He wouldn't let her try to banish him along with her ghosts. She didn't speak and sweat beaded on his brow. He could not hold himself back much longer. *'Please.'*

Her expression softened and the sudden tears that shimmered in her eyes nearly broke him. 'Khalis,' she whispered, and with a primal groan of satisfaction he drove inside her, felt her welcoming warmth wrap around him. 'Khalis,' she said again, her nails digging into his shoulders, her body arching upwards, and triumph tore through him as they surged towards a climax. Grace cried aloud, her head thrown back as her legs wrapped around him. His name sounded like both a supplication and a blessing as her body convulsed around his. *'Khalis.'*

CHAPTER EIGHT

GRACE lay in the cradle of Khalis's arms and could not keep the tears from silently slipping down her face. She closed her eyes, but still they came, one after the other, tears of poignant joy and bitter regret. She'd never felt so close to a man before…and yet so unbearably far away. She'd been so afraid to open her heart and body and soul to him, afraid of the strength of her own feelings. Right to the end she'd resisted, and then…

Then her heart had cracked right open and instead of feeling like the end it had been a beginning. Life instead of death. Hope instead of fear. How could she not have realised how different it would be with Khalis, how wonderful?

And yet how could it last?

She thought she was crying silently, so Khalis, his arms wrapped around her as he drew her back against his chest, wouldn't hear, but he did. Or perhaps he just sensed it, as he had so many other things. Gently his hands came up towards her face and his thumbs wiped away her tears. Neither of them spoke. After a long moment Grace drew in a shuddering breath, her face still damp although at least the tears had stopped.

Khalis pressed a kiss against her shoulder, his arms still wrapped around her. 'Tell me,' he said quietly.

Grace closed her eyes. Another tear leaked out. She wanted to tell him, tell him everything about her disastrous marriage, her own stupid, selfish folly, her painful divorce, the endless aftermath. She'd given him the barest of details, made herself look far more of a victim than she was. Now she imagined telling him all of it, having every sordid secret spill out of her, and while it would be a relief, like a blood-letting, it would also be messy and painful. And it would change the way Khalis looked at her. Why that should even matter since she didn't intend to see him again after tonight, Grace couldn't say. It just did.

She drew a deep breath and rolled over onto her back, Khalis's arm heavy across her. 'It's just been a long time,' she said, attempting a smile. 'I'm kind of emotional.'

Khalis studied the tracks Grace knew her tears had made down her face. 'You're sad.'

'And happy.' She pressed a kiss against his palm. 'Very happy.'

Khalis didn't look convinced but, to Grace's relief, he let it go. He pulled her more securely against him and she lay there for a long time, his arms wrapped around her as she stared into the darkness, savouring the steady warmth of him next to her, the reassuring rise and fall of his chest. Eventually she slept.

When she woke the tent was washed in sunlight and Khalis was gone. She knew he couldn't have gone far—they were on a deserted island, after all—and so for a few seconds she just lay there against the pillows, recalling the sweet memories, enjoying this brief happiness. Then she rose, wrapping a cashmere throw around her, for her gown— the only clothes she'd brought—was lying discarded and damp on the sand some metres away.

Khalis appeared, coming from the beach, looking energised and alert, a towel slung low round his hips. His hair was damp and spiky, and when he smiled Grace started to melt.

'Good morning.'

'Good morning. You had a dip in the sea?'

'A very refreshing way to start the day,' he confirmed. 'Sleep well?'

'Yes.'

'It took you a long time to go to sleep.'

Surprised, her grip loosened and the throw slid down revealingly. She hitched it up again. 'How did you know that?'

'I just sensed it, I suppose.'

'It felt strange to sleep next to someone,' Grace admitted. 'But nice.'

'Good.' Without a modicum of self-consciousness, Khalis dropped his towel and began to dress. Grace watched as he pulled on a pair of faded jeans, his legs long, lean and sprinkled with dark hair. 'Where did you get those clothes?' she asked, more to distract herself from the sight of his naked body than any real sense of curiosity.

'I brought a bag with a change of clothes for both of us.' He gave her a quick grin. 'Just in case.'

'Rather confident, weren't you?' she said, smiling and blushing at the same time.

'I like to be prepared.' He reached for a T-shirt and Grace leaned back against the pillows and watched him dress. It was a glorious sight. 'I thought we could have a look round the island this morning,' he said as he fastened his jeans. 'Not that there's much to see.'

'That sounds nice.' Anything to extend their time together.

Khalis sat down next to her on the pillow, his expression turning serious. He rested one hand on her knee. 'And tonight I want to fly back to Paris with you.'

Shock rendered her momentarily speechless. 'You… what?'

'I put a call in to the head of my legal team,' Khalis continued, 'and asked him a few questions. There's no way this custody arrangement is legal, Grace. We can fight it. We might even be able to dig something up on Christofides. I don't think he's squeaky clean. My team is researching it now—'

Grace just stared at him, her mind frozen. 'How did you know his last name?' she asked. 'I never told you.'

'I did some research.'

'I thought you didn't like internet stalking.'

His expression hardened. 'Sometimes it's justified.'

She let out a short laugh. 'Is it?'

'What's wrong, Grace? I thought you'd be happy to hear this. I want to fight for you. And your daughter.'

She shook her head, wanting to deny the fierce hope his words caused to blaze within her. 'You should have told me you were doing those things.'

'I wanted to have some information before I said anything—'

'I don't like being bossed around.' Her words came out sharply—sharper than she intended. 'I *really* don't like it.'

Khalis was silent for a moment. 'Is that what he did to you?' he asked quietly. 'Ordered you around? Kept you imprisoned on some island?'

Grace stared at him, the fierce light in his eyes, the hard line of his mouth. 'Something like that.'

'I'm not your ex-husband.'

'I know,' she snapped. This conversation was scraping her emotions raw, making her feel more exposed than ever. Exposed and hidden at the same time, for everything about their relationship was a mess of contradictions. A paradox of pleasure and pain. Secrets and honesty. Hope and despair. She took a deep breath. 'I know,' she said again, more quietly. 'But, Khalis—it's not that simple. You should have told me what you were doing before you interfered.'

'Interfered? I thought I was *helping* you.'

'There are things—' She stopped, bit the inside of her cheek hard enough to taste blood. 'Things I haven't told you.'

'Then tell me. Whatever it is, *tell* me.'

She stared at him, trying to find the words. Form them. A few simple sentences, that was all, but it could change everything. And even now, when she'd lain sated in Khalis's arms and he'd wiped away her tears, she was desperately afraid.

'Grace,' he said quietly and reached for her hand. His hand was warm and dry and strong, and hers felt small and icy in it. Still she didn't speak. 'Whatever it is, whatever happened between you and your husband, I can handle it. I've seen a lot of things in this world. Terrible things.'

'You're talking about your father.'

'Yes—'

'But you walked away from him. From all that.'

'Of course I did.' He was silent for a moment, struggling for words. 'I don't know what your husband did to you,' he said quietly, stroking her fingers, 'but I hate him for it. I'll never forgive him for hurting you.'

Slowly Grace lifted her gaze to his. He looked intent and utterly sincere. He'd meant his words as some kind of comfort, an assurance that he was on her side. He didn't realise just how cold that comfort was. *I'll never forgive him for hurting you. I'll never forgive. Never forgive.* She heard the relentless echo of that hard promise in her mind, and she pulled her hand from his.

'There's no point in discussing this,' she said, and struggled up from the bed of pillows, wished she was wearing more than a cashmere throw. 'Did you say you brought me some clothes?'

Khalis had gone very still, his grey-green stare tracking her movements as she hunted for the bag of clothes. 'Why is there no point?'

With relief Grace pulled a pair of trousers and a T-shirt from a duffel bag. She straightened and turned to face him, the clothes clutched to her hard-beating heart. 'Because I don't want you to fly to Paris with me. I don't want you to call your legal team and tell me what to do. I don't want *you*.' She stared at him, each word a hammer blow to her heart—and his. They were lies, and yet she meant them. This, Grace thought numbly, was the worst contradiction of all: she was breaking the heart of a heartless man. She loved someone who couldn't love her back, even if he thought he did.

He didn't know her.

Khalis didn't answer for a moment. His face was devoid of expression, although the corners of his mouth had whitened. 'I don't believe you,' he said finally.

'Do I have to spell it out for you?'

'You're afraid.'

'Stop telling me what I feel,' Grace snapped. 'Stop deciding just what it is between us. You keep telling me what I feel, as if you know. Well, you don't. You don't know anything.'

'If I don't know something,' Khalis answered, his voice so very even, 'it's because you haven't told me.'

'And maybe I haven't told you because I don't want to,' Grace retorted. How could she feel heartbroken and furious at the same time? She was afraid he'd reject her if she told him the truth, and yet at that moment she was angry enough to reject him. Nothing made sense. 'Just take me back to Alhaja,' she said. 'And then I'll find my way back to Paris myself.'

Anger sparked in Khalis's eyes, turning them golden-green. 'And how will you do that? Swim?'

'If I have to,' Grace flashed back. 'If you think you can keep me on that damned island—'

'I told you before,' he cut her off icily, 'I am *not* your ex-husband.'

'There's a startling resemblance at the moment.' As soon as she said the words Grace knew she didn't mean them. Khalis was nothing like Loukas. He'd been so gentle and kind and *loving*, and she was the one pushing him away. Pushing him away because she didn't want to be pushed away first. *Coward*.

The silence between them felt taut with suppressed fury. Khalis stared at her for a long moment, his face unreadable, his chest heaving. He drew a deep breath, and Grace watched as he focused his anger into something cold and hard. 'I thought,' he said, staring into the distance, his body now angled away from her, 'we had something special. That sounds ridiculously sentimental, I know. I didn't really believe in *special* until I felt it with you.' He turned to face her and Grace flinched from the bleakness in his eyes. 'But all that *we sense each other's emotions* stuff, this connection between us—that was just crap, wasn't it? Complete rubbish.'

Grace didn't answer. She couldn't. She didn't have the strength to deny it, and yet she could not tell him the truth. She wasn't even sure what the truth was any more. How could she fall in love with someone who was so hard and unyielding? How could she truly believe in his gentleness and all the good things he'd shown her? 'There's no point to this conversation,' she finally said flatly. 'We could drag it all out, and do a post-mortem on everything we've ever said, but since we're not going to *have* a relationship—' she drew in a ragged breath '—why bother?'

'Why bother,' he repeated softly. 'I see.'

She forced herself to meet his icy stare. 'Yes,' she said, 'I think you do.'

He stared at her, his face so blank and pitiless. Slowly he shook his head. 'I thought I knew you, or was at least coming to know you, but you're really a stranger, aren't you? A complete and utter stranger.' He might as well have said *bitch* instead. 'I don't know you at all.'

'No,' Grace agreed softly, 'you don't.' She drew in a deep, shuddering breath. 'Now I think you should take me back to Alhaja, and then I'll go home.'

He stared at her, and for a moment he looked like a different man, everything about him hard and unyielding and angry. The core revealed. Grace had known it was there, had known he possessed it, yet that cold, hard fury hadn't been directed at her...until now.

'Fine,' he said shortly. 'I'll get the boat ready.' And in two swift strides he'd left the tent, disappearing down towards the beach.

Khalis didn't speak to her again except for a few terse commands when she boarded the boat. She glanced at him, his jaw bunched as he stared out at the endless blue horizon, and again she felt that ridiculous, desperate longing for things to be different. To tell him everything, to take a chance. Maybe it wouldn't matter. Maybe he'd accept and understand and—

She watched as his eyes narrowed against the now-blazing sun and all the things he'd said tumbled back into her mind. He didn't forgive. He didn't want to forgive. He was a man with high and exacting standards for himself as well as everyone else. She fell far short of them and nothing could change that. Nothing could change the fact that she didn't deserve his love.

Tears thickened in her throat and stung her eyes and, furious with herself, Grace blinked them away. Was she really going to have a pity party *now*? The notion was ludicrous, idiotic. And far too late.

Alhaja Island loomed in the distance, a green crescent-shaped speck, and then the walls with their barbed wire and broken glass became visible, the ugly concrete compound behind.

Khalis docked the boat and cut the engine and in the sudden silence they both sat there, neither speaking or even looking at each other.

'Get your things,' he finally said. 'I'll have someone take you back to Paris.'

'I can get transport from Taormina. If someone could just—'

'I'll get you home,' he told her brusquely. He paused, and as he turned to her Grace saw a welter of emotion in his agate-coloured eyes and its answer rose up in her chest, a silent howl of anguish and loss. If only things could be different. If only *they* were different. His lips twisted in something close to a smile and he lifted his hand, almost as if he were going to touch her. Grace tensed in anticipation and longing, but he didn't, just dropped it back to his side. 'Goodbye, Grace,' he said, and then he vaulted out of the boat and strode down the dock.

Fury drove Khalis to the pool. He needed to work off his frustration…and his pain. Stupid, to feel so hurt, like a kicked puppy. And it was his own damn fault.

He dived in and cut through the water with sure, swift strokes, his emotions driving him forward. Even as he swam he winced. He'd been so sentimental, so stupidly romantic, and she'd been the one to spell it out. *I don't want you.* He felt pathetic. Pathetic and bruised.

He'd blinded himself all along, he knew, turned deaf ears to what she was saying. *I couldn't be in a relationship with you.* He'd thought she was just afraid, wounded by her ex-husband, and maybe she was. Maybe it was fear that had made her reject him, but the fact still remained, hard and heartless. She didn't want him. He'd wanted to rescue her as if she were some princess in a tower, but she didn't want to be rescued. Or loved. And, really, did he even know her at all? How could you fall in love with someone so quickly and suddenly? Wasn't it supposed to grow over months and years, not a mere matter of days?

Khalis completed another lap and hauled himself, dripping, onto the side of the pool. Even now, his chest heaving and his lungs burning, he couldn't get her out of his mind. Those chocolate eyes, dark with pain or softened with humour. Her mouth, swollen and rosy from being kissed. The pure, clear sound of her rare laughter, and the way she looked at him, her attention so focused and complete it made him feel a hundred feet tall. The pliant softness of her body against his, and the way he'd felt when he'd been inside her, as if he'd finally found the home he'd long been looking for.

With a groan of frustration Khalis pushed off the side of the pool and started swimming again, harder and faster than ever, as if exercise could obliterate thought. In the distance he heard the sound of the helicopter taking off.

An hour later, showered and dressed, he strode into his office. His frustration and hurt had hardened into something cold and steely that lodged inside him like a ball of iron.

Eric was waiting for him with a sheaf of papers as he

sat behind his desk. 'You look,' Eric remarked mildly, 'like you want to rip someone's head off. I hope it's not mine.'

'Not at all.' He held out one hand for the papers. Eric handed them to him with his eyebrows arched.

'If not me, then who?' He rolled his eyes. 'Wait, I think I can guess.'

'Don't,' Khalis said, cutting him off. 'It's not up for discussion.'

'This island is really doing a number on you, isn't it?'

Khalis suppressed his irritation with effort. Eric was one of his oldest and most trusted friends, and he generally appreciated his levity. Yet, since coming to this island, tension had been wrapping itself around him like a steel band, choking all the life and hope from the air. Grace had distracted him, he realised. She'd *helped* him. And her rejection had made everything worse, the memories darker, the pain more intense.

'It's not the island,' he said shortly. 'I'd just like to wrap up this whole business quickly and get back to my real life.' Except he wasn't sure he could do that any more, or at least not easily. Not since Grace.

'I wouldn't mind a few more weeks lounging in the sun,' Eric said, although Khalis knew his assistant had done precious little lounging since arriving on Alhaja. 'Is there anything else for now?'

'No—' Khalis dropped the papers on his desk and raked a hand through his hair. 'Yes,' he amended. 'I want you to find everything you can on Grace Turner.'

'Everything?' Eric asked dubiously. 'You sure you want to go there?'

He gritted his teeth. 'Yes.'

Eric gave him a considering look, then shrugged. 'It's your party,' he said, and left the room. Resolutely, Khalis pulled the papers towards him. Grace had told him he could find out what he needed to know with one simple internet search. Well, he thought grimly, maybe now he'd take her up on that.

By the time Grace arrived back at her apartment in Paris's Latin Quarter, she felt exhausted, both emotionally and physically. Khalis's helicopter had taken her to Taormina, and then he'd arranged a private jet to take her directly to Paris. Even at the end, when he must have hated her, he was considerate. She almost wished he wasn't. When he'd been arrogant and controlling it had been far easier to stay angry and to let that carry her. Then he softened into gentleness and she felt all tangled up inside, yearning and fear tying her heart into knots. Why couldn't he make it easy for her to let go? Simple not to care? Yet nothing about her time with Khalis had been simple or easy.

Yes, it had, she corrected herself. It had been all too easy to fall in love with him.

Resolutely, Grace pushed the useless thought away. She had no space or freedom in her life for love. Khalis might have cracked open her heart, but she could close it again. Love led to pain. She knew that. She'd seen it with Loukas, when he'd left her alone on his island, trapped and miserable, half-mad with loneliness.

And as for Andrew…

No, she wouldn't think about Andrew.

Slowly, each movement aching, she dropped her bag and kicked off her heels. She curled up on the sofa, wishing she could blank out her mind. Stop thinking, stop remembering. Not Loukas or Andrew, but Khalis. Khalis smiling at her, teasing her, making her laugh.

Frankly, that looks like something my five-year-old goddaughter might paint in Nursery.

Even now Grace's mouth curved into a smile as tears

stung her eyes. Khalis looking at her, heavy-lidded with sensual intent. Kissing her so softly, so sweetly. Finding ways to make her feel safe and treasured.

Now the tears spilled over and Grace buried her face in her hands. Had she made a mistake, not trusting him? If she'd told him what she'd done, would he have forgiven her? And wasn't loving someone worth that risk?

She drew in a shuddering breath and other memories came to her. Khalis's eyes narrowed, his mouth a hard, compressed line.

You're very forgiving, much more forgiving than I am.

No, he wasn't forgiving. And he wouldn't forgive her. And even if she'd fallen in love with him, it didn't change who he was. And who she couldn't be.

CHAPTER NINE

GRACE transferred her untouched glass of champagne to her other hand and tried to focus on what the ageing socialite across from her was droning on about. She caught a word here and there and she thought she was making the appropriate noises of interest, but her entire body and brain were buzzing with the knowledge that Khalis would be here tonight. After two months, she would see him again.

Tension coiled through her body, twanging like a wire. She had had no contact with Khalis these last few months, although she'd exchanged a few emails with Eric, arranging for the art collection to be transferred. Khalis had, of course, obeyed all the legal procedures in authenticating the artwork in his father's vault and turning it over to the proper authorities. Tonight was a gala celebrating the return of several important paintings to the Louvre, as well as Khalis's generous donation of a Monet that had been one of the few paintings in his father's collection that had not been stolen.

The party was being held in the Louvre's impressive courtyard, the distinctive glass pyramids glinting in the last rays of the setting sun. It was early summer and the air was sun-warmed and fragrant. Grace took a sip of champagne to ease the dryness in her throat and glanced around the milling crowd for Khalis. He hadn't arrived. She would know it if he had.

And when he did arrive, Grace asked herself yet again, what would she say to him? How would she act? Prudence required that she keep a professional distance, yet two months had only intensified her longing and regret and she was afraid she'd betray herself when she saw him again.

She attempted to turn her attention back to the socialite, yet within seconds it felt as if someone had suddenly turned a spotlight on her, even though nothing had noticeably changed. She felt a prickling between her shoulder blades, a tingling awareness creep through her entire body. He was here.

Barely aware of what she was saying, she excused herself from the conversation and turned away, trying to search the crowds discreetly. It didn't take long; it was as if he were equipped with a tracking device to her heart, for she saw and felt him right away. He stood alone, his figure tall and proud, his gaze sweeping over the crowd. Then that cold gaze fastened on her and Grace's breath hitched. For an endless moment they stared at one another, and from across the crowded courtyard Grace could not discern his expression. She didn't even know what the expression on her own face was, for both body and brain seemed to have frozen.

Then Khalis looked away, his gaze moving on without any real acknowledgement of her presence. Head held high, she turned away and walked towards another knot of guests, forced herself to listen to their idle chatter. What had she expected? That Khalis would run over and greet her? Kiss her? She wouldn't even have wanted that. She *couldn't* want that. Yet it still hurt, not the pain of disappointment, for Grace hadn't really expected anything from him tonight, but the agony of remembered loss.

Somehow she made it through the next hour, listening and nodding, murmuring platitudes although she barely knew what she was saying. Her body ached with the knowledge of Khalis's nearness and, even without looking, she was certain she knew exactly where he was. Amazing, and still alarming, to share this connection that they'd both acknowledged…and then she'd denied.

The evening dragged, every moment painfully slow as Grace instinctively tracked Khalis's progress around the courtyard. He looked amazing in a dark suit and silver-grey tie, as lean and powerful and darkly attractive as ever, and just glimpsing him out of the corner of her eye reminded her how warm and satiny his skin had been, how complete she'd felt in his arms.

By the end of the social hour, and then another half hour of speeches, she felt ready for bed. Tension knotted in her shoulders and her head pulsed with the beginnings of one of the stress-related headaches she'd been getting ever since her divorce. The party had moved inside to the Pavillon Denon, and Grace stayed near the back of the gallery as the director of the museum praised Khalis's civic service in restoring so many famous works of art to their rightful places. Her heart twisted like a wrung rag inside her when Khalis stepped to the podium and spoke eloquently about his duty 'to redeem what has been forsaken, and find what has been lost'.

Pretty words, Grace thought with a sudden spike of spite, but he hadn't been much interested in redemption when she'd been talking to him. When it came to his father, he'd been cold, hard and unforgiving.

And you were so afraid he'd be the same with you. That's why you ran away like a frightened child.

Not that it mattered. The only child she could think of was Katerina. Just the thought of her daughter's apple-round cheeks, her dark plaits and her gap-toothed smile made Grace blink fiercely. She had to forget about Khalis, for Katerina's sake as well as her own.

The speeches over, Grace excused herself from the party. She saw Michel give her a sharp glance from across the room; she didn't think she'd fooled him since she'd returned from Alhaja.

The rest of the museum was quiet and dark, and it felt strange to be wandering alone among all this priceless art. Of course, everything was wired to a central security system and there were guards at every exit, but Grace at least had the illusion of solitude.

She headed down the stairs, past the ancient statue of Winged Victory of Samothrace, when a voice caused her to still.

'Leaving already?'

She half-turned, saw Khalis coming down the stairs to meet her. 'I wanted some air.' She needed some now, for the sight of him had stolen the breath right from her lungs.

He stopped a foot or so in front of her and in the dim lighting Grace could not quite read his expression. His eyes were narrowed, but whether in concern or anger or mere indifference she could not say. 'Are you getting one of your headaches?'

She shrugged. 'It's been a long day.'

'You look tired.'

'I am.' She wondered why he cared, knew she wanted him to. 'I should go.' Still she didn't move.

'I haven't forgotten you, Grace.' His voice was pitched low, assured and so very sincere. She angled her head away from him, another wave of loss sweeping through her, nearly bringing her to her knees.

'You should have.'

'Have you forgotten me?'

'No, of course not.' She took a step away from him. They shouldn't be here, having this conversation alone.

'Of course not?' Khalis repeated. He'd stepped closer to her, blocking her escape route down the stairs. She glanced back at the statue of Nike, armless and headless yet still magnificent, the only witness to this encounter. 'That surprises me.' She said nothing, unwilling to continue the conversation even as her gaze roved over him, drinking him in, memorising his features. God, she'd missed him. Even now, when he looked so intent and angry, she missed him. Wanted him. 'The last time I saw you,' he said, 'you gave the distinct impression you wanted to forget me.'

'I did want to,' Grace answered. She couldn't be anything but honest now; the sheer closeness and reality of him was too much for her to be able to prevaricate. *Lie.* 'But I couldn't.' He'd stepped closer, so close she could breathe the achingly familiar scent of him, feel his intoxicating heat. She closed her eyes. 'Don't—'

'Don't what? Don't make you remember how good it was between us?' Slowly, deliberately, he reached out one hand and traced the line of her cheek. His thumb touched the fullness of her mouth and Grace shuddered.

'Please—'

'We still have it, Grace. That connection between us. It's still there.'

She opened her eyes, furious and afraid and despairing all at once. 'Yes, it is, but it doesn't matter.'

'You keep saying that, but I don't believe it.'

'I told you—'

'You didn't tell me anything. I'm still waiting for that, Grace. Waiting—and wanting to understand.' She just shook her head, unable to speak. 'I want,' he said, his teeth gritted, 'to give you a second chance—'

And she'd wanted to believe in second chances, even if she couldn't have one. 'Don't, Khalis.'

'You still want me—'

'Of course I do!' she shouted, her nerves well and truly shattered. 'I'm not denying it. So are you happy now? Satisfied?'

'Not in the least.' And, before she could protest or even think, he'd pulled her to him and his mouth came down hard and relentless and yet so very sweet on hers.

Grace gave in to the kiss for a blissful fraction of a second, her hands coming up to grip his shoulders, her body pressed so wonderfully against his, before she jerked away, her chest heaving. *'Don't!'*

Khalis was breathing as hard as she was, his face flushed, his eyes flashing fire. 'Why did you walk away from me?'

Tears pricked her eyes and her head blazed with pain. Truth spilled from her lips. 'Because I was afraid you'd hate me if I stayed.' A sound of someone on the stair above her made Grace's insides lurch in panic. She shook her head, unable to look at him. 'Just leave me alone,' she whispered. *'Please.'*

And then she fled down the stairs.

Back in her apartment, Grace peeled off her cocktail dress and took a long, hot shower, tried to banish the imprint of Khalis's mouth on hers, the blaze of desire his touch had caused her. She couldn't believe he'd still pursued her, still wanted her. She thought he'd hate her by now, and the fact that he didn't made it so much harder to forget him.

After her shower, dressed in her most comfortable worn pyjamas, Grace pulled out the photo album from the top shelf of the bookcase in her bedroom. She tried not to look at this album too often because it hurt too much. Yet tonight she needed to look at the beloved pictures, remind herself just what she had lost—and still had to lose.

Katerina at birth, her face tiny and wrinkled and red. Six weeks old, fast asleep in her pram. Six months, one chubby fist in her mouth, her eyes the same brown as Grace's own. A year, taking her first toddling steps. After that there were no photos except the ones Grace took when she saw her daughter once a month, in Athens. She gazed at these hungrily, as if she could fill in the many missing pieces of her daughter's last four years. Loukas had arranged it perfectly, she thought not for the first time, too weary now to be bitter. She saw Katerina enough for the girl to remember her, but not enough to love her as a child loved her mother. As Grace loved her daughter.

A sharp, purposeful knock on the front door startled her out of her thoughts and quickly she closed the album and slid it back on its shelf. Her heart had begun beating with hard, heavy thuds for she knew who was knocking at her door.

'Hello, Khalis.' Colour slashed his cheekbones and he held his body tensely, like a predator waiting to spring. He looked, Grace thought with a spasm of hopeless longing, as wonderful as always.

'May I come in?'

Wordlessly she nodded and stepped aside so he could enter. Khalis came into her little sitting room with its slanted ceilings and rather shabby antique furniture, seeming to dominate the small space.

To her surprise, he took a pile of folded papers from his inside pocket and dropped them on the coffee table with a thud.

'What is that?'

'Your file.'

'My *file*?'

His mouth tightened. 'After you left, I had Eric research your background.' He gestured to the thick pile of papers. 'He gave me that.'

Grace took in his hard expression, the narrowed eyes and tightened mouth, and she swallowed dryly. She knew what kind of articles the online gossip sites and tabloids had run. Sordid speculation about why Loukas Christofides, Greek shipping tycoon, had divorced his wife so abruptly and denied her custody of their daughter. 'It must have made some interesting reading,' she managed.

'No, it didn't, actually.'

She stared at him in confusion. 'What do you mean?'

'I didn't read it.'

'Why…why not?'

'Because even now I believe we shared something on that island, something important and different. I don't know why you ran from me, but I want to understand.' He stopped, his chest heaving, his gaze blazing into hers. 'Help me understand, Grace.'

How could she refuse when he asked her so rawly? And maybe…maybe he did understand. He *could.* She swallowed, her heart beating so hard it hurt. 'It's a long story,' she whispered.

'I have all the time in the world.' He sat down on her sofa, his body seeming relaxed although she still felt his tension. 'Why did you say I might hate you?' he asked quietly when the silence had ticked on for several minutes.

Grace knew he'd painted her as a victim, the most innocent of portraits. Now she would have to tell him the truth, in bold, stark colours. He would know, and he might leave here hating her more than ever before.

Or he might understand, forgive and love you more than ever before.

Did she dare hope?

Swallowing, she sat down across from him, her hands tucked between her knees. 'I've told you a bit about my marriage. About Loukas.'

'A little,' Khalis agreed neutrally. She hadn't said anything yet, and still it was so hard. Every explanation felt like an excuse.

'And that our marriage was troubled.'

'Yes, I'm aware of that, Grace.'

'I know.' She closed her eyes. He knew a little of how unhappy she'd been, trapped on that wretched island. Yet to go into detail now, to try to explain how desperate and lonely and scared she'd felt—wouldn't it all just sound as if she were justifying her actions? Khalis would certainly think so. He had given himself no excuses for accepting his father's help even after he'd realised the extent of his corruption. She wouldn't give herself any, either.

'Grace,' he prompted, and impatience edged his voice. Grace sighed and opened her eyes. There was, she knew, only one way to tell him the truth. Without any explanations, reasons or excuses. Just the stark, sordid facts. And see what he did with them.

'You've probably wondered how Loukas managed to gain complete custody of Katerina.'

'I assumed he worked the system, bribed a judge.' He paused, his voice carefully even. 'You implied as much.'

'Yes, but there was more to it than that. The truth is, he painted me as an unfit mother.' She gestured to the packet of papers he'd thrown onto her table. 'If you'd read those articles, you'd see. He made me seem completely irresponsible, negligent—' She swallowed and forced herself to go on. 'By the time he'd finished, anyone would think I hadn't cared about my daughter at all.'

Khalis's gaze remained steady on hers. 'But they would be wrong, wouldn't they?'

'They'd be wrong in thinking I didn't care,' Grace said in a low voice, brushing impatiently at the corners of her eyes. 'But they wouldn't be wrong in thinking I'd been negligent.' She drew in a shuddering breath. 'I was.'

Khalis said nothing for a moment. Grace forced herself to hold his gaze, but she couldn't tell a thing from his shuttered eyes, his expressionless face. The tears that had threatened were gone now, replaced with a deep and bone-weary resignation.

'Negligent,' he finally repeated. 'How?'

Again Grace hesitated. She wanted to rush to her own defence, to explain she'd never meant to be negligent, she'd never actually put Katerina in danger—but what was the point? The fact remained that she had betrayed her husband. Her family. Herself. She took a breath, let it out slowly. 'I had an affair.'

All Khalis did was blink, but Grace still felt his recoil. He was surprised, of course. Shocked. He'd been expecting something sympathetic, something perhaps about post-partum depression or her abusive husband or who knew what. All along he'd been thinking that she'd been hurt, not that she'd done the hurting. Not an affair. Not a sordid, sexual, adulterous affair.

'An affair,' he said without any expression at all.

'Yes,' she confirmed, tonelessly now. 'With the man who managed the island property. Gardening, house repairs—'

'I don't care what he *did*.'

'I know. I just...' She shook her head. 'I told you I didn't want to tell you,' she said in a low voice.

Khalis didn't speak, and neither did Grace. The silence that yawned between them now was worse than any words could have been. Finally he asked, 'And while you had this affair...you were negligent of your daughter?'

'I never put her in danger or anything like that,' she whispered. 'I loved her. I still love her.' Her voice wavered and she strove for control. Khalis needed to hear the facts without tears or sentiment. 'That whole time is a blur. I was so unhappy—I didn't knowingly neglect her, of course not. I just…I just wasn't the mother I wanted to be.'

'Or the wife, apparently.'

His cool observation was like a dagger thrust straight to the heart. Grace blinked hard. 'I know what it sounds like. Maybe it's a blur because I don't want to remember.' Yet she'd never been able to truly forget. How could you not remember and not forget at the same time? More contradictions. 'I'm not trying to make excuses,' she said. 'How can I? I'm just trying to explain—'

'Why you had this affair.'

'How I don't really remember.'

Khalis let out a rush of breath that sounded almost like a laugh, yet without any humour in it at all. 'How convenient,' he said, 'for you not to remember.'

'I'm not lying, Khalis.'

'You virtually lied to me from the moment I met you—'

'That is *not* fair.' Her voice rose, surprising her. 'Why should I have told you such a thing when I barely knew you?' She stuck out her hand in a mockery of an introduction. 'Hello, my name is Grace Turner, I'm an art appraiser and an adulteress?'

Khalis rose from the sofa, prowling around the room with a restless, angry energy. 'There were plenty of times after that,' he said, his words almost a growl. 'When you knew how I felt about you—'

'I know—' she cut him off with a whisper '—I know. And I was afraid, I admit that. I didn't want you to look at me…the way you're looking at me now.' With his face so terribly expressionless, as if he could not decide if she were a stranger or someone he knew, never mind loved.

And she loved him. She'd fallen in love with him on the island, with his tenderness and gentleness and understanding. She'd fallen in love with him despite that hardness inside him that she was seeing and feeling now. And she didn't know if her love was enough. She said nothing, simply waited for his verdict. Would he walk away from her just as he had from his family, no second chances, no regrets?

'How long?' he finally asked.

'How long…?'

'How long did you have this affair?'

She hesitated, the words drawn reluctantly from her. 'About six weeks.'

'And how long were you married?'

'Nearly two years.'

Khalis said nothing. Grace knew how awful it all sounded. How could she, with a little baby and a new husband, have gone and sought out another man? How could she have deceived her husband and lost her daughter? What kind of woman did that?

She did. Had. And if she hadn't been able to forget or forgive her actions, how could a man like Khalis?

Khalis stopped by the window, his back to her as he stared out at the darkness. 'And I suppose,' he said in a detached voice, 'your husband found out about the affair. And was furious.'

'Yes. He didn't want anyone to know he'd been… That I'd…' She stopped miserably. 'So in the courts he painted me as a negligent mother instead.'

'But you weren't.'

His observation, even when delivered in such a cold

voice, gave her the thinnest thread of hope. 'I don't *think*…
I don't know what I was.'

Khalis didn't answer. His back was still to her. 'How?'
he finally asked.

Grace blinked. 'How…?'

'How did he find out?'

'Do you really need to know all these details?' she asked
rawly. 'How does it help anything—?'

'He walked in on you, didn't he?' Khalis said. He turned
around and Grace quelled at his icy expression. This was
the man who had faced down his father, who had walked
away from his family. 'On you and your lover.'

Her scorching blush, she knew, was all the answer he
needed. Khalis said nothing and Grace gazed blindly down
at her lap. She couldn't bear the look of condemnation she
knew she'd see on his face.

He let out a shuddering breath. 'I thought you'd been
abused,' he said quietly. 'Emotionally or physically—
something. Something terrible. I hated your ex-husband
for hurting you.'

Grace blinked hard, her gaze still on her lap. 'I know,'
she said softly.

'And all along…' He stopped and then, through her
blurred vision, from the corner of her eye, she saw him
pick up his coat.

Her throat was so tight she could barely choke out the
words. 'I'm sorry.'

The only answer was the click of the door as Khalis
shut it behind him.

CHAPTER TEN

'You look,' Michel told Grace a week later, 'like a plate of warmed-up rice pudding.'

'That doesn't sound very attractive.' She closed the door to her employer's office, eyebrows raised. 'You wanted to see me?'

Michel stared at her hard. 'I mean it, Grace. You look terrible.'

'Clearly you're full of compliments today.'

He sighed and moved around to his desk. Grace waited, trying to keep her expression enquiring and friendly even as her body tensed and another headache began its relentless pounding. This last week had been horrible. She had not seen or heard from Khalis since he'd walked out of her apartment without a word, leaving her too empty and aching even to cry. She'd drifted through the days, feeling numb and yet possessing a terrible awareness of what lay beneath that nothingness—an awful, yawning expanse of grief and despair. Just knowing it was there, like the deep and frigid waters beneath a thin layer of black ice, kept her awake at night, staring into the darkness, memories dancing through her mind like ghosts.

Memories of her marriage, the deep unhappiness she'd felt, the terrible mistakes she'd made. Memories of holding Katerina for the first time, the joy so deep it almost felt like pain as she'd kissed her wrinkled, downy head. Memories of the court hearing that had left her as close to longing for death as she'd ever been.

Memories of Khalis.

She'd taken her one night knowing she would only have the memories to sustain her, but they did not. They tormented her with their tenderness and sweetness, and she lay in bed with her eyes closed, imagining she could feel his arms around her, his body pressed against her, his thumb brushing the tear from her cheek.

Sometimes sleep came, and always dawn, and she stumbled through another day alone.

'Is there something you wanted?' Grace asked, keeping her smile in place with effort. Michel sighed and steepled his fingers under his chin.

'Not precisely. Khalis Tannous has donated the last two works in his father's collection.'

'The Leonardos?'

'Yes.'

Grace affected a look of merely professional interest. She had no idea if she succeeded or not. 'And where is he donating them?'

'The Fitzwilliam in Cambridge.'

The Fitzwilliam in Cambridge was practically a second home.

Grace angled her face away from Michel's narrowed gaze. 'A rather odd choice,' she said.

'Is it? I thought it quite spectacularly appropriate.'

'What do you mean?'

'Come now, Grace. It's quite obvious to anyone with eyes in his head that something happened between you and Tannous on that island.'

'I see,' Grace said after a second's pause.

'And that it made you more miserable than ever,' Michel

continued. 'I had hopes that Tannous might bring you back to life—'

'I wasn't *dead*,' Grace interjected and Michel gave her a mirthless smile.

'As good as. I'm your employer, Grace, but I've also known you since you were a child, and I care about you. I never liked seeing you so unhappy, and I like it even less now. I thought Tannous might help you—'

'Is that why you insisted I go to that island?'

Michel gave a dismissive and completely Gallic shrug. 'I sent you there because you are my best appraiser of Renaissance art. But I must confess I don't like the result.' He stared at her rather beadily from behind his desk. 'You're enough to make the Mona Lisa lose her smile.'

Grace thought of Leda's sorrowful half-smile and shook her head. 'I'm sorry. I'll try to—'

'Don't be *sorry*,' Michel cut her off impatiently. 'I didn't bring you in here to ask for an apology.'

'Then why?'

Michel was silent for a long moment. 'What did he do to you?' he finally asked.

'Nothing, Michel. He didn't do anything to me.' *Except make me fall in love with him.*

'Then why are you looking—?'

'Like a bowl of warmed-up rice pudding?' She gave him a small sad smile. 'Because he found out,' she said simply. 'He found out about me.'

Khalis gazed down at the financial report he was reading and tried to make sense of the numbers for the third time. In disgust at his own lack of focus, he pushed them away and stared out of the window of his father's office in Rome's EUR business district. Below him tourists and office workers bustled about their business, whether it was snapping photos or grabbing their lunch.

He should have forgotten her by now. Or at least stopped thinking of her. He'd been able to do that for his own family; why couldn't he do the same for a slip of a woman who had virtually lied to him and betrayed her own marriage vows?

Instead he kept remembering everything about her. How her eyes had lightened with sudden humour and her lips had curved as if she wasn't used to smiling. Her passion and strength of purpose for her work, her focus which matched his own. The softness of her breasts pressed against his chest, her body so wonderfully yielding against his.

And how she had deceived and duped him into thinking she was innocent, a victim like Leda. She should have told him. At some point during their time together, she should have told him. No, he realised with sudden savagery, it wasn't the telling that mattered. It was the doing. He wanted her not to have had the affair at all. After such a huge betrayal...how could he trust her? *Love* her?

His intercom buzzed, disrupting his pointless recriminations. 'A phone call for you, Mr Tannous, on line one.'

'Who from?'

'He didn't say, sir. But he said it was urgent.'

Khalis felt a flicker of irritation. He paid a receptionist to field his calls, not just pass them on. 'Very well,' he said tersely and picked up his phone.

'Yes?'

'Hello, Khalis.'

Khalis's fingers froze around the phone as his mind blanked with shock even as he registered that familiar voice. A voice he hadn't heard in fifteen years. His brother.

His brother who was supposed to be dead. Khalis's

mind raced in circles. Was his father alive as well? What the hell had happened? Swallowing, he finally managed to speak.

'Ammar,' he said without expression. 'You're alive.'

His brother let out a dry, humourless laugh. 'You don't sound pleased I am back from the dead.'

'You died to me fifteen years ago.'

'I need to talk to you.'

Khalis fought down the tide of emotion hearing his brother's voice had caused to sweep over him. Shock, anger, pain, and both a joy and regret he didn't want to acknowledge. 'We have nothing to say to each other.'

'Please, Khalis,' he said, but it still sounded like a command, the older brother bullying him into submission once more, and his resolve hardened.

'No.'

'I've changed—'

'People don't change, Ammar. Not that much.' Khalis wondered distantly why he didn't just hang up.

'Do you really believe that?' Ammar asked quietly, and for the first time in Khalis's memory he sounded sad rather than angry.

'I…' *Did* he believe that? He'd been living that truth for the last fifteen years. His father wouldn't change. Couldn't. Because if he had…if he could…then maybe Khalis wouldn't have had to leave in the dramatic fashion that he did. Maybe he could have stayed, or returned, or worked something out. Maybe Jamilah wouldn't have died.

Khalis swallowed, forced the agonising thoughts back. 'Yes,' he said stonily. 'I do believe that.' And then, his hand trembling, he hung up the phone.

The ensuing silence seemed to reverberate through the room. Khalis stabbed at his intercom. 'Please block any calls from that number,' he told the receptionist, who bumbled through an apology before Khalis severed the connection. He rose from the desk and paced the office restlessly, feeling caged not by the four walls but by his thoughts. His memories.

Had Ammar changed? He'd changed once before. Khalis had a sudden sharp memory of when his brother had turned eight. Their father had called him out of the nursery where they'd been playing with Lego together, neither of them knowing it was to be the last day of boyish pleasures. Khalis didn't know what Balkri had said or done to his oldest son that day, but when Ammar returned his lip was bleeding and the light had gone out of his eyes. He never had a kind word or action for Khalis again.

As the years had passed the rivalry between them had hardened into something unforgiving and cruel. Ammar always had to win, and not just win but humiliate Khalis. He was older, stronger, tougher and he let his little brother know it at every opportunity. Grace had asked him if Ammar was a bully, but it hadn't been a simple case of sibling rivalry. Ammar had been driven by something darker, and sometimes Khalis thought he'd seen a torment of emotion in his brother's eyes he knew he didn't understand. If he tried to, Ammar just turned away or hit him. There was no going back to those simple days of childhood. There was no going back at all.

Do people change?

Ammar might not have changed, but could he make that kind of assumption about everyone? About Grace?

Khalis halted his restless prowling and stared unseeingly out of the office window. He pictured Grace as he'd last seen her, her head bowed in regret, tears starting in her eyes. Did he believe she'd changed, or was he going to freeze her in her weakest moment, refuse to allow her to move past it? How much was his experience of his father and brother colouring his perception of Grace?

She was different, he realised with a shaft of self-recrimination. Of course she was. He still didn't like the stark reality of it, he knew. He wished things could be different. But he'd told Grace there was no point in looking back, no point in useless regrets. He wanted to look forward.

He turned away from the window, a new resolve hardening inside him. He needed to see Grace again. Speak to her. *Help me understand*, he'd asked. But he hadn't understood, not then. Maybe they both needed a second chance.

Grace straightened her simple grey sheath dress and glanced round the crowd of art enthusiasts and academics that comprised the guest list for tonight's reception at the Fitzwilliam Museum. Khalis was once again being hailed a hero for donating his father's works of art, in this case the two Leonardos of Leda.

'You must be thrilled,' one of her old professors told her as she plucked a glass of champagne from one of the circulating trays. 'Such important works of art being exhibited so close to home!'

'Yes, it's wonderful news for the museum,' Grace answered dutifully. Cambridge didn't really feel like home although she did still possess the house on Grange Road where she'd grown up. She let it out to visiting academics. And as for Khalis donating the works to the Fitzwilliam… *why* had he done that? Grace had wrestled with that question for many sleepless nights. It almost seemed like the kind of tender, thoughtful gesture that had made her fall in love with him—but he hated her now. So what kind of message was he trying to send?

She continued her progression around the grand en-

trance hall of the museum, chatting to guests, keeping an
eye on the door. Even though she knew there was no real
point, she still could not keep herself from looking for him
and wanting to know when he was here.

Even if she hadn't felt it—that curious prickling between her shoulder blades—she would have known he'd
arrived by the speculative murmurs that rippled through
the crowd. Tall, imposing in an immaculate navy suit and
utterly gorgeous, Khalis would draw admiration wherever
he went. Grace stepped back against the wall, holding her
untouched glass of champagne in front of her like some
kind of shield. She saw Khalis's grey-green gaze search
the crowd and knew he was looking for her. And then he
found her, his unwavering stare like a laser that pierced all
of her defences. She stood there, still clutching her glass,
unable to move or even think.

Khalis's face was neutral yet his eyes seemed to blaze
right into her, searing her soul. He really did hate her. With
effort Grace turned away, walked on wobbly legs towards
the next knot of people and tried desperately to seem unconcerned as their chatter washed over her in an incom-
prehensible wave.

Regret lashed him as Khalis watched Grace walk away.
Her back was straight, her figure lithe and slender in the
simple silk sheath she wore. Had she lost weight? Her
face had been so pale, her eyes huge as they'd gazed at
each other.

He'd had plenty of time to acknowledge how his past
had coloured his perception of the present, of Grace. He'd
duped himself, just as he had with his own father. He'd
wanted to believe only the best of her and so he'd refused
to heed her warnings, insisted on painting his own rosy
picture.

And when she'd finally worked up the courage to give him the truth, he'd walked away. He'd wanted her trust—demanded it, even—only to abuse it at the first opportunity.

Why, he wondered bleakly, should she ever trust him again?

CHAPTER ELEVEN

GRACE felt her nerves tauten throughout the evening, so by the time the reception came to an end she felt as if they were overstretched threads, ready to snap. Her body ached with the effort of appearing interested and unconcerned, as well as thrilled that Khalis had donated such magnificent works of art to the museum.

Khalis, she'd observed, had circulated around the room in distinct counterpoint to her rotation; there could be no question he was avoiding her—or at least that she was avoiding him. Perhaps he was simply indifferent to her now. Yet, despite the distance between them, she remained constantly and agonisingly aware of him. Even as she chatted with guests she strained to hear his low, husky voice, felt every one of his easy movements reverberate through her own body.

At least she wouldn't see him again. The Leonardos had been the last two works from the Tannous collection. There would be no more receptions or galas, no need to encounter him at all. No risk, no danger. The thought should have brought blessed relief, not the wave of devastation Grace felt instead.

Finally the guests were trickling out into Trumpington Street and Grace found an opportunity to slip away. Khalis, she'd seen, was still chatting with a few hangers-on. She hurried out of the entrance hall, grabbing her coat, and into the damp night. It was midsummer, but the weather was wet and chilly and she wrapped her coat more firmly around herself as she headed down the street, her heels clicking on the slick pavement.

So that was that, she thought dully as she walked towards the hotel in the centre of town where she'd booked a room for the night. She'd probably never see him again. Talk to him again. *Touch* him again…

'Grace.'

For a second Grace thought she must be imagining things. Fantasising that she'd heard Khalis because she missed him so much, even though she knew she shouldn't—

'Grace.'

Slowly, stunned, she turned around. Khalis stood there, his hair damp and spiky with rain. He'd forgotten his coat.

Grace simply stared, her mind empty of thoughts. Why had he sought her out? He didn't look as if he was angry but she could not think of a single reason why he would come and find her. Surely everything had been said that awful night at her apartment?

'Are you staying at your father's house?' he finally asked after they'd simply stared at each other for an endless moment.

Grace shook her head. 'I've let it out. I booked into a hotel, just for the one night.'

'Tomorrow you go back to Paris?'

She nodded. 'Thank you for donating the Leonardos to the Fitzwilliam,' she said awkwardly. 'The museum is thrilled, of course.'

'Well,' Khalis answered with a crooked smile, 'the Louvre has the Mona Lisa, after all. And I know how much you care about these paintings. I thought they should go to your second home.'

Sudden tears stung Grace's eyes as she slowly shook her head. 'Thank you,' she said. 'It was kind of you, especially considering—' Her throat closed up and all she could do was stare at him, knowing her heart was in her eyes. Her heartbreak.

'Oh, Grace.'

In one fluid movement Khalis strode forward and pulled her into his arms, wrapping her in a gentle yet fierce hug. Grace felt the damp wool of his suit against her cheek, her mind frozen on the fact that he was here, hugging her, and it felt unbelievably, unbearably wonderful.

With effort she pulled away. 'Someone will see—'

'To hell with that.'

'I don't understand you,' Grace whispered. 'Why are you here? Why are you—?' *Hugging me. Looking at me as if... Almost as if you love me.*

'Because I'm sorry, Grace. I messed up. A lot.' His voice wavered on the last word and she stared.

'*You* messed up?'

'I shouldn't have walked out on you. I was shocked, I admit that, but I…I wanted you to trust me and then I threw that trust away with both hands.'

She blinked, taking in his words, the self-recrimination that lanced each one. 'You judge yourself pretty harshly.'

'I had no right to judge you.'

'I know what I did, Khalis—'

'I know you do. Everything you said and did is marked by guilt, Grace. I couldn't believe I didn't see that before.'

She angled her face away from him, knowing he was right. Wishing he wasn't. 'I don't know how to let go of it,' she whispered.

'I asked you to help me understand,' Khalis said quietly. 'And you told me the truth, but I don't think you told me all of it.'

She nearly choked. 'What more do you want me to say—?'

'Help me understand,' Khalis said as he drew her to him, his arms enfolding her and holding her close. Accepting her, even now. Especially now. 'Not just the things you regret or wish were different. Help me understand *you*.'

'I don't know how—'

'Tell me. Tell me everything.'

It wasn't until she was lying in his arms that she started to speak. Khalis knew he had to be patient. Gentler than he ever had been before. He'd thought it had been hard to get her to trust him before, when she hadn't told him anything and he'd thought she was perfect. Now he knew there were things he wouldn't want to hear, facts he would be reluctant to accept. And still he needed to hold her close and justify this fragile trust she'd placed in him.

She stirred, her hair brushing against his bare chest. He'd brought her to the luxury hotel he'd booked in town, the windows of the penthouse suite overlooking the River Cam. She'd come into the room warily, her eyes wide as she took in the huge four-poster bed piled high with pillows and a silken duvet.

He'd been about to reassure her that they could just talk, that all he wanted was to talk—well, sort of. After nearly three months apart, he wanted *her* desperately.

'Grace—' he began, and then she turned to him suddenly and wrapped her arms around him. He pulled her close, buried his face in her hair, inhaling its sweet fragrance.

'I missed you,' she said in a whisper. 'I missed me with you.' And he knew what she meant. He'd missed her, too, missed the sense of rightness he felt when he was with her. He kissed her then and, though he meant to keep it gentle, neither of them could control the tide of desire that swept over them as their lips met and met again. They'd missed each other too much to go slowly. In one fluid movement Khalis undid the zip of Grace's dress and she wriggled out of it, laughing a little as it snagged round her ankles.

'Another dress bites the dust,' Khalis said with a grin as he tossed it aside. Grace kicked off her heels. He pulled her towards the bed, his breathing turned harsh and ragged as they both fell upon its softness and each other, hands roving over skin with an urgent need to remember, to feel, to know.

Grace arched upwards as Khalis slid his hand between her thighs, his own voice coming out in a moan of longing. 'Oh, Grace. I missed this. I missed you.'

'Yes,' she panted, her head thrown back, her fingers digging into his shoulders as she urged him closer. And then he was filling her, making her gasp and his heart fill with the wonder of it, with the knowledge that the connection they'd both experienced was finally, joyously restored.

Afterwards she lay in his arms, her heart thundering against his as he brushed her dry cheek. 'No tears,' he said softly, his hand cupping her face, and she smiled against his palm.

'No tears,' she answered, and then neither of them spoke for a long moment. The weight of the words she hadn't said lay between them, but as Khalis held her he knew they bore it together. And then she stirred, settled herself against him and began.

'I first met Loukas when I was just fourteen,' she said softly. She ran her hand down his arms, her fingers curling around his bicep, holding onto him like an anchor. Khalis pulled her closer and waited. 'My mother had died the year before and I suppose I was lonely. My father was wonderful, but he was also easily distracted, absorbed by his books. And Loukas was so kind then. He was full of important plans about how he'd make his fortune, but he still made time for me.' She sighed and her hair whispered against his chest once more. 'The next time I saw him was at my father's funeral. I was twenty-six, and I'd just finished my doctorate. I was about to join an auction house in London, and before he died I felt like I had everything before me. But then...' She paused, shaking her head. 'I felt so alone. I realised I had no one left, and when Loukas invited me out, listened to me...well, it felt wonderful. I hadn't had any really serious relationships; I'd been too involved in my studies. And at that moment...' She paused. 'Sometimes I wonder if we'd met at a different point, if I would have noticed him at all. Maybe that's just...wishful thinking, I don't know. I don't think my head would have been quite so turned.'

'You were vulnerable.'

She shook her head. 'That's just an excuse.'

'We're not talking about excuses,' Khalis reminded her. 'Just understanding.'

'We were married within six weeks. It was far too fast, I see that now. I barely knew what I was doing. I was still grieving, really. I still thought of him as the university student with a kind word for me and a friendly smile, but he'd changed. He was wealthy now, terribly wealthy, and I think...I think he saw me as a possession. A prized one, but...' She stopped, swallowing, before she continued in a voice heavy with remembrance. 'He took me to his island for what I thought was a honeymoon. I thought we'd go back, live in London, have a normal life.' She stopped again, and he felt her body tense. He ran his hand down her shoulder and arm, pulled her closer to him. 'He left me there,' Grace confessed in a whisper. 'He informed the auction house that I wasn't taking up the post, and told me he wanted to keep me safe. He made it sound like he was trying to take care of me, but I felt—' She drew in a ragged breath. 'I felt like Leda, trapped in that little room with no one to see her or even know she was there.' She gave something that Khalis supposed was meant to be a laugh, but it wobbled too much. 'It sounds so ridiculous because I wasn't really a prisoner. I mean, I was a grown woman—I could have arranged transport or something. I wasn't *trapped*.'

'But?' Khalis prompted when it seemed as if she wouldn't go on.

'But I was afraid. Loukas felt like the only person I had in the world and, even though he wasn't there most of the time, I didn't want to lose him. And sometimes I convinced myself that it was all reasonable, that living on an island paradise was no hardship.'

'No wonder you hated Alhaja with all of its security and walls.'

'I don't like feeling trapped. Or managed. Loukas was always telling me what to do, even what to think.' She sighed, shaking her head. 'I think I was working up the courage to leave when I found out I was pregnant. I knew I couldn't leave him then. He wouldn't let me, and I still wanted our family to work.' She rolled over to face him now, her eyes clouded with sadness and yet so heartbreakingly clear. She hid nothing from him now. 'After Katerina was born, I thought it would be enough. It should have been enough. But she didn't sleep or nurse well and I was tired. Loukas had hired a nanny to help me but she was awful, as bossy and controlling as he was. At times I felt like I was going out of my mind.'

Khalis said nothing, just kept stroking her back, her shoulder, her arm. Touches to show he was listening. He understood. 'And then,' she whispered and stopped. She rolled back onto her side, tucked her knees up into her chest. The silence ticked on. 'Loukas hired him, you know,' she whispered. 'To tend the property. Sometimes I wonder... I think maybe...maybe he was testing me, and I failed.'

'That's not how a marriage is meant to work.'

'No,' Grace said after a moment, her voice no more than a scratch of sound. 'None of it was meant to work that way.' Her shoulders shook then and he knew she was crying, not just tears trickling down her face, but sobs that wrenched her whole body.

Khalis didn't say anything. He just held her, rubbing her back, his cheek pressed against her hair. The sound of her sorrow made his own eyes sting. How could he have ever doubted this woman? Thought he couldn't love her?

He loved her now more than ever.

Finally her sobs abated and she gave a loud sniff, a trembling laugh. 'I'm sorry. I haven't cried like that since... well, since forever.'

'I thought as much.'

She rolled over to face him again. Her eyes were red and puffy from weeping, her face completely blotchy. Khalis smiled and pressed a gentle kiss to her lips.

'You're beautiful,' he told her. 'And I love you.'

Her mouth curved in a trembling smile. 'I love you, too.' She laid her palm against his cheek. 'You know,' she said softly, 'for the first time I feel like the past isn't hanging over me. Suffocating me. I almost feel...free.' She stroked his cheek and another tear slid down her cheek. 'Thank you,' she whispered.

* * *

When Grace awoke the bed was empty and sunlight flooded the room. She lay there, the memories of last night washing over her in a healing tide. She never would have thought telling Khalis everything would feel so good, so restorative. Surely there were no secrets between them now.

What about your daughter?

Grace rolled over onto her side. Loukas would have found out about last night. Somehow, some way, he would know she'd been indiscreet. And even as her heart ached at this knowledge, she realised she no longer lived in the kind of terror he'd kept her in for four long years. With Khalis's help, she could fight the custody arrangement. She didn't know how long it would take or how they would do it, but for the first time in four years she had hope. It was as powerful and heady a feeling as the love she felt for Khalis. Smiling, she rose from the bed. She heard the sound of the shower from the bathroom and saw a tray with a carafe of coffee, a couple of cups and a newspaper. She poured herself a cup and reached for the paper.

Ammar Tannous survives helicopter crash.

It wasn't even on the front page, just a corner of the second page, hardly noticeable, and yet the words seemed to jump out and grab her by the throat. Khalis's brother was alive.

She'd barely processed this information when the bathroom door opened and Khalis emerged, dressed only in boxers, a towel draped over his shoulders.

'Good morning.'

She looked up, the paper still in her hands. 'Khalis… Khalis, I've just read…'

'Something amazing, it would seem.' He smiled as he reached for the carafe of coffee.

'Look at this.' She thrust the paper at him, pointing to the article about Ammar. And in the second it took Khalis to read the headline, his mouth compressing, she felt her hope and joy being doused by the icy chill of foreboding.

He glanced away from the paper and finished pouring his coffee. 'What about it?'

'*What about it?* Khalis, that's your brother. Isn't it?' For a second she thought she must have got it wrong. Surely he couldn't be so cold about *this*.

'It appears to be.' He sat across from her and sipped his coffee. Grace would have thought he was completely indifferent except for the tension radiating from his body. The bone china cup looked as if it might snap between his fingers. 'I went to file a custody appeal this morning.'

Grace blinked, trying to keep up. 'A custody—'

'My legal team thinks the trial judge abused his wide discretion,' Khalis explained. 'And because there was so little finding to support the court order, it's manifestly in error. I think you could have complete custody.'

Even as that thought caused new hope to leap within her, Grace shook her head. 'You're just changing the subject.'

'I'm talking about your daughter.'

'And I'm talking about your brother. You don't even seem surprised that he's alive.' She saw a wariness enter his eyes, felt his hesitation. 'You knew, didn't you?' she said slowly. 'You already knew.'

Khalis glanced away. 'He phoned me a few days ago.'

'And what…what did he say?'

'I didn't really talk to him.'

'Why not?'

He snapped his gaze back to her. 'Because he was up to

his neck in the same illegal activities as my father. I don't trust him, don't even know him any more. As far as I'm concerned, he's my enemy.'

She stared at him, saw the taut, angry energy of his body, and knew there was more to this than Khalis was saying. More darkness and pain and fear. He'd helped her look into the abyss of her own past regrets and mistakes last night; maybe it was her turn to help him.

'Couldn't you at least talk to him?' she asked.

'I don't see any point.'

'Maybe he's changed—'

Khalis gave a short, hard laugh. 'He suggested the same thing. People don't change, Grace. Not that much.'

She felt a sudden shaft of pain pierce her. 'Don't they?'

Khalis glanced at her, his lips pressed in a thin line. 'You know I didn't mean you.'

'I don't really see the difference.'

'You don't see the difference between you and my brother? Come on, Grace.'

'What *is* the difference, Khalis? It sounds like we're two people who made mistakes and regret them.'

'You think Ammar regrets—'

'You said he told you he'd changed.'

Khalis looked away. 'This is ridiculous. You made one single mistake which you regret bitterly, and Ammar made dozens—'

Grace felt herself go cold. 'Oh, I see,' she said. 'There's a maximum on how many mistakes you can make? I'm all right because I just made the one?'

'You're twisting my words.'

'I don't understand why you can't just talk to him at least.'

'Because I don't *want* to,' Khalis snapped. Colour

slashed his cheekbones. He looked angry, Grace thought, but he also looked afraid.

'You don't *want* to forgive him,' she said slowly. 'Do you?' Khalis didn't answer, but she saw the truth in his eyes. 'Why not?' she asked, her voice soft with sorrow. 'Why do you want to hold onto all that anger and pain? I know how it can cripple you—'

'You *don't* know,' Khalis said shortly. He rose from the table and moved to the window, his back to her. 'I don't want to talk about this any more.'

'So I'm meant to tell you everything,' she said, her voice rising. 'I'm meant to completely open my heart and soul but you get to have certain parts of your life be off-limits. Well, *that* seems fair.'

The very air seemed to shiver with the sudden suppressed tension, tension Grace hadn't even really known existed between them. She'd thought they'd both been laid bare and healed last night, but only she had. Khalis was still living in the torment of his past, holding onto his hard heart. How could she not have seen that? She'd seen that unyielding iron core the very first day they'd met. It didn't just magically melt or disappear. She'd been dreaming of happy endings, but now she saw that as long as Khalis held onto this anger they were just fairy tales.

'Khalis,' she said quietly, 'if you aren't willing to forgive your brother, if you can't believe that he might have changed, how can I believe you think I have?'

Khalis let out a ragged breath. 'It's completely different—'

'No, it isn't. It really isn't.' She shook her head sadly. She wanted to help him, but she didn't know if she could. If he'd let her. 'I almost wish it was. But don't you see how this—this coldness in you will affect anything we have together?'

He turned back to her, his eyes flashing a warning. 'You don't know my family, Grace.'

'Then tell me. Tell me what they did that's so bad you can't give your brother—your brother whom you thought was dead—a second chance.'

Khalis swung away from her and raked a hand through his hair. 'You are trying to equate two very different situations. And it simply doesn't work.'

'But the principles are the same.' Grace rose and took a step closer to him. 'The heart involved in the relationships is the same—yours.'

Khalis let out a sound that was close to a laugh, but filled with disbelief and disgust. 'Are you saying I can't love you if I don't forgive my brother?'

Grace hesitated. She didn't want to make ultimatums or force Khalis to do something he wasn't ready for or capable of. Yet she also knew that they could have no real, secure future as long as he harboured this coldness towards his family. 'Ever since we first met,' she began, choosing her words with care, 'I sensed a darkness—a hardness in you that scares me.'

He turned around, eyebrows arched in cynical incredulity. 'I *scared* you? I thought you loved me.'

'I do, Khalis. That's why I'm saying this.'

'Cruel to be kind?' he jeered, and Grace knew she was getting closer to the heart of it. The heart of him, and the thing—whatever it was—he was afraid of.

'I'm not trying to be cruel,' she said. 'But I don't understand, Khalis. Why won't you even talk to your brother? Why do you refuse to mourn or even think of your family? Why are you so determined never to look back?'

'I told you, the past is past—'

'But it *isn't*—' Grace cut him off '—as long as it controls your actions.'

He stared at her long and hard and she ached to cross the room and hold him in her arms. 'You helped me face my demons,' she said softly. 'Maybe now you need to face yours.'

His features twisted and, with a lurch of mingled hope and sorrow, Grace thought she'd won. *They* had. Then he turned away and said tonelessly, 'That's just a lot of psychobabble.'

Her eyes stung. 'Do you really believe that?'

'Don't make this into something it isn't, Grace. This isn't about us. We can be perfectly happy without me ever seeing my brother again.'

'No. We can't.' Her words fell slowly into the stillness, as if from a great height. Grace imagined she could almost see the irrevocable ripples they created, like pebbles in a pond, disturbing the calm surface for ever.

He turned back to face her, shock replacing anger. 'What are you saying?'

'I'm saying,' Grace said, each word a knife-twist in her heart, 'that if you can't even talk to your brother—your brother whom you thought was dead—then I can't be with you.' He looked as if she'd just punched him. Maybe she had. 'I'm not trying to give you some kind of ultimatum—'

'Really?' he practically snarled. 'Because it looks that way from here.'

'I'm just stating facts, Khalis. Our relationship has been a mess of contradictions from the beginning. Keeping secrets even as we had this incredible connection. Amazing intimacy and terrible pain. Well, I don't want a relationship—a love—that is a contradiction. I want the real thing. Whole. Pure. Good. I want that with you.'

He let out a shuddering breath. 'When we first met, I put you on a pedestal. I thought you were perfect, and I was disappointed when you showed me your feet of clay.

But I accepted you, Grace. I accepted you and loved you just as you are. Yet now you can't do the same for me? I've got to be perfect?'

'No, Khalis.' She shook her head, blinked back tears. 'I don't want you to be perfect. I just want you to try.'

His mouth curved in a disbelieving and humourless smile. 'Try to be perfect.'

'No,' she said, her heart breaking now, 'just try to forgive.'

Khalis didn't answer, and that was answer enough. He couldn't do it, she realised. He couldn't even try to let go. And they couldn't have a future together—a secure, trusting future—as long as he didn't.

Slowly Grace walked over to the bed, where her clothes from last night still lay discarded on the floor. She reached for her dress. 'I think,' she said, 'I have a flight to catch.'

Khalis stared at the nondescript door of the hotel room where his brother was staying. It had taken two days to work up the courage to call Ammar, and then fly to Tunis where he was staying. Now he was here, standing in the hallway of a nameless hotel, the cries and clangs from the busy medina of metalwork and craft shops audible on the hot, dusty air.

Even now he was tempted to walk away. Grace had demanded answers, yet how could he explain his reasoning for refusing simply to speak to his brother? What kind of man could be so hard-hearted?

Apparently he could.

Yet the feeling—the *need*—to keep himself distant from his family was so instinctive it felt like a knee-jerk reflex. And when he'd heard Ammar's voice on the telephone, sounding so ragged and even broken, that deep-seated instinct had only grown stronger. Grace was right. He didn't want to forgive Ammar. He was afraid of what might happen if he did.

It had taken her leaving him—*devastating* him—for him to finally face his brother. His past.

Khalis raised one trembling fist and knocked on the door. He heard footsteps, and then the door opened and he was staring at his brother. Ammar still stood tall and imposing, reminding Khalis that his brother had always been older, stronger, tougher. Ammar's face looked gaunt, though, and there was a long scar snaking down the side of his face. He stared long and hard at Khalis, and then he stepped aside to let him in.

Khalis walked in slowly, his body almost vibrating with tension. The last time he'd seen Ammar he'd been twenty-one years old and leaving Alhaja. Ammar had laughed. *Good riddance*, he'd called. And then he'd turned away as if he couldn't care less.

'Thank you for coming,' Ammar said. He sounded the same, surly and impatient. Maybe he hadn't changed after all. Khalis realised he would be glad, and felt a spurt of shame.

'I'm not sure why I did,' Khalis answered. He couldn't manage any more. Raw emotion had grabbed him by the throat and had him in a stranglehold, making further speech impossible. He hadn't seen his brother in fifteen years. Hadn't spoken to him or even looked at a photograph of him. Hadn't *thought* of him, because to think of Ammar was to remember the happy days of their childhood, when they had been friends and comrades-in-arms. Not competitors. Not enemies.

To think of Ammar, Khalis knew with a sudden flash of pain, was to think of Jamilah and to regret. To wonder if he might have made a mistake in leaving all those years ago. And that was a thought he could not bear to consider for a moment.

'So,' he finally said, and his voice sounded rusty, 'you're alive.' As far as observations went, it was asinine. Yet Khalis felt robbed of intelligent thought as well as speech. Part of him wanted to reach forward and hug the brother he'd lost so long ago. The other part—the greater part, perhaps—still had a heart like a stone.

The heart involved in the relationships is the same— yours.

And he wanted that heart to belong to Grace. For her— for them—he had to try. 'Why did you want to talk to me?' he asked.

Ammar's face twisted in a grimace. 'You're my brother.'

'I haven't been your brother for fifteen years.'

'You'll always be my brother, Khalis.'

'What are you saying?' Khalis tried to keep his voice even. It was hard with so many contrary emotions running through him. Hope and fear. Anger and joy. *I don't want a relationship...that is a contradiction.* He swallowed. He had to see this through.

Ammar released a shuddering breath. 'God knows I have made many mistakes in this life, even as a boy. But I've changed—'

Khalis let out a disbelieving laugh, the sound harsh and cold. Grace was right. There was a coldness inside him, a hard darkness he did not know how to dispel. *She only wanted you to try.* 'How have you changed?' he managed.

'The helicopter crash—'

'A brush with death made you realise the error of your ways?' Khalis heard the sneer in his own voice.

'Something like that.' He gazed levelly at Khalis. 'Do you want to know what happened?'

He shrugged. 'Very well.'

'The engine failed. I think it was a genuine accident, although God knows our father always suspected someone of trying to kill him.'

'When you deal with the dregs of society, that tends to happen.'

'I know,' Ammar said quietly.

Khalis gave another hard laugh. 'As well you should.'

'I was piloting the helicopter,' Ammar continued. 'When we realised we were going to crash, Father gave the one parachute to me.'

For a second Khalis was stunned into silence. He had not thought his father capable of any generosity of spirit. 'Why was there only one parachute?' he asked after a moment.

Ammar shrugged. 'Who knows? Maybe the old man only wanted there to be one so he could be sure to take it in case of an accident. I always thought he'd be the last one standing.'

'But he changed his mind?'

'He *changed*,' Ammar said quietly, and Khalis heard a note of sorrow in his brother's usually strident voice. 'He was dying. He'd been diagnosed with terminal cancer six months ago. It made him start to really think about things.'

'*Think* about things?'

'I know he had a lot to answer for. I think that's why he decided to hand the company over to you. He only did that a month or so before he died, you know. He talked about you, said he regretted being so harsh with you.' Ammar gave him a bleak smile. 'Admired what you'd done with yourself.'

It seemed so hard to believe. Painful to believe. The last time he'd seen his father, Balkri Tannous had spat in his face. Tried to hit him. And recklessly Khalis had told him he was taking Jamilah with him.

Over my dead body, Balkri Tannous had said. Except in the end it had been Jamilah's.

And still Khalis had left. Without her.

Pain stabbed at him, both at his head and his heart. This was why he never thought about the past. This was why he'd cut himself off from his family so utterly, had insisted his father or brother could not be redeemed. So he wouldn't wonder if he should have stayed. Or returned sooner. Or taken her anyway. Anything to have kept his sister alive.

'You're thinking of Jamilah,' Ammar said quietly and Khalis swung away, braced one hand against the door. He wanted to leave. He was *desperate* to leave, and yet the thought of Grace—the warmth of her smile, the *strength* of her—made him stay. 'It was an accident, you know,' Ammar said. 'Her death. She didn't mean to kill herself.' He paused, and Khalis closed his eyes. 'I knew you'd wonder.'

'How do you know it was an accident?'

'She was determined, Khalis. Determined to live. She told me so.'

Khalis let out a strangled sound, choking off the cry of anguish that howled inside him. 'If I'd come back for her—'

'You could not have prevented an accident.'

'If I'd stayed—'

'You couldn't have stayed.'

His hand clenched into a fist. 'Maybe I should have,' he said in a low voice. 'Maybe if I'd stayed, I could have changed things for the better.'

His back to Ammar, Khalis didn't hear his brother move. He just felt his hand heavy on his shoulder. 'Khalis, it took an act of God and my own father's death for me to want to change. It took Father's diagnosis for him to even think about changing. Do not attempt to carry the world on your shoulders. We were grown men. We were not your responsibility, and neither was Jamilah.'

Khalis didn't speak for a long moment. He couldn't. 'So what happened next?' he finally asked.

'I parachuted into the sea and managed to get to land. A small island south of here, closer to the coast. It had fresh water, so I knew I could survive for a few days at least. I dislocated my shoulder when I landed, but I managed to fix it.' Ammar spoke neutrally enough, but Khalis was humbled anyway. He could not imagine enduring such a catastrophe.

'And?' he asked after a pause.

'After six days I managed to flag down a fishing boat, and they brought me to a small village on the coast of Tunisia. I'd developed a fever by that point and I was out of my mind for several days. By the time I knew who I was and I remembered everything, weeks had passed since the crash. I knew I needed to speak with you, so I flew to San Francisco to find out where you were, and then to Rome.'

'How did you even know about my company?'

'I've kept track of what you've been doing,' Ammar said. 'All along.'

And meanwhile Khalis had deliberately refused to read or listen to anything about Tannous Enterprises. Again he felt that hot rush of guilt. He couldn't bear the thought of his brother or father regretting his departure, watching him from afar. He couldn't bear the thought he'd been wrong.

'I know I wasn't a good brother to you,' Ammar said.

Khalis just shrugged. 'Sibling rivalry.'

'It was worse than that.' He didn't answer. He knew it was. 'Please forgive me, Khalis.'

Ammar couldn't say it plainer than that. Khalis registered the heartfelt sincerity in his brother's gaunt face, and said nothing. The words he knew his brother wanted to hear stuck in his throat.

If I forgive you then the past can't be the past any more and I'll have to live with the guilt and regret of knowing I should have stayed and saved Jamilah. And I don't think I can survive that. I'm not strong enough.

But Grace was strong. Grace made him strong. And he knew, just as Grace had known, it wasn't only Ammar he needed to forgive. It was himself.

You helped me face my demons. Maybe now you need to face yours.

His throat worked. His eyes stung. And somehow he found the words, raw and rusty, scraping his throat and tearing open his heart. 'I forgive you, Ammar.' *And I forgive myself.*

Ammar broke into a smile and started forward. Clumsily, because it had been so long, he reached to embrace Khalis. Khalis put his arms around Ammar, awkwardly, yet with a new and hesitant hope.

He couldn't have done it, he knew, without Grace. Without her strength. She'd been strong enough to walk away from him. And now he prayed she would come back to him when he found her.

Ammar stepped back, his smile as awkward as Khalis's hug. This was new and uncomfortable territory for both of them. 'It is good,' he said, and Khalis nodded.

'What will you do now?' he asked after a moment. 'Tannous Enterprises should by rights be yours.'

Ammar shook his head. 'Father wanted you to have it—'

'But I don't want it. And your whole life has been dedicated to the company, Ammar. Perhaps now you can make something of it. Something good.'

'Maybe.' Ammar looked away. 'If it is possible.'

'I'll sign my shares over to you—'

'I need to do something first.'

Surprised, Khalis blinked. 'What?'

'I need to find my wife.'

'Your *wife*?' He had not known his brother had married. But of course he had not known anything about these last fifteen years.

'Former wife, I should say,' Ammar corrected grimly. 'The marriage was annulled ten years ago.'

Curiosity sharpened inside him, but the hard set of his brother's features kept Khalis from asking any more probing questions. 'Still,' he said, 'you should take control of Tannous Enterprises. Turn it around, if you will.' Perhaps then the company could be redeemed, as Grace had suggested. Redeemed rather than dismantled and destroyed.

'There is time to discuss these matters,' Ammar said, and Khalis nodded.

'You must come to Alhaja. We can celebrate there.'

Ammar's mouth twisted. 'I've always hated that place.'

'As did I. But perhaps we can redeem even that wretched island.'

'You are full of hope,' Ammar observed wryly. He did not sound particularly hopeful himself. His brother might have changed, but he still looked haunted.

'I am,' Khalis answered. His heart felt light, lighter than ever before. He felt as if he could float. And he needed to find Grace. 'And while you need to find your wife, I need to find my—' He paused. 'My love.' Smiling, he embraced his brother once more. 'And tell her so.'

Six hours later, Khalis strode into the head office of Axis Art Insurers. A receptionist flapped at him, saying she'd have to check if Ms Turner was available, but Khalis just flashed her a quick smile and kept walking. Nothing was going to keep him from Grace now.

He'd wandered down several wrong corridors before he finally found her in one of the labs. She was standing in front of a canvas—he couldn't see what it was and, frankly, he didn't care—and his heart swelled with love at the sight of her. She wore a crisp white blouse and navy pencil skirt, reminding him of when he'd first seen her. Her hair was up in its classic chignon, but a few tendrils had escaped and curled around her neck. She gestured to the unseen canvas with one slender arm, and he felt pride swell along with overwhelming love. She was so strong. So amazing, to have come so far and done so much on her own. To have not just survived, but triumphed.

Khalis opened the door.

Grace heard the door open, felt that prickling along the nape of her neck that had alerted her to Khalis's presence before. Her body was wired to his in some elemental way, and yet...

Surely he couldn't be here.

He was. She turned and saw him looking as mouth-dryingly gorgeous as ever, his expression intent and serious as he gazed at her. And Grace gazed back, drinking him in, knowing that even though it had only been a few days she'd missed him. Terribly.

He nodded towards the canvas on the stainless steel table. 'Forgery?'

'No, it appears to be genuine so far.'

Khalis gave her a crooked smile. 'I don't know much about art, but thank God I know the real thing when I see it.' He closed the space between them in two long strides and swept her into his arms. 'You.'

Grace's arms came around him as a matter of instinct even as she searched his face. 'Khalis—'

'I found my brother. I talked to him.'

Her arms tightened around him. 'I'm glad.'

'So am I. Mainly because losing you over something like that would have killed me. But also because you were right. I did need to face my past. Face my family, and that darkness in myself.' His throat worked as his voice choked just a little. 'I needed to forgive myself.'

She laid one hand against his cheek. 'Sometimes that's the most difficult part.'

'But worth it. Most definitely worth it.' He bent his head and, smiling, Grace tilted her own back as he kissed her softly, a promise. 'Now,' Khalis said as he lifted his head, 'we really can look towards the future. Our future.'

'That sounds like a wonderful idea.' Grace's gaze widened when she saw him retrieve a small velvet box from his pocket.

'And I think,' Khalis said with a smile, 'it can begin with this. Grace Turner, will you marry me?'

She let out a shocked and joyous laugh. 'Yes. Yes, I will.'

'Then,' Khalis said, sliding a gorgeous diamond and sapphire ring onto her finger, 'the future looks very bright indeed.'

EPILOGUE

GRACE stared at the imposing villa in one of Athens's best neighbourhoods and felt a flutter of nerves so strong it was more like a kick in the gut.

'What if she's forgotten me?' she whispered. 'What if she doesn't want to go with me?'

Khalis slipped his hand into hers and squeezed. 'We'll take it together, one step at a time. One second at a time, if need be.'

Grace let out a slow breath and nodded. It had taken six months to get to this moment. Her ex-husband had been brought to court in a custody appeal, and after a lengthy trial Grace had been awarded main custody of Katerina, with Loukas having her every other weekend. Furious that he'd been thwarted, her ex-husband had relinquished all claims on his daughter. Even though Grace was saddened that he'd rejected Katerina, she was thrilled to have her daughter back. Thrilled and terrified. After years of stilted and unsatisfactory visits, she'd finally tuck her in at night. Sing her songs. Hold her close.

If Katerina would let her.

'I'm so scared,' she whispered and Khalis put his arm around her as he guided her up the front steps.

'The past really is the past,' he reminded her. 'We're looking towards the future now—as a family.'

A family. What a wonderful, amazing, humbling thought. Gulping a little, Grace nodded and pressed the doorbell.

Katerina's nanny answered the door; she had remained on as the child's carer while the trial went on. Now, with trepidation, Grace introduced herself and then waited as the nanny went to bring her Katerina.

The first sight of her daughter in several months nearly brought her to her knees. She'd grown several inches and, at nearly six years old, she was starting to lose some of that toddler roundness. Her eyes were wide and dark as she stared at Grace.

'Hello, Katerina,' Grace said, her voice only just steady. Khalis squeezed her hand in silent, loving encouragement. 'Hello, darling.'

Katerina gazed at her for a long moment, and then glanced at Khalis curiously before turning back to Grace. She offered a shy, hesitant smile. 'Hello, Mama,' she said.

*   *   *   *   *

AN INNOCENT
IN PARADISE

KATE CARLISLE

To my four favorite plotters, Susan Mallery,
Maureen Child, Christine Rimmer and Theresa
Southwick. Thank so much for the inspiration,
motivation, support, threats and laughs.
Drinks are on me, ladies!

One

Logan Sutherland was strolling toward the hotel lobby of the exclusive Alleria Resort when the jarring sound of shattering glass reverberated from the cocktail lounge.

"Price of doing business," Logan muttered. But he stopped and listened for another moment.

And heard nothing. Not a sound.

"Hell," he said, and checked his watch. The conference call was scheduled to start in fifteen minutes. He didn't have time for this. But the ominous silence made him change direction and head for the bar.

Logan and his twin brother, Aidan, had made their fortunes designing and operating exotic, upscale cocktail bars in high-end hotels all over the world. So the sound of breaking glassware was rarely a cause for alarm. But in his experience, the breakage was invariably followed by raucous cheers, jeers and laughter. Never silence.

Silence meant something was wrong. And Logan

Sutherland was not a man who allowed things to go wrong without doing something about it.

He walked into the casually elegant bar and noted that the sound level still hadn't risen, even though the place was busy and most of the tables were occupied by hotel guests having a good time. Cocktail waitresses and waiters moved swiftly from table to table, serving drinks and appetizers. The quiet was disconcerting.

A small group of his people were gathered in a knot at the far end of the long bar, all of them crouched on the floor. He approached the head bartender on duty. "What's going on, Sam?"

Sam flicked his chin toward the other end of the bar. "New cocktail waitress dropped a full tray of drinks."

"Why is it so quiet?"

Sam took a few seconds to study the drink station halfway down the long bar where two junior bartenders were efficiently refilling the drink orders. Then he turned and made eye contact with Logan. "We're all a little worried about her, boss."

"Why?" Logan glanced again at the small crowd. "Did she cut herself?"

He lifted a shoulder. "Naw, she's just a real sweet kid. It wouldn't be nice to laugh at her."

Logan frowned at the brawny former Marine, then turned to get a better look at the new employee.

The small group of servers and busboys picked up the last of the big chunks of broken glass and dispersed, heading back to their own stations. One waitress remained as a busboy swept the residual shards of glass into a dustpan. Then she knelt down and, with several bar towels, sopped up the rest of the liquid.

"Thank you so much, Paolo," the waitress said, and squeezed the busboy's arm affectionately. He took the clump of towels from her and she headed back to the drinks station. That's when Logan got his first look at the "real sweet kid." And felt a solid wall of heat almost knock him off his footing.

His *second* thought was: *Hope she's wearing sunblock,* because her skin was so pale and smooth and creamy.

His *first* thought had been vividly X-rated and not suitable for discussion in mixed company.

And none of that made him happy.

She was a classic redhead with a peaches-and-cream complexion and a light dusting of freckles across her nose. Thick, dark red hair tumbled down her back in rich, lustrous waves. In her official uniform of bikini top and filmy sarong, Logan couldn't help but notice she had a world-class butt and perfect breasts.

She was tall, a quality Logan preferred in his women—not that it mattered, since he didn't have time for or interest in a relationship right now. On the other hand, who said anything about a relationship? He could always make time for sex. Maybe he ought to rethink his schedule since staring at her was causing him to calculate how quickly it would take to get her into his bed.

She walked with the sort of poise that some tall women possessed naturally. That made the fact that she'd spilled a large tray of drinks even more baffling to him, since she didn't seem clumsy at all. On the contrary, she appeared confident and self-assured. Smart. Hard to believe she'd ever spilled anything in her life.

So what kind of game was she playing?

Logan thought of his tough bartender, Sam, calling her sweet and worrying about her sensitivities. Well, Sam wouldn't be the first man drawn in by a conniving, manipulative woman.

The woman in question finally noticed Logan and her

eyes lit up as she smiled directly at him. Okay, she was a stunner for sure. Logan felt as if he were the only man in the room and understood how his burly bartender had turned into such a pussycat in her presence.

Her mouth was wide and sexy, her lips full and lush. Her eyes were big and green and twinkled with an open friendliness that seemed genuine. She'd probably been practicing that generous smile forever. If nothing else, it would certainly help her garner the big tips.

Of course, she wouldn't be getting many tips if she kept spilling the customers' drinks. And that's why he was here, lest he forgot.

Before he could step up and introduce himself, the two bartenders finished her drink order and called her over.

"Oh, thank you, guys," she said, her voice as appealing as her smile. "You're both so sweet."

Logan watched the experienced bartenders' faces redden at the simple compliment, just as the woman pulled a small notebook from her waistband and studied it for a moment. She slipped the notebook away, then began arranging the drinks carefully on the tray in some kind of circular order. When she was finished, she grabbed the tray with both hands and started to lift it. There was a sudden hush around the room as the large tray bobbled awkwardly and the woman's eyes widened.

Without thinking, Logan rushed to her. He whisked the tray out of her hands, lifted it onto his shoulder and held it in place with one hand. Then he looked down at her. "Where's this going?"

"Oh, aren't you wonderful?" she said with another wide-eyed smile. "It goes right over here." She led the way to a four-top by the wall of windows overlooking the white-sand beach. She gestured with her hand. "These drinks are for Mr. and Mrs. McKee and their friends."

"Hey, doll," the older man said. "I told you I'd come and get those drinks for you, but it looks like you found yourself a helper there."

A guest of the Alleria resort was willing to get his own drinks for her? Okay, that was bad enough, but did this guest actually think Logan was the waitress's lackey? It was about time he and Ms. Clumsy had a long talk.

"Oh, Mr. McKee, thank you for offering," the waitress said, then turned and patted Logan's arm. "But all the servers here are so helpful that—"

"It's no problem at all, sir," Logan interrupted, lowering the drink tray onto the edge of the table. He quickly passed the drinks out, then said as affably as he could manage, "Enjoy your cocktails."

"You betcha, pal," Mr. McKee said and took a big sip of his banana daiquiri. "Man, these go down smooth."

"Here you go, sweetie," Mrs. McKee said, and tucked a fifty-dollar bill into the waitress's hand. "That's for all your trouble."

"Oh, my goodness," the waitress said, staring at the money, then back at her customers. "Thank you so much."

"No, thank *you,* doll." Mr. McKee winked. "You're a cutie-pie and we're just sorry we loaded you up with our orders."

She waved off the apology. "Oh, that's—"

"Thank you, Mr. and Mrs. McKee," Logan interrupted. "Please enjoy your day." Then he grabbed the waitress's arm and led her gently but firmly away from the table. He stopped at the bar, where he dropped off the tray, then scooted her across the room and out the door.

"Wait," she protested, squirming against him. "You have to let me go. I can't leave the lounge right now. I'm working."

"We're going to have a little talk first," Logan said,

smiling grimly as he led her down the hall toward his office.

"Stop," she insisted as she struggled to pull her arm from his grasp. "Honestly, who do you think you are?"

"At the moment I'm your employer," he said, glaring down at her. "But I don't expect that status to last much longer."

Grace cringed at his revelation. Of all the people to have rescued her from another spilled tray of drinks, why did it have to be one of the Sutherland brothers?

Before leaving for Alleria, Grace had done some cursory research on Logan and Aidan Sutherland. They'd risen to the top of the surfing world in their teenage years, then parlayed their winnings into fancy nightclubs and bars all over the world. Rumor had it they'd won their first bar in a college poker game; but Grace didn't believe that story was anything more than an urban legend.

The most recent story she'd read about the Sutherland twins centered on them joining forces with their cousins, the Duke brothers, who owned a number of luxurious resorts on the West Coast.

Grace had seen photographs of the Sutherland men online, but those pictures were all action shots of the brothers surfing or sailing. None of them had shown how good-looking they were up close, nor had the photos given her even one, tiny warning of the disconcerting amount of physical power and dynamism the man striding next to her would exude in person.

Halfway down the hall, her new boss stopped at a set of double doors and flicked a plastic card through a security slide. He ushered her through the door and into a large, beautifully furnished hotel suite. An attractive sofa and several overstuffed chairs in muted shades of chocolate-brown and rich taupe were clustered at one end of the large room. The other half of the room contained a set of large, elegant office furniture along with all the usual equipment necessary to run a twenty-first-century office.

"This is where you work?" She turned around slowly to take it all in. Plantation shutters were opened to reveal an entire wall of sliding glass doors that led to a wide private terrace and showed off the spectacular view beyond of palm trees, sunshine, pristine white sand and clear, turquoise water.

It was one of the most beautiful sights Grace had ever seen and she stopped to admire it for several long seconds.

"Nice view, isn't it?" Mr. Sutherland said.

"It's stunning," she said, and turned to look at him. "You're so lucky."

"Yeah, it's good to be king," he said, and flashed her a confident grin that made her knees go weak. She rubbed her stomach and wondered if maybe she should've had more to eat for breakfast than just granola and mango juice, because her knees had never gone weak before in her entire life.

But looking at him again, she realized she would just have to learn to live with rubbery knees. He was tall and imperious, she thought, with dark blue eyes that glimmered with cynicism. She hoped there was some glint of empathy underneath that cynicism.

He picked up the phone and when someone answered, he said, "Reschedule the conference call for four o'clock." Then he hung up and stared at Grace. She knew she was in trouble but it didn't stop her from enjoying the sight of those riveting blue eyes that seemed to see right through her. His jaw was firm and strong and he had a small cleft in his square chin. His nose was just slightly crooked, which gave him a raffish charm she found nonsensically alluring.

"Sit," he said brusquely, indicating one of the plush chairs that faced the massive mahogany desk. She sat quickly, then noticed that he'd chosen to remain standing. The better to intimidate her, of course.

But that was fine. If these were to be her last few minutes on the Caribbean island, she would be perfectly happy to spend them staring at Mr. Sutherland. The man was stunningly handsome and muscular—not that she'd seen any of his actual muscles in person. Sadly, his impeccably tailored black suit covered his rugged frame completely. But Grace knew the man was built because of the way he'd so casually taken that heavy drink tray from her hands and lifted it up onto his shoulder so effortlessly.

Granted, before this trip to Alleria she hadn't gotten out of her laboratory much, but she'd never seen anything quite like him. His arms and shoulder muscles had to be in remarkable condition. She itched to squeeze them.

And that was an absolutely ridiculous thought, she scolded herself.

"I'm going to go out on a limb here," he said, interrupting her pleasant daydream, "and bet that you've never worked as a cocktail waitress before. Am I right?"

She took a deep breath or two as she considered lying to him, then changed her mind. She'd never been very good at prevarication. Still, it wouldn't do to tell him everything. But then she argued with herself, Oh, why not? Finally she said, "Yes, you're right, but—"

"That's all I wanted to know," he said pleasantly. "You're fired."

"No!" she cried, gripping the arms of her chair. "You can't fire me. Not yet."

"Not yet?" he repeated. "Why not? Because you haven't had a chance to break my entire supply of glassware?"

Her shoulders sagged. "No, of course not. But...I can't go home."

His eyes focused in on her. "What's your name?"

"It's Grace. Grace Farrell."

"Wait a minute." He cocked his head as though he hadn't heard her correctly. "Your name is *Grace?*"

She nodded gravely. "That's right."

"You're kidding." He chuckled, then leaned his hip against his desk and began to laugh, a deep rich sound that caused tingles to stir in her stomach.

What the heck was so funny about her name?

"Oh," she said, finally getting the joke. The very *lame* joke, she might add. "Yes, well, I suppose I wasn't very graceful out there."

"You think?" He snorted.

She blinked and sat up straighter in her chair. "You don't have to be rude."

"Sweetheart, you're the one who lied on your job application."

"I didn't— How did you know I lied?" She groaned inwardly. She couldn't even lie about lying. That was just sad.

"Easy." He folded his arms across his impressive chest in a move Grace knew was meant to daunt her. And it was working, sort of. She was more than a bit overwhelmed by him, if her inability to breathe was any indication.

"I don't hire inexperienced waitresses," he continued. "Since we did hire you, your application must've stated that you knew what you were doing. And you obviously don't, which means you lied. And since you no longer work for me, I can be as rude as I want."

"I hope you'll reconsider," she said, sniffing with annoyance at the logic of his argument. "I had a very good reason for lying—er, fudging the truth."

"Fudging?" He leaned one hip against the edge of his desk. "I can't wait to hear this."

She frowned at him. "Are you willing to listen to reason?"

"I'm a reasonable man," he said, waving his hand at her as if granting her permission to speak. "Just make it fast. I was on my way to making a very important phone call when I was interrupted by your little scene out there."

"Oh, I'm really sorry about that."

"Yeah, me, too. So?"

"Right. Well, it's simple, really." She took a quick moment to wish she was dressed in something more professional than a bikini top that revealed most of her breasts and a thin wisp of cloth that was knotted well below her belly button. But since she couldn't exactly run back to her room and change clothes, she took another deep breath and blurted, "You have spores."

He stared at her for a length of time, then shook his head. "No, I don't. I bathe daily."

She blinked, gasped, then laughed. "Oh, no, not *you* personally. Your island. There are rare spores growing here on Alleria that will save lives someday. I'm a research scientist and I've come here to collect and study them."

He continued to stare her down as he seemed to consider the situation. She thought she saw something akin to a hint of reasoning in his eyes. But then he checked his watch and said, "Okay, nice try. I'll expect you off the island within the hour."

"What? No!" She jumped up from her chair. "Mr.

Sutherland, you don't understand. I refuse to leave this island. I need to stay here and work."

He shook his head. "I'm afraid you're the one who doesn't understand, Ms. Farrell."

"You're wrong. I do understand," she insisted, shaking her finger at him. "I know I lied and maybe you think you have every right to fire me, but I am not leaving this island until I get what I came for."

Logan couldn't help but admire the fire of righteous vehemence in Grace Farrell's eyes. It seemed to light up her entire body and made him wonder if she would show that same level of passion in bed. When he thrust himself into her, would she scream with pleasure?

His eyes narrowed at the mental picture and he shook himself back to reality. What the hell was he doing, thinking of her in terms of a sex partner? She'd lied on her résumé, broken his glassware and wasted his time. She had no business staying on his island a minute longer than necessary.

But the vivid sexual image took a few knots of wind out of his sails and he took a moment to reconsider the idea of throwing her off the island. Yes, she was a liar, but she was a gorgeous one. Why not enjoy a few rounds of mutually enjoyable sex before tossing her off the island?

Hell, that idea was growing more appealing by the minute. Maybe he'd been working too hard lately, because he realized he wasn't quite as ready to get rid of her as he was a few minutes ago. Didn't mean he trusted the woman for a second, but frankly, he hadn't been this amused or intrigued—or aroused—in months. That was worth a few minutes of his time. It wouldn't hurt to let her talk.

"So tell me about these spores you're so anxious to find," he said, as he sat and made himself comfortable on the overstuffed couch. Might as well enjoy the show for as long as it lasted, he thought.

She was pacing now and pounding her fist into her palm, clearly committed to her cause. "Allerian spores flawlessly mimic human reproductive genes and are essential to my continued experimentation in gene replication. I've been working on this project every day for almost ten years and have been using the same batch of spores for the past two years. It's imperative that I acquire a fresh consignment in order to obtain new funding and continue my studies."

"Gene replication?"

She stopped midpace. "You know what that is?"

"Well, sure." He frowned. "Generally. Yeah."

"Oh, that's good. That's wonderful!" She clasped her hands together and pressed them to her breastbone. "Then you understand how important my work is and how vital it is that I find new spores. My dissertation detailing their meiotic patterns and the ability to exploit the resulting haploid cells has already gained international interest. I'm positive that further study will ultimately lead to unlocking the secrets to curing some of the worst diseases known to modern man."

"Oh, yeah?" He'd lost her at "meiotic patterns" but wasn't about to mention it.

"Absolutely." She held up her thumb and forefinger and squeezed them together. "I'm this close to finishing the preliminary studies and I've applied for further grant money in order to move to the next level. It's urgent and important work. But I need fresh, large batches of spores and I need them soon."

"I see," he said, stretching his arm out across the back of the sofa.

Clearly frustrated by his blasé tone, she stopped her

pacing and said quietly, "Look, Mr. Sutherland, I am a scientist, a very good one. And I…I need this job here in order to conduct my studies. Your resort is the main source of employment on the island."

"It's the *only* source of employment, Ms. Farrell, but let's not nitpick." Staring out the sliding glass doors, he carefully avoided making eye contact as he returned to his original argument. "So the reason you lied on your résumé was so that I would hire you so that you could live here at my resort for free and study our spores."

"Well, yes, and—"

"And you thought you'd coast right into the mindless job of waitress in our cocktail bar to cover your costs."

"I suppose that's right, but—"

"And yet, you've never been a cocktail waitress."

"Well, no, but—"

"Well, then." He lifted his shoulders in a move meant to indicate only one conclusion. "At the risk of repeating myself, you're fired."

"Wait!" She rushed over and sat on the couch mere inches from him, her breasts rising and falling with her rapid, anxious breathing. Her scent, some exotic blend of spice and…was it orange blossoms?…enveloped him. Up close, he could see a pale smattering of freckles on her shoulders. He had the most bizarre urge to touch them.

"Haven't you heard a word I've said?" she said. "I'm not leaving."

"You don't have to leave," he said genially. "Feel free to book a room at the resort and study spores as much as you want. But don't expect me to subsidize your trip."

"But…" A heavy frown marred the smooth surface of her forehead and her lower lip was in danger of quivering. She wasn't going to cry, was she? If she did, Logan swore he would throw her out of here faster than she could say *meiotic*...whatever. Crying was the ultimate weapon of female manipulation. He'd learned that the hard way.

"I can't book a room here," she confessed. "It's too expensive. The only way I can stay is if you'll let me work for you."

He raised one eyebrow. "No."

"Fine," she said defiantly, and jumped up from the couch. "I'll sleep on the beach, but I'm not leaving."

"Wait just a damn minute," he said, standing. "Nobody sleeps on my beach."

She turned. "*Your* beach?"

"That's right. I own most of this island and I say who comes and goes. And I don't want vagrants setting up camp on my beach."

"I'm not a vagrant," she muttered as she folded her arms tightly across her chest. Her lower lip stuck out in a pout and as much as he hated the manipulation game, he had to admit he wanted to run his tongue over those pouty lips of hers. He had to give her points for that.

She swallowed nervously and took another deep breath and it seemed to help her regain some inner resolve. Her lips tightened and she faced him head-on. "I'm not leaving, Mr. Sutherland. I need to find those spores. I won't go home without them."

He observed her quietly for a long moment. "You don't look like a research scientist."

She rolled her eyes. "What do my looks have to do with anything?"

He almost laughed. Her looks had almost everything to do with why he'd allowed her to make her case in the first place. If she didn't understand that, then maybe she *had* been hiding out in a stuffy laboratory for the past ten years.

Wait. Ten years? He knew she couldn't be much older

than twenty-five, which meant she'd been doing her so-called research since she was fifteen. If she was telling the truth, that is. Obviously, she wasn't.

She was a liar, plain and simple.

Before he could comment aloud, she waved her arms and forged ahead. "Fine. I may not look like your notion of a research scientist, but that's exactly what I am. And I have every intention of staying here until I've got everything I need to finish my work."

"Is that right?"

"Yes."

He noticed she was barely able to keep from squirming under his sharp gaze. Good.

Then, without warning, she stepped even closer and stared hard at him, eye to eye. Well, eye to chest was more accurate, since he towered over her. But that detail didn't seem to intimidate her.

"Look, I'm not above begging," she admitted. "I intend to stay on this island and I'm willing to do anything you want me to do. If you refuse to let me be a cocktail wait-ress, I'll clean hotel rooms or wash dishes or…or water your plants. I just ask that my mornings be kept free for the spores. That's why the cocktail waitress job is ideal, but there must be something else I can do around here. Oh, I can cook! Well, I'm not a great cook, but I can make salads or cut up fruit or…"

Anything he wanted her to do? Did she realize how dangerous that offer was? Was she truly that naive? For a second or two, Logan wondered about her and her wide-eyed innocence, then roughly shook the thought away. He didn't believe it. Grace Farrell was as manipulative as every other woman he'd ever met. Intriguing, gorgeous, sexy, but a manipulative liar just the same.

Damn, his brain was fogging over from her erotic scent. Maybe he was crazy, but he wanted his hands on her.

"Fine," he said. "You've got one week to prove you can handle the cocktail waitress job. If not, you're off the island."

"Oh, thank you!" Without warning, she threw herself into his arms. "Thank you so much. I can do it."

He drew in her scent and warmth, then forced himself to take hold of her elbows and nudge her out of his arms. "Just make sure you don't break any more glasses."

"I won't, sir."

"And don't call me sir."

She smiled tentatively. "Mr. Sutherland."

"Nobody calls me that, either. It's Logan."

"Thank you, Logan. And please call me Grace." She surprised him by taking hold of his hand, then gazed up at him, unsmiling. "You have no idea what this means to me and to the world at large. And I promise, I'll be the best cocktail waitress you've ever hired."

"Oh, yeah?"

"Oh, yes," she said with confidence, then let go of his hand and whipped out her small notebook. "I'm very smart and a quick learner. I've already memorized the ingredients of every drink in the bartenders' guide I bought. And as far as lifting the trays? Well, it's just physics, after all. Simply a matter of determining the correct spatial placement of the glassware on the tray. Look."

She flipped the pages and showed him a diagram. "As you can see, it's an exact duplication of our own solar system. In miniature, of course. My theory is that if the drinks are dispersed in this pattern on the tray, equilibrium will be achieved and there shouldn't be any spillage."

His mouth twisted in an acerbic grin. "Interesting theory."

"Yes." She stared at the diagram, then back at him. "I was just a little surprised to find out how heavy the tray was when I lifted it. But I know I can—"

"That's right, Grace, it's more than just physics," he said deprecatingly. "There's also a little matter of balance and proper weight distribution, not to mention the right application of upper-body strength."

"Oh, that's good," Grace said, eagerly grabbing a pen from his desk to make some notes in her pad. "That's very good. So you agree, it's a perfectly simple job once you get the dynamics hammered down."

He shook his head and wondered when, exactly, he'd lost control of the conversation.

"Thank you so much, Mr. Sutherland." She slipped her notepad into her waistband, then gave his arm an encouraging squeeze. "I promise you won't be sorry."

"It's Logan," he repeated. "And you've got one week to improve or you're out."

Two

She'd escaped banishment by the skin of her teeth.

Shivering slightly at the recollection of yesterday's lecture from Mr. Sutherland, Grace continued folding and organizing her clothes in the sleek bureau drawer.

Despite the fact that she expected to be here at least a month, everything she'd brought barely filled two of the drawers. But, back in Minnesota, when she'd packed her suitcase, she'd figured she wouldn't need much more than a few shirts and shorts to wear while searching for spores during her off-hours. And the hotel provided a uniform for its cocktail waitresses.

"Uniform." She shook her head at the term. Serena, the lounge manager, had asked her size, then handed her two brightly patterned bikinis and a see-through scrap of cloth they laughingly called a skirt.

But Grace was desperate to stay, so she didn't really mind wearing the outfit. And she didn't mind carrying ten to fifteen pounds of drinks on her shoulders if it meant she could work and live in the hotel for a month while she collected her precious spores.

The fact that she only had a few days to prove she could carry those trays on her shoulders was something she didn't want to contemplate too closely. Needless to say, she'd begun an intense upper-body workout that morning, knowing she needed more strength in her arms and shoulders.

Glancing around the luxurious hotel room with its elegant white wainscoting, coffered ceilings and wide-open view of the sparkling Caribbean waters, Grace allowed herself to revel in a moment of happy amazement. How in the world had she landed in such a beautiful place?

Of course the question was rhetorical, she thought with a smile, since she knew exactly how she'd arrived.

But it was remarkable that less than forty-eight hours ago, she'd been racing through the Minneapolis airport to make her flight. It had been difficult to run in her wool coat and thick sweater, heavy jeans, gloves and boots.

What a difference between then and now. Today she wore a bright pink tank top, thin linen shorts and sandals.

The frantic energy she'd felt two days ago on her way out of town was still coursing through her veins. Even though she recognized the source of the energy, it was disconcerting all the same. She'd always lived a quiet, well-ordered, disciplined life. Predictable. Safe. But now she was flying blind with absolutely no idea of what would happen next. Logan Sutherland had made it more than clear that she was here on borrowed time.

She was annoyed that none of her research on the Alleria Resort had uncovered the fact that the Sutherland brothers actually owned most of the island. That little fact had taken her by surprise and Logan had known it and used it to his advantage. She would have to stay alert to any other revelations if she found herself in his company again.

As she brushed her long hair back into a ponytail, she took careful note of the fact that her neck and shoulders were warming up at the very thought of Mr. Sutherland. No surprise there. Despite his threats and ultimatums, he was the most wickedly attractive man Grace had ever seen.

Not that she'd seen all that many attractive men in her lifetime. She would've remembered. Her mind was a steel trap, after all. But, no, gorgeous men like Logan Sutherland didn't tend to hang around the university research laboratory much. More like, never.

She knew he'd expected her to cower when he'd issued his ultimatum. But Grace never cowered. She'd been challenged countless times in the past and had always risen to the occasion. Mr. Sutherland—Logan—had simply thrown down a different sort of gauntlet than she'd been faced with before.

No worries. Because what Logan hadn't taken into consideration was that Grace Farrell was nothing if not a fighter. She relished obstacles; the higher level of difficulty, the better. To her, this was a new game to play, a new puzzle to be solved. She would learn the rules of the game using logic and reasoning, just as she'd done throughout her life. Then she would decipher the puzzle and win the game. To do otherwise was inconceivable.

She glanced at the clock on the nightstand. It was time to go to work. But as she glanced out the picture window at the stunning views, she wished for just a moment that she could stop all the clocks, take all the time in the world and just enjoy herself. She wanted to feel the sun on her back, walk barefoot in the white sand and frolic in the blue waters of Alleria Bay. She wanted to drink champagne and kiss a handsome man under the Caribbean moon.

"Oh, don't be ridiculous," she admonished herself. Those kinds of thoughts were not only foolhardy, they were dangerous. The clock was ticking. Time was of the essence.

There was no place in her life for fun and frolic, never mind kissing. Her entire life, her research, everything she'd ever worked for, would go down the drain if she didn't act quickly to staunch the damage already done.

She checked her kit bag to make sure she had everything she needed, then grabbed a towel from the bathroom and left the hotel room.

Crossing the bright, tropical-themed lobby, Grace stepped outside and felt the first rays of the warm sun on her skin. She adjusted her sunglasses and walked a dozen yards along the rows of swaying palm trees until she reached the edge of the white sand beach.

Now this was paradise.

She allowed herself thirty seconds to breathe in the spectacular view of the tropical island. Startlingly clear water stretched as far as the eye could see. Behind her, farther inland, were rolling green hills studded with more palm trees and lush vegetation. Sailboats bobbed at their moorings in the bay and sea birds flew overhead.

Her thirty seconds were up. Taking another deep breath, she hunkered down for the next forty minutes. Walking from palm tree to palm tree, she searched the base of each trunk where the roots divided, looking for a sign of the rare Allerian spores she'd come here to observe.

The sun was already warm at eight o'clock in the morning and she was glad she'd doused herself in sunblock. She should've brought a hat with her, too; but she'd been in such a hurry to pack and leave Minnesota that she hadn't fully considered the effects of the tropical sun on her sensitive skin. At times like this, she was forced to admit she wasn't quite as smart as everyone thought she was.

Another case in point, her awkward conversation with Logan Sutherland yesterday. She cringed inwardly, knowing that most of what he'd accused her of was true. Yes, she'd lied on her résumé, although that was for a good cause. But what she really hated admitting was that she'd foolishly underestimated the job of cocktail waitress. That wasn't smart. She wouldn't make that mistake again, especially after seeing firsthand how hard everyone in the bar worked.

"Just let that go," she murmured. At least Logan had relented and allowed her to stay, thank goodness. She had a full week to redeem herself and she vowed to do just that, if only for the sake of the spores.

Now if she could only find the darling little critters.

A sailboat under full sail skimmed across the bay and Grace stopped to watch it. Everywhere she turned on this island, in any direction, she could find something new and wonderful and exotic to look at. She stretched and allowed the sunshine to permeate her skin. Had she ever felt this warm and cozy without the benefit of a down jacket?

She'd lived in Minnesota her entire life and she was perfectly happy there, of course. But she was just beginning to realize that she'd spent a good portion of her life being cold. No, not just *cold,* she thought. *Chilled to the bone.* She was so tired of being cold, so weary of bundling up in heavy coats and mittens and long underwear and wool scarves for more than half the year.

Alleria was beautiful and, more important, it was *warm.* If she couldn't truly let herself go and relax and enjoy her time here, she could at least savor the warm weather. It was so completely different from anything she'd ever experienced before.

Standing in a cozy patch of shade cast by a huge cluster of coconuts hanging in a nearby palm, Grace took another minute to stretch out her muscles. She rolled her shoulders and raised her arms up in the air, then bent at the waist to touch her toes. She was starting to ache a little from her upper-body workout and it felt good to stretch and bend.

Once Logan had pointed out the need for balance and upper-body strength, Grace had known what she had to do. She'd begun with thirty push-ups when she first got out of bed this morning. She was in decent condition physically, but she needed much more strength in her upper arms if she expected to lift those hefty cocktail trays every night.

She was determined to make Logan Sutherland acknowledge that she took her waitressing job seriously. She couldn't afford to be sent home. She absolutely had to get her funding; and to do that, she had to find and collect enough Allerian spore specimens to conduct her lifesaving experiments for the next few years.

As she straightened up and moved to another tree, she pondered the sadly obvious fact that Logan Sutherland couldn't care less about her scientific work. No, he just cared that she performed her job as cocktail waitress as well as anyone else in the company. But if that's what it took to keep her here, that's what she would to do.

At each coconut palm tree, she knelt down and examined the juncture where the thick palm roots crisscrossed and divided. Feathery fern leaves sprouted here and there and that was where her spores were known to propagate. But tree after tree, frond after frond offered exactly nothing.

She wandered away from the shore and deeper into what looked like a jungle of wild plants and palm trees. Here the thicker vegetation created more shade, but instead of being cooler, it was warmer and muggier. The overabundance of plant life kept the sea breezes from filtering through and cooling the air. Humidity was a good thing if you were a spore.

Sure enough, minutes later in a shady cluster of coco palms, surrounded by the soft fern leaves that protected them, Grace finally came across the spores she'd traveled thousands of miles to find.

"Ah," she whispered, "there you are, my lovelies."

She spread the clean towel on the sand and unzipped her spore kit. Kneeling on a corner of the towel, she used her most powerful magnifying glass to study the precious plant life more closely.

Unlike many plants, these types of spores could thrive without sunlight, but they still needed a warm, moist environment. Glancing around, Grace saw that this part of the island was indeed ideal. The sun was only beginning to shine here so the spores had a part of the morning to thrive in the muggy shade. They seemed happy, reproducing madly even as she watched them through the ultramagnified glass.

Grace smiled at the thought of happy spores. A sense of calm came over her as she observed the microscopic world. She had been experimenting on this rare strain of Allerian spores for so many years, ever since old Professor Hutchins, her teacher and first mentor, showed her his excellent treatise based on the first spores he brought back from the island. That dissertation had led Grace to begin her own experiments using the potential lifesaving properties of these little guys.

Grace glanced up at the clear blue sky and marveled at how far she'd come in her studies of the Allerian spores. They were valuable for so many reasons, including the gene replication studies she'd mentioned to Logan. But she was even more excited by the fact that the mitochondria found within the spore cells contained a rare type of phytohormone that carried potential medical applications. Her latest experiments had proven that these hormones could have an adverse effect on human cancer cells, causing certain cells to be suppressed or, in the case of her most recent lab trials, to die altogether.

The possibility that Grace's studies could lead to the destruction of cancer cells thrilled her as nothing else had before. She could no more stop this important research than she could stop breathing.

She thought back to the day she first walked into the university laboratory when she was eight years old. She'd spent hundreds of lonely hours in the lab since then, but knowing that all those years of research might ultimately lead to so many lives being saved made her forget her own pain. It had all been worth it.

Recently, Grace had entered a new and critical phase of her research. And even though some of the Professor's last batch of spores were still producing decent progeny, they were beginning to die out. Grace required a fresher, stronger crop of the rare organisms to meet her current needs.

"Current needs," she grumbled, shaking her head in disgust. If it weren't for Walter Erskine trying to steal her entire life's work, including taking credit for her latest experiments and proven theorems, she wouldn't be so desperate right now. Her cheeks still burned as she recalled how easily Walter had charmed her, how quickly she'd grown to like him, how fervently she'd hoped they would be together always. And she'd actually believed he reciprocated her feelings. Could she honestly have been that naive?

She shook herself free of those unhappy thoughts. She refused to blame herself for falling for his lies. Walter had been quite the smooth operator, after all. Almost everyone in the department had been fooled. But it was *Grace's* job that was on the line now, not anyone else's.

Snapping on a pair of disposable gloves, she pulled out one of her sterilized petri dishes. With her forceps, she carefully plucked a thick clump of spores from the fibrous base of the frond and held it over the dish. After tapping the forceps against the side of the dish, she watched the spores drop into the dish along with bits of moss and sand.

For the next hour, she repeated the process several more times. She numbered each petri dish and noted in her book the location and features of the palm tree, the angle of the sun and the temperature at the precise time she gathered each of the groups of spores.

Her stomach growled and she realized she was famished. Earlier, she'd eaten breakfast with other members of the hotel staff in their private cafeteria. Everyone was so nice to her and she'd felt almost decadent as she chose the colorful fruit platter with its dollop of yogurt. She hadn't seen such gorgeous fruit in Minnesota in a long time, if ever. But now, as she worked under the hot sun, she felt a little dizzy and determined that she would need to eat a bigger breakfast each morning. The last thing she wanted to do was pass out on the beach. She could only imagine what Logan Sutherland would say about that.

Checking the dishes stacked in her kit bag, she decided she had enough spores from this particular tree. It was a good start. She pulled off the gloves, packed up her kit and pushed herself up off the ground, anxious to return to her room where her microscope and portable lab equipment waited for her.

"Wow," she said with a laugh, as she brushed the fine grains of sand off her legs. "Do you know how to have a good time or what?"

She turned and almost collided with Logan Sutherland, who grabbed hold of her shoulders to steady her.

"What are you doing out here without a hat on?" he demanded, glaring at her.

She'd been so absorbed in her work that she hadn't heard him approach, but she should've sensed his forceful presence. He wore cargo shorts with a faded Hawaiian shirt and waterproof sandals. His skin was tanned a deep bronze and there was a hint of beard stubble on his jaw. He was laid-back and casual, so why did he look even more dangerous today than he had in his thousand-dollar suit yesterday?

She realized that the sun had shifted and she was now standing in bright sunlight. "I've been in the shade most of the time," she said lamely.

"You'll soon find out that doesn't make much difference this close to the equator." He took his baseball cap off and handed it to her. "Here, wear this. It's not much, but it'll protect your face for a while."

"It's not necessary," she said, taking a step back from him. He was so big and masculine, it was a bit overwhelming so early in the morning. And it was unnerving to realize that he was studying her as carefully as she would examine a particularly fascinating germ under her microscope. Maybe that's why she felt so shaky. "I'm going back to my room right now."

"Ten minutes out here is enough to make a difference. Put the damn hat on."

"All right." He was pushy, but he probably knew what he was talking about. Besides, she didn't want to give him any reason to think her uncooperative. She slipped her ponytail through the strap in back and adjusted the cap on her head. "Thank you. I'll get it back to you this afternoon."

"No hurry," he said. "We've got a gift shop filled with

wide-brimmed hats. You'll need one if you're planning to work outside every morning."

With a nod, she said, "I'll be sure to buy one this afternoon."

"Good. And buy more sunblock," he added brusquely. "I'd hate to see your skin get burned."

"Thank you." *I think,* she added under her breath, since he sounded almost angry about it. But she decided not to blame him. He'd probably seen his share of hapless tourists suffering from second-degree sunburns.

He stuck his hands in his pockets. "So you've been out looking for spores?"

"Yes. I've found a thriving colony right here," she exclaimed, energized all over again. Kneeling back down at the base of the palm tree, she pulled out her magnifying glass and handed it to him. "Come and see."

"Spore porn?" he said dryly. "I can't wait."

She smiled at him. "I'm sure you think it's odd, but I actually find it quite fascinating to watch them reproduce."

He knelt down next to her, so close that their shoulders and hips were touching. Taking the glass from her, he bent down and stared for a while. Then he straightened and gazed at her. "So they're basically having sex right now?"

Her eyes widened. His face was a mere inch away from hers. If he leaned in… But he wouldn't, of course. What was she thinking? She took a moment to swallow around her suddenly dry throat. "Um, yes. I suppose you could call it that. They do it around this time every morning."

One eyebrow shot up. "I guess you've got to admire their discipline."

"Oh, I do, I do," she murmured, mesmerized by his flirtatious smile. He had beautiful, straight, white teeth and his mouth had a sexy, sardonic curve to it that she found nearly irresistible. Oh, my, she thought. Was he moving closer to her? He stared into her eyes, then his gaze shifted to her lips. Was he going to kiss her? She could feel herself melting. She really should've worn a hat.

Standing abruptly, she said, "I've got to go. Got to get these back to the room. Got to… Well, goodbye."

She took off like a startled bunny and could actually feel his gaze locked on her as she ran down the beach. On her mad dash back to the hotel, she berated herself for behaving so foolishly. Had her emotions shown on her face when she realized his mouth was a few millimeters away from hers? She hoped not, but she knew she wasn't sophisticated enough to fake a look of bland disinterest in a moment like that.

Despite knowing he wanted her off the island, despite knowing he would use any excuse to get rid of her, she still found him irresistible.

"But you will resist him," she said sternly. She had no choice. She might've spent the past fifteen years working in near isolation in the university biogenetics laboratory, but she hadn't been completely cut off from real life. She read books and magazines; she socialized somewhat, if you could call it socializing when her current mentor—who was also her closest friend—invited her over once a month to have dinner with her big, boisterous family. Grace was grateful for those invitations since she was rarely invited to spend time with her own odd family.

The point was, Grace was savvy enough to know that where a man like Logan Sutherland was concerned, she was in way over her head.

From now on, she would keep her distance from her fine-looking boss. She would be polite and do what she had to do to impress him in the cocktail bar. But, outside of work, she would avoid him, evade him, do anything she had to do to stay away from him. She couldn't forget that he wanted her gone, off the island and away from the spores that were critical to her life's work.

And yet, dealing with Logan Sutherland would be a piece of cake compared to the hell she'd lived through the past six months. All she had to do was remember the bottom line: she wasn't leaving this island until she was damn good and ready to.

Three

The cocktail lounge was packed with happy people drinking, laughing and dancing. The music was mellow jazz, just loud enough to enjoy but not so overbearing that people had to shout to be heard. The lighting was subtle enough to make everyone look good and was embellished this evening by the glow of a full moon reflecting off the dark blue waters of the bay.

Logan had a dozen other things he could've been doing tonight. He usually made a point of stopping by the bar most evenings to say hello to guests and lend his presence in the rare instance that someone was causing trouble. But he didn't usually linger for long. He and his brother had hired the best, most trustworthy and well-trained employees, who knew the service business inside and out. They didn't need Logan hanging around, standing sentinel like an overanxious mother hen, driving his bartenders and staff crazy. Or worse yet, making them think Logan had no confidence in them.

But he was here anyway—and he wasn't leaving. He attempted to look casual as he leaned his elbow on the bar and sipped his thirty-year-old single-malt scotch. He let the smooth liquid heat its way down his throat and tried like hell to pretend he wasn't here to keep an eagle eye on his newest employee.

"Order up, Grace," Joey, one of the bartenders, called.

"Thanks, Joey," Grace said, rewarding him with a generous smile as she placed one of the wide trays on the bar and began to load it with drinks.

Logan noted that, as promised, she hadn't spilled a drink tonight. But that was only because her customers and the other waiters had been so willing to step in and help her carry her trays. One guest had even bussed a few tables for her. It was the strangest thing Logan had ever seen.

Usually, his waitstaff were territorial about their customers and tips. But with Grace, they all chipped in and helped her. Logan grudgingly admitted it was to her credit that she was quick to split her generous tips with all of them.

She loaded the drinks onto a large tray in that spiral pattern she'd insisted was cosmologically sound. Logan had to shake his head at that cockamamy theory, but sobered as he watched her shoulders tense up. She licked her lips and tested the tray's weight. Was she really going to try to carry it? There had to be at least ten drinks on the tray. What was Joey thinking?

Logan pushed off from the bar and moved toward her. But before he could get close enough to grab the tray, Clive, a witty Englishman and one of his top waiters, slipped smoothly behind Grace and rested his hands on her hips.

"Brace your knees, love," Clive said, "and put all your strength right here." With that, he skimmed the edges of her slender thighs all the way down to her knees. Then he moved around to face her and patted his own stomach. "Breathe from here. Muscles nice and tight."

Logan froze in place, his teeth clenched, determined not to step in and save her again. Instead, he would allow Clive to instruct her, unless it started to look like she would need more skilled intervention from Logan himself.

He watched Grace's breasts move in rhythm with the deep, anticipatory breaths she took. Then she was flying solo, following Clive's instructions, steadying her legs and lifting the tray onto her shoulder.

Clive and several other waiters watched with apprehension as Grace moved slowly across the room to a table of guests sitting near the window. Bending her knees, she set the tray down on the table. Half the staff applauded and Logan's tight jaw relaxed.

Grace's face lit up as she glanced around at her odd group of supporters. When her gaze met Logan's, her happy smile faltered.

Hell. He hated to be the cause of her bright eyes dimming, so he quickly grinned at her and flashed a thumbs-up sign. Her eyes widened and, as her smile grew, the entire room seemed to light up, as well.

Satisfied that she was happy and would survive the night, Logan turned back to the bar and took a last sip of his drink. But before he could even swallow, reality smacked him upside the head and he noted with disgust that she'd manipulated him again. Who cared if she smiled, for God's sake? She wasn't here to be happy. She was here to earn her paycheck or go home, damn it.

Waving down the head bartender, he snarled out his order, "Pour me another scotch, Sam."

Taking advantage of the early-morning quiet, Logan hauled his windsurfing board down to the deserted beach just as the sun was cresting over Alleria Peak. He slipped the board into the water, adjusted the mast and sail and then slid on top and started paddling.

It might've sounded strange to someone who didn't know him, but from the first time he swam in these waters, Logan had recognized Alleria as home. It was warm all year round so he never had to wear a wet suit. And it was clean. Even at twenty feet, he could see the sandy bottom of the sea. That was a minor miracle after years of surfing and sailing the rough and churning waves off the coast of Northern California—where he and his brother had grown up and where, when they were seven years old, their father had taught them how to surf.

Logan paddled a few more yards out. Then in one quick move, he rose to a standing position on the board and yanked the uphaul rope, pulling until the sail was upright. Grabbing hold of the mast and boom, he angled the sail until it caught the barest hint of wind. Balancing his weight on the board, he turned and headed for open water beyond the tip of the peninsula that formed the bay.

Alleria Bay itself was a tranquil inlet with few waves and the mildest of winds. But out beyond the break, the eastern trade winds provided plenty of excitement for any resort guests interested in windsurfing or sailing.

In a few hours, Logan would have contracts to study and phone calls to make. But right now, surrounded by wind, water and speed, he tried to blow off all thoughts of business and enjoy the moment. It wasn't easy; he was hardwired for success and had had a difficult time relaxing lately.

An unexpected swell crested and broke into a wave inches from his board. Logan took instant advantage, raking the sail back, then throwing the mast hard into the wind while jumping and lifting the board into the air and twirling it over the wave.

"Hot damn," he shouted with good humor. He'd managed a one-hundred-eighty-degree flaka, a hotdog maneuver he hadn't pulled off in years. He laughed as the wind picked up. The move reminded him of the days when he and Aidan had lived to surf. Back then, Logan had considered surfing the closest he would ever get to spirituality. It was all wrapped up in the notion of man and nature coming together through the elemental forces of the universe, the movement of water against earth, the changing of the tide, the passing of time.

He could still recall that exact moment in his youth when he'd stared into the eye of a twelve-foot wave and realized that if he could stand up on a flimsy piece of fiberglass and ride over the spuming water like Poseidon on a dolphin-teamed chariot, he could damn well conquer anything.

That understanding had kept both brothers at the top of their game as they traveled the world and competed in—and won—numerous international competitions. Because they were identical twins competing at the highest echelon of surfing circles, they were often treated like celebrities with all the perks that came with the territory. Especially women. They were everywhere and temptation was strong.

It was a wild life that might've eaten them up if they hadn't taken to heart the life lessons their father had taught them early on. Thanks to Dad's good example, they didn't take the lure of the high life too seriously. They also followed the number-one rule of surfers everywhere: *Never turn your back on the ocean.*

In other words, Logan thought: *Pay attention.* A guy never knew when a wave might knock him down or a shark would eat him alive.

Logan had learned the hard way that the rule applied to women especially. He'd let down his guard five years ago when he met Tanya and convinced himself he was in love with her. When he asked her to marry him and she said yes, he thought his life was complete. A year into their marriage, she was killed in a car crash and he thought he might die along with her. It wasn't until the funeral that Logan found out she had been driving off to meet her lover, some clown that had worked in the twin brothers' accounting office.

Never turn your back on the ocean. If his wife's betrayal wasn't enough to remind him that women, like sharks, were not to be trusted, Logan only had to remind himself that his own mother had deserted them when he and Aiden were seven years old.

With a determined pull on the boom, Logan angled the sail around and headed back to land. For the past few years, his emotions had drifted between grief that Tanya had to die and guilt that he'd never really loved her anyway. He had finally resigned himself to the fact that he just wasn't capable of love—and that was fine with him. Women were in plentiful supply and he certainly enjoyed them. A lot. The more the merrier. But that didn't mean he would ever fall in love and he sure as hell would never trust another woman again.

As he sailed closer to the beach, he spotted Grace Farrell walking through the clusters of palms growing in profusion along the bay. The muscles of his hands tightened around the mast and boom as he watched the gorgeous research scientist pause at each palm tree to study the roots and base. He was glad to see she'd taken his advice and worn a wide-brimmed hat today, along with a loose shirt with sleeves that would protect her sensitive shoulders from the unrelenting heat of the sun.

But there was barely anything covering up her long, shapely legs and even from this distance, he could appreciate the view of those legs and her luscious bottom as she bent over to search for spores.

Spores, for God's sake.

After a moment, she straightened up, then noticed him and waved. He grinned and aimed the board in her direction and sailed to within a few feet of the beach.

"Good morning," she said.

"Same to you." Logan folded the rigging and secured it to the board with a Velcro strap. Then he pulled the board onto the sand far enough to insure that it wouldn't slip back into the water.

"Hunting for more spores?" he asked.

"Yes," she said. "Have you been out long?"

"About an hour," he said.

She stared at the board, then back at him. "How in the world do you stay upright on that thing?"

Logan ran both hands through his wet hair, pushing it back from his forehead. "It's magic."

"It would have to be," she mused. Her gaze slipped down to his wet, bare chest. "Would you like my towel?"

"No, thanks. I'm okay."

She held it out for him. "But you're so wet and, um, well, it's your towel, actually, since I took it from my hotel room."

"Well, since it's mine," he said, chuckling as he took the towel. Maybe she hadn't seen many dripping-wet men in swim trunks back at her research lab because she seemed awfully flustered. He hoped like hell that he made her uncomfortable. It would serve her right for manipulating and lying to him.

He took his time drying himself off as he studied her. She'd been on the island four days now and true to her word, she spent each morning hunting for spores, then worked the cocktail lounge in the afternoons and evenings. And she hadn't dropped a single glass since the first day's fiasco.

He noticed her cheeks had a rosy pink glow from her mornings in the sun. He liked the glow almost as much as he liked her fabulous legs and perfect rear end. Even knowing the woman was a liar and not to be trusted, Logan found her incredibly appealing. He wanted her in his bed with an urgency that was going to reveal itself any second now if he didn't get the hell out of here.

"I've got work to do," he muttered finally, and handed her the towel as he walked away.

Grace clutched the damp towel as she stared at Logan's backside until he disappeared through a door into the hotel. Then she pressed the towel to her face to cool herself off. She was certain she'd never met such a formidable man. Certainly not one with a body like that. Or eyes like that. Or hair, so adorably short and blond and spiky when wet.

But for goodness' sake, did that mean she had to practically drool in front of him? And could she possibly have thought of anything dumber to say to him? *How in the world do you stay upright on that thing?* What was wrong with her?

She blamed it on his smile. This was the first time he'd smiled at her without showing his sarcastic or ironic side. The sweetness of it had nearly blinded her. And talk about upper-body strength. The man was built. She'd wondered what he looked like under his business suit and now she knew. The knowledge was life affirming, to say the least.

She turned back to her task but was still trying to shake off the effects of Logan's smile ten minutes later. She silently recited the periodic table of elements, an effective trick she used whenever she was having trouble concentrating. Unfortunately, it wasn't working today. She feared that smile of his might have a half-life of more than several hours because she was still caught up in its spell.

With a sigh, she walked away from the beach and deeper into the forest of vegetation. Despite the heat, she appreciated the extra layer of humidity, knowing it was the best breeding ground for her beloved spores.

"Beloved spores," she uttered aloud, shaking her head. Did that sound pathetic or what? But the truth was, sometimes she felt closer to the tiny, one-celled meiotic organisms than she did to people. Well, except for Phillippa, of course. Her lab partner and mentor had been her friend for years and right now, she could use someone to talk to. One thing she loved about Phillippa was that she always had an opinion about everything. Grace wondered what her friend would think of Logan Sutherland.

Grace was certain Phillippa would declare him "hawt."

Okay, he was hot, all right. But as she pushed past a giant fern, Grace gave herself a good talking-to. It didn't matter whether Logan was hot or not. He was her boss and Grace had no business thinking of him that way. All she needed from Logan Sutherland was his approval of her work in the cocktail lounge, nothing more.

She forced all thoughts of Logan away and got to work, backtracking to the palm trees where she'd found spores yesterday. Close to the base of each tree, she pounded a discreet wooden marker into the sand so she would know the trees from which she'd already extracted specimens. She planned to remove the stakes on her last day here; but, until then, they would provide a handy map for her to follow.

An hour later, she left the palm trees behind and headed back to the hotel. After running into the staff commissary to grab a sandwich, she returned to her room to document her findings and refrigerate several more petri dishes filled with fresh specimens. She showered and dressed for work, happy she'd been assigned to the swing shift from two o'clock to ten. The bar stayed open until three in the morning and the servers on the late shift got the best tips, but Grace preferred to wake up early and go to bed relatively early.

As she walked through the lobby toward the cocktail lounge, she passed a pretty young woman sitting on one of the smooth rocks that surrounded the tropical waterfall, crying. Grace paused, wondering if she should say something. Would the management frown on a cocktail waitress approaching a hotel guest? Did it matter? The woman was clearly distressed, so Grace went with her instincts and walked over to the woman.

"Are you all right?" she asked.

The woman looked up and pressed her lips together to stop from blubbering in front of a stranger. "I'm fine."

"We both know that's not true." Grace sat next to her. "Is there anything I can do for you?"

Fresh tears dripped down her cheeks. "I'm on my honeymoon."

"Then you should be happy, not sad," Grace said.

"But...I can't talk about it."

"Sure you can." Grace patted her knee. "I'm not sure I can help, but I can certainly listen."

* * *

Logan halted halfway across the lobby when he spotted Grace deep in conversation with one of the hotel guests. They sat by the tropical waterfall and he approached cautiously, not wanting to make a scene. But caution wasn't necessary. The women were so engrossed in their chat, they didn't notice him.

Grace was dressed for work in her bikini top and sarong, and Logan knew without checking his watch that her shift was about to begin. So what was she doing out here? He stepped closer.

"So if he spends more time right here at this spot," Grace said, tapping her notepad with her pen, "I think you'll be very happy."

The young woman took Grace's notepad and stared at some diagram she'd drawn. "Are you sure it's right there? He didn't seem to get anywhere near that spot."

"But he will," Grace said. She took the notepad, tore out the page with the diagram and handed it to the woman. "It'll make a big difference, I promise."

"I hope so," the woman said with a watery smile. "I don't want to spend my entire honeymoon crying."

"I'm sure your husband doesn't want that, either."

The woman hugged Grace, then jumped up. "You're so smart. Thank you."

Grace looked at her wristwatch and stood. "Please let me know how it goes. I work in the cocktail lounge in the evening or you can find me on the beach most mornings."

"I will." She waved the piece of paper as she hurried away.

Grace waved, then turned toward the cocktail lounge—and gasped. "What are you doing here?"

"I own the place," Logan said, folding his arms across his chest. "What was that all about?"

She fluttered her hands in the air. "Oh, nothing. Sorry I can't talk now. I have to get to work."

"It's okay. I know the boss." He grabbed hold of her arm. "You can be a few minutes late. Now tell me what's wrong with that woman. Did someone from the hotel bother her?"

"From the hotel? Oh, no. Absolutely not."

"You sure?"

"Yes, I swear it. She just had a…a little disagreement with her new husband. I saw her crying and I tried to comfort her."

"That's it?" Logan glanced in the direction the woman had gone, then back at Grace. "Is she all right?"

"I think she'll be fine," Grace said.

"Good," he murmured. "That's good. I don't like to see my guests crying in the lobby."

She nodded earnestly. "I can see how that would be a problem. But she's okay, I promise. Now I'd better get to work."

"Fine." Logan watched her walk all the way across the lobby and into the lounge. No doubt about it, the woman had a world-class backside and he itched to get his hands on her. He wasn't particularly happy about it because she was basically a pain in his neck. But as he walked back to his office, he resolved to seduce her as soon as possible. And then he'd kick her off his island.

"Six piña coladas, Joey," Grace said, and wished she could sit down and rub her feet. Anyone who ever thought waitressing was an easy job should be forced to do it for a week wearing high heels.

"Coming up, Gracie girl," Joey said.

She smiled at her coworkers' nickname for her. Nobody had ever called her Gracie until she arrived in Alleria. She liked it. She'd never thought much about it before, but back home, everyone took her so seriously. A few people called her Grace, but usually she was addressed as Doctor Farrell. Even by her parents, who were completely intimidated by her title and her intelligence. Nobody here called her Doctor Farrell, thank goodness. They had no idea she had four PhD's and would probably laugh their butts off if they found out.

"Hunk alert at three o'clock," said Dee, a pretty, dark-haired waitress from New Jersey, as she sidled up next to Grace.

Grace glanced at her watch. "What happens at three o'clock?"

Joey and Dee exchanged grins, then Dee put her arm around Grace and said, "Poor baby's led a sheltered life."

"I guess I have," Grace admitted.

Joey leaned over and whispered, "She's alerting you that the boss just walked in."

"And he is looking hunk-a-diddly-dumptious," Dee said, smacking her lips.

Grace laughed. "Oh, wait, three o'clock, I get it." She turned to her right and saw Logan, then quickly turned back and tried not to show she was flustered. "Does he come in every night?"

"He usually stops in, but never stays long," Dee said, then frowned. "Until recently, anyway. Last night he was here for a couple hours. Not sure what that's all about. I hope we're not getting laid off."

"The place is filled to capacity every week, so nobody's getting laid off," Joey said, then cast a less-than-subtle stare at Grace.

Dee frowned at him. "You think?"

"Oh, yeah," Joey said as he opened a new bottle of rum.

"What?" Grace said, glancing from one to the other.

Dee raised both eyebrows. "Has the boss got his eye on you, Gracie girl?"

She grimaced. "He just wants to catch me making a mistake so he can fire me."

"We'll make sure that doesn't happen, honey," Dee said, patting her shoulder. "Although, I gotta say, if I caught the eye of someone that hunkalicious, I'm not sure I'd be able to keep my cool." She waved a hand in front of her face. "Mmm-mmm. Is it getting hot in here or what?"

Grace elbowed her. "You're crazy."

"I don't think so," Dee said, chuckling.

"Here's your piña coladas, Gracie," Joey said. "You need help with the tray?"

"You're sweet, but I've got it."

"I'll say you've got it," Joey said, wiggling his eyebrows at her. "Now work it."

She laughed as she walked away with her drinks, fairly certain she'd never "worked it" in her life. But she was more than willing to try.

"I had three orgasms!" a woman cried.

Logan whipped around, shocked to recognize the young woman who'd been crying in the lobby yesterday afternoon. She had Grace wrapped in a fierce hug and she was jumping up and down.

Logan had just returned from an early-morning run up the peninsula and back. When he saw Grace walking toward the palmetto grove, he started to follow her, but her new best friend grabbed her first.

"Thank you, thank you," the woman gushed. "You were so right! He found that spot and it was miraculous!"

Fascinating. Logan watched Grace glancing around the

beach, probably checking to see if anyone had overheard the effusive woman. When she spied Logan standing ten feet away, she shook her head and closed her eyes in resignation.

Grinning, Logan continued to observe the exchange with interest, listening to every word as the woman gleefully described her husband's successful foray. It was clear now that Grace had instructed the young honeymooner on how to make love with her new husband. Very interesting.

His gaze narrowed and focused on her. It appeared that all those years Grace Farrell had spent studying the sexual and reproductive habits of spores and other creatures—including humans, obviously—had given her a level of sexual expertise he wanted to explore.

The thought made him grit his teeth. He wanted her right now. It was taking every ounce of control he had to not drag her into the palmetto grove, back her up against a tree and give in to the desire he knew they both felt for each other.

Grace hugged the woman and congratulated her, then watched her skip away. Once she was gone, Grace turned to Logan. "I suppose you heard all that."

"Pretty much."

"It's not what you think."

"Yeah?" he said. "Because I'm thinking you pretty much made her day. And night, apparently."

"Yes, well." She brushed her hair off her forehead, then fiddled with her sunglasses. "I didn't do anything she couldn't have… Well, I just…" She glanced up at the sky. "It's late. I really should get to my spores."

"Wait."

She froze and he took immediate advantage, stepping closer, invading her personal space.

"What is it, Logan? Is something wrong?" Her pink

tongue slid across her lush lips again and he almost groaned.

"If you lick your lips again," he warned, "I'm going to haul you over my shoulder and take you to my room."

She swallowed slowly. "I—I can't help it. You make me nervous."

"Do I?"

She glared at him. "You know you do. And I think you do it on purpose."

"Yeah, maybe I do." He skimmed his fingers across her shoulder and was gratified when she shivered. "That was a nice thing you did for her."

She tilted her head, clearly baffled. "You think so?"

"Yeah." His smile grew. "Do you often go around explaining the G-spot to clueless women?"

"Um, no." She shook her head slowly. "That was definitely a first."

He studied her, taking notice of the small scar over her left eyebrow, another smattering of pale freckles on the upper ridges of her cheeks, the perfect cupid's bow of her upper lip. "What the hell makes you tick, Grace Farrell?"

Puzzled, she said, "I might ask the same of you."

"Hey, I'm an open book."

A frown line marred her brow. "Not to me."

"The thing is," he said, "I'm usually a pretty easygoing guy. But ever since you showed up, I've been feeling a little edgy."

"That's not my fault," she said heatedly, poking her finger at his chest. "And I'm not leaving the island."

He grabbed her finger to stop the jabs. "It's not that kind of edgy." He kept hold of her hand, rubbing his palm against hers, shaping it and molding it to his.

"Oh."

"Yeah."

Awareness had her licking her lips again and a bolt of pure heat lit up his insides.

"What do you want?" she whispered.

"This." He leaned forward and kissed her, wrapping his hand around her nape to press her closer to him. Her mouth was as sweet as anything he'd ever tasted and he had to fight to keep the contact light. But his control was slipping as the heat of her body invaded his own. Visions of her lush, naked skin danced through his mind and he groaned.

He would've stopped, but a delicious sigh escaped her throat and her lips parted for him. He plunged inside her warmth and her tongue met his instantly, eagerly. Logan felt his heartbeat stagger and every muscle in his body hardened with need.

He wanted her, wanted to strip her clothes off and touch her breasts, her thighs, her slick core. He wanted his hands and mouth on every inch of her body. Now.

The images jarred him back to reality and he remembered they were standing outside in view of anyone who walked by. That's when he pulled back, but not completely. He took his time, kissing the corners of her mouth, her cheeks, the line of her jaw, the silky length of her neck.

"Let's go to my room," he murmured against her skin, then took her hand and started walking back to the hotel.

She stopped and pulled her hand away. "I can't do that. I have to go."

He turned and looked at her. "No you don't."

"I do. I'm sorry, I shouldn't have…" She paused to catch her breath. "You don't know me."

"No," he said carefully. "But I do know you want me and I want you."

She looked so serious. "You don't, really."

"You're wrong, Grace," he said, reaching for her.

She put both hands up to stop him. "If you really knew me, you never would've kissed me. You would've run for the hills." She took two steps backward. "I'm saving you the trouble."

"Nice of you."

"Oh, you have no idea." Then she gave a firm nod. "It's definitely best that we stop right now."

"Yeah?" He closed the gap between them. "I say we test that theory." Yanking her close, he covered her mouth with his and kissed her roughly at first. Then he softened his lips against hers and they moved together, deepening the kiss until they were both shaking with need.

When she moaned again, he let her go, then watched her lick her lips and taste him there. The move was innocent and skilled at the same time, and he scowled as an irrational wave of tenderness washed over him.

Finally, she opened her eyes and stared at him in wonder. "Wow."

"Yeah," he said gruffly. "That's what I'm talking about."

"Well, don't ever say I didn't warn you." Then she turned and jogged away as swiftly as her feet could move in the deep white sand.

He didn't follow her, just watched as she disappeared through the thick fronds at the far end of the beach.

What the hell was she talking about? He'd never had to work this hard to convince a woman to make love with him. *If you really knew me, you never would've kissed me.* He shook his head at the memory of her words. Oh, he knew her, all right. She was a woman and therefore a master manipulator. She could give lessons, no doubt about it.

That didn't seem to negate the fact that he was currently sporting a massive hard-on, thanks to her. Now that was something his entire staff would notice if he strolled into the hotel at that moment. So instead, he pulled off his shirt and tossed it on a chaise, then walked straight into the water to cool himself off.

Four

"Ladies and gentlemen," Logan said to the others participating in yet another conference call. "With the opening of the new Alleria sports center, the island will become a premier destination for world-class sporting events such as tennis, gymnastics and boxing."

Aidan, sitting in the brothers' penthouse offices two thousand miles away in New York City, picked up the conversation. "As you'll note in the prospectus we've sent you, the main court will have a tiered seating capacity of five thousand. We'll have ten deluxe private-viewing suites, a press booth, locker rooms, a four-thousand-square-foot commissary and private dining rooms for players and visiting dignitaries."

Eleanor, their senior vice president who was working out of the New York office with Aidan, jumped in. "There are six adjacent practice courts, as well. And the main court is easily converted to a boxing ring, gymnastic floor, a concert stage, or whatever is required. This project is shovel-ready, gentlemen. As soon as the contracts are signed, construction can begin."

"We've more than proven the viability of Alleria as a sports destination," Aidan said. "The Alleria Palms Golf Tournament is now third in worldwide television viewing audience, surpassed only by the Masters and the British Open. Our airport is world-class and we've recently expanded the resort by another five hundred rooms."

Part of the prospectus they'd sent their handpicked investors included a pictorial story of the island itself. It mainly featured their own bayside resort as well as the tiny Victorian port town of Tierra del Alleria. There, attractive shops and eclectic restaurants lined the beach and pier that formed the harbor where multimillion-dollar sailboats docked side by side with the local fishermen who sold their daily catch.

Logan and Aidan had created a ten-year, slow-growth plan to attract small businesses and specialty tourist groups. The sports center would attract the type of high-end traveler who, in theory, would appreciate the eco-friendly environment and rustic charm of the island.

There was silence on the line for a moment, then Tex McCoy spoke up. "You boys have got yourselves a pretty decent situation down there."

Logan had known Tex forever and could hear him puffing on his Cuban cigar as he participated in his favorite sport: wheeling and dealing. Logan could almost smell the thick, expensive cigar smoke. The billionaire Texan was one member of the consortium of wealthy investors who had invested in the brothers' past projects.

"You know you can count on me and my boys," Malcolm Barnett said amiably. "The wives are all itching to get back to Alleria since visiting this past year."

"That's always nice to hear, Malcolm," Logan said to the man who was regularly featured on the pages of *Forbes* and *Fortune*. Malcolm's two sons had gone to college with Logan and Aidan.

"Count me in, too," Tex said. "I'll have my people look over the contracts and get back to you."

Aidan said, "You know we appreciate it, Tex."

"Thank you, Tex," Logan chimed in. "You won't be sorry."

"You can both thank me by shaving a few points off my next golf game with y'all."

"Not sure we can do that, sir," Logan said with tongue in cheek.

"Sorry, Tex." Aidan chuckled. "We know you'd never want us to cheat."

The older man grumbled. "Damn your straitlaced father for raising such a pair of sticklers."

Everyone laughed, then several other investors jumped in to voice their desire to get in on the action. The conference call ended fifteen minutes later and Logan quickly called his brother on his cell phone.

"I think that went well," he said, grinning as he stated the obvious. Eleanor was probably in the New York office kitchen, popping open the champagne as they spoke.

Aidan ignored the statement. "What's going on with you?"

"What're you talking about?" Logan asked, stretching back in his chair. From here, he could see a catamaran drifting across the bay and wondered how soon he could get out of this suit and tie and into a pair of running shorts. "Everything's fantastic."

"I hear it in your voice, man. Something's bugging you."

"You're delusional," Logan drawled. "Everything's fine.

Perfect. We're about to close on a billion-dollar deal. Life is good."

Aidan paused, then said, "I'll drag it out of you eventually so you might as well save us both the trouble and tell me now."

Logan stared at the phone, wishing for once that he and his twin brother didn't have quite so tight a bond. It had been that way all their lives. They often finished each other's sentences and there were times when they could practically read each other's minds. They usually used it to their advantage, but right now, Logan didn't need anyone homing in on what he was thinking. Namely because he wasn't so sure of what was going on himself.

"Nothing's wrong, dude," he said, trying to convey a relaxed attitude he no longer felt.

Aidan snorted. "Fine, keep it to yourself, but I'll be back next Thursday and I expect to hear the whole story."

"Great," Logan said with a scowl. "I'll be sure to dream up something interesting to make you think you're right."

He disconnected the call and felt a twinge of irritation. He hadn't fooled Aidan one bit. But what was he supposed to tell him? How could he explain that a hot, sexy, spore-hunting research scientist had invaded their island and sucked up every last ounce of Logan's common sense?

He couldn't explain it. But once Aidan got here and saw Grace for himself, he would reach his own conclusions. Whatever his brother concluded, Logan intended to make it clear that Logan had seen her first and Grace Farrell was *his.*

Logan jerked forward and sat straight up.

"What the hell?" He shook his head in disgust. Where had that thought come from? He was rarely possessive when it came to women. In fact, he couldn't remember a time when he and his brother had been jealous of each other. It helped that they'd rarely ever gone after the same woman, but the few times they had, one of them had always acquiesced to the other. It just wasn't that important and, after all, there were plenty of women to go around.

But with Grace, Logan was willing to draw a line. It was mostly about business; after all, he and Grace had a deal. It was his responsibility to handle her situation. Aidan had nothing to do with it.

Okay, fine, he might be willing to admit that something about Grace tugged at him. The passionate way she'd defended her actions that first day still intrigued him. Logan sort of admired her quirky but logical way of thinking, even when it drove him nuts. And, he admitted, there was the basic fact that the woman was gorgeous.

"And scheming, and a liar," he added aloud, then shook his head in defeat. The schemes and lies didn't seem to matter. He still wanted to bury himself inside her.

Ever since that damn kiss he'd been unable to get her out of his mind. Several times he'd caught himself daydreaming, for God's sake, wondering what she was doing. Was she conducting a class in the joys of the G-spot to a new group of unsuspecting honeymooners? Was she hunting down spores in the rain forest? Was she balancing twenty-seven strawberry margaritas on her slim shoulders?

He thought about the other night in the bar, when Clive had trained her how to balance those heavy trays and she'd picked right up on his advice. Logan frowned with the sudden thought that Clive might be watching her a little too closely. He hoped not. He would hate to have to fire his top waiter.

He clawed his hands through his hair in frustration. Hell yeah, he was distracted, as Aidan had been quick to notice. But he was also discreet. Aidan would be the only person in the world who would have ever heard it in his voice. No one else would have a clue, and that's the way he wanted it. He didn't want or need anyone on his staff knowing his personal business. And, frankly, right now that included Aidan. Yeah, they were twins; but that didn't mean he was willing to kiss and tell, especially over the phone.

The main thing was, he didn't want Grace's reputation damaged. Not that he particularly *cared* about the woman one way or the other. He just *wanted* her. Once he'd had her, all these idiotic distractions would fade away and he would be able to get his head back on business and complete the sports-center deal.

In the meantime, Aidan would be home in three days and Logan was determined to have Grace Farrell for himself before that. It would help if he could just figure out a way to keep her from running in the opposite direction the next time he kissed her.

"Tequila, triple sec, sweet and sour, squeeze of lime," Dee said, and handed Grace a shot glass.

"Oh, I know this one," Grace said, taking a tiny sip. "Margarita, right? Mmm, that's good."

"That was too easy," Dee said, her tanned arm flexing as she lifted another bottle and poured. "I still can't believe you memorized the entire bartenders' guide but never tasted the drinks before."

Grace downed the rest of the margarita. "I suppose I've always been more of a reader than a doer."

"Guess those days are over," Dee murmured, grinning.

They faced each other at the small table in Dee's hotel room. Between them was a cocktail tray filled with different bottles that Joey had smuggled out of the bar for their enjoyment. But this was business as far as Grace was concerned. On the tray were chunks of fruit and several shot glasses, as well.

She had already taken sips of a martini, a gimlet, a Brandy Alexander, Sex on the Beach and a whiskey sour. She'd written the names down, followed by her own descriptions and reactions to the flavors of each drink, but her notes were looking a little fuzzy. Still, she was determined to learn as much as she could from Dee.

Mixing a new concoction in a clean shot glass, Dee slid it across the table. "This one's vermouth, bourbon and bitters."

Grace frowned as she tasted. "It's too strong."

"It's usually shaken with lots of ice and a cherry on top. Makes it really tasty."

"I hope so." She made a face. "Is that a Manhattan?"

"Yes," Dee said, sitting back in her chair and fluffing her long, dark hair. "You won't get a lot of orders for that down here since it's more of a big-city winter drink. But it's a classic."

"Then I should know how it tastes," Grace said firmly, and forced herself to take another sip. After almost a week of working together, she had finally confessed to Dee that she didn't have much experience as a cocktail waitress. Dee had wrapped an arm around Grace and revealed that everyone in the bar already knew that. Grace had begged for a few more tips about the job.

When Dee questioned her further, Grace had confessed that she rarely went out to bars and didn't really drink. That's when Dee had gleefully suggested they have a cocktail quiz.

"You might like this one better," Dee said, and handed her another tiny glass filled with a bright pink liquid. "Vodka, cranberry juice, lime juice and triple sec."

"Oh, I know this one," Grace said as she downed the

entire drink. "That's yummy, but I can't remember what it is."

"Cosmopolitan."

"Oh, yeah." Grace nodded slowly. "I get lots of orders for those. I can see why."

"They're smooth, but dangerous." Dee mixed another small cosmo and handed it to Grace, then put the caps back on all the bottles. "I think we're done."

"Oh." Grace frowned in thought as she stared at the notepad, trying to discern her scribbling.

"So you don't ever go out to bars, Gracie?"

"Not really," she said, and pushed her notepad aside.

"Do you have a boyfriend?"

"No." Grace grimaced. "I thought I did, but I was wrong."

Dee nodded sagely. "He was a jerk?"

"Oh, yes. Big-time."

"Goody," Dee said, rubbing her hands together. "Tell me all about him."

Grace laughed as she took a sip of her cosmo. "His name is Walter."

"Oh, sorry. But I have a creepy uncle Walter and that name is not a good sign," Dee said darkly. "He already sounds like a jerk, for sure. So how did you meet him?"

"You really want to know?"

"God, yes. Spill everything."

"Okay." She stretched her arms up for a few seconds, then pushed her hair back off her forehead, wondering where to begin. "Well, you know I work in a lab, and I've been so busy this past year that my boss decided to hire a new associate to help me. As soon as Walter started, we hit it off. It was nice, because we were spending long hours together. My experimentation phase was reaching a critical point." It was odd, but her tongue felt numb.

"Sounds very exciting," Dee said, sipping her mini-margarita.

"It was." Grace took a moment to remember how it was in the beginning. "Walter was wonderful. We talked about so many things. He seemed to really like me and he was always telling me how much he admired my intelligence."

"That's so sweet."

"It was," Grace said. "I don't get that a lot."

"Well, you should," Dee declared. She tried to rest her chin in her hand but her chin slipped twice before she was able to get comfy. "So keep going. I want to hear every last ghastly detail."

"Oh, it's ghastly all right," Grace admitted. "So, anyway, I suppose it was silly to be so flattered by Walter's attention, but he's very nice-looking and I've never had much of a love life before, so what did I know?"

"He took advantage of that."

"Yes. After two months of working together, he finally asked me out and I was over the moon. He took me out for a romantic candlelight dinner at a restaurant overlooking the lake. Then later when he took me home, he wanted to come inside. I was a little hesitant to let him in."

"It was your first date, right?"

"Right."

"He should've kissed you good-night and left."

"That's sort of what I thought. But he said we'd known each other long enough and he wanted to spend the night with me. Except he used a much cruder expression than that." She frowned, remembering that night. But at the moment, Walter's face in her memory was as fuzzy as her mind felt. She realized she liked him better that way. "Anyway, I told him I wasn't ready to take that step and he got angry. He said he knew I wanted it, so what kind of game was I playing? He said he'd spent almost two hundred dollars on me and wanted to get his money's worth. I ended up smacking him hard and while he was recovering, I ran inside my house and locked the door on him. He took it badly. Work became a nightmare with him around."

"Worse than a jerk," Dee said. "I hate him."

"Thank you. Me, too. But at the time, I felt like an idiot."

"It wasn't your fault," Dee said, jumping up and grabbing two bottles of water off the dresser. "He was a toad."

"I know." Grace popped open one bottle and took a long sip. "But I felt like such a cliché."

"Oh, been there, done that."

"Anyway, he finally quit, thank goodness, but he stayed in Minnesota. He's at a rival university and he's trying to claim my studies as his own."

Dee gasped. "What a total jackass."

"Yes, that describes him nicely." Grace couldn't sit still thinking about Walter, so she stood and walked over to Dee's window. She stumbled, but caught herself, then frowned at the rug, looking for whatever had tripped her. She didn't see anything. "I found out after he left that he'd stolen a small batch of my spores and some of my papers, and now he's applied for new funding to allow him to work on the exact same line of research as mine."

"Can we kill him?"

Grace blurted out a laugh. "Oh, Dee, you are the best."

"Hey, it's an option."

"I wish," she said, only half kidding. "No, all I can do is collect lots of new spores and continue my research when I get back. Thank goodness I never told him exactly where these rare spores could be found."

"A good thing for Walter," Dee said with a decided edge to her voice. "Because if he showed up here, he'd be very sorry."

"I really appreciate that," Grace said with a smile, then added, "even though you scare me a little."

She laughed. "I'll scare Walter a lot worse and that's a promise. I got your back, girlfriend."

Grace felt sudden tears prickling her eyes. Nobody had ever had her back before. Oh, she knew Phillippa would support her, if it came down to that. But somehow the way Dee had said it so simply and unconditionally, made Grace feel all warm and snuggly inside.

And even though she trusted Dee, she couldn't bear to confess the worst part to her. Yes, her university had promised to defend her against Walter's lies, but Grace knew that if she couldn't get the spores and raise the level of her research and experimentation to new heights, her reputation would suffer.

She also had to prove to the foundation that her work was her own and that she was the one deserving of the funds, not Walter. Otherwise, within a month she could lose her funding, her job and, most important, her reputation.

"Forget about stupid Walter," Dee said, interrupting her worries. "What about Mr. Hunkadelic?"

"What? Who?" Grace wondered if she'd had a few too many sips of Dee's cocktails because the lightning-quick change of subject made her head spin.

"You know who." Dee stared meaningfully at Grace. "The hunky man who is our boss? Mr. Big?"

"Oh, Logan." Grace stared intently at the label on her water bottle. The letters looked wobbly. Very odd. "What about him?"

"Something happening between you two?"

"Nothing."

"Then why aren't you looking at me?" Dee said, chuckling. "Do you have something to hide?"

Grace whipped around. "No! I mean…okay, he kissed me, but—"

"He kissed you?"

She sighed and flopped down on the bed. "Yes, and I warned him not to do it again."

"You…wait." Dee moved her chair so she could rest her feet on the bed. "Okay, I've got to hear your explanation for this one."

Grace stared at the ceiling as if help might be sent down from up above. But none came, so she finally met Dee's gaze. "It was for his own good."

"I don't get it. Is he a bad kisser?"

"Oh, no," Grace said, shaking her head. "He's really good."

"Well, then…"

"I ran away," Grace said, and buried her face in her hands. Humiliation swept through her. She still couldn't believe that she'd run from Logan like a teenager afraid of her own hormones.

Dee's eyebrows shot up and her feet thumped to the floor. "You ran away? Honey, are you crazy? Nobody runs away from Logan Sutherland. We're all running toward him."

She had known that, deep down of course. But hearing Dee say it out loud only confirmed that once again, Grace was "not normal." She didn't do anything like your average woman did. Heck, she hadn't even been able to stand her ground when a gorgeous man kissed her. It was pitiful. Just pitiful.

Still, she had to try to defend herself, pointless though it might be. "Dee, he doesn't know me. He's the one who would go running if he knew…"

"If he knew what?"

Grace gritted her teeth and forced herself to say it. "If he knew how smart I really am."

Dee came over to the bed, grabbed a pillow and sat next to her, resting her back against the headboard. "Honey, I confess I'm not sure how smart you are, but what does it matter? He kissed you. He likes you. Why are you running away from that?"

Grace folded her arms across her chest, anxious to make Dee understand. "Men don't like smart women."

"Oh, Gracie, that's just plain prehistoric. These days, men love smart women."

Grace shook her head stubbornly. "Not when they're as smart as I am."

Dee's mouth twisted in confusion. "Just how smart are you?"

"I have an IQ of 172," she said, annoyed with the slight whine in her voice.

"Oh, Gracie." Dee reached out and grabbed Grace's hand. "You realize that means nothing to me, right?"

"Yes," Grace said, laughing. "That's just one reason why I like you so much."

"I like you, too, Gracie," Dee said, "but really, is 172 good? I mean, what's average?"

"Well, that's difficult to say, really, since IQ scores have been gaining three points every decade now for some time, but—"

"Ballpark figure," Dee interrupted. "What's average?"

"About 100," Grace admitted with a sigh.

"Whoa." Dee blinked. "And what's genius?"

Grace groaned as she said, "One forty and above."

"Damn." Dee grinned at her. "So, you're like, what? *Über*genius?"

Stunned to discover that Dee's opinion of her hadn't

changed, Grace relaxed and for the first time in her life, actually giggled. "*Über*genius? I like that."

"You could be a superhero or something," Dee continued. "You could be Smartgirl!"

Relief and gratitude rushed through Grace as she returned Dee's smile. She had been so worried that once Dee knew the truth about Grace, she wouldn't want to be anywhere near her. After all, her own parents had run the other way from her, and that was a memory she really didn't want to dwell on just now. No, right now she wanted to concentrate on the amazing sensation of having her fears dissolve. For the first time, she was being accepted and liked, completely, for exactly *who* she was, not how *smart* she was—although Dee seemed to think that was pretty cool, too.

"Smartgirl? Sometimes I wonder," she muttered, then brightened. "But I do have four doctorate degrees."

"Wow! Four?" Dee laughed. "I lasted about six weeks in college. I was so bored, I ran screaming."

"Really?"

"Oh, yeah. So how long did it take you to get four degrees, cuz you look really young."

"I did all four of them concurrently."

"Wow." Dee shook her head, then took a sip of her drink. "Your classes must've been intense. But now you're like a PhD?"

"Yes, times four."

"Holy moley."

"I know," Grace whispered, then said, "Do you think we could have another mini-margarita?"

"I think I need one, too." Dee bounced off the bed and returned to the table to mix the drink. "So you work in your lab every day. But what do you do in your spare time?"

"I don't have much spare time," Grace said as she joined her at the table and squeezed a lime into the shot glass. "My work in the lab is very important, so—" she shrugged "—that's mostly what I do."

"Okay, I know you don't go out to bars," Dee said. "Do you like to shop or go to movies?"

"I've never really had much time to do either," Grace said, feeling more inadequate by the second.

"So you've only ever gone to school and worked in a lab?"

"That's pretty much it." She smiled cheerfully. "But I love my work."

"Oh, I like my job, too," Dee said, as she mixed another mini-margarita for herself. "But I like shopping, too, and, well, lots of things. But especially shopping."

"School and work are all I've ever known," Grace said, sipping her drink. "I started college when I was eight years old."

Dee's gaze was awash in sympathy. "That's terrible. College is hard enough on grown-ups, let alone a kid."

Grace blinked. She'd never shared that part of her background with anyone besides Phillippa. But that didn't mean there had ever been a moment when she'd considered herself unfortunate. Far from it. "I was lucky. I got to live at school and study and learn."

"Your parents let you live at school? When you were eight?"

"Well, I wasn't alone. I lived with the head of the Science Department and his wife."

"But your own parents sent you away?" Dee said.

"Oh, they were happy to do it," Grace said lightly. "I belonged in college. And it worked out well for them because the university paid them for me to go to school."

Dee stopped in midpour. "Your parents got money for you?"

"They didn't have a lot of money," Grace explained, "so I was glad to help them get by."

"But it sort of sounds like they sold you."

"Oh, no." Grace laughed. "I wanted to go."

"Gotta say, Gracie…I think somebody needs to go back in time and give your folks a swift kick or two."

"No, no," Grace said, pleased that her new friend would defend her, but knowing her parents had done the best they could. Maybe she hadn't quite understood it at the time, but now she knew that her mom and dad were nice, simple, hardworking people who had never understood her at all. "I appreciate it, but everything worked out."

"Wow," Dee said, taking an experimental sip, then another. "When I was eight, my big excitement was cutting all the hair off of my Barbie dolls. Guess we come from two different worlds."

"But we can still be friends," Grace said, hating to sound so tentative.

"Most indubitably," Dee said, giggling as she held her glass out in a toast. "We are friends, Gracie. Never doubt it. To my friend, Gracie."

"To my friend, Dee." Grace wiped away a happy tear as they clinked their glasses together.

Grace wasn't sleepy at all. So after leaving Dee dozing in her room, she walked out to the terrace and down to the beach. She couldn't get over how beautiful it was here, even at night. The moon was as big and clear in the sky as Grace had ever seen. The water was as smooth and shiny as the heavy-gauge stainless steel table in the lab's radiation room.

"You're hopeless," she muttered, shaking her head at

that comparison. Would her head always be stuck in the laboratory? She hoped not. She wanted to think carefree thoughts, dream frivolous dreams, like drinking champagne and kissing a handsome man under the Caribbean moon.

Had she always harbored a secret wish to be so frivolous? No, she was absolutely sure this was something new for her. But it felt good.

She hadn't drunk any champagne yet, but she'd had plenty of mini-margaritas. And as far as kissing a handsome man? Well, she'd done that, too, except for the moonlight part.

"And the part where you went scurrying away like a mouse," she reminded herself. Other than that, the kiss had been pretty darn dreamy.

The mild breeze whispered across her shoulders, ruffling her hair. Nudging her sandals off, she walked in bare feet through the cool sand. Oh, yes, she'd definitely had one too many mini-drinks, but she felt wonderful. At the water's edge she stopped, then had the strongest urge to keep on going. Touching the water with her toes, she discovered it was tepid. Not too cold, not too warm. Just right. And wouldn't it be delightful to swim in the moonlight?

"It's not safe to swim alone at night."

She whirled around. Logan stood behind her. "Oh, hello. I didn't hear you coming."

Logan came closer. "The sand swallows the sound of footsteps."

She smiled at his poetic words. "Are you taking a walk in the moonlight?"

"It appears I am."

"Isn't it beautiful?" she said, and spun around to take it all in.

Logan grabbed her before she stumbled straight into the shallow water.

"Oops," she said, and giggled.

"Have you had a few drinks tonight, Grace?" he asked as he pulled her closer to him. She wished he would smile again. He had such a nice smile. She couldn't seem to get it out of her mind.

Had he asked her a question? Oh, yes.

"I have," she said, resting her head on his chest because it seemed so inviting. "But it was strictly for business purposes. I was taking a test."

"A test?" he said, rubbing her back in a slow circle. "Which test was that?"

She could hear in the tone of his voice that he was smiling. She liked that tone, too, and gazed up at him. "Dee calls it the cocktail quiz."

"Ah. And how did you do?"

"I passed with flying colors because I'm very smart. Do you know how smart I am?"

"You've mentioned several times that you're very smart indeed," he said.

"But you don't know how smart I really am," she said, pointing her finger at his face, which was slightly blurry around the edges. "If you knew, you'd run for the hills."

"You said that before, too," he murmured, wrapping his hand around her finger. "But you're wrong."

"I think you're very handsome," she said, staring at him keenly.

He chuckled. "And I think you're toasted."

She thought about it, then nodded. "I think you're right. And I'm okay with that."

"Glad to hear it," he said, his arms wrapped securely around her waist. "Shall I walk you to your room now?"

She looked up at the night sky, then at him. "Aren't you going to kiss me again?"

"Do you want me to kiss you?"

"Yes, please," she whispered. "Under the moonlight, if you don't mind."

"Well, since you ask so politely..." He touched his lips to hers in a kiss so gentle, so sweet, so warm, Grace wanted to melt in his arms.

"Just like a dream," she uttered, feeling as if she were floating on air. Was she melting for real? She felt as light as a feather. Then she felt nothing at all.

Logan caught her as she slid downward, boneless and out cold. Lifting her effortlessly into his arms, he was thankful he'd decided to take a walk out to the beach to catch a few minutes of fresh air before heading to his suite for the night. Otherwise, he wouldn't have had a chance to rescue Grace from a night spent sleeping on the sand.

As he carried her across the terrace, he hoped like hell she wouldn't wake up with too bad a hangover in the morning. He had a feeling she didn't indulge very often, so she was probably going to pay for taking the cocktail quiz.

He reached her room and used his own master-key card to open it. Stepping inside, he let the door close behind him and carried her over to her bed to lay her down. Once she was settled, he glanced around her room and saw the elaborate setup she'd arranged on her table and across the top of her dresser. It was a portable laboratory complete with a serious-looking microscope, state-of-the-art laptop and some contraption with a toggle switch and digital read-out screen that measured something or other. There was a small scale next to a plastic thing that held glass cylinders suspended in a row, several of which had tubes attached that wound around and emptied into nearby beakers.

If he didn't know her better, he might've thought she'd set up a still to make whiskey.

He glanced back at Grace, who was snoring softly. She would probably freak out when she woke up in the morning and realized that her boss had been the one who'd carried her to bed.

She wore cropped pants and a thin blouse and he pondered the idea of taking her clothes off. She would sleep better wearing just her underwear, right?

He enjoyed the image of her waking up and seeing herself in panties and a bra. How quickly would she grasp that it had been Logan who'd undressed her?

Ah, well, it was a nice fantasy. One he wouldn't be carrying out tonight.

But soon. Very soon.

This time, though, he would allow her to keep her clothes on because that's the kind of guy he was. Pulling the lightweight comforter over her, he turned off the lights and left her alone to sleep off the cocktail quiz.

Five

He found her late the next morning, sitting in an over-stuffed rattan chair in the shady portion of the terrace. She wore dark glasses and a light pink sweater and was sipping something thick and red.

"Is that a Bloody Mary you're drinking?" he asked.

Grace looked up at him and tried to smile, but it was a bit shaky. "Dear God, no. No alcohol for me, thank you." She stared with suspicion at the concoction, then back at Logan. "It's something Joey mixed up. Supposed to be good for me because of my…um, hay fever."

"Hay fever." He grinned. "Is that what they're calling it these days?

"All right, fine," she said, pouting. "I'm a little under the weather. But it's all your fault."

He barked out a laugh. "My fault?"

"Of course."

"This I've got to hear." He sat in the chair next to her. "How is your hangover my fault?"

She turned slowly in her chair and faced him. "I was investigating ways to improve my job performance last night."

"Ah. And in order to improve your skills at carrying drinks, you got drunk, apparently deciding to carry those drinks on the *inside*. And since I'm the boss, it's my fault."

She frowned briefly. "Exactly."

He chuckled. "That's a new one."

She hunched a bit lower in her chair and glared at him. "It's true."

"Sweetheart, nobody said anything about you having to drink the same stuff your customers order."

"But I thought it would be good to know how the different drinks taste. That way I can give advice to people who ask for recommendations."

"That's thoughtful of you, but it doesn't excuse Dee from overserving you."

Grace grabbed his arm. "Don't you dare yell at Dee. She's my friend."

Logan's eyes focused on her soft hand on his arm. "I have no intention of yelling at her."

"Oh. Good." She pulled her hand back. "It's not her fault anyway. She didn't realize what a lightweight I am." She looked away. "Neither did I, I guess. And the drinks were in such tiny glasses, I never thought about how much I might be drinking and…"

The vulnerable look on her face almost did him in and he decided to change the subject. "Grace, do you remember seeing me on the beach last night?"

She frowned again, avoiding his gaze as she licked her lips. "I have a vague memory of that."

"Are you sure it isn't more than a vague memory?"

"Why?" she asked, turning to look at him. "Did I say something ridiculous? Should I apologize?"

"Of course not. You were on your best behavior. We had a nice conversation about the moonlight."

"Oh, good," she said with relief.

"And then you asked me to kiss you."

She cringed. "Oh, no." Then, taking a deep breath, she said, "Apparently I shouldn't be allowed anywhere near liquor without a keeper. I'm so sorry if I embarrassed you."

"You're kidding, right?" He regarded her intently. "The only thing I'm sorry about is that you were too tipsy to take the next step with me."

She flashed him a look he couldn't read because of those dark glasses blocking her eyes. But she seemed to dwell on his words, letting them sink in. He hoped so, anyway, because he intended to take that next step as soon as possible.

"What are you thinking, Grace?"

She cleared her throat. "Nothing much."

He scooted his chair closer to hers. "Are you thinking about that kiss? About what else we could share?"

She didn't answer, but he could see a faint blush rise on her pale cheeks.

"Because I'm thinking about it," he said softly, touching her shoulder with his fingers, then trailing a path up her neck and along her jawline. "I can't stop thinking about it. I want you in my bed, Grace, wrapped up in nothing but me. And once we're in bed together, I'll take my time with you. I want to touch and feel every inch of your body with my hands and my mouth and tongue. I want to make you feel everything I'm feeling. I want to make you hot. I want to make you scream."

Her breath shuddered out and she shifted uncomfortably in her chair. She swallowed hard and murmured, "Oh, God."

He leaned closer and whispered in her ear, "Say when,

Grace. Tonight? Say the word and we'll be together. To-morrow night? I won't wait much longer. I've got to have you soon." Then he bit her earlobe and soothed the bite with his tongue. "Yes?"

"Yes." She let out a soft moan. "Soon."

"Good." He touched her cheek, then stood. His body was tight and hard and he knew he'd suffer for an hour or more because of this little seduction scene. But it had been worth it. Even with the dark glasses covering her eyes, Logan could tell she had been as affected as he and that was, after all, the point. Right?

Smiling, he turned to leave. "You have a nice day, Grace."

She watched him walk away and had to resist the urge to call the hotel doctor. Her heart was stuttering so wildly from his incendiary words—not to mention that nibble on her ear—that she wasn't sure it would ever calm down again.

"Wow," she whispered. The man was potent. Maybe too potent. Because now she had to ask herself, was she ready for someone like Logan Sutherland? She had barely dated in the past ten years and after the debacle with Walter, she'd lost some confidence in herself as a woman. Of course, Logan's flattering words over the past few days had gone a long way toward helping her get some of that confidence back.

He'd also confused her completely. A few days ago, he'd made it more than clear that he didn't trust her. Lately, though, he seemed to have changed his mind. And today... She shivered again, then winced when her head pounded in response. Why had he chosen *today* of all days, to tell her he wanted her in his bed? She had been in no mental shape to argue him out of it. She certainly would have, she consoled herself, if she'd been able to.

But no, even she didn't believe that.

The memory of his mouth at her ear, his warm breath on her skin, made her feel nearly boneless with the want rampaging through her.

So now the question was, did she trust him enough to, well, allow him to do all those things his whispered promise had suggested?

Just thinking about giving herself up to him caused ripples of lust to waft through her stomach and roam even lower.

Oh, who was she kidding? She wanted him so much, she could barely sit still. She'd never felt this way about a man before, not even Walter. And she had trusted Walter!

"That proves you're a dunce," she muttered. She had trusted Walter and he had betrayed her, so how could she base her feelings for any man on the amount of trust she felt for him? She couldn't, so she might as well throw caution to the wind and do what she wanted to do. And, right now, all she wanted to do was Logan Sutherland. Heck, if she couldn't have trust, she would settle for lust.

"Yes," she murmured with a cautious smile. "Soon."

"He didn't mean it," she muttered to herself that night in the bar. She refused to be disappointed, chalking it up to her own naïveté when it came to men.

After garnishing four mai tais with pineapple chunks and maraschino cherries, Grace carried the cocktails over to one of her tables and passed them around to her customers.

She'd been on duty for four hours already and Logan hadn't shown up. After seeing his imposing presence in the bar every night for the past week, she was a little frustrated that he wouldn't show up tonight. Especially after propositioning her that afternoon.

If he didn't appear, should she go to his room? But what if he was with someone? Oh, God. She needed to forget he'd ever mentioned anything to her. Forget he'd whispered all those provocative suggestions in her ear. Forget the smoldering lust she'd been suffering all day.

He'd obviously been teasing her.

But why? Was he trying to set her up for a fall? If she came on to him, would he have his excuse to fire her? Was that his plan? If so, it was sneaky and mean.

It wasn't as if she wanted to work in the bar forever, but she had friends here now and she still cared about doing a good job. She had at least another week or two of spore collection before she would feel right about leaving, so she needed to protect herself against the possibility of losing her job.

So it was settled. She wouldn't act on her attraction to Logan. She'd already behaved like an idiot with one man. She didn't need to do it again. Walter had been handsome, too, although nowhere near as gorgeous as Logan. And look where her attraction to him had gotten her.

At least she and Walter had had something in common, for whatever that was worth. She and Logan, on the other hand, had nothing in common. He certainly had no interest in spores—that much was clear. Wasn't it important to have shared interests? What if he asked her about herself and she mentioned her fascination with biological dispersal and meiosis in the sporangium? His eyes would glaze over and he would zone out.

Of course, Grace was used to people outside of the lab dozing off when she began waxing microbiological. She could handle the general disinterest, although, privately, she didn't understand why the whole world wasn't utterly captivated by the subject of Allerian spores and their regenerative properties.

But she *really* didn't want Logan to do the zone-out thing with her. She wanted him to look at her and see more than a scientist. She wanted him to feel the same pulse-pounding desire that had been charging through her all day.

When she found herself staring out the window near the last table she'd served, she shook herself back to reality. She really needed to concentrate on her job or she'd find herself on the next plane off the island.

Back at the bar, she collected a larger order of ten drinks and arranged them on a tray. After a few deep breaths to keep her nerves at bay, she whispered the words that always helped relax her. "Helium, argon, xenon."

Positioning her feet on the floor and flexing her leg muscles as Clive had taught her, she lifted the tray in one smooth movement onto her shoulders. Then she blinked. "Wait, neon comes before argon. And Krypton comes before… Oh, dear."

She steadied the tray and began to walk carefully toward her next table. She would have to take extra care with her drink trays tonight because she was obviously flustered. Otherwise, she never would've mixed up the order of noble gases in the periodic table. She forced herself to concentrate as she crossed the room, talking to herself as she walked. "Now where was I? Oh, yes, krypton, xenon, radon. Now the alkali metals. Lithium, sodium, potassium—"

"Looking good, Gracie girl," Dee said with a wink as she passed her in the aisle between tables.

"You, too, Dee." Grace grinned. She'd never had a friend like Dee before, someone who was smart and funny and so much fun to talk to. Grace's closest friend in Minnesota was Phillippa, and while they had a good time at work together, Grace didn't have many friends outside of the lab. Not a friend like Dee, anyway. She hadn't known her long but already felt so close to her.

Grace didn't know what she'd do without Dee, once she went back to Minnesota. They could email, of course, but that wasn't the same. The thought depressed her enough that she had to put it out of her mind. For now, she would think positively. She was here on the island because of the spores, of course, but Dee was near the top of her list of best reasons to come back to Alleria someday soon.

Grace made it to her customers' table and back to the bar before she realized she'd forgotten to name the rest of the alkalis.

What was wrong with her? It was a good thing she'd gone back to her room to rest for a few hours that afternoon. Lord knows how much more loopy she'd be tonight without that nap. She vowed never to overindulge again, knowing what a mess it made of her memorization skills, among other things.

A low-level buzz stirred its way through her system and Grace turned around to see what was causing it.

Logan.

Glancing around, she realized nobody else in the room was taking an interest in his presence but her. Where in the world had that buzz come from? She didn't know, but her insides were tingling and the pale hairs on her arms were standing up.

He stood a few feet inside the doorway and stared at her with an intensity that nearly had her knees collapsing. As she gripped the edge of the bar, he jerked his chin toward the door. Did that mean he was leaving?

"I'll take over your tables," Dee whispered in Grace's ear as she took hold of her drink tray. "Go."

Her friend nudged her away from the bar and Grace stumbled toward the door where Logan stood waiting. The bar crowd became a vague shadow and the raucous laughter faded to a soft drone. All she saw was him.

Heart pounding, she met him at the door. Were his eyes always that compelling, she wondered. Or was tonight special? Was there something more in the way he looked at her? She saw the tension in his features and knew he was experiencing everything she was. The sexual pull between them was off the charts, no matter what periodic table she might use to try to define it.

But oddly, Grace had zero interest in quantifying anything that lay between them. The fact that their feelings for each other existed was enough. The look in Logan's eyes said it all. He'd come for her. He'd meant what he said. He wasn't setting her up for a fall or trying to fire her. He wanted her. And in that moment, all her earlier worries dissolved. She knew she was safe with him.

He took her hand and they strode out of the bar side by side. She gazed up at him and thought, *well, not exactly safe*. She was in over her head. She knew it. She'd never been with a man like Logan Sutherland before and barely knew her next move. But she *was* a genius, after all, so she would surely figure it all out soon.

And if not, she would never let him know it.

Her scent enveloped him and fueled his craving for her. Logan had almost stayed away tonight, thinking she'd come up with some excuse to refuse him. But in the end, he had to see her. It didn't mean anything. *Couldn't* mean anything. It just meant that he needed a woman and she was the one his body happened to require.

It barely registered that some of his staff were watching him. He'd noticed Dee taking Grace's tray, knew they were friends and he was grateful for it. As for the others, if his behavior stirred up any gossip among them, they would have to get over it.

As Grace walked toward him, he was pitifully glad he'd come. Her thin sarong was backlit by the lights of the bar and Logan could see the outline of her gorgeous legs as she sauntered toward him. His gaze was riveted to the apex of that silhouette, the subtle brush of those slender thighs as she moved closer, the curvaceous shape of her hips, the subtle rise and fall of her breasts that seemed to signal her own need.

She'd worn her dark red hair loose tonight and it fell in bouncing waves over her shoulders. He wanted to gather it in his hands and bury his face in those lustrous locks while he lost himself in her hot core.

It took every bit of control he had—control that slipped with every step they took together—not to lead her into the nearby utility room, pull off her bikini bottom, thrust himself inside her and quench this hunger. But the cold wall of a janitor's closet wouldn't do for their first time together. He intended to spend a long, long time savoring her—and for that, he wanted complete privacy. And a damn strong mattress.

They entered his suite and he wasted no time. As the door clicked closed, he flipped the lock, then turned and lifted her into his arms, giving in to the need to hold her again as he had the night before. With her pressed against him, he could recall all over again the feminine softness of her body skimming his hard chest.

She wrapped her arms around his neck and nestled her head against his shoulder as he moved quickly through the front salon and into the bedroom. Once there, he covered her mouth in a hot, devouring kiss that she met with equal fervor. Then he placed her gently on the bed and watched as her eyes searched his face and her arms reached out for him.

"Come to me," she said. It was the first time she'd spoken since he'd grabbed her hand and led her out of the bar. Now, as he stared hungrily at her lips glistening wet from their kiss, he knew he was about to reach the end of his famous control.

Kneeling on the bed, he straddled her, took hold of both her hands and pulled her arms up over her head. The action caused her breasts to thrust out for his pleasure. He reached behind her back to untie her bikini top, then slipped it over her head and tossed it aside. He stopped and took a moment to gaze at her exposed, perfect breasts.

"Gorgeous," he muttered, taking both breasts into his hands to mold them gently, using his thumbs to stroke her rosy nipples to stiffness.

He bent to take one nipple into his mouth, sucking gently, licking and teasing it with his teeth and tongue. Then he switched his attention to her other breast, plying her sensitive nipple with sensual nips and licks until she moaned deep within her throat. She was writhing beneath him now and he slid himself up to claim her mouth in another kiss so heated, it could end things here and now if Logan didn't force himself to step back and slow down.

He untied the knot of her sarong and pushed it aside, then slid his fingers under the edge of her bikini bottom, seeking her most intimate spot. When he slid one finger inside her, she groaned in need.

"Tight," he murmured. "And so hot." He eased another finger in, then moved both fingers out and back in again as her flesh grew even more heated and moist with her need.

"Logan," she whispered. "Please."

Her hair moved in waves around her head like a dark red halo and her intoxicating taste and scent filled his senses. As her sweet body twisted against him, tempting him beyond the edge, his mouth sought hers blindly, renewing his claim on her. His hard length pressed against her, demanding entry.

"I need to have you now," he said, barely recognizing the uncivilized rumble in his voice.

"Yes, yes," she urged him.

He jumped off the bed and quickly removed his clothes. Reaching into the top drawer of his dresser, he grabbed a condom and slipped it on.

Then he returned to her, yanked her bikini bottom down and threw it across the bed. Grasping thick strands of her hair in his hands, he urged her to meet his gaze. "I want you too much, Grace. It'll have to be hard and fast this first time."

She nodded, her eyes glazing with desire. "Yes."

"Finesse will have to come later."

"God, yes, just touch me," she demanded, lifting her mouth to cover his in a kiss so laced with sweet passion it brought an unfamiliar ache to his chest; and it forced him to ease back on his relentless urge to lose himself inside her.

Instead, he kissed her again, meeting her sweetness with his own demanding assault on her mouth, her lips, her tongue. Finally, though, that kiss, as deep as it was, wasn't enough to stay him any longer. He broke free, pulled his head back and stared down at her.

"Look at me," he whispered. "I want to see you lose control with me."

She complied and he stared with masculine satisfaction at the fierce glimmer of heat and need in her eyes. Holding her gaze, he plunged into her with one strong thrust.

She gasped and her eyes widened in shock.

"What the hell?" he shouted, then grimaced as he fought to hold himself completely still.

"Don't stop," she insisted, wrapping her arms around his waist. She lifted both legs, resting her thighs against his hips, and that movement beneath him was a sensual wave that threatened to consume his last ounce of brain-power.

But Logan forced himself to stop anyway, his eyes locked on hers as he struggled to speak. "You're a virgin?"

"That's not really important right now," she said tightly, and raised her hips to urge him deeper inside her.

"But…the G-spot," he uttered, resting his forehead on hers as he focused every ounce of his energy on keeping perfectly still. "What about when you—"

"Can we discuss this later?" she said, and wound her legs around his to keep him bound to her.

"You're killing me," he said with a groan.

"Don't make me," she said through clenched teeth.

"When did you get so pushy?" he said, biting back a grin as he reached out and smoothed a strand of hair away from her cheek.

She sighed. "Nobody warned me that men talked so much during sex."

He laughed despite the awkwardness of the moment. "Fine, but we're going to have a long talk afterward."

"I figured we would."

He began to move again, slowly at first, then with building speed. He tried to keep his strokes long and smooth in order to ease inside her without causing too much pain. But when she skimmed her hands across his back and locked her legs around his waist, he lost whatever last bit of control he'd managed to maintain thus far.

She matched him move for move and her heart pounded in rhythm with his. He pushed harder, pumped faster as they both climbed higher, his need igniting more and more with every thrust.

She rocked against him and Logan drove into her with savage delight, stroking and gliding as she urged him on. Then, with a sudden sharp intake of breath, she uttered his name and shattered beneath him.

Logan watched her surrender in his arms and an innate need to join her overtook him. Thrusting harder, faster, deeper, his breath grew ragged as he used every muscle in his body to push again, then again, until an explosive wave of pleasure engulfed him and he was hurled over the edge with Grace.

Exactly where he most wanted to be.

Six

Grace wasn't sure how long she slept. Eventually, she opened her eyes and found Logan leaning on his elbow, watching her. A frown marred his handsome features.

"I hurt you," he said, as his fingers edged along her hairline. He was still stretched out next to her with his leg thrown over hers. It felt perfect.

"No," she said, struggling to sit up and regain some dignity. But it was impossible because he wouldn't budge, so she plopped her head back down on the pillow with a sigh. Dignity was overrated anyway. Besides, she was *naked*. How much dignity would she really be able to find?

And who really cared? She had finally lost the big V she had carried around inside her mind for years. Her virginity was gone and frankly, she had never expected to enjoy losing something so much. Grace looked up into Logan's eyes and felt her heart give a soft, warm flutter. He had been wonderful, even though, right now, he didn't exactly look pleased to be her deflowerer.

"You didn't hurt me at all, Logan. It was…"

"Why didn't you tell me?" he asked.

It would be silly to pretend not to know what he was referring to, but she considered playing dumb for a half second. Then she gave it up. "You mean why didn't I tell you I was a virgin? Honestly, I didn't think it would be an issue. And I confess I was so wrapped up in the moment, I didn't want to stop. I'm glad we didn't stop."

He smiled at that. "Me, too, Grace. But I still wish you'd said something." His voice was repentant as he stroked her hair. "I would've been more gentle, taken my time to make you feel more at ease."

She was surprised to see regret reflected in his eyes and she reached up and touched his face. "You did everything right, Logan. It was wonderful."

"No," he said meaningfully, taking hold of her hand. "But it will be."

He lowered his mouth to hers, kissing her with a tenderness she'd never thought to experience. Desire trembled within her all over again, rising inexorably as he tormented her with gentle warmth, lavished her with whispered endearments, tempted her with slow, openmouthed kisses. He touched her with a softness born from regret, she knew, that he'd neglected to use enough care with her before.

The sweetness of his actions touched her heart and she met his passion with a wholehearted joy she'd never known before. Oh, she tried to hold on to a dash of detachment for her own good, but it was useless. Logan effectively destroyed all her defenses until she was left with nothing but shivering need for his hands and mouth on her skin.

Was this what love felt like? Oh, she wasn't stupid enough to imagine she'd fallen in love with him. But she'd often heard that being in love was the best feeling in the world, and right now, she felt pretty darn fabulous.

"I'm just going to hold you for a while, Grace," he said softly, tucking her in close to his side.

"We're not going to—" Even she could hear the disappointment in her voice.

He smiled against her hair. "Not right this minute."

"Oh," she said, snuggling her head against his shoulder. "Why?"

Logan chuckled and she smiled even as she closed her eyes.

"Because you wore me out, Grace," he said, still smiling.

"I did?" She sighed, and stretched out one arm across his broad chest. Even though it had been her first time, she must have done everything right. Good to know. "That's nice."

As they dozed off to sleep, she issued her naive self a warning. This wasn't love. She hoped she was smart enough to know that much. But several times during the night, when she awoke and found herself in his arms, she had to wonder if she hadn't already slid effortlessly into something very close to love with him.

As daylight began to lighten the room, Grace quietly rose from the bed and got her first real look at Logan's elegant bedroom. Pale gold walls and terra-cotta floor tiles gave the space a lovely, open feeling, while thick, colorful area rugs provided warmth and a touch of charm. White plantation shutters covered a wall of windows that when opened would no doubt reveal an unsurpassed view of blue water and lush green hillsides. A comfortably overstuffed taupe sofa with striped brown and coral pillows sat against the wall facing the bed. The room was casual, elegant and expensive, and completely suited its owner.

Logan sprawled sound asleep under the covers, all rumpled and warm and sexy. Shards of sunlight streamed in through the windows illuminating the king-size bed and lending a romantic aura to the scene.

"No, no," Grace whispered, taking quick pains to sweep all thoughts related to romantic auras out of her mind. What she and Logan were having was sex. Wild, exciting and passionate, for sure, but not a romance. Romance was for some other couple, not for them. And that was just fine and dandy with Grace. She could be as sophisticated as the next girl, right? So she vowed to be perfectly happy and enjoy her time with Logan for as long as it lasted.

And once she was back in Minnesota, whenever she found herself feeling a little bit lonely, she would be able to look back at these moments with him and remember this time as the most thrilling of her life.

Not everyone could say they'd had such a time. She was lucky. And happy.

She took one more glance at Logan, then tiptoed to the bathroom. Staring at herself in the mirror, she gave herself a little squeeze because she felt so wonderful. She'd never guessed that sex could be so... Well, now she totally understood why the spores did it every morning like clockwork.

She finished freshening up, then quietly opened the bathroom door. And shrieked.

"Not staying for coffee?" Logan said casually, as he stood there waiting for her. He wore a gorgeous smile, but otherwise, he was completely naked.

She scurried backward and yanked a bath towel off the rack to wrap around herself. Naked in the middle of the night while she was wrapped around him was one thing. Naked while standing in the morning sunlight having a conversation was something else altogether. "I didn't think you'd… Well, good morning."

"Good morning to you," he said, still grinning. "You do know I saw your naked body all night long, Grace."

"That was different," she said, clutching the towel in a death grip. "Now it's…it's morning." She almost groaned. So smart, yet, oh, so lame.

"Yes, it is," he said agreeably. "I ordered coffee and breakfast. No need to rush off."

"Oh, thank you. But I should…" She had no idea how to complete that sentence. Her lack of knowledge when it came to sexual etiquette was disheartening.

"Stay," he said, settling the matter. He walked past her into the bathroom. "I'll be right out."

They had breakfast on his private terrace. He'd ordered eggs, bacon, sausage, hash browns and toast for both of them, along with a variety of pastries, juice and coffee.

Grace knew she wouldn't be able to eat half of the food on her plate, but took a bite of egg and a sip of coffee.

One half hour later, her plate was empty and Logan was pouring her another cup of coffee.

"I guess I was hungry," she said, as she stirred a teaspoon of cream into her coffee. Logan had graciously loaned her his bathrobe so she would feel more comfortable.

He stretched back in his chair. "It's refreshing to be with a woman who enjoys eating as much as you do."

"I take it you haven't been up to Minnesota lately," Grace said wryly. She popped the last bite of toast into her mouth and dabbed her lips with her napkin.

He laughed. "You're right…I haven't."

"We have to eat to stay alive up there," she explained. "And we live by those words. Minnesotans believe you need an extra layer of body fat or two, just to keep warm through the long winters."

"Ah." He leaned closer, untied her bathrobe and skimmed his fingers across her stomach, causing a shiver of excitement to race through her like lightning. "But you don't have an extra layer of body fat on you, Grace."

"I…I suppose I work it off in the lab." She wished she could drag him back to bed right then. But, once again, she had no idea what constituted proper behavior the morning after.

"Your lab job sounds like it would be fairly sedentary. Is it?"

"I suppose it can be for some people, but I do a lot of running around."

They both reached for the same croissant and she almost screamed from the shock of tingling heat she felt as their hands touched. What was wrong with her?

She stared at Logan but he didn't seem to be at all affected by the touch. Instead, he grinned, took the croissant, tore it and handed her half.

"So tell me why someone like you is still a virgin."

The question surprised her. "Someone like me?"

He broke off a piece of the flaky pastry and munched on it. "You're beautiful, Grace. What's wrong with the guys up there in the tundra? Has all that snow frozen their brains?"

"Maybe." She felt her cheeks warm up, but she had to smile at the unexpected compliment. "Thank you. But the most likely answer is that the men I work with are lab geeks like me. They're only interested in my theories."

She wasn't about to tell him how Walter had pretended an interest he didn't really feel. Instead, she added, "Other than that, I don't get out of the laboratory much."

"Why not?"

"It's my job," she said simply, but it was more than that. "It's my life."

"Life is more than a job," he countered.

"I suppose it should be," she said, and knew she could've left it at that. But, for some reason, she wanted him to know more about her. "But I grew up there. I'm most comfortable when I'm surrounded by science. Even though much of it is theoretical, it's so much more real than anything else in my life. It's tangible. I totally understand it, too. It's nothing like the world outside the lab where everything is confusing and I always feel like I don't know the rules." And that sounded pathetic, didn't it? She took a breath and added, "The lab is safe—and unemotional, for the most part. Except when I get excited about some result or finding."

He studied her as he sipped his coffee. "What do you mean, you grew up there?"

She shrugged. "I've lived at the university since I was eight."

"Eight?" His eyes narrowed and he set his coffee cup down and leaned in. "You mean, eight years old?"

On the other hand, maybe she shouldn't have been quite so forthcoming because now he was staring at her as if she'd suddenly grown a second head. Her imagination took flight as she envisioned the headlines: *Two-headed scientist found on tropical island.* Eyewitness reports would deem it scientifically significant, but gruesome nonetheless. She and her two heads would be put in a cage and displayed at zoos around the world. And everyone would look at her the way Logan was right this minute.

Grace reeled her thoughts back to planet Earth and held her chin up high. "That's right, I was eight years old. I told you I was smart."

"Yeah, you did," he said slowly, sitting back and crossing one leg over the other. "Told me I'd run for the hills if I knew how smart you really were."

"That's right. Well…" She folded her napkin, placed it carefully on the table and stood. "I'll be going now."

He grabbed her hand. "Not so fast, Grace."

"Logan, I think we've said all there is to say."

"I don't." He yanked her down onto his lap and met her mouth with his in a hard, wet kiss that involved teeth and tongues and lots of zapping electrical currents zooming through her body. Then he pulled his mouth away and she knew she would've collapsed if he hadn't been holding her so tightly.

"I may not be Einstein," he said gruffly, his eyes narrowed on her, "but I'm not an idiot. I like you just fine. And I don't run."

Looking into his eyes, all she could think was that she was the one who probably should run—but she really didn't want to. As soon as she caught her breath, she whispered, "I'm glad."

"Good." Then he grinned. "Now let's go hunt for spores."

She had been a virgin.

Logan was still shaking his head in disbelief two days later as he sat at his office desk. He'd just received the revised set of blueprint renderings of the proposed sports center and he pulled them from the large mailing tube. Unrolling the thick stack of drawings across his conference table, he used his stapler and a hardbound dictionary to secure the ends and prevent the stack from curling up.

Grace was the last woman on earth he would've guessed would be a virgin. If he'd known, he sure as hell wouldn't have taken her to bed the other night.

But how could he have guessed? The woman had come

across as though she'd written the book on sex. She studied a species' sexual habits, for God's sake. She gave lectures to newlyweds on how to find their G-spot—or whatever they were calling it these days. Who would've guessed that Ms. Sexual Expert had been faking it this whole time?

"Hell." He wiped a hand across his jaw. He should've been pissed off with her deception, but instead he caught himself laughing out loud as he recalled her demands in bed the other night. He'd tried to be a nice guy when he discovered she'd never done the deed before. He'd been willing to stop altogether, or at least slow down. But not Grace. She was full steam ahead. Thank God.

Logan shook away the image of Grace naked in his bed and tried hard to focus on the sports center blueprints.

He and Aidan had learned long ago that projects like the sports center would cause problems at every step. And whenever a new problem reared its ugly head, a whole new set of drawings had to be rendered. So not only had the design of the center itself changed three times now, but they'd been forced twice to completely move the site of the project. The new site was based on the latest geological survey and the environmental impact reports they'd received last month.

Logan turned to the next blueprint to study the architect's three-dimensional rendering.

Most of the problems with building a sports center on the tiny island of Alleria had to do with the geological makeup of the island itself. The beaches, the natural bay and the rocky coves were the features that brought most of the tourists here. But also, the island had been formed by an ancient volcano, now dormant, and the land around the volcano had been ravaged by ancient lava flows. Now, over one square mile of north island coastline was barren except for the scrub that managed to grow there. In contrast, much of the southern part of the island was covered in lush rain forest.

The original investors had suggested that the brothers put the sports center adjacent to the hotel and within walking distance of the edge of the rain forest. The theory was that sports enthusiasts would be able to enjoy not only the beauty of the rain forest, but also the hiking and zip-line features offered.

But early on, Logan and Aidan had nixed that location and considered canceling the entire project. Who wanted to look at or spend time at a concrete sports center when they could simply enjoy the natural beauty of the island itself? But when the brothers decided they could relocate the sports center to the north side of the island, closer to the dead zone at the foot of a dormant volcano, the project was revived and revamped.

The brothers wanted a hotel built closer to the sports center, as well. They had invited developers to the island to check out the possibilities, but none of those builders had brought the sort of entrepreneurial spirit and sensibility that Logan and Aidan envisioned for their island. But then, this past year, they'd met their Duke cousins for the first time.

Adam, Brandon and Cameron Duke owned Duke Development and after touring a few of their California properties, the Sutherland brothers had decided that the Dukes would be the perfect partners in a new boutique hotel on Alleria.

The Duke family would be arriving next weekend and Logan and Aidan had already planned an extensive private tour for them in order to show off all the special qualities that had originally attracted them to Alleria.

In fact, there were several island features that had never been advertised in the hotel brochures or on the website, such as the hot springs that bubbled in various places around the island. The ancient volcano had created thermal pockets that still provided heat to the small pools. One secluded lagoon was located in the rain forest, within hiking distance of the hotel. But the hike was treacherous enough that few hotel guests had ever ventured far enough into the forest to discover it.

Logan suddenly wondered if the scientist in Grace would enjoy exploring the hot springs. Logan grinned, knowing the scientist in *him* would definitely enjoy exploring her naked body as it soaked up the heat.

"Damn," he muttered. It was getting impossible to concentrate on work as the thought of Grace crossed his mind again. She was definitely unlike any virgin he'd ever known before—not that he'd known all that many. Frankly, he tried to avoid virgins whenever possible. They were just too much damn responsibility. After all, if he somehow ruined a woman's first sexual experience, it would traumatize her for the rest of her life and leave a black cloud over her memory of him and all other men on the planet. Who needed that kind of pressure? Not Logan.

Grace didn't seem at all traumatized, he thought, then chuckled. Far from it. In fact, Logan had been blown away by her natural passion and enthusiasm for trying new things. He had originally planned to walk her back to her hotel room later that night; but, the truth was, he hadn't wanted to let her go. The feel of her in his arms, the soft sigh of her breath as she drifted into sleep. The woman got to him on levels he hadn't even been aware of.

They'd spent every night since then together.

He couldn't get enough of her and damned if he knew what to make of that.

The only thing that concerned Logan was that once his brother and their corporate staff returned to Alleria, he was a little uncertain about how he and Grace would arrange to spend time together. Getting their latest project up and running was going to keep both Logan and Aidan busy.

But, hell, maybe it wouldn't be an issue; his need for Grace might fade by then. It would certainly fade eventually. It always did. And, of course, sooner or later, she would have to go home. And that would be the end of it.

But that didn't matter right now. For now, he wanted her in his bed at night. Once Aidan was back, Logan and Grace would simply have to be as discreet as possible. After all, he didn't need his brother tormenting him about sleeping with the staff. On the other hand, Grace wasn't really part of the staff anyway, considering the fact that she'd arrived on the island under false pretenses. So it wasn't a problem, was it?

Yeah, that was his story and he was sticking to it.

"I still can't believe you've never been sailing before," Logan said as he held Grace's hand and helped her aboard the sailboat.

"The closest I ever got was when I very young and went fishing with my father."

Logan watched her glance around and take everything in. "How'd that go for you?"

She stepped up next to the mast and studied the rigging and hardware. She seemed to be weighing her words before she finally gazed at him and spoke. "I spent most of the time calculating the velocity of the wind versus the barometric pressure, then trying to angle my fishing line in the direction I'd theorized would produce more biting fish."

Logan laughed as he hauled the large picnic basket on board, then led the way down into the cabin. The thirty-foot Catalina sailboat belonged to Logan and Aidan and they'd had some great adventures—and some awesome parties—sailing around the Caribbean together. But with business obligations and scheduling problems, it had been a few months since Logan had taken the boat out.

Grace followed him down and glanced around the sleek main cabin. "It's so nice down here."

"Yeah, it's a cool design," he said, strapping the picnic basket under the galley table.

"So did you catch any fish?" he asked.

"Yes, I caught twelve," Grace admitted, frowning.

"Twelve fish for a little kid is a pretty good haul," he said, flashing her a grin. "How'd your dad do?"

She made a face. "He didn't have much luck. He told me I scared the fish away."

Logan was taken aback. "Hardly sounds fair."

"It wasn't his fault," she said quickly. "I talked a lot. I guess it freaked him out sometimes."

"What do you mean?" He climbed the ladder back up to the deck, then turned and gave her a hand up.

"I was such a pain," she said with a rueful laugh. "I seemed to know so much about everything, except I didn't know enough to shut up once in a while. Little kids like to talk, you know? But my parents didn't seem to have a clue what I was talking about. I intimidated both of them."

She said it lightly, but Logan could see the hurt in her eyes. He could relate to the pain she must still be suffering from her parents' inability to love and understand their child.

"I thought parents love it when their kids are smart." He tossed her a life jacket and she slipped it on over her tank top. "Their reaction doesn't sound right."

She sighed. "When I was five years old, my cat broke her leg and I set it in a plaster cast. My parents took the cat to the vet to have it x-rayed and he said it was a picture-perfect set."

Logan laughed. "Wow, they must've been proud of you."

"Oh, no, that scared them to death."

"I can't believe that. I mean, there are plenty worse things you could've done. At least you used your power for good."

"I tried," Grace said, laughing, then sobered. "My parents used to say that I belonged to the world. I think it was their excuse to get me out of the house because they didn't know how to deal with me."

"You don't seem all that difficult to deal with."

She smiled and stared out at the water, but Logan had a feeling her thoughts were a few thousand miles away. After a moment, she turned and looked at him. "I've never admitted this to anyone, but when they told me I was going to go live at the university, I was scared to death. I cried and begged them not to send me away. I promised I'd behave better, but they insisted that it wasn't about my behavior. It was about me having this great opportunity. That was how they justified it, I guess, by telling themselves they were doing it for me. But they looked so relieved and happy about their decision, I knew they'd simply given up on me. So I let them think I was excited to be going."

"Sounds like you were the grown-up in that house."

"Maybe."

"I'm so sorry."

She shook her head and waved his words away. "No, I'm sorry. Nobody likes a whiner."

"Grace." He sat down, took her hand in his and said quietly, "Don't apologize. Tell me what it was like for you at school."

She smiled. "You don't want to hear all that melo-drama."

"Tell me."

"Okay," she said, and took a deep breath. "At first it was awful. I was afraid every day, and I was so lonely. I had no friends my own age and everyone looked at me like I was an alien or something."

"Did you tell your parents?"

"Oh, no," she said quickly. "I knew they didn't want to hear anything bad. But it turned out okay. I loved work-ing in the laboratory, and, slowly but surely, the university became my life. It's where I belong."

She gazed up at him and tried to smile. "I guess I sound pretty weird, don't I?"

Logan shrugged. "Who isn't weird?"

She beamed at him and squeezed his hand. "That's so nice of you to say."

"Hey, it's true. And trust me, I'm not that nice." He stood and stepped onto the pier to untie the rope, then shoved the boat off and jumped back onto the deck. "Just watch me turn into Captain Bligh."

Saluting, she said, "Aye aye, Captain."

Logan used engine power to steer the boat through the small marina and out into the bay, explaining the basics of sailing to Grace and assigning her certain duties. As soon as they cleared the last pier, he unfurled the sails and they headed for open water.

It had taken every ounce of willpower he had to stay calm as Grace talked about her parents. He couldn't imag-ine growing up in a house like that. Hell, his own mother had walked out when he was seven, but at least he and his brother had always had their father. Dad had been their biggest champion and always showed them nothing but love and support, even when they behaved badly.

But Grace's parents? Sounded like all they'd shown her was contempt. They'd never supported her at all. In fact, it sounded like they might've tried to stifle her constant search for knowledge; but, knowing Grace, she probably couldn't be stifled.

So her parents couldn't handle it and they shipped her off to some university where she'd been put to work from the age of eight, conducting research and writing papers that would bring acclaim and new funding for the university. But it sounded like she'd never been allowed to have a life outside of the school. She'd certainly never had a boyfriend, or she wouldn't have still been a virgin. On the other hand, she didn't seem unhappy with her life. In fact, she seemed happy, loving, well-adjusted. She got along great with everyone at the resort. So maybe he just needed to stop worrying about it.

"Ready to come about," he shouted, and watched Grace scramble to get out of the way of the boom, then pull the mainsheet taut as he'd showed her.

"Good job, mate," he called out.

She laughed. "Thanks, Captain."

Once the boat was on course, Grace moved aft and sat with him on the small padded bench where he showed her how to steer and steady the wheel.

"You're a natural," he said after Grace had been steering the boat for a few minutes.

"I'm just a good student," she said, smiling as she gazed up at the full sail, resplendent against the blue tropical sky.

Logan had to agree. Hell, maybe she really had been better off at school than at home with her parents. Sounded to Logan like they were the real oddballs, not Grace.

Yes, she was really smart, but she was also funny and

sweet. She had a great attitude and enjoyed learning new things. She'd taken to the cocktail waitressing gig as well as any of the other waiters on staff. Okay, she still got a lot of assistance from the others, but that was because they all liked her and didn't want to see her get fired.

He still had to laugh whenever he thought back to their first conversation about the spores. She'd been so adamant about staying on the island, and now he was glad she had. Not that it mattered, of course. She would leave eventually. Logan figured the timing would be just right for him to move on to the next woman anyway. That's how it had always been and it would keep on going that way. Women were a plentiful commodity. And as he and Aidan had always said, the more the merrier.

For now, though, for as long as it lasted, he was more than satisfied to spend his time with Grace.

"It's so beautiful," she said, pointing to the coast.

"Yeah, it is," Logan murmured, then realized he wasn't even looking at the shoreline.

"This chicken salad is delicious," Grace said after taking her first bite.

"The kitchen does a great job with picnics and box lunches," Logan said, as he spooned more coleslaw onto his plate.

They'd dropped anchor in a small deserted inlet a mile beyond the picturesque port town of Tierra del Alleria, and Grace and Logan had unpacked the picnic basket the hotel kitchen had prepared. Along with chicken salad sandwiches, there was orzo salad and Asian-style coleslaw. It was simple food expertly prepared, and Grace's mouth was watering by the time she'd filled her plate. The kitchen staff had also tucked a half bottle of crisp white wine into the basket, along with brownies for dessert.

They ate and talked, and Grace felt a little tug at her heart as she replayed Logan's earlier words when he'd defended her against her parents. Grace no longer blamed her parents for anything they'd done, but it still gave her a warm feeling to know that Logan was on her side.

He and Dee were the first people she'd ever shared her background with, outside the university, and they had both rushed to support her unconditionally. Nobody in her life had ever done that for her before and she felt so much love for them because of it. And of course she'd used the word *love* in the friendliest sense possible. Nothing more. Good grief, she'd known these people for less than two weeks. And yet, she had to admit she felt closer to Logan and Dee and Joey and Clive and some of the others, than she did to the lab colleagues she'd known for years. And what did that say about her life up to now?

"Everything okay, Grace?" Logan asked, rubbing her knee gently. "You look a little anxious all of a sudden."

She gazed at him with what she hoped was a carefree smile. "I'm fine. Wonderful. I was just, um, a little worried that we'll never finish all this food."

He took another big bite of his sandwich and grinned at her. "That's never been a big problem for me."

They napped in the shade of the mainsail, then made love below deck in the well-appointed, mahogany-lined forward cabin where a cool breeze wafted through the open brass portholes. Grace had enjoyed exploring the cleverly arranged space, but all those fun design details drifted into the ether as Grace lost herself in the exquisite sensation of having Logan sheathed inside her.

Pleasure built as he drove into her again. They gazed at each other and Logan's mouth curved in a smile of satisfaction that indicated pure male approval. Then his face shifted, his jaw tightened, his eyes squeezed closed as his breath grew ragged and passion rose to a fever pitch. His murmured endearments awakened her innermost desires and Grace's heart beat even faster as every nerve ending inside her was stretched to the limit. Then in an instant, they all flew free in an explosion of joy more colorful than any Fourth of July celebration she'd ever experienced.

Seconds later, waves of tension rippled through him and he cried out her name, then joined her in this place that was beyond anywhere she'd ever been before.

A while later, he gathered her in his arms and dozed for a time. His pounding heart grew quiet and steady against her chest and she felt completely cherished for the first time in her life. If they never left the boat again, she knew she could be perfectly happy here. Then her eyes fluttered open and she gazed up at his expression. Maybe she was dreaming, but she would've sworn she was looking into the face of serenity, pure and simple.

And that's when she knew she was in big trouble.

It was early afternoon the following day when Grace glanced around at the fertile hillside of palm trees and couldn't believe her amazing good luck. Fumbling in her bag for her forceps, she kept her focus on the profusion of spore-rich fronds she'd just discovered. The groupings looked slightly thicker and darker than the others down in the palmetto grove. Was that due simply to the lack of direct sunlight on the hill or were these new spores a different subspecies? Would these more prolific creatures provide even more insight into the scientific puzzle she was on the verge of solving? She could only hope and pray that they would.

She'd spent the morning collecting samples from the palmetto trees. Then, on a hunch, she'd walked a few hundred yards along the trail that led into the rain forest, stopping when she reached a fork. Instead of the wider trail she'd taken before, she chose the narrow, less worn path that clung to the side of the rugged green hill and meandered even farther into the vast canopy of verdant trees, thick vines and wild green ferns.

It was hot and close, with sunlight only managing to peek through the heavy trees occasionally. The thick scents of the rain forest wrapped themselves around her and she smiled despite the sweat she felt rolling along her spine.

The path continued climbing up and around one hill to another area of the forest where she found more palm trees growing in scattered profusion up and down the hillside. She stopped to study the fronds at the base of one tree that grew close enough to the path, since she didn't dare veer off in her lightweight sandals. Next time she decided to hike into the hills, she would wear appropriate shoes.

After collecting as many spores as her forceps would grab, she stacked her petri dishes in her bag and looked around at her surroundings.

With a short laugh, she realized that after walking for at least an hour, she'd barely risen thirty or forty feet above the forest floor. But the view was incomparable anyway. From here she could see a slice of coastline in the distance. Unlike the calm, protected waters of Logan's bay, there were waves swelling and tumbling onto that faraway beach. Did Logan ever go surfing there?

She turned and stared at the tops of the trees and felt tears sting her eyes. That's when she hugged herself, knowing she'd never seen a view more exotically beautiful in her life. After a few minutes, she pulled out her smartphone and took some pictures, despite knowing they could never convey the true colors and natural splendor of the real thing. That was okay. The photos would at least provide a reminder to Grace that she had, indeed, stood in this place once upon a time.

A movement caught her eye and she glanced to the nearest hill across the expanse of trees. A narrow rush of water fell over rocks and shrubs on its way down the hill and formed a waterfall that splashed into a small, secluded pool at the base.

Surrounded by thick plants and greenery, the tiny pool wasn't visible at first. But now she could barely wait to see it up close. She wondered if Logan knew it was here. Then she wondered if he would come back here with her. She shivered at the thought of the two of them frolicking in their own private lagoon.

Her next thought caused her to shiver again, and not in a good way. Were there alligators? Snakes? She would have to find out for certain before she dared step foot in the water.

"What would paradise be without a snake?" she muttered aloud, and shivered all over again. But it was too lovely a day to be harboring sucky thoughts of reptiles, so with a mental shove, she rid her mind of all images of slithery creatures. Instead, she went with the much more pleasant daydream of lazing the day away with Logan in their own private rain forest swimming pool. As she picked up her kit and headed out of the forest, she smiled in anticipation.

Seven

Logan stood beside the limousine and watched Aidan jog down the stairs of the brothers' Gulfstream G650 jet before strolling across the tarmac. He was followed closely by their Senior VP, Eleanor, and two corporate staffers as a crew of airport workers began unloading luggage from the plane onto a cart.

"Welcome home, bro," Logan said, and grabbed his brother in a bear hug. Then he shook hands with Eleanor and the two staffers. "You all did a great job in New York. Thanks."

They all piled into the limo and while they waited for their luggage to be loaded into the trunk, Logan passed around bottles of beer to anyone who wanted one. He knew he did. He'd spent the past two hours dealing with Pierre, his irate hotel manager, and the entire housekeeping staff, who were in various stages of tears and anguish after Pierre had reamed them for stealing from a hotel guest.

Nobody had confessed and Pierre was on the verge of firing every one of them. But armed combat was unexpectedly averted when the hotel guest called Logan's office to announce that, oops, she'd found her diamond necklace after all, in another handbag she'd forgotten she brought.

Pierre was still simmering and the staff were all nursing grudges that would eventually fade. Pierre tended to hit pretty high on the drama meter, but he was also savvy enough to make it up to the staffers for insinuating there was a thief among them. They were all used to Pierre's over-the-top reactions, but the fact that he cared so very much about the guests' safety and comfort was what made him an excellent manager.

Still, that was the last time Logan would ever make the mistake of casually asking the hotel manager how things were going.

After the short drive back to the hotel, Logan and Aidan waved off the staffers and headed for Aidan's suite.

While his brother changed from a business suit into a pair of cargo shorts and a T-shirt, Logan pulled two more bottles of beer out of the refrigerator, opened them and handed one to his brother.

"Thanks," Aidan said, and took a long drink. "Damn, feels like I've been gone a month."

Logan sat in an overstuffed chair and rested the beer bottle on his knee. "And to me, it's as if you'd barely left."

"Ah, feel the love," Aidan said, laughing. The two brothers grinned at each other, staring into identical blue eyes that reflected the exact same image back at them.

They had grown up so identical that no one besides their father had ever been able to tell them apart. Even close friends and family members, people who should've been able to tell the difference, couldn't. Their mother, for instance, had always mixed them up, from the time they were born. But then, she'd never really bothered to get to know them. And when she disappeared when the twins were seven, no one was too surprised.

Ancient history, Logan thought, and shook off the grim memory. Aidan wanted an update on anything new that was happening at the hotel and Logan brought him up to date on each department.

As he spoke about the latest housekeeping kerfuffle and filled his brother in on new staffing and such, Aidan unpacked. He made several piles of laundry on the bed, then put in a call to housekeeping.

"Tomorrow after the conference call, we need to finalize the Dukes' visit," Logan said as soon as Aidan was off the phone.

"Good thinking." Aidan found his briefcase and pulled out a thick, leather-bound notepad. "I've made some notes."

Logan still couldn't quite believe he and his brother had never met their Duke cousins until this past year. Adam, Brandon and Cameron Duke were the adopted sons of Sally Duke, who was the widow of the twins' father's brother, William.

Logan grinned. The convoluted nature of their relationship confused him sometimes, too.

But a year ago, Logan's father, Tom, had received a call out of the blue from Sally Duke, explaining the connection.

Brothers William and Tom had lost their parents in a car crash and been sent to live in an orphanage in San Francisco for a few years until William was adopted. In those days, there was no concern for keeping siblings together, so the boys never saw each other again.

Once he was old enough, William tried to contact the orphanage to find his brother, but the place had burned to the ground five years earlier and all the records had been lost.

Sally had picked up the lost trail after William died and spent years trying to track down Tom. Thanks to the miracle of internet search engines, she finally found him, along with his two boys who were now grown men. Sally had arranged for a family reunion and now they all tried to get together as often as possible. And it seemed to Logan that their father might've developed a bit of a crush on Sally.

Since the Duke brothers built hotels, it had been a natural move for Logan and Aidan to eventually invite them to Alleria to see if they might be interested in expanding their empire to the Caribbean.

They'd be here next weekend, and Logan and Aidan intended to pull out all the stops and show them the best that Alleria had to offer. And thinking about that, Logan was reminded that he really needed to show Grace the hot springs in the rain forest.

Putting thoughts of a wet, naked Grace out of his mind, Logan watched his brother move around the room putting his things away. In that moment, Logan realized that a part of him felt much more relaxed now that Aidan was back on the island. It was almost as if he'd been missing a body part or something. It was no big deal, just another weird twin phenomenon he and Aidan had laughed about their entire lives.

"You want to go for Mexican food?" Aidan asked.

"How'd you know?"

Aidan just grinned as he used his foot to straighten the line of shoes in his closet.

Logan lined his shoes like that, too, he thought, and added the quirk to the list of oddities that went along with being a twin. Although, watching Aidan go down the line of shoes again, nudging them minutely, he wondered if this particular quirk wasn't more like a case of mutual OCD.

He finished his beer and tossed the empty bottle into the recycling can. "Let's go."

After returning from the rain forest, Grace had tried to track down Logan to tell him about the temptingly secluded pool she'd seen and what she'd like to do about it with him. But one of the clerks had told her he'd gone to the airport to pick up his brother, so she went to her room instead and had been studying spores ever since.

At least, she'd tried to study the spores when thoughts of Logan weren't interfering. She wondered if she would see him in the lounge tonight. Would he introduce her to his brother, Aidan? Would Aidan like her? She hoped so. She knew that the two men were twins. Everyone on the staff talked about them, especially the women. Apparently, it was impossible to tell them apart.

That's when another thought suddenly interfered: How would Grace know which one was Logan? Would she embarrass herself in front of his brother?

She couldn't imagine not being able to tell the difference between the man she'd spent so many hours laughing and talking and making love with, and his brother. What kind of woman would that make her?

She couldn't wrap her mind around that possibility, so she forced herself to concentrate on her work. She'd studied slide after slide of the new spores and under the microscope, these new batches appeared to have the exact same qualities as the original group. But time—and her ultrapowerful electron microscope back in the laboratory—would tell.

She jolted when the buzzer on her travel alarm went off. She pressed the off button, then closed up her notepad and began to prepare to take a hot shower before heading out to her evening job in the cocktail lounge.

Removing her clothes, she folded them on top of her bed, then walked into the bathroom. A sudden image of Logan standing in the shower with her, his broad chest glistening with soapy water, brought a shiver to her spine and a smile to her face as she waited for the water to get hot.

"At this rate, you'll need a *cold* shower," she told her reflection in the rapidly fogging mirror, then stepped into the shower stall.

As she washed and rinsed her hair, Grace's thoughts drifted back to Logan's reaction at finding out how smart she was. Most men she'd known would've brushed her off. For goodness' sake, if she was being honest about it, even her own father and mother had brushed her off. But Logan seemed to enjoy the fact that she was knowledgeable, that she paid attention and enjoyed learning new things. It was heartening that he seemed to like her and to want her to stay with him, because the feeling was mutual. She'd never wanted anything quite as badly as she wanted him. Even temporarily, which was all she could really hope for anyway.

She'd given up trying to lecture herself on falling in love with him since she was pretty sure it was too late. Maybe she should've tried a little harder; because, after all, in case she needed to be reminded, she really couldn't be trusted when it came to her feelings for men. Remember Walter.

But as she rinsed her hair one last time, she realized that she couldn't exactly recall Walter's face. How odd was that? It would be wonderful if Walter and his face were truly just a vague memory now. If she was lucky, she would never have to see the man again.

Logan was another matter altogether. His face was etched in her memory so clearly, she was pretty certain she would never forget him. Still, she thought it might be nice to ask Dee to take a surreptitious photograph of Grace standing next to Logan. It would be lovely to have something to look at and remember him by. But even if she couldn't get a picture, she would never forget his face. Or his body. Or his voice. Or his kiss.

She really would need that cold shower at this rate.

Turning off the water, she grabbed a towel and dried off. She couldn't help it if her thoughts continually turned to Logan. He was simply the loveliest man she'd ever known and part of her wished, foolishly, that she would never have to leave Alleria.

Her more practical mind argued that nothing lasted forever. Even if she stayed on the island, Logan might very well grow tired of her. And what would happen then? Would he fire her? Or would he just make it so impossible for her to be happy here that she would end up leaving anyway?

That thought was such an unhappy one that it left an achy feeling in her chest. She absently rubbed her sternum to ease the pain as she told herself firmly that it was better all the way around to leave when she planned. Before Logan began to look at her with boredom, or, worse... irritation in his eyes.

Shaking off the heaviness around her heart, she applied a touch of mascara and lip gloss, then walked over to the dresser and pulled out the bikini and sarong that made up her uniform. And since she was standing by the dresser anyway, she checked the microscope slide again.

Then she checked it one more time.

"That can't be right," she said. She rechecked her notes. Had she made a mistake in notating the circumference around the edges of the new spore gathering? She didn't think she had, so she looked back at the slide. Then her notes.

Either she was seeing things, or the spores were replicating at least three times faster than the ones back in the lab at the university. If it was true, if she wasn't hallucinating, then these new spores from the top of the rain forest were stronger, faster and more efficient than any she'd found before.

She did a little happy dance. It was an unexpected breakthrough, a development she couldn't have foreseen in a million years. She should've been itching to get back to the laboratory and the more precise equipment she could use to measure things more accurately. But all she wanted to do was track down Logan and share her news with him. After all, it was Logan who'd allowed her to stay on the island, thus providing her with the opportunity to find these spores and accelerate her experimentation. She thought it only fair that she thank him for that.

Her face heated up as she considered the many inventive ways she could show him how grateful she was.

Lively mariachi music floated out to the patio of Casa Del Puerto, where Aidan and Logan sat enjoying the three items the restaurant was most famous for: fajitas, homemade tortillas and an unsurpassed view of the picturesque harbor of Tierra del Alleria. The margaritas weren't bad, either.

The quaint Tierra marina was where Logan and Aidan had first docked their boat on their original visit to Alleria. They'd needed to have their boat overhauled and intended to stay a week while the work was done. It had never crossed their minds to buy land here, least of all the entire island.

But when the week was over and their sailboat was ready, they decided to stay another week, slowly falling in love with the sleepy harbor town, its charming residents, miles of white-sand beaches and an amazing rain forest.

They learned during that visit that one of the smaller cruise lines featuring sailing yachts had recently negotiated to add Tierra to its itinerary. The brothers recognized that the island was on its way to becoming a key Caribbean destination within a few years. They made an appointment with the major landowner on the island about buying property and that's when they found out that the island itself was up for sale.

The brothers had survived on their gut instincts long enough to have a sixth sense for knowing when something sounded right. They spoke to their fledgling investor group and within two months they were the proud owners of their very own Caribbean island. Once the ink on the contracts was dry, the first order of business had been the design and construction of a luxury resort that would truly establish Alleria as a premier destination for the most discerning travelers in the world.

Now, seven years later, that goal had been met, and the hotel also served as the corporate headquarters for all the Sutherland enterprises. They had offices in New York and San Francisco, as well; but Alleria was the home as well as the heart of their operations.

Logan smeared a fresh tortilla with a hearty spoonful of refried beans and a healthy dab of hot sauce, then wrapped it up and bit into a little taste of heaven.

Aidan sat back in his chair, patting his stomach. "That's it for me."

"I'll be done after this last bite," Logan admitted.

"Good," Aidan said. "Then we can talk."

"We've been talking all night," Logan said, gazing at his brother with suspicion as he took a sip of his drink.

"Yeah, but, funny thing, this subject never came up," Aidan said, stretching his legs out to the side of the table. "You see, Ellie was talking to Serena day before yesterday and she mentioned a certain new cocktail waitress you've been spending time with."

It was a good thing Logan had swallowed his margarita or he would've spewed it all over the table. And that would've been a waste of good alcohol. His eyes narrowed on his brother. "So now you're listening to employee gossip?"

Aidan shrugged. "When the source of the gossip comes from the management level, I'm willing to pay attention."

Just his luck, Logan thought. Serena was manager of catering which included the cocktail lounge and the various restaurants throughout the hotel. And Ellie was one of her best friends. "So what's the problem?"

"Dude, you're dating an employee?" Aidan said. "Are you out of your mind?"

"She's not really an employee."

Aidan snorted. "Interesting that you'd say that since she's on the payroll. And, according to Serena, she actually does work in the cocktail lounge. Sounds like an employee to me."

"*Temporary* employee," Logan said.

One wary eyebrow shot up. "What's that supposed to mean?"

Logan pushed his plate away and sat back in his chair. It had only been a matter of time before the subject of Grace came up, so he figured he'd better deal with it here and now and put a stop to the gossip.

He explained to Aidan how the new cocktail waitress had come to the island under false pretenses and how he'd fired her, then spelled out the circumstances under which he'd allowed her to stay on.

"Okay." Aidan nodded agreeably. "I get how she arrived and I'm willing to go along with her staying, if you think it's justified."

"It is."

"But I haven't heard how all that turned into you *dating* her."

"Because she's…"

Aidan leaned forward. "Sorry? I didn't catch that. What'd you say?"

Logan scowled. "None of your damn business."

"Ah." Aidan nodded, his mouth twisting in a grin. "So she's hot."

"Shut up."

Aidan chuckled. "I'll take that as a yes." His smile faded and he said, "Look, when we talked the other day, I heard something in your voice I don't remember hearing before. So sue me for being concerned."

"Nothing to be concerned about."

Aidan studied him for another long moment. "I'm not convinced."

"Tough. It doesn't matter anyway. Grace doesn't expect anything from me but great sex. Besides, she'll only be here for another few weeks and then she's leaving."

"You sure she's leaving?"

"Yeah. She's leaving." Saying the words aloud brought a frown to Logan's face. Strange, but he didn't want her to leave just yet. He was still having a good time with her. Why break it off when they were having a good time?

Okay, yeah, Grace was unlike any woman he'd ever known; so, yeah, he could admit he was, well, sort of captivated by her. Who wouldn't be? She was a beautiful woman with an amazing brain and an even more incredible heart. He liked her.

But that's all this was. It wasn't like he *cared* for her. He didn't *care* for any woman. It was just that she was… unique. Funny. Smart. And sexy as hell. They'd been having fun together and that would continue for as long as it lasted. Then she'd go home. Things would be over between them and that would be the end of it. No harm, no foul.

But Aidan had been watching him carefully and now he shook his head in disgust. "Crap, man. You're falling for her."

"What?" Shocked at the idea, Logan snorted a laugh. "That's a load of bull. I'm not falling for her."

"Yeah, you are."

Irritated by his brother's scrutiny, Logan grabbed his margarita and chugged it down. "How stupid do you think I am? I haven't forgotten that she lied and manipulated her way onto the island, so why on earth would I ever trust her, let alone fall for her? So let it go."

"You're sleeping with her."

"So what?"

"You of all people should know how women are." Aidan sat forward with his elbows resting on his knees and shook his head. "Once you're sleeping with them, they think they've got you by the balls. And, damn it, what do you really know about this woman? She comes here under false pretenses with this bizarre story about spores, which is damn strange to begin with, by the way. I mean, really. Spores? Is she into biological warfare or something?"

"They're good spores," Logan muttered.

"Oh, I feel so much better, thanks." Aidan shook his head. "So, anyway, once this woman gets here, she latches onto you faster than a tic on a hound dog and now you're falling for her. How did that happen?"

"I'm not falling for her," Logan repeated through gritted teeth. "It's nothing like that. And seriously? Tic on a hound dog?"

"I just spent two days on the phone with Tex," Aidan said with a shrug. "I've gone country."

"Good to know."

"Okay, now look," Aidan said slowly. "I understand if you have feelings for this girl."

"You don't understand squat."

"No really, there's nothing wrong with that."

"You're completely off base," Logan said. "Just drop it."

But Aidan was on a roll. "I'll drop it as soon as you hear me out. Has it occurred to you that she's after your money?"

Logan barked out a laugh, then laughed harder at the very idea. Grace? A gold digger? Come on. "You're so wrong it's not funny." He relaxed in his chair. "Look, you don't know her, so I'll give you a pass on that. But trust me, it's impossible. She's not like that. Her whole world is wrapped up in her research. You should see her room. She's got a microscope and all this equipment and reams of notes. There's no way she's…"

Aidan continued watching him as Logan mentally replayed a few conversations he'd had with Grace.

"Well?"

Logan shook his head with firm resolve. "Nope. Absolutely not."

"I think you're not looking at her from an objective point of view."

"Duh." Logan glared at his brother. "Just because I'm not being objective doesn't mean I'm some naive idiot, either."

"Fine. Prove it to me, then."

"Yeah? How?"

Aidan smiled and his eyebrows lifted high on his forehead. "Easy enough. I say we need to pull the Switch."

Logan leaned forward and pounded the table with his fist. "No way. Don't even think about it."

Over the years, the brothers had occasionally pulled the Switch on women, usually just for fun or when one of the brothers seemed to be getting too serious about a woman. Aidan had always called it a test, implemented merely to see if a woman was paying attention to which brother was which.

The last time they'd employed the Switch was when Logan suspected that his wife, Tanya, was being less than faithful to their marriage vows. He'd asked Aidan to pull the Switch on her. Tanya didn't pass the test.

"Fine," Aidan said, holding up his hands in surrender. "You win. But I still want to meet her. Let's just swing by the lounge on the way back so you can introduce me to her."

"You're not meeting her."

"You know how stupid you sound?"

Logan clenched his teeth together, then blew out a heavy sigh. "Yeah, I'm pretty clear on that. Fine, we'll swing by, I'll introduce you, you'll say hello, then you'll shut up and leave."

Aidan grinned. "You're not doing yourself any favors here."

"I know," Logan muttered. What was wrong with him? It was no big deal if Aidan met Grace. But there was no way he'd allow his brother to pull the Switch on her.

"So what's her name?"

He hesitated, but his brother's expression switched to

one of such abject *pity,* he finally blurted, "Grace. Her name's Grace."

Aidan smile in satisfaction. "Pretty name. Where's she from?"

Logan rolled his eyes. "Minnesota."

"Ah, a farm girl," his brother murmured.

"No, a scientist," Logan said flatly.

"Oh, right, the spores. Tell me more."

"They're rare spores only found on Alleria. Grace is studying their replication patterns in hope of curing diseases and saving lives someday."

"No kidding?"

"Yeah."

Aidan folded his arms across his chest. "Seems to me you know a hell of a lot about spores all of a sudden."

"Yeah, I do," Logan said, taking a long sip of his drink. "We've got miracle spores on Alleria and I'm swollen with pride over that."

Aidan choked on a laugh. "Damn, it's good to be home."

"I've missed you, too," Logan said dryly.

"Right." Aidan grinned. "You sure you don't want to reconsider the Switch? It's always worked for us before. And wouldn't you rather know the truth for sure?"

Pissed off now, Logan flopped back in his chair. Knowledge was power, even when the truth sucked. Besides, he had more than a sneaking feeling that Aidan would carry out the Switch whether Logan approved or not. And there was the added fact that once Aidan had met Grace and seen how sincere and real she was, he'd back off and leave Logan to enjoy her for the short amount of time he had with her.

"Fine," he said, lifting his margarita glass in a toast.

"Give it your best shot. But if you hurt her, I'll have to kill you."

"Fair enough," Aidan said with a laugh, and called for the check.

Eight

"Hey, babe," he said from close behind her, his tone warm and intimate. "I missed you last night."

Grace whipped around and laughed with joy. "Oh, Logan, I missed you, too. I'm so happy to…" Her voice faded and she smiled curiously as she studied him more carefully.

He'd called her late last night after her shift had ended to let her know he couldn't see her. He'd sounded as disappointed as she'd felt, so Grace hadn't worried too much that he was losing interest or whatever equally foolish scenario she could've dreamed up in the moment.

And now, just knowing that he'd come looking for her this morning and that he knew her well enough to know she'd be walking on the beach toward the palmetto grove, was sweetly heartening.

Would it be too outrageous if she dragged him off to

the shelter of the rain forest and had her way with him? Her body tingled at the thought.

But…something was wrong. Logan wasn't… Hmm. She gazed at him, trying to figure out what was different. Was it his ears? Was it…?

"Babe," he said, his handsome smile fading to a look of concern. He reached out and lightly gripped her upper arm. "Are you all right?"

Yes, she was all right, but he was…different somehow.

"Ah," Grace said slowly and her smile broadened. "You must be Aidan. Hello." She reached out and took his hand in a warm handshake. "How do you do?"

"Babe, that's crazy." He took a half step back. "I'm not—"

"I've often wondered what it would be like to be a twin, especially an identical twin. It must be fascinating to look at another person and see your own face staring back at you." She took her time and circled all the way around him, trailing her hand along his waistline as she examined his posture, the fine laugh lines around his compelling eyes, the shape of his head, the way his chiseled jaw met his strong, square chin. All of it was so appealingly rugged. "Well, it's extraordinary, isn't it? You look exactly like Logan."

"But I *am* Logan," he insisted, scowling now.

"Oh, that's so funny," she said, laughing at his joke as she patted his arm. "I've always found the concept of twins so interesting. You two must've been able to play the best tricks on people."

"We don't play tricks," he ground out as his forehead furrowed in annoyance.

"Really? I certainly would've if I had a twin sister." She sighed at the thought. "We could have practiced smiling the same way—unless you do that anyway? Do you?

I mean, you and Logan of course. Do you instinctively do things in the same manner or was it learned behavior? You know, they do twin studies all the time and identical twins are in high demand. Have either of you ever thought of donating some time to scientific exploration?"

"Scientific…" He sounded confused.

Well, Grace was used to that kind of reaction, but not from Logan, she realized, and that made her smile even brighter.

She threaded her arm through Aidan's and they walked along the shore for a bit before she stopped and squeezed his arm enthusiastically. "You do know that identical twins come from the same egg. Of course you know that. Why wouldn't you? Oh, but what a thrill to imagine the fertile egg separating in the womb. To watch a zygote's first cellular division as it becomes two living beings. What miracle of nature triggers the split? Do you often ask yourself that question? It's incredible on every level, isn't it?"

He stared at her as if she'd sprouted antennae, but again, she was used to that.

"Grace…"

"Oh, it's all right, Aidan. I understand why you would want to play a trick on me! If I had a twin sister, I would want to test her boyfriends, too. In fact, I'm sort of thrilled that the two of you would take the time to plan this out. Makes me feel sort of special, you know?"

"You're not mad?"

"Oh, no, this is fun."

"It was my idea," he muttered.

"Of course it was." She grinned up at him. "I'm just so pleased to meet you. Logan speaks very highly of you, you know."

"He does?"

"Oh, yes."

His eyes narrowed. "Seriously, how do you know I'm not Logan?"

"What a silly question," she said, smiling. "Walk with me, Aidan."

They continued walking companionably and she gazed sideways at his powerfully built chest and muscular shoulders so clearly outlined by his T-shirt. With a sigh, Grace noted that Aidan and Logan Sutherland were simply magnificent-looking men. Staring up at Aidan's handsome face, she smiled again. It was remarkable that he was so identical to his brother, yet, somehow, so very different.

Logan had never called her "babe" before. And despite their first confrontation shortly after she'd broken all those glasses and Logan had appeared so cynical and grim, Grace could see that Aidan had an even more sardonic wit than his brother.

There was more, of course. Though their features were identical, Logan held his head differently. And it might be her imagination, but his mouth quirked a bit higher on one side when he gave her that devastating half smile. And his eyes seemed to shine more brightly. His hair, she thought, looked thicker to her. More…touchable.

And yet, none of that took away from the fact that they were both ridiculously stunning specimens of masculinity.

But Aidan continued to stare at her and his mouth twisted in puzzlement. He stopped walking finally and turned to gaze out at the water as he let go of a heavy sigh.

"Are you all right, Aidan?" she asked, clutching his arm. "You look a little flushed. It might be the heat. You should probably be wearing a hat."

"I'm…fine," he mumbled, pushing his hand through his closely cropped hair. Even their haircuts were identical. "Look, Grace, it's been great meeting you, but I've gotta get back to…you know." He waved his hand in the general direction of the hotel.

"It was so nice meeting you, too, Aidan." She stood on her tiptoes and kissed his cheek. "I hope we can talk again soon."

"Yeah. Soon." And he walked away, still shaking his head.

"Damn it, it's not funny."

But Logan threw his head back and laughed anyway. "She's priceless. She took it down to the zygotes? You gotta love that."

"It's not funny," Aidan repeated emphatically as he paced in front of Logan's wide desk. "Nobody but Dad has ever been able to tell us apart before. I don't know what it means, but it's a cause for concern."

"Grace is just more observant than most people. Cut her some slack." Logan sat back in his office chair and asked the question he'd been stupidly worrying about all morning. "So, did you like her?"

Aidan thought for a moment, then shrugged. "Yeah. She was kind of sweet. And gorgeous, of course, but you knew that already. Damn, those eyes of hers. And that hair color is amazing. Do you think it's real? Wait, I guess you would know the truth."

"That's enough."

Aidan rolled his eyes. "Dude, you're pitiful."

"I'm pitiful? You're the one making rude comments."

"Sorry. But you know, when she first turned around and saw me, she looked at me like she wanted to eat me alive—in the best possible way, just so you know." Aidan scraped his knuckles across his jaw in contemplation. "Of course, she thought I was you at the time. But within seconds she'd busted me. And after that, it was just weird to see her staring at me like I was something she might find under her microscope."

"Hey, it's your own damn fault for trying to trick her. At least she didn't smack you, even though you kind of deserved it."

"Huh," Aidan said, as he studied him. "You're taking her side. What's up with that?"

Logan chuckled. "Anyone who can cause you to flip out this much? I'm on their side."

Aidan's eyes narrowed in thought and he began to pace again. "What if she couldn't really tell us apart, but she's been watching us? You know, like maybe she stalked you this morning. You keep your window wide-open half the time. Maybe she saw you in the business suit and knew as soon as I showed up in khakis that I wasn't you."

"You know what? You're losing it."

"Yeah, maybe." Aidan sighed. "But what can I say? It was weird."

Logan laughed again. "You're an idiot."

"No, you're an idiot," Aidan said. "Because you really like her."

"I do like the way she took you down a notch."

"Yeah. I guess it was probably funny from a strictly objective point of view." Aidan stopped in midpace and turned. "But what are we going to do about her?"

"*We* aren't going to do anything about her."

"I'm only thinking of you, bro," Aidan said. "She could still be a stalker."

"The fact that Grace was too perceptive to fall for the Switch doesn't make her a stalker." Logan laughed at that ludicrous thought. "Just let it go, man."

"Okay." Aidan slumped down into the visitor's chair. "But I never thought I'd see the day when the Switch would fail me."

"It's a sad day, all right." Logan shook his head, pulled a file out of the credenza and spread it open on his desk. "We need to get this meeting started. I'll buzz Ellie to let her know we're ready to go."

"You promise there are no snakes?"

"Cross my heart." Logan grabbed her hand as the path widened and they were able to walk hand in hand. "We don't have poisonous snakes on Alleria. Yes, we have little green-and-brown snakes that eat bugs and stuff, but that's it. We have a very nonconfrontational ecosystem here on the island."

Grace's eyes widened and she laughed. "Really? Non-confrontational ecosystem? That's so impressive."

"I sound like a science geek, don't I?"

"Yes." Grace sniffled. "I'm so proud."

They both laughed as Logan grabbed her and swung her into his arms. "Come on."

Clouds flitted across the blue sky as they followed the narrowing path that switched back and forth around the hills through the forested area. They found the hot springs twenty minutes later, after cutting their way through the thick fronds and giant leaves of the banana trees that grew close to the source of the thermal heat.

They stopped at the edge of a small pool that had been carved over the centuries into the base of the rock-covered hill. Hot bubbles rose to the surface from the thermal pockets while cool water cascaded down over smooth boulders and splashed into the clear water.

Thick vegetation grew in abundance under the canopy of the rain forest, assuring them of utter privacy.

"It's like our own private paradise," she said, and gazed at him. "Can we go in?"

"Absolutely." Logan stripped off his T-shirt, then pointed

up at the waterfall. "Just so you know, the water coming from the hill is much cooler than the springs itself, so don't be shocked to find pockets of cold mixed in with the hot once you step in."

"So the cold spots aren't from the alligators swishing their tails underwater?"

He bit back a grin. "No alligators."

"I'm trusting you," she said, shaking her finger at him. "I have a deep-seated fear of alligators."

"You and me both, sweetheart." Logan stepped to the edge of the pool. "And I swear the only predatory beasts are the small lizards who only want to sun themselves down in the flatlands."

"Okay. Is the water shallow?" she asked.

"No, it's more like five or six feet deep."

She slipped out of her hiking shorts, then adjusted the strap of her bathing suit where it wrapped around her neck.

Logan, being a mere human, slid his gaze down to her breasts, where the strap adjustment caused them both to lift in a sensual movement that was surely meant to search and destroy every last one of his brain cells.

When her nipples suddenly perked up at his scrutiny, he grinned. Always nice to know the attraction wasn't one-sided.

With little blood left to nourish his brain, Logan was helpless to prevent his gaze from traveling farther down her well-shaped torso, taking in her nicely toned stomach, perfectly rounded hips and long, lovely legs.

When he finally realized that she was watching him as he took his little side trip, Logan forced himself to make eye contact once again.

Sure enough, Grace glared back at him with eyes narrowed and hands pressed to her hips in a mock display of insulted dignity.

"Hey, I'm just a guy," Logan said, laughing. "An uncouth clod of a guy, for sure, but still a guy."

"Have you seen enough?" she demanded to know.

"Not nearly."

Grace smiled. "Maybe you'll get a chance to see more if you behave."

"Not a chance you'll get me to behave out here."

"Well, then." Grace whipped around toward the water. "Last one in the pool is a dirty rotten protozoan."

She jumped into the pool and Logan followed her, creating a riot of waves and splashes as they surfaced. They grabbed blindly for each other and once he had her in his arms, Logan kissed her slowly, deeply, wrapping his tongue around hers as all his pent-up fervor began to unfurl.

In unspoken synchronicity, they began to peel off what little clothing they wore. Logan flung his trunks and her bikini onto the nearest rock, then, despite an aching yearning to be inside her, he turned all of his attention to first satisfying her completely. He was determined to move unhurriedly, though she was so damn tempting with her lovely breasts cresting on the surface of the water.

With both hands on her face, he kissed her again. When she swept her tongue along his lower lip in a move that was both innocent and seductive, his mind emptied of all thought but pleasure, pure and unadulterated.

He took his time with her, working his hands along the sides of her breasts, teasing her nipples to fullness, then moving down her firm stomach to the apex of her thighs where he stroked her soft folds until he heard her blissful sigh. The sweet sound brought his erection instantly to attention and he groaned with desire for her. She reached down and stroked his rigid length until he had to pull away or fall apart in her hands.

Gripping her behind, he squeezed and kneaded lightly as he moved his mouth to cover hers, kissing her long and hard as he continued to touch her all over.

"I need you, Logan," she murmured, and stretched her arms around his neck. "Please."

"I just have to do this first," he whispered, cupping her breasts in his hands, then bending to taste first one, then the other, taking his time to enjoy her soft fullness. "Now wrap your legs around me, sweetheart."

She did as he asked, her breasts pressing against his chest, driving him to madness as he eased her down onto him, then held his breath when she drew him in to the hilt.

Her eyes fluttered closed as passion overcame them both. Logan began to move inside her, thrusting faster and harder, plunging deeper, then deeper still. She cried out her pleasure as she moved with him. Her heated need threatened to drive him to completion too quickly, so he willed himself to go slowly, carefully, dragging each second out as he stroked her innermost core.

But need consumed him once more and pure instinct took over. His movements grew faster, deeper, more frantic as his body pulsated within hers. She screamed his name and moments later, he groaned in response as a wild rapture overtook him and he plunged with her over the edge.

Spent and sated, they lay sprawled on one of the smooth boulders that lined the edge of the pool.

"You're right—this is paradise," Logan said, touching her cheek with his fingers. Then he rolled up onto his elbow and leaned over to kiss her.

She stared at his long, powerful body lying next to her, aching to touch him again. She just wasn't sure she had the strength to move a muscle.

They dozed for a few minutes, then slid into the water

again. She swam toward the waterfall, needing the coolness to quench the heat she felt inside her body and out.

He came and stood behind her and let the water cool them both. He smoothed her hair back with his hands. Then she turned and he pulled her into his arms, holding her against his chest, his solid strength a counterpoint to her soft roundness. She ran her hands along his shoulders and down his back, marveling at the silky smoothness of his skin against the solid firmness of his muscles.

Paradise. Against all odds, she'd found it. And her heart stuttered, knowing it was only a matter of time before she would have to leave it forever.

Two days later, the twins' father, Tom, arrived with Sally Duke and the three Duke brothers and their wives.

The limousine picked all eight of them up at the airport and delivered them back to the hotel in time to get checked in, then meet Logan and Aidan in the cocktail lounge for drinks before dinner.

As they toasted the cousins' arrival with various cocktails and fruit drinks, Logan spied Grace working at the bar.

She should be sitting here with me and my family, he thought. The realization caused him to jolt. Had he really been thinking that? No. He brushed the thought away. Grace wasn't a part of his family. She just worked here. Yes, they were sleeping together. And, yes, he liked her. But, damn, he needed to get real.

Not that it mattered, but Aidan would never let him live it down if he ever found out what Logan had been thinking.

"You must get the cream of the crop in terms of workers," Adam said, glancing around the well-appointed, wide-open room.

"I was just thinking the same thing," his wife, Trish, said. "Your employees are all such beautiful people, and so accommodating."

Brandon's wife Kelly smiled. "And who wouldn't want to work in a tropical paradise?"

"It really is a spectacular location," Sally said, pointing toward the wide wall of windows. "I love this view."

Julia, Cameron's wife, glanced around, then directed a playful scowl at Logan. "So is everyone on your staff required to be gorgeous?"

Everyone at the table laughed, and Logan said, "I've never considered that a job requirement. But I will point out that serving cocktails and food requires the servers to be on their feet for hours while lifting heavy trays the entire time."

"You've got to have great upper-body strength for that job," Brandon said.

"Which means they're all in excellent shape to boot," Kelly said, and laughed despite her look of dismay.

"Besides being so pretty," Sally added.

Logan glanced at Aidan, then gazed around the room and realized it was true. They had a darn good-looking group of people working here. Why hadn't they ever discussed that fact? Maybe they could feature it in one of their online newsletters.

Aidan bit back a grin. "Contrary to every human resources dictate ever written, we have a very strict Pretty People policy here at the Alleria Resort."

"Yeah, right," Logan said, rolling his eyes. "He's kidding. Our Senior Vice President and most of our managers would have our heads if that were true."

"Well, the hotel is beautiful," Sally said, sipping her piña colada. "And everyone has been more than helpful."

"I'm glad," Logan said.

"I can't wait to swim in that clear turquoise water," Julia said dreamily.

"I'm starting with a massage first thing tomorrow," Sally said, then sighed. "All my beautiful grandbabies are taking a toll on my muscles."

"Oh, I'll join you," Kelly said, rubbing her neck. "I'm pretty sure my shoulder was yanked out of its socket when I lifted Robbie yesterday."

"I know what you mean, sweetie." Sally cast a wary glance at Brandon. "I'm afraid that little guy is going to grow up to be a linebacker."

Brandon grinned. "That's my boy."

"I was hoping to get a golf game in first thing," Tom said as he grabbed a chip full of guacamole.

"I'll be glad to join you," Adam said.

"Me, too," Brandon chimed in. "And Kelly's no slacker on the golf course, either."

"Massage first," Kelly said. "But I'd love to play golf the next day."

"I'll go swimming with you, baby," Cameron said, wrapping his arm around Julia's shoulder. With a smile, she closed her eyes and rested her head on his chest.

Logan felt a tug of envy at his cousins' good luck at finding three such beautiful, accomplished women to marry. He knew they each had one or two really cute kids, too. So they'd clearly never had a qualm about trusting a woman enough to marry and settle down with her. Of course, they'd grown up with Sally, who was a fantastic mom and must've provided them with a happy home despite her husband's untimely death. The Duke brothers had never known a mother's betrayal or experienced the treachery of a manipulative, lying woman.

Lucky dogs.

* * *

Logan wiped away the sweat from his eyes as he ran to the end of the peninsula and rounded the slow curve of white-blond sand. He headed back toward the hotel, his heart pounding in rhythm with his feet. He observed a few others out this morning, running or walking to the beat of the music blasting into their heads through tiny earbuds.

He tried to concentrate exclusively on his breathing, but the thought of Grace's lush, naked body still warming his bed caused his body to tighten. It had seemed like a good idea to force himself to get up and go running this morning, but now he couldn't quite figure out why.

Pacing himself, he marked time and distance as he passed the familiar landmarks of life here on Alleria. The paddle tennis courts where he and his brother took turns beating each other. The grassy pavilion where concerts were held during the high season. The tiny marina where the hotel kept a fleet of sleek catamarans for guests to rent and where the brothers docked their sailboat.

Thinking of the sailboat reminded him of Grace and their recent picnic. And her lush, naked body.

"Damn," he muttered, and tried to focus on the sound of his shoes pounding against the damp, hard-packed sand. The bay water smelled briny this morning and he wondered if the local fishermen might be reeling in more bluefish in the near future.

The colors of the sunrise were muted pink and coral and so rich it almost hurt to gaze at the swirling hues. He would never admit to a single soul that it was those colors and the island scents that brought him out here at this absurdly early hour of the morning. Exercise was simply an excuse.

"Hey, cousin," a voice called out.

Logan turned and saw Brandon Duke running toward

him and slowed his pace. "Morning, Brandon. You're up early."

"Couldn't sleep," Brandon said, then shook his head. "Don't laugh, but I miss my kid."

"I'm not laughing. That's nice to hear."

Brandon turned and headed back to the hotel with Logan. "Kelly tells me I'm crazy and that it's good to get away for a few days. But she misses him, too. I caught her staring at all of his pictures on her phone."

"How old is he now?"

"Just seven months," Brandon said. "Doesn't seem right to just leave him with the nanny, does it? But here we are."

"You got pictures?"

"Aw, jeez, don't ask. I've got a phone loaded with his photos, too. And I'm willing to bore—I mean, share them with anyone foolish enough to ask."

Logan laughed. "You're a good dad."

"Yeah," Brandon said, shaking his head in wonder. "Who would've thought."

"Well, you had a great mom growing up to show you how it's done."

"Not exactly," Brandon said, grimacing.

"What do you mean?" Logan asked.

"We all came from different screwed-up families and landed in the foster system around the same time," he explained. "Sally adopted the three of us when we were all about eight years old."

Logan stared at him. "I didn't know that."

"Yeah. Before that fateful day, I'd spent eight years living with a crack addict mother and a subhuman piece of crap I hesitate to call a father. He beat the hell out of us from the first moment I could remember. After a few hundred brutal beatings, dear old mom hit the road, leaving me alone with the monster. Luckily, a good neighbor turned him in to child services and I ended up in foster care. But I never forgot the lessons his fists taught me. Adam and Cameron had similar experiences. We're all damn lucky Sally found us."

Logan stopped walking. Troubled, he glanced around the shore, gazed at the hotel in the distance, then looked back at his cousin. "I…I don't know what to say. Last night I was thinking you and your brothers were the luckiest guys on earth for getting to grow up with a mom like Sally. I was feeling sorry for myself, comparing my life to yours. I figured you guys didn't have a care in the world. Guess I didn't know what I was thinking."

"That's okay," Brandon said. "Sally really did change everything for us. And I *am* the luckiest guy on earth. But it took a few drop kicks from Sally to get me to realize that."

"Yeah? What happened?"

"I was ready to walk away from Kelly."

Logan frowned. "But you two seem perfect for each other."

Brandon grinned as they began to walk again. "Don't get me wrong. I was crazy in love with her and she loved me, too, in spite of the fact that I was a complete knucklehead for thinking I wasn't good enough for her. My thing always was, I didn't want to get close to anyone in case I came up short, you know? Sally's the one who finally smacked some sense into me."

Logan shook his head, pulled a hand towel from his back pocket and wiped more sweat away. "So let me get this straight. You weren't going to marry Kelly because you figured your parents had screwed you up so much that you could never be a decent husband and father?"

"That about covers it."

Logan nodded grimly. He knew Brandon had spent years

in the NFL as a star quarterback, then worked in broad-
casting before joining his brothers in their multimillion-
dollar business. He defined the word *successful*. Besides
that, he was smart, had a great sense of humor and loved
his family. The guy was a virtual paragon.

But he'd grown up thinking he was all screwed up?

And now he was well-adjusted and secure enough to
admit the mistakes he'd made? Logan was starting to view
his cousin in a whole new light.

Through gritted teeth, Logan said, "Our mom walked
out on us when we were kids."

"Damn," Brandon said, shaking his head. "Some people
are just not meant to have children."

"No kidding."

"But look on the bright side." Brandon chuckled. "At
least she did you the favor of leaving you in the hands of
a great father."

"That's true." Logan hadn't thought about it from that
angle. And now he couldn't help but picture Brandon as
the kid who'd been used as a punching bag by a vicious
man who never should've been allowed to be a father.
But he'd survived. No, he'd more than survived. Brandon
had thrived. Logan couldn't help but admire the man he'd
become.

He shook his head slowly as he realized he'd completely
misjudged his cousins. He was also a little stunned to
admit that because of his mother, he'd spent most of his
life carrying a chip on his shoulder where women were
concerned. Now, after talking to Brandon, he was almost
glad she'd left them.

"Damn," he said. "I've been an idiot."

Brandon laughed and slapped his cousin's shoulder
companionably. "Welcome to my world, dude."

Nine

"It takes less than two hours to circumnavigate the island," Logan told his cousins after instructing their driver to take the main highway that looped around Alleria. "But that's with no stopping."

"We'll be making four stops, right?" Brandon said, paging through the detailed itinerary Logan's assistant had typed up.

"That's right," Aidan said. "Three possible hotel sites and the proposed sports-center site. Then we'll stop for lunch in Tierra before heading back to our hotel."

Adam put his arm around his wife, who sat next to him in the spacious limousine. "Glad you ladies decided to come with us."

"Me, too," Trish said, glancing around at the other wives. "We can get massages anytime, right? This is much more interesting."

"We like to think so," Aidan said with a grin.

"If you're on the lookout," Logan said, pointing out the window that faced the coast, "you'll be able to see water most of the time."

"Sometimes the growth gets too heavy to see through," Aidan said, "but we're still only within a few hundred yards of the shore at all times."

"That's so cool," Kelly said.

"It's a really small island," Aidan said. "But that's part of its charm."

The first two stops were brief. Everyone agreed that neither of the locations were ideal for the type of hotel that the Dukes specialized in.

"We've got one more spot to look at," Logan said as they continued driving north.

When the limo stopped a few miles later, everyone stared in hushed silence.

"It's perfect," Trish whispered before they'd even climbed out of the limousine. The driver had maneuvered the car down a narrow dirt road and pulled to a stop at the bottom of a rugged hill, inches from the edge of the sandy beach. Tropical palm trees lined the shore and swayed in the soft breeze.

Once they were out of the car and walking around, Kelly pointed in amazement at the hillside above them where flowering vines of every color, shade and variety cascaded down the fertile green surface.

"It's like a painting," she cried, then turned to Brandon. "Isn't it beautiful?"

"Fantastic," he said, pulling her close to him.

"It's incredible," Trish agreed.

Logan had always enjoyed this tranquil cove with its flowering cliffs and wondered why he hadn't brought Grace here before. Someday soon he would take her for a drive and show her the beauty of his island.

As he listened to his cousins and their wives, Logan had every confidence that the Dukes would build the perfect small hotel here that would blend in with the beauty of the land and the sea. He wondered if Grace might come back to visit sometime and see the completed project.

He quickly shook his head, wondering where that thought had come from. Once Grace left, she wouldn't be coming back to visit the island unless she needed more spores. It would be smart for him to keep that in mind.

Julia wandered closer to the water, then turned. "Can I live here?"

Cameron laughed, then said to the others, "This beach is perfect."

"It's on a slight inlet," Aidan explained, pointing to the land that extended out on both sides of the water. "So you're protected from the stronger trade winds. But you've still got more waves coming in than we have on the other side of the island. And there's a nice breeze, so you'll attract a good sailing crowd."

"As long as they bring their money along, we're happy to have them," Adam said with a laugh, always the businessman.

They spent almost an hour exploring the area. They checked the shallow cliffs for erosion and found none. The twins had already commissioned an environmental-impact study and a geological-viability assessment of the land itself. Adam asked how fast and high the tide came in and Aidan had an answer for him.

"But we don't expect you to go by our word alone," Aidan added. "We welcome your independent surveyors and inspection crews."

"Dude," Brandon said, "first of all, you're family, so we're not worried. But, also, you're part of our investment group, so you've got skin in the game, too."

Logan flashed a grin at his brother, then looked at his cousins. "The truth is, we would be building our own hotel here if you hadn't been interested."

"We're interested," Adam said, then glanced at his brothers. "Am I right?"

Cameron and Brandon answered with firm nods, then Cameron said, "Let's have the bean counters work the numbers and we'll draw up the papers."

After a brief stop at the proposed site of the sports center, they had lunch outside on the patio of a small, friendly French bistro that specialized in local fish and shellfish. A colorful market umbrella protected the entire party from the rays of the sun as they enjoyed the views of the lively harbor along with the exceptional food.

"Oh, my God, I'm stuffed," Trish said, pushing her dessert plate away. "All I'll be capable of doing this afternoon is passing out on a chaise longue on the beach."

"Me, too," Julia said, dabbing her lips with her napkin. "But this was lovely. I've never tasted a richer, more delicious sauce than the one on the Coquilles St. Jacques." She squeezed her husband's arm. "Sorry, sweetie, but I'm going to dream about it tonight."

Cameron chuckled, then took a bite of the tarte tatin they were sharing. "How in the world did a chef with so much talent for haute cuisine wind up in this tiny place?"

"He's the son of a local family," Logan said. "Studied in France at several three-star-rated restaurants, then came home to marry his childhood sweetheart."

"She's our waitress," Aidan added with a grin.

"That's so romantic," Kelly said, causing Brandon to smile as he took her hand and kissed it.

As he watched his cousins flirt with their wives, Logan had the strangest urge to drive straight back to the hotel and find Grace. He missed her and wished, not for the first time, that he'd invited her along, knowing she would fit in perfectly with his family.

"Guess there's not much chance of stealing the guy away, is there?" Adam asked, as he finished the last bite of his chocolate mousse. "We could use someone this talented at the new hotel."

"Not a chance," Aidan said firmly.

"We know," Logan chimed in, chuckling. "Because we've tried."

"What other secrets does this fabulous island hide from the rest of the world?" Kelly asked, intrigued.

"Well, since you're family," Aidan said, winking at her, "I guess it'll be okay to disclose a few secrets. For one thing, we've got amazing hot springs up in the rain forest."

"I haven't read anything about that," Kelly said, frowning.

"We've never put it in any of the brochures," Logan admitted. "Don't want anyone trampling on our own little piece of paradise."

"We won't advertise it, either," Brandon said.

"It sounds so romantic," Trish said.

"Definitely," Julia said, and gave Cameron a playful tap on his shoulder.

Cameron returned her smile, then explained, "We've got a secluded pool and a grotto on the grounds of our resort in Monarch Bay. It's pretty cool."

"And very romantic," Julia said.

"Well, our hot springs aren't quite that accessible," Aidan said, "but believe me, they're off the scale in terms of providing a romantic setting. Lush foliage, waterfalls, completely secluded."

"Oh, yeah," Logan said. "It takes some time and exercise to find them, but they're totally worth the effort once you're there."

Aidan continued describing the hike to the hot springs but Logan tuned him out. His mind had already returned instead to thoughts of Grace and the day they'd spent making love in the rain forest. He wished again that she were here with them enjoying the day and realized he hadn't yet brought her into Tierra for lunch or dinner. She would love it here, and he vowed to bring her soon.

Strange that his desire for her continued to grow instead of diminishing as he'd once thought it would. He was beginning to wonder if he would ever grow tired of her.

Logan walked into the lounge at five o'clock and was greeted by Aidan, who grabbed his arm and said without preamble, "We need to talk."

"What's up?" Logan said amiably. He was in a cheery mood, having spent the past two hours with Grace in her room. In her bed, to be more accurate. He followed Aidan to the far end of the bar, where Brandon was sitting alone, nursing a bottle of beer.

"Sit down," Aidan said to Logan, pointing to the stool next to Brandon. Then he nodded at Brandon. "Go ahead. Tell him."

Before Brandon could speak, Joey appeared in front of Logan. "What're you drinking, boss?"

"I'll have what he's having," Logan said, pointing his thumb toward the bottle in front of Brandon. "Thanks, Joey."

Aidan grabbed his own beer and stood behind the two men. "I want you to listen to Brandon."

Logan turned and eyed his brother. "I will, as soon as he says something."

Brandon swiveled his stool around and faced Logan.

"Aidan seems to think you might have a problem. So here's the deal. I want you to look across the room, over by the windows, where my mother is sitting with your father."

Logan picked out the couple in the crowd, then smiled. "Yeah, I've noticed they've been hanging out with each other, practically since the first day we all got together. You think we'll be hearing some kind of announcement pretty soon?"

"That's not the point," Aidan said sharply.

Logan whipped around. "What the hell is wrong with you?"

Brandon grinned at the two of them. "It's such a kick to see you guys together. How does anyone ever tell you apart?"

"That's not the point, either," Aidan groused.

Brandon laughed and turned back to Logan. "It's about my mom. She likes to play matchmaker."

"Are you listening?" Aidan said pointedly.

Logan ignored him. "Go on, Brandon."

Brandon nodded. "For the past half-hour, while Aidan and I have been talking here at the bar, Mom's been chatting with that pretty redheaded cocktail waitress. She's over there at the bar right now."

Logan didn't have to look to know he was talking about Grace. "Yeah, I know her," he said, his voice edged with suspicion.

"When I mentioned to Aidan that Mom had this thing about making sure everyone in her life was happily married and having babies, he thought I should warn you."

Logan turned his stool slowly around until he was facing Aidan. "You're kidding. That's what the big emergency is?"

To his credit, Aidan held up both hands in surrender. "I admit that hearing Brandon talk about it now makes it all sound a little far-fetched. But you didn't see the way Sally was talking to Grace. They were tight and it looked serious. They were making plans, I'm telling you."

"You've lost your mind," Logan muttered, shaking his head. Joey brought him his beer and Logan took a long, hard drink.

Aidan scowled. "Okay, maybe I got a little carried away in the moment."

"Maybe?"

Brandon jumped in. "Hey, I'm right there with you, Aidan. Believe me, I watched Sally take down both of my brothers and I was determined not to let it happen to me."

"But you're happily married now," Logan said in protest.

"I know." Brandon laughed. "I'll be damned if Mom didn't show up at my hotel in Napa one day, say a few words, and the next thing I knew I was walking down the aisle, happy as a clam."

"There she is," Aidan whispered loudly. "Check it out."

Logan rolled his eyes again, but turned in time to see Grace walk over to Sally's table and hand her a note. Sally stood and gave Grace a hug, then slipped the note into her small purse. Then Grace walked back to the drink station to place an order.

"Okay, that was weird," Brandon admitted.

It was, Logan had to admit. Frowning to himself, his gaze locked on Grace, he wondered what the note was all about.

"What the hell is she up to?" Logan wondered aloud.

"Thank you," Aidan said, gazing skyward, then back at his brother. "I feel slightly vindicated. I hope you're going to get to the bottom of whatever's going on."

Logan nodded, unsure of what to say or think about what he'd just seen. So, for now, he kept quiet and sipped his beer as he mulled over the possibilities and considered his next move.

Hell, it wasn't like Sally had magical powers or anything.

Oh, for God's sake. The fact that his mind had actually put those words together in a sentence meant that he had just stepped into the loony zone. Right next to his brother. The difference was, Aidan really belonged there; Logan didn't.

Contrary to Aidan's opinion, there was nothing going on between Sally and Grace. Sally was a lovely lady who took a friendly interest in all the people around her, including Grace. That was all that was going on there. Who knows, maybe Grace gave Sally her phone number so they could keep in touch. Or maybe the note held the name of some store where she liked to shop. Who the hell knew? And who cared? Besides Aidan, of course.

The real problem was that Aidan didn't trust Grace. He thought she might be after Logan's money. Logan knew it wasn't true but he hadn't done a good enough job convincing his brother. But what would be the point? This thing with Grace was temporary and he knew it. All too soon, she'd be leaving Alleria and Logan behind.

But in the meantime, Aidan had glommed on to Brandon's matchmaking conspiracy theory. Great. And Grace wasn't helping matters much since it did look like she really was going to Sally for advice. And Sally seemed happy enough to help Grace. But help her with…what? Perform a voodoo marriage chant? Sprinkle his dinner plate with aphrodisiacs? He almost laughed out loud at the thought. Grace was too down-to-earth, too literal, to buy into anything so absurd. And damn it, Sally was, too. This was all Aidan's crap and Logan needed to call him on it. Besides, the bottom line was, there was absolutely nothing that Grace—or Sally, for that matter—could do to coerce Logan into marrying her.

He would just need to do a better job of convincing Aidan of that. And then he would get off Logan's back about his relationship with Grace.

And yet, Logan had to admit that seeing Grace slip Sally that note had struck him as a little odd. But he was sure it could be easily explained. All he had to do was ask Grace about it and she would tell him the whole story. He knew Grace had a hard time lying, so it wouldn't be difficult getting the truth out of her.

But not tonight. Tonight, all he wanted to do was make love with her. Tomorrow would be soon enough to question her about Sally and the note. It was probably something completely innocent, but he knew his brother would continue tormenting him until Logan found out the truth.

Ten

"I'm going to marry her."

As Aidan's eyes widened in shock and dismay, Logan almost laughed himself silly.

"You're kidding," Aidan whispered.

"Why are you so surprised?" Logan asked. "Haven't you noticed they've been in love practically from the first day they met?"

"You noticed?" his father asked, his grin broader than Logan had ever seen it.

Logan laughed and slapped Dad on the back. "We all noticed, Dad. Except Aidan, apparently."

"Sorry, Dad. I've had a lot on my mind." Aidan scowled at Logan as he threw down the toast he'd been about to bite into. Shaking his head to rid himself of what seemed to be a pretty weird mood, Aidan pushed away from the table and walked over to Dad, who stood and wrapped him up in a bear hug.

Logan jumped up and grabbed them both fiercely. "I'm thrilled for you and Sally, Dad. She's the greatest."

"She is," Aidan said quickly. "I guess I was shocked because I never thought I'd see the day."

"Me, neither, son," Dad said, and his eyes grew misty. "But she's the woman for me. I'm in love with her and I want to be with her always. Took me long enough, but I got it right this time."

Logan felt his own eyes tear up and he willed himself to get a grip. "Where is Sally right now, Dad? I want to give her a big kiss."

"Me, too," Aidan said.

"She'll love that." Dad wiped away a happy tear. "Right now she's off making plans for us to go somewhere special for a picnic."

"Sounds great," Aidan said. "You two will have a fun day."

"But we'll celebrate tonight, right?" Logan said. "I'll reserve the table in the wine cellar and we'll all go a little crazy."

"Sounds perfect," Dad said.

Before Logan went off to find Sally, he wanted to find Grace and invite her to the family party that night. He didn't care what Aidan thought of his decision, he just wanted Grace to be with him for as long as she was on the island. He still didn't know what had gone on between her and Sally last night and while he was anxious to find out, he realized that he trusted Grace enough to know it wasn't anything sinister.

Logan turned for one last look at his dad who was still grinning from ear to ear. He hoped and prayed his father would be wearing that grin for the rest of his life. Nobody deserved happiness more than he did. When Logan thought about all the years when he and Aidan were growing up, all he could see was his father, always there. Always steady. Always loving his sons enough to make up for the loss of their mother.

Yeah, Sally Duke was perfect for Dad because Logan could see in her eyes how much she loved his father. And that made her perfect, period, as far as Logan was concerned.

The following day, the Duke brothers and their wives, along with Sally and the twins' dad, Tom, flew back to the West Coast.

"Damn, I miss them already," Aidan said as they stood together on the tarmac.

Logan agreed, staring at the sky as the jet climbed higher then curved gracefully toward the west. "Funny how we all became a family in an instant. It's like we've known them all our lives."

"I know," Aidan said. "It's comforting. A little weird, but nice."

"Really nice," Logan murmured. "Glad we got to party last night with everyone. Dad was in his element." Logan was especially glad that Grace had agreed to accompany him to the party. She'd looked beautiful and he'd been so proud to introduce her to his entire family. She'd fit in as well as he'd imagined she would.

"Yeah, it was great to see Dad and Sally together," Aidan said. "Can't wait for the wedding. It's going to be one hell of a celebration."

"Dad really deserves that."

"Yeah, he does."

Logan didn't say it out loud, but he was starting to wonder why they *all* didn't deserve that kind of happiness. Shaking his head, he said, "I was thinking...how about we build a house for Dad and Sally up on the bluff?

I know they won't live here full-time, but they might like their own place on Alleria."

"I like it. You know," Aidan said with a grin, "you're smarter than you look."

"Ah," Logan countered, with a matching grin, "twin joke. Good one."

"Okay, bro, let's get going," Aidan said, and they strolled over to the limo. Once they were settled and the driver took off, he broached the subject they'd left hanging last night. "So, did you find out about the note Grace slipped to Sally?"

"No, I didn't get a chance to ask her yet."

"Dude, you were with her all night."

"I had other things on my mind." Such as getting Grace back to his suite and into his bed. That note had been the last thing he was thinking about by then, and he smiled at the memory.

Aidan snorted. "Fine, but you'll ask her today, right?"

"Of course." Though he wasn't real anxious to open up that line of conversation and he couldn't really say why.

"Because I'll ask her myself if you don't."

"No, you won't," Logan said, jabbing his finger in the air. "Just…back off. First of all, it's probably nothing to get excited about. And second of all… Damn it, just…back off."

Aidan held his hands up in surrender. "Jeez, power down. Fine. I won't ask her. As long as you do."

"I said I would, didn't I?"

"Good. It's cool. I trust you."

"Yeah, right."

The car pulled to a stop outside the hotel entrance. Both men thanked the driver and climbed out, then Aidan checked his watch. "Look, I've got to go pack."

"Oh, hell," Logan said, rubbing his head in frustration.

"I do, too. In all of the excitement over Dad and Sally, I forgot we're leaving for New York tomorrow."

He didn't want to leave.

Logan had been dragging his ass around his bedroom, throwing socks and T-shirts into his open suitcase and counting out the required number of dress shirts and suits for the hanging bag. But the realization didn't hit him until he started pulling shoes out of the closet and lining them up next to the suitcase.

Damn. He would never disclose this to Aidan, but Logan had the strongest urge to blow off New York and stay here with Grace. They'd spent almost every night together and he was forced to admit—to himself only— that he'd grown damned close to her. He liked having her around and knew he was going to miss her while he was gone.

"Get a grip," he muttered to himself. He was only going to be gone for three days.

The problem was, he didn't know how much longer Grace intended to stay. Checking his calendar, he realized she'd been here almost three weeks. He'd never asked her how long she planned to stay. But he wanted her to be here when he got back.

If she did have to go home for a while, maybe Logan could convince her to just drop off the spores and come back right away.

"Ah, jeez." When had he turned into such a sap? Shaking his head in disgust, he stuffed his shoes into the soft cloth shoe bag, fitted them into the suitcase and zipped it closed. Nope, he definitely wouldn't be mentioning any of that to Aidan.

"What are you looking at?"

Grace jolted, startled by the voice. She hadn't heard

footsteps approaching, but that was because she tended to recede into her own little spore world when she was out here among the palms.

"I'm looking at these tiny creatures." She turned over one of the palm fronds and pointed them out to the little girl who stood a few feet away. "Can you see them?"

She took a step closer. "The little red dots?"

"That's right, although they're not actually red. More of a brownish-green. But when they're clustered together, they appear to be brick colored."

The girl frowned. "Who are you?"

"I'm Grace," she said, sitting back on her feet. "I'm a scientist and I collect these spores to use in experiments. Who are you?"

"I'm Swoozie," she said, and folded her arms across her narrow chest. "I'm staying at the hotel with my parents."

"I like your name," Grace said. "Do you like science?"

Swoozie made a face and shook her head. "I'm failing math and science."

"Oh, that's interesting. Those are my two favorite subjects." She smiled good-naturedly. "But I've always been kind of weird."

"My friend Charlotte likes math, too, but I don't get it."

Swoozie looked about ten years old, thin, with long, brown hair and big brown eyes.

"What's your favorite subject?" Grace asked as she packed up her bag.

"I guess I like English."

"Do you like to read?"

"Yes, but mostly, I just want to graduate high school so I can go and be a model in Europe."

"You want to be a model?"

"A supermodel," she specified.

"You'll need to know math and science if you're going

to be a model," Grace said casually as she stood and brushed the bits of sand and dirt off her legs.

"No, I won't."

"You will." Grace began to walk with her back to the hotel. "Say you're in Paris and you want to have dinner after your photo shoot with Pierre, the world famous French photographer. You'll need to calculate the daily exchange rate to make sure you're on budget and not overtipping your waiter. So if you know that the day's rate is 1.44 euros to the dollar, and your meal is twelve euros, you'll be able to figure out that you're about to spend over seventeen dollars, and that might not be within your budget."

"Oh." Swoozie frowned, then her face screwed up in deep thought. A few seconds later, she grinned. "But I'll be with Pierre and he'll be happy to calculate all those numbers for me."

"Well." Grace laughed and waved her hand in the air. "As long as Pierre is with you, he should just pay for your dinner."

Swoozie laughed. "That's even better."

They walked through the palmetto grove until they reached the beach. "So what are you studying in math right now?"

"Multiplication tables," Swoozie said miserably. "I'm supposed to memorize them while I'm on vacation, but I suck at memorizing stuff."

"Oh, there's a better way to learn multiplication," Grace said, leading Swoozie over to a shaded table on the terrace. "I'll show you."

Logan stood at the bar sipping his single-malt scotch as he waited for Grace to finish her shift. This would be their last night together for a few days and he didn't want to waste a minute of time, so he'd decided to camp out at the end of the bar and watch her in action until it was time for her to clock out.

She was balancing cocktail trays like a champ these days, as long as she only carried two or three drinks at a time and moved very slowly. The customers didn't seem to mind. Hell, half the time they followed her to the bar and grabbed the drinks on their own. It was a bizarre way to do business, but Logan was no longer complaining.

A thirty-something couple walked into the lounge and headed straight for the bar. The woman called the bartender over and said briskly, "Which one of your waitresses is Grace?"

Logan's hackles stiffened as he watched Sam scan the room. Spying Grace across the room wiping off a four-top for a small group of guests who waited nearby, Sam pointed her out to the couple.

"Oh, yes," the woman said, nodding. "I was told she was a redhead."

As Grace walked back toward the bar, the couple met her halfway. Logan followed them. He didn't know what this was all about, but he didn't want any trouble, especially if it involved Grace.

"So you're Grace," the woman said.

"Yes, I am," she said, smiling. "Can I help you?"

"You spoke to my daughter Swoozie this morning."

"Oh, yes. She's a sweet girl." Grace's eyes suddenly widened and she looked mortified. "Oh, I'm so sorry I suggested that Pierre pay for her dinner. I was thinking about that later and realized—"

"Thank you so much!" the woman exclaimed, and grabbed Grace in a tight embrace.

"Oh, well," Grace said, nonplussed.

"You have no idea what we've been through," Swoozie's mother cried.

The woman's husband glanced around the room nervously. When he made eye contact with Logan, he shrugged, clearly clueless.

When the mother finally let her loose, Grace raked her hair back self-consciously. "But I really didn't—"

"She came back to the room and did three pages of math homework!"

"Three pages." Grace smiled and nodded. "That's nice."

"She was so excited," the woman continued. "She kept saying 'I get it!' over and over again. When I asked her what happened, she told me you explained it to her in a way that finally clicked for her."

"I'm so glad," Grace said. "I just showed her an easy way I have of remembering number systems. I can show it to you if you'd—"

"No, no," the woman said quickly, holding up her hand as she took a step back. "Whatever you did, it worked and I'll just leave it at that. Swoozie has seen the light! That's all that matters to me. Thank you so much."

"You're welcome."

Logan stood next to Grace as the couple walked out of the bar.

"Isn't that sweet?" Grace murmured. Logan wasn't sure what had just happened, but he knew right then that Swoozie wasn't the only one Grace had helped to finally see the light.

"Come with me to the airport," Logan said early the next morning. "The driver will bring you back."

Grace was dressed in shorts, tank top and sandals, ready to leave his room. But Logan decided he didn't want to say goodbye just yet.

"Are you sure you want me there?" she asked.

"Yeah." He grabbed Grace with one hand and his suitcase with the other, and they left the suite to meet the limousine out front.

He and Grace were already waiting in the limo when Aidan climbed inside. Logan ignored his brother's fulminating glance and breathed a sigh of relief when Eleanor arrived a few seconds later. They all drove to the airport in companionable silence.

Aidan assisted Eleanor out of the car and they walked to the jet, leaving Logan to say goodbye to Grace.

Standing on the tarmac, Logan kissed her goodbye. "You'll still be here when I get back?"

"Yes, of course," Grace said with a smile. "I still have a few weeks of work to do before I have to go back to Minnesota."

"Good. I'll see you in a few days, then." He kissed her again, then turned and walked away.

"Have a good trip," Grace called.

"Hell," he muttered. A glance at the plane and his twin standing in the open doorway watching him reminded Logan that he still hadn't asked Grace about the stupid note. And if he didn't, Aidan would rag his ass for the next three days. He turned back to her. "I keep forgetting to ask you something."

"What is it?"

"You passed a note to Sally the other night in the bar. What did it say?"

She flinched and her face turned pale. "You saw that?"

"Yeah," he said, warily watching her reaction to what should've been a simple question. "What was in that note?"

Grace turned around and grabbed the limo's door handle, trying to escape. "I don't have to tell you."

"Grace," he said, reaching for her, "do you have something to hide from me?"

She glared at him. "Well, of course I do. And you have

things to hide from me. People have their secrets. It's human nature."

"What was in the note, Grace?" he asked, his tone deadly quiet.

Her jaw was set in a stubborn scowl and as much as she tried to hold to her convictions, Logan continued to stare her down. Finally, she broke, and exhaled heavily. "Fine. I gave her directions. Are you happy?"

"Directions to what?" he shouted. "Her G-spot?"

"Oh, for God's sake, Logan," she said, throwing up her hands in exasperation. "Sally doesn't need help finding her G-spot."

Oh, he so didn't need to know that about his soon-to-be new mother. "Then what? Just tell me."

She huffed and puffed and fumed, and Logan had the strongest urge to kiss her senseless. But first he needed to know the truth.

She wrapped her arms tightly around her middle. "She wanted directions to the hot springs. There, are you happy?"

Seriously? The hot springs? That was the big secret? Logan frowned at that. "Why would she want to go there?"

"You're kidding, right?" Grace rolled her eyes, then slapped her hands on her hips and said, "She wanted to take your father there, but she didn't want anyone else to know that they were sneaking off to have wild jungle sex."

"Oh, no, no, no." Logan stumbled back a half step, pretty certain that his own face had grown pale, too. Grace had just painted a picture in his mind that he would've been perfectly happy never to have seen in his entire life.

And if not for Aidan bugging him to find out, he never would have. It would be his pleasure to share that horrifying mental image with his twin.

"And don't you dare tell her I told you," Grace said, her voice stinging with aggravation.

"I won't, don't worry. In fact, I'm going to do everything I can to forget you ever told me." He stared at her for another ten seconds, then began to chuckle. "Jesus, Grace." He laughed out loud, then yanked her close and planted a hot, wet kiss on her lips. "God, I'm going to miss you."

She pressed her palm against his chest. "I'll miss you, too, Logan."

He gave her one more hard, fast kiss, then turned and jogged to the plane. Still laughing, he climbed the stairs, then spun around and waved goodbye one last time.

Eleven

Grace was a pathetic mess. She missed Logan terribly, and he'd only been gone one day. What in the world would she do once she was back home in Minnesota? Once she left Alleria, she would never see Logan again. So wasn't it about time she pulled herself together and figured out the best way to deal with the pain?

But a long, sleepless night wasn't the way to get used to anything. Every time she closed her eyes, she saw Logan. A tight ball of misery lodged in the pit of her stomach, reminding her with every breath that this was just the beginning. That leaving Logan would be the hardest thing she had ever done.

By morning, she was exhausted and feeling sorry for herself, so she spent several hours in the rain forest, hiking and searching for more spore sites. But even her research couldn't fill the void that was building inside her. That evening, she worked tirelessly in the cocktail lounge and even stayed an extra hour later to help the others.

She loved the camaraderie among the waiters and bartenders and busboys. Sometimes she wished she could just go and be a waitress because the people were so much more fun than academics. Sad but true.

But even though she wished she could stay on the island forever, she knew she needed to get back to the laboratory. She had important work to do there. Besides, this wasn't her world. Was it? She'd lived her entire life in academia. Could she honestly leave it all behind? Could she really see herself living here in paradise?

"Oh, dear," she whispered, and tried to swallow around the sudden lump in her throat as she watched Dee laugh at something Joey said. She thought of Logan and all the nights he'd stood at the end of the bar waiting for her. And that's when it struck her that she really could live here forever. And the realization scared her to death.

Working all these long hours had done little to take her mind off missing Logan. It didn't help that tonight everyone was talking about the possibility of a tropical storm off the coast of South America turning into a hurricane as it headed north toward Alleria. She didn't want to be in a hurricane without Logan.

The very notion of riding out a hurricane was terrifying to her, but some of the staff were taking it in stride. They had experienced severe storms and hurricanes in the past and were confident that Logan's hotel was so well built that it could withstand the worst that Mother Nature could throw at it.

As Grace returned to the bar for another drink order, she noticed it had grown breezier in the lounge. The manager asked some of the men to close the casement windows along the outer perimeter of the room so the guests would be more comfortable.

"It's so chilly tonight," Dee said, rubbing her arms as they waited together at the bar for their orders. "And I've got a jacket on."

"I wish I had my sweater," Grace said after noticing that several of the waitresses were covered up. Dee's denim jacket looked cute over her sarong.

"Why don't you run and get it?" Dee said. "I'll watch your tables for a few minutes."

"Are you sure?"

"Absolutely. If you're sticking around to help us, we don't want you freezing to death."

"Okay, I'll hurry back."

"No worries."

Grace left the bar and started walking back to her room, but remembered she'd left her pink sweater in Logan's suite the other night. He'd recently given her a copy of his key card to use when she worked late, so she hurried over to his side of the hotel and used the card to slip inside.

She switched on the light, glanced around the room and saw her sweater on the chair near his desk. She grabbed it, then noticed the thick set of architectural drawings spread out on his desk.

Her curiosity was piqued and she rounded the desk to see what they were. Grace had never seen blueprints before and appreciated the architectural precision of the lines and angles. She smiled as she realized that these were the plans for the sports center Logan and his brother were going to build. He was excited about creating a destination for sports enthusiasts here on Alleria and had described it in detail. That was the reason he'd gone to New York, to meet with the investors and finalize these plans.

Studying the blueprints made her feel closer to Logan somehow. She knew he had studied the same drawings and probably pictured the finished creation in his mind. She tried to do that as she gazed at all the little side drawings and various site descriptions.

And that's when she saw it: the map and description of the location of the gigantic sports complex in relationship to the hotel. North side. Adjacent. Palmetto grove.

"No," she whispered.

She walked around the desk, certain at first that she was interpreting the drawings all wrong. But she wasn't a dummy, and after ten minutes of studying every sheet in the stack, she knew she had been betrayed. He had lied to her. Okay, he hadn't lied exactly, but he'd clearly avoided telling her the truth as he let her gather her spores and talk about the importance of her research, all the while knowing that he planned to pave over the whole site.

Logan and his brother had every intention of building their sports center directly on top of the land where the spores grew.

She backed away from the desk. Maybe there was some mistake. But she knew there wasn't. So why hadn't Logan said something to her? He knew how important her research was. Had he simply been using sex as a way of distracting her from his plans for eradicating the very spores she'd come there to study?

Or maybe he'd simply been carrying out what he'd promised her from the very beginning. He'd wanted her off the island and he would do whatever it took to get rid of her.

Oh, but that was ridiculous. This wasn't personal. It wasn't about her. It wasn't about her spores. It was just the way businessmen conducted business. Destroy a few billion spores to build a few tennis courts? Sure, if that's what made money. Never mind the possibility of curing disease and saving lives.

"Oh, God." Not only would this plan eviscerate the spores but it would destroy the foundation of her life's work. Her funding would dry up and there would be no possibility of continuing her research.

"Stop," she cried. She needed to calm down and think instead of going crazy. Of course there would still be spores. Logan wouldn't destroy the entire rain forest, for goodness' sake. But the fact remained that he knew how important it was to Grace that the palm trees and their spores be kept safe and intact. And he'd blithely decided to destroy a large swath of it.

"How could he do it?" she mumbled over and over. And how could she have trusted him? That question was more easily answered than the first. She was simply a dim-witted woman who'd fallen in love with a man who didn't respect her or her life or her goals.

With a sharp cry, she ran from Logan's suite and headed for her own. Friends smiled and tried to talk to her as she passed, but Grace hardly saw them. Her mind was churning, her vision blurry with unshed tears and her heart was heavy with a pain she wasn't sure she could survive.

She ran inside her room and slammed the door shut. Then she crawled onto the bed, shivering in humiliation.

She might've lain there for a few minutes or a few hours, she would never be sure. Finally, she stumbled across the room and fumbled in her purse for her cell phone. Stabbing the buttons, she called her friend and mentor, Phillippa, and prayed that she would pick up before it went to voice mail.

"Grace, is that you? It's so late. What's going on?"

Grace quickly explained the situation and was gratified when Phillippa blurted an expletive.

"Why, that lousy spore killer," she said stoutly, and Grace could picture Phillippa's glasses sliding down her nose. "How could he do this to you? Were you aware that he was so environmentally unfriendly?"

Maybe he was, but despite everything, Grace couldn't bear to hear any criticism of Logan. She just wanted to save the spores. "Do you know how to stop him?"

"Oh, yeah," Phillippa said. "It's called an injunctive order and we're going to slap it on him so hard, he won't know what hit him."

Before she hung up, Phillippa took a minute to warn Grace that Walter's funding had come through. Grace slid down onto the chair, unable to speak. Yes, she would go back and face the grant committee and tell them how he had lied. And she would present them with her own latest findings based on her new collection of super spores. But still, how could the committee have fallen for Walter's lies? How could they have awarded him one cent?

It was a double blow. Now she'd been betrayed on two fronts. She could care less about Walter, but she hated to go back to the university and face all those sympathetic stares. But that would be a piece of cake compared to the way she would feel if she stayed on the island. There was no way she could face Logan after finding out he'd been playing her for a fool all this time. Walter's lies were nothing compared to Logan's betrayal. She'd thought he was different and it hurt to know how very wrong she'd been. So much for all that intelligence she was so famous for.

With a bitter sigh, she pulled her bags out of the closet and began to pack. It was difficult because her eyes were blurry from the tears she didn't seem able to stop.

There was a knock on the door.

For one second she thought it might be Logan. Then her brain cleared. He was still in New York arranging for the money to kill her career. That would take him another day or two at least. Without even realizing it, anger began to film over some of her pain as she hurried to the door and opened it.

"Oh, Dee," she cried. "I'm so sorry."

"Gracie, you never came back to—" Dee stopped and glanced around the room.

Grace realized it looked like the hurricane had already struck. "I'm packing. I need to go home."

"What's going on?"

"Nothing," she said, then realized how absurd that sounded, even to her. Sitting down on the edge of the bed, she told Dee the whole story.

"It just doesn't sound like Logan," Dee murmured, shaking her head.

"I didn't think so, either," Grace said miserably. "But I saw the plans myself, Dee. There's no mistake."

Dee pulled her close for a hug. "I hate that you're leaving, Gracie, but I understand. It's no more than he deserves, the lying rat-dog. I'm sorry he hurt you."

"Me, too."

"Will you call?" Dee asked, standing up and stepping back. "Let me know you're okay? I mean, just because you're leaving doesn't mean we can't still be friends, right?"

One bright spot in a completely hideous day, Grace thought, and hugged Dee fiercely. "Thank you! I will call. I promise."

After Dee left, Grace continued packing. When she was finished, she called the concierge to ask about flights. That brought on another dismal round of tears. She'd grown to love it here. She loved her friends and her job and the palm trees and the rain forest and the beach and her poor little spores.

And she loved Logan.

In spite of what he'd done, she'd fallen in love with him. And while that meant she had to be the biggest twit in the universe, she loved him and knew she always would. And the fact that he was never going to be hers brought another sharp pain to her chest.

She spent a long night staring out the window at the ebbing storm, and early the next morning, Grace left a polite note for Logan with the concierge, then took the first flight off the island.

The jet reached cruising altitude and Logan stretched his legs out on the seat facing him. The meetings were over, the investors' checks were deposited, and the Alleria sports center would soon be a reality. Eleanor walked into the cabin and handed Logan and Aidan each a glass of champagne.

"Thanks, Ellie."

The mood was festive as they toasted to their success and drank down the cold, bubbly liquid.

"That's good," Aidan murmured, grinning. "We did good."

"Yeah, we did good," Logan said.

Ellie giggled. "Life is good."

They all laughed, then Logan said, "Man, I can't wait to see Grace."

"What?" Aidan twisted around to stare at him.

"Aww," Ellie said, and smiled warmly at him.

Logan frowned. "Did I say that out loud?"

"Yeah, you did."

He glanced from Ellie to Aidan. "Huh."

"Ah, hell," Aidan said in disgust. "Now you've done it."

"Done what?"

"You've gone and fallen in love with her."

"Don't be—" He started to protest automatically, then stopped. And thought about it. Hard.

Love. Just saying the word in his head didn't strike the same raw nerve it had in the past. Did that mean it was true? Was he in love with Grace? The idea didn't rankle him as it had in the past. In fact, it made him smile.

Ever since he'd talked to Brandon out on the beach, Logan had been thinking about things. The past. The future. Love and life. Risk. Trust.

He'd spent half of his life fearing to trust in love. He'd talked himself into marrying Tanya, thinking he should give love a try. But he'd never loved her. The fact that she'd cheated on him was as good an excuse as any to never try again.

But these few days away from Grace had made him realize how much he wanted to try. The thing was, his world felt empty without her. He couldn't wait to get home to see her. He wanted to know how she'd spent her days, wanted to hear what was new with the spores.

It was staggering to realize that he'd actually fallen in love for the first and last time in his life.

He tested the words over and over again in his mind and when he was certain that he wasn't going to be struck by lightning, he decided to say them aloud.

"I'm in love with her."

Aidan buried his head in his hands.

As they climbed down the stairs and stepped onto the tarmac, Aidan slung his arm around Logan's shoulder and said, "Wonder if Dad and Sally are in some hot tub in San Francisco right now…how did Gracie put it? 'Having hot jungle sex'?"

"Oh, man." Logan slapped his hands over his ears and started humming loudly.

Aidan laughed uproariously, then calmed down and admitted, "Okay, I'm going to say something I never thought I would. I like her, bro."

"Good," Logan said, knowing he was talking about Grace. "Because I'm in love with the confounded woman and that's all there is to it."

"If you had to take the fall, she was a good one to pick. So if it matters to you, you've got my blessing."

"It matters," Logan admitted, glancing at his twin. "Thank you."

Aidan grinned. "Let's go tell her the good news."

The brothers strolled across the lobby wheeling their luggage behind them.

"Oh, Mr. Sutherland," Harrison, the concierge, called out. "I have a letter for you." He pulled an envelope from his desk and rushed over to the twins.

Aidan took it, glanced at the envelope and handed it to Logan. "It's for you."

Logan stared at his name on the envelope. He might've waited to open it when he was alone, but something niggled at him and he opened it right there. A minute later, he let the note drop to the floor.

Aidan picked it up and read the words. "She left? She just left? What did you do to her?"

Logan shook his head, too dumbfounded to answer.

"Come on," Aidan said, pushing him forward. "We'll go to your room and call her."

They made it to Logan's room, but before they could get inside, Dee came running up the hall. "There you are! Why did you do it?"

Logan scowled at her. "Close the damn door."

Aidan pulled her inside and led her over to the chair in front of Logan's desk. "Sit. Talk. Tell us what you know."

"I don't care if you're my boss. What you—he—you—" she looked from one to the other of them. "What Logan did to Gracie was just plain mean and underhanded and—"

"What did Grace say?" Aidan demanded since Logan was staring into space.

"He knows what he did," Dee said, pointing at Logan. Then she pointed at Aidan. "For Pete's sake, which one of you is which?"

"I'm Aidan," he said. "Now tell us everything that happened."

Logan sat behind his desk with his elbows resting on the surface and listened to Dee's story.

When she was finished, Aidan scratched his head. "What the hell?"

"We're not killing any spores," Logan muttered.

"That's what she said," Dee insisted, then shook her head in confusion. "She left the bar to get her sweater and the next thing I knew, she was in her room crying her eyes out about you paving over the rain forest."

"It was her pink sweater," Logan murmured. "I remember seeing it and meant to bring it to her."

"Right," Dee said. "She came in here to get her sweater and all hell broke loose. It wasn't enough for that creep Walter to break her heart, but then you had to come along and—"

"Who the hell is Walter?" Logan said, his voice belonging more to a growling animal than a normal human.

Dee told them the whole ugly story of Walter's betrayal and how much it had messed up Grace's life. Then Dee took off, leaving the men to brood on their own.

Logan stared at his desk for a long time, until he realized it wasn't his desk he was seeing but the thick pack of old blueprints he'd left spread out here. The new ones

were on his desk in the corporate office down the hall.
"Oh, crap."

"What?" Aidan said.

"She saw the old plans," he said, tapping the blueprints.

Aidan got closer and peered at them. "Those are two
years old."

"I know. They're completely obsolete. But she must've
seen them and jumped to the conclusion that I was going
to pour cement over the freaking palmetto grove."

"She thought you betrayed her."

Aidan frowned as he beat the edge of the desk with his
knuckles. "Now we know why she left in such a hurry."

"Damn it," Logan said, letting loose a sigh loaded with
frustration.

"Look, just call her and tell her she's wrong."

"Hell, no," Logan said, his eyes focused on the blue site
map in the corner of the wide sheet. "She didn't even trust
me enough to ask me about any of this. She just assumed
the worst and took off. Who's betraying whom?"

There was a knock on the door.

"Now what?" Aidan said. He opened the door and a guy
slapped a blue-backed form at him.

"What is this?"

"Injunction," the guy said. "You've been served."

Logan prowled his office like a caged animal. It had
been three days since Grace had left, three days that he'd
spent chastising himself for falling for a woman who was
willing to leave him without a word. Grace had walked
out on him as easily as the mother he barely remembered.
As easily as his cheating wife had driven away from him
that night four years ago.

So much for love. *Love*. He laughed without humor.
What a great cosmic joke. Hopefully this was the last

lesson needed to prove to him that love simply didn't exist. Not for him. Ever.

As he paced around his desk for the tenth time, he saw the injunction sitting there and his anger festered all over again. He stared at the new blueprints and the contracts stacked on the conference table, then back at the original site map that had caused all the trouble in the first place.

And a plan began to form in his mind.

Grace was miserable and utterly confused. Always in the past, she'd been able to count on science to clear up any questions for her. But what she still felt for Logan simply wasn't logical. If this was love, why did it have to hurt so much?

She had tried to bury herself in university life again but she found that world was no longer a good fit. Heck, maybe it never had been, only she hadn't had a choice. Now, all she could do was remember Alleria and how she'd spent her days working and her nights loving Logan.

Still, that part of her life was over and so she'd applied for funding and was waiting to hear back. It had warmed her heart to hear that Phillippa and two department heads had written to protest Walter's funding, threatening legal action. Phillippa promised that as long as she had breath in her body, Walter wouldn't get away with stealing Grace's work. Knowing Phillippa, Grace was sure it was only a matter of time before Walter was dragged into court with his tail between his legs. A good thing, because now more than ever, Grace needed her research funding. It was all she had left.

She forced herself to work. It was the one thing that had been there for her throughout her life. And now that she'd lost Logan, work was especially important.

But then, she hadn't really lost Logan, had she? How

could she, when he'd never been hers to begin with? And that line of thinking just made her hurt all over again, so she stared into the eyepiece of the electron microscope and lost herself in the world of spores.

In the background, she heard the door open, followed by several sets of footsteps. It was probably Phillippa and some other lab tech. Whoever it was, she wasn't interested in talking to them. She just wanted everyone to leave her alone to find her way back to some sense of normalcy.

Grace continued to stare at the slide in front of her, marveling at the pace of replication the new spores were exhibiting.

"She's right over there," Phillippa said.

"Yes, I see her," a man said.

Chills skittered across Grace's shoulders at the sound of that voice. She pulled away from the microscope and turned in time to see Phillippa step out of the room and close the door behind her.

"Logan?"

"How are you, Grace?"

"I'm…" What was she? Not fine, certainly. Lonely? Miserable? Unhappy? In love?

He didn't seem to need an answer, just walked over and handed her a folded document. "This is for you."

She stared at the papers in her hand, then back at him. He looked wonderful, although his eyes and mouth showed signs of strain. It didn't matter. He was still the most handsome man she'd ever seen. And the only man she'd ever loved. Tears swam in her eyes, blurring her vision. She whipped around so he wouldn't see her swipe her hand to brush away the tears.

"What is it?" she asked numbly.

"It's a deed to the palmetto grove and that hillside in the rain forest where the wild palms grow. If you'd stuck around a few more days, I could've given it to you before you left."

Her hand fisted on the papers and she gawked at him. "What? Why? Why would you do this?"

"Why?" He folded his arms across his chest. "Because now you'll always know for sure that the spores are safe."

"They're safe?"

He shook his head in annoyance. "Damn it, Grace, you served me with an injunction against building anything on that land in perpetuity. So yeah, they're safe. What I don't understand is why you felt like you had to have sex with me to save the damn spores. You could've just asked me."

She gasped. "I didn't have sex with you to save the—"

"You didn't trust me, Grace. Don't you know I would never destroy anything that was so important to you?"

"I didn't—"

"Look, Grace. To be honest, it was never about you or the spores anyway. We moved the site of the sports center two years ago."

She frowned at him. "But I saw the plans."

"You saw an old set of blueprints that I was just looking at for reference. So next time you're snooping, check the dates."

"You were never going to build near the spores?"

Logan studied her for a long moment, his face unreadable. "No."

She exhaled heavily. "I thought…"

"You assumed I was such a jerk that I would unceremoniously tear up the rain forest and destroy the entire ecosystem of the island just to build a few tennis courts. That makes me sound like a pretty big jackass, all right. No wonder you took off."

"I—I thought…"

"You thought I was too stupid to understand what it meant to you."

"No. I've never thought you were stupid." She groped for the words. "I just thought you didn't care."

"I cared," he said tightly. "It was you who didn't care. It was you who didn't trust."

She tried to blink back the tears but it was too late. Her cheeks were wet with them. "Logan, I'm so sorry. I didn't think you cared about my research."

"I care about *you,* Grace. You should've trusted me." He came up close and tapped the deed in her hand. "There are your damn spores. You got what you wanted."

He turned to leave.

"I wanted you," she whispered.

He turned back around and laughed shortly. "You're way too smart for that."

Then he left.

The room was silent except for the sound of Grace's heart shattering. Grabbing a fistful of tissues, she collapsed onto her lab stool and buried her head in her arms.

She didn't know if a body could survive this much heartache. And the fact that she'd inflicted so much pain on Logan made her pain even worse. She wanted to crawl into a hole and hide, she felt so awful. Could her crippled heart withstand this much agony?

A minute later, she felt a hand on her back.

"Logan?"

"It's me, Grace," Phillippa said. "I eavesdropped through the door. I'm so sorry."

"Oh, God, I'm an idiot," she wailed.

Phillippa grimaced. "Yeah, I kind of think that might be true."

Grace looked up through her tears. "Whose side are you on?"

"Sorry, honey." Phillippa patted her back again. "But wow, that guy must really love you to give up that land for you. And to come all this way just to tell you so? How do you feel about him?"

Sniffling, Grace rubbed her stomach. "I feel sick and dizzy and clueless and stupid. My heart aches and my throat feels like there's a boulder stuck in there. It's hard to swallow. Everything hurts and I can barely stand up, I feel so miserable."

"Ah," Phillippa said, nudging her glasses up her nose. "Sounds like you're in love with him, too. I would say you're probably going to have to do a lot of groveling to get him back."

Back on the island, Logan was making everyone crazy. He would complain to anyone who was willing to listen that he felt used, abandoned and betrayed. And since he was the boss, everyone felt compelled to listen.

He grumbled to Aidan about how pissed off he was that once again, he'd trusted the wrong woman and he would never risk his heart again.

He didn't mention to a living soul that he missed Grace more than he would have ever thought possible. The days were miserable, but the nights without her were torture. He couldn't sleep. Couldn't eat. Hell, he couldn't even enjoy a damn walk on his own damn island because he kept *seeing* her there.

Aidan popped open two beers and handed one to Logan.

"Thanks," Logan muttered, and took a big gulp.

Aidan sat down in the chair across from him. "Dude, you've gotta stop bitching and moaning to the staff. You're starting to sound like a girl and I think you're scaring the housekeepers."

"Tough," Logan said.

Aidan didn't speak for a time and they both drank their beers in peace and quiet. But it couldn't last.

"You know," Aidan said, "you once told me that part of Grace's charm was that she didn't expect anything from you."

Logan's eyes narrowed on his brother. "I never said that."

"Yeah, you did," Aidan said. "But listen, there's nothing charming about having low expectations. It's heartbreaking, is what it is. Grace obviously learned the hard way to lower her expectations when it comes to a man having feelings for her."

"Since when did you become a philosopher?"

Aidan spoke through clenched teeth. "I'm just trying to help you out here, bro. It's painful to see you acting like such a jerk."

"Look," Logan said, "I made a mistake falling for Grace and I'm determined to put that mistake behind me. It might take a little time so I would appreciate some damn patience from my twin."

"Time isn't gonna help you, Logan," Aidan told him solemnly.

Logan didn't believe it. He would conquer this. Any day now.

But he continued to walk around in a fury for the next few days until Aidan and most of the staff were no longer talking to him.

The phone rang and Logan punched the speaker button. "What is it?"

"We've got a situation in the cocktail lounge," Aidan said. "Get out here now."

Logan shook his head in irritation. Why couldn't anyone handle anything around here without him? Muttering an expletive, he pushed away from the desk and took off down the hall.

As he came within a few yards of the doorway into the lounge, the strident sound of breaking glass resounded from inside the bar.

"What the hell?" Logan groused, and walked into the large, open room. The first and only thing he saw was Grace in an impossibly sexy bikini and see-through sarong. She stood a few feet away, staring down at a pile of broken glass and liquid oozing across the sleek wood floor.

"Oops," she said.

"Hello, Grace," he said.

She looked up. "Oh, hello, Logan."

"You're fired." He turned to leave before he did something stupid like sweep her up against him and kiss her until neither of them could breathe. He'd already learned that sex wasn't the answer, though he wanted her more than ever. The fact that she was here didn't mean a damn thing had changed.

"You can't fire me."

He whirled around. "Oh, yeah? Why not?"

"Because I love you."

Logan glared at her in spite of the fact that his heart took a hard lurch at her words. "Oh, really? I thought you were way too smart to fall for someone like me."

She smiled. "As it turns out, I'm a complete idiot."

He sighed. "No you're not, Grace."

"It's true." She walked up close to him and pressed her hand against his chest.

He was helpless to move. Damn it, he didn't *want* to move. Just her touch was enough to ease away the pain of the past few days. "Grace."

"It's no excuse for the way I behaved," she said, "but

I've grown used to men walking away from me in my life. I just assumed you would do it, too."

"You didn't trust me."

"I did, Logan. I trusted you with my heart."

"But not with your spores." Logan wondered if this conversation sounded as weird to everyone else in the room as it sounded to him. It didn't matter. He wanted to get it over with. "Grace, you didn't trust me enough to do the right thing."

"I know and I'll never forgive myself. I was wrong. I admit it. Can you ever forgive me and let me back into your life?"

"I'm not sure."

"Oh, for God's sake," Aidan shouted in exasperation from across the room. "Just kiss the girl and get on with it."

Logan pierced him with a look. "You of all people should understand why trust is so important."

"Yeah, yeah, your ex-wife cheated," Aidan said, shaking his head. "Blah, blah, blah."

Logan bared his teeth and Grace gasped, but Aidan ignored it all. "And not only was she a cheat, but thanks to the Switch, we found out she was too self-involved to take the time to learn the differences between you and me."

"What's your point, Aidan?" Logan said.

"My point is that Grace could see the differences from the first minute she met me. That's because Grace is in love with you. Even I figured that out. And I think she's earned your forgiveness. Haven't you, Grace?"

Grace flashed Aidan a sweet smile that pissed off Logan even more.

"Logan," Grace said, forcing his attention back to her. "It never occurred to me that you would care. Nobody's ever cared, so I didn't know what that looked like or felt like. I should've, but I didn't. And that makes me as stupid—"

"You're not stupid."

"Yes," she said earnestly. "I'm as stupid as a big bag of dirt."

Logan was taken aback. "That's a little harsh, Grace."

"It true, a big bag of dirt, with sphagnum and peat moss thrown in there."

"Sounds like potting soil."

She clapped her hands. "See how smart you are? No wonder I love you so much."

Logan laughed and pulled her into his arms. "So are you, because you came back to me."

"Kiss me, please?"

He kissed her. "I love you, Grace."

"Oh, Logan, I love you, too." She stretched up on her toes and met his mouth in a kiss meant to seal a promise.

Logan touched her cheek. "But you're still fired, Grace. I can't afford the breakage bills."

"Fine," she said, laughing. "But I'm not leaving here, ever again."

"What about your laboratory?"

"I don't care," she said. "I'll...well, to be honest, I don't know what I'll do. But I'm not worried."

"I'm not worried, either," he said, wrapping his arms around her. "Because I'm going to find a nice spot to break ground on a new research lab right here on the island."

She gazed up at him. "You'd build a lab for me?"

Logan saw a sheen of tears in her eyes and his heart overflowed with joy for this very smart woman who'd stolen his heart. "I'd do just about anything for you, Grace. If you hadn't come back to me, I would've gone to get you in another day or two. I can't live without you, spores and all."

Applause broke out in the bar as Logan and Grace sealed their love with another long kiss and a whispered promise to each other that they would always be together.

* * * * *

IMPOSSIBLE
TO RESIST

JANICE MAYNARD

To Judy Flohr – Thanks for all you do to support
authors, books and your wide circle of friends!
You are a special woman!

One

Jacob Wolff had seen more than his share of naked women. He knew the female body inside and out. After all, he was a doctor.

But when Ariel Dane set foot in his office, fully clothed, he reacted like a man, not a physician.

Jacob retreated behind his pewter-colored metal desk and motioned for her to sit. "Make yourself comfortable, Ms. Dane."

She might as well have been deaf for all the notice she afforded his pleasantries. With quick, nervous steps, she approached the broad picture window and stared out at the forest, her hands clasped behind her back.

Jacob took the opportunity to study her. She was thin, too thin. But that was no doubt the influence of Hollywood. Ariel Dane was a star. And seeing her in the flesh for the first time, he understood why. She was exquisite. Ethereal.

Her pale blond hair often flowed across the pillow of a leading man. Today it was confined in a simple ponytail. The severe style lent emphasis to her finely-drawn features, and drew attention to the delicate curve of the nape of her neck.

Jacob shifted restlessly, leaning back in his chair. The silence didn't bother him. She would speak when she was ready. What disturbed him was the way his sex stirred and his breathing quickened. He had not been with a woman in years. But that meant nothing. He'd learned to subdue his sexuality at will. Rarely did he allow his body to best him. Now, in the presence of a woman whose image had no doubt fueled a million male fantasies, he found that he was human after all.

Her silence outlasted his curiosity. "How did you know to contact me, Ms. Dane?"

She half turned, finally deigning to answer, her expression pensive. "You know Jeremy Vargas, don't you? The actor?"

"Slightly. My new sister-in-law, Olivia, is a close friend of his."

She nodded, returning her gaze to the lush jungle of hardwood trees, rhododendron and laurel. "He saw me at a party recently and told me I looked like sh—"

She stopped short. He saw her shoulders tense.

Turning to face him, she winced. "Sorry. Let's just say that Jeremy was not particularly flattering in his assessment of my current attractiveness. He told me I should come to see you. Insisted on giving me your contact information."

"There are doctors in Hollywood."

She lifted her chin, her expression hunted. "Jeremy says that because of what your family has endured from the press over the years, you're unfailingly discreet. Was he wrong? I'm well aware that a copy of my medical records would fetch a handy sum from the paparazzi. I have nowhere else to turn. No one else I can trust completely."

"I don't need your money, Ms. Dane. And my family and I have no great fondness for the gutter press. So yes, your secrets are safe with me."

"Thank you." A tiny, hiccupped sob escaped her throat.

"You don't know what that means to me." She wrapped her arms around her waist. The pale-pink silk shirtdress she wore halted just above her knees and displayed a pair of slim, spectacular legs. The thin fabric outlined pert, though small, breasts. If she wore a bra, it was flimsy, because he could see the outline of her nipples.

His throat dried, and he cursed inwardly. *Get a grip, Jacob.*

"I have to tell you, Ms. Dane, that I don't have much experience with eating disorders. But I could refer you to a private facility."

Shock flashed across her face. "I must look worse than I thought."

Her voice didn't match her fragile appearance. It was low and husky and made a man think about sex. Which was, perhaps, part of the reason her career had skyrocketed. After a string of well-paid childhood gigs, she'd landed her first "adult" starring role at seventeen.

"You are incredibly lovely," he said, his tone deliberately devoid of emotion. "But clearly, you are ill. It's my job to notice things like that."

She cocked her head, staring at him with an intensity that made him sweat beneath his crisp white dress shirt. Humor seasoned her words. "I love milkshakes, greasy fries and pizza. My metabolism runs at full tilt. And I hate to throw up. I don't have an eating disorder." A tiny, but recognizable, grin lifted the corners of her unadorned mouth. "Show me a plate of junk food, and I'll prove it to you."

Relief flooded his stomach. Anorexia and bulimia were damned serious. And not really his area of expertise.

But then another, even less palatable thought occurred to him. Was she addicted to recreational drugs? Her reputation was no secret, even for a man who lived in self-imposed exile. Party girl. Serial dater. Shallow princess.

He wasn't an idiot. He knew that the media loved to exaggerate both the good and the bad. So he would give her the benefit of the doubt. "Speaking of food," he said. "Would you like something? I can provide light fare here, or a quick call up the hill will net us something fancy."

"I'm fine." Now she prowled, picking up a book here, a photo there. She stopped, holding a framed image that was one of his favorites. "Who's this?"

"My brothers and I. When we were teenagers. Dad let us do a rafting trip on the Colorado. As far as I know, it was our only true vacation."

"Why?" she asked, frowning. "Is he super frugal?"

"It wasn't a question of money. Our mother and our aunt were kidnapped and killed when we were young. My father lived in fear that his children would be targets."

"I'm so sorry," she whispered, huge periwinkle eyes filled with distress. "I've heard bits and pieces about your family's struggles, of course, but meeting you makes it seem more real."

He shrugged. "It was a long time ago. Most people know the story. How old are you?"

"Twenty-two."

Good lord. She hadn't even been born when the Wolffs suffered their very public tragedy.

Her eyes narrowed. "I sent you all that info in my email. Every bit of your incredibly thorough seven-page form."

"My fault entirely. I wasn't expecting you so soon." The message had only come through on his computer the evening before. "I'll read it over later." He was rarely inclined to get personal with a patient. But for some reason, he wanted to reassure her. "We have more in common than you might think, Ms. Dane. My family has been the target of the paparazzi for years, ever since my mother and aunt were murdered. The perpetrators were never caught, so occasionally the story surfaces again."

"I'm sorry," she said, her tone formal. "And I know I should have waited for you to contact me about an appointment. But I don't have much time."

His stomach pitched in irrational fear. "You already have a diagnosis?"

She nodded, pacing the length of the room. As she moved, he scanned her body for evidence of a terminal illness. Though she could stand to gain twenty pounds, her color was good, and he could see no immediate sign that cancer had ravaged her body.

Thinking about it made his gut clench with terror. He fought back the memories and inhaled a sharp breath. "Are you dealing with addiction or something worse?" The words came out bluntly and sounded more judgmental than he had intended.

She froze, halfway between his desk and the door. Approaching him slowly, she sank into the chair he had offered and frowned. "My God, you don't pull any punches, do you?"

With only inches separating them, he was close enough to detect hints of lavender and gray in her clear irises. In a black-and-white film, she could have been a younger Ingrid Bergman. Her beauty was timeless, classic. Unfortunately, most movie directors chose to turn her into a sexed-up nymphet for their summer blockbusters.

Jacob kept his pose casual, though his emotions were anything but at the moment. "I can't help you if I don't know the truth."

Her hands were graceful, long fingers bare, the nails French-manicured. She wore no jewelry there, not even a watch. The only adornment she had allowed herself was a modest pair of diamond stud earrings that caught the light when she moved her head.

Her gaze skittered away as if disconcerted by his visual examination. She sighed, her hands resting on the arms of the chair. "I've been told that you see only high-profile patients whose utmost need is privacy."

"Yes."

"So you understand why I need your help."

"I understand the need for discretion. I've yet to hear your actual reason for coming to me."

Without waiting for an answer, she rose to her feet and paced again. "Why did you become a doctor?" she asked, her back toward him.

Jacob swallowed, fighting the urge to draw her back to the chair so he could inhale her scent. "When my mother was killed, I remember crying and asking my father why the doctors didn't do something. At the time, I didn't really understand that she had died instantly of a gunshot wound. Dad told me no one could have saved her."

Ariel faced him, eyes shadowed with concern. "But you didn't buy that?"

Jacob shrugged. "I was a little kid. I decided then and there that I would become a doctor so other families wouldn't have to deal with the heartache that was tearing us apart."

"Sweet."

"But misguided."

"Surely you realize that your healing skills are valuable."

"Doctors are not gods, despite what some of my colleagues might believe. We run the numbers, make our best guesses, and pray."

"Why do you do it, then, if you're so dubious of your worth?"

"I know what it's like to have no private life, to have the whole world speculating, sometimes even lying, about those I love. So when I can help people who can't go anywhere else for medical care, I provide a service. When I'm not seeing patients, my passion is leukemia research. I have the time and the money to make a difference there."

"Why leukemia specifically?"

"When I was six or seven, my best friend, other than my cousins and siblings, was the son of a man who was in charge of the stables and all our animals. The boy's name was Eddie. He was diagnosed with leukemia, and despite the fact that my father and uncle brought in the very best doctors and paid

for every available treatment, Eddie died at the age of eight.
I already knew, even then, that I wanted to be a doctor. Later
in life, the memory of losing Eddie fine-tuned my medical
training."

"That's very admirable."

He shrugged. "I love my work. But it's not glamorous." He
stopped and grinned. "At least not until today."

Ariel ignored his compliment. "And what about the poor
and not so famous?"

"If you're talking about medical care in general, I can assure
you that the Wolff family invests heavily in Doctors Without
Borders. My brother Kieran and I have built several clinics on
our own both here and abroad. You needn't feel guilty that ac-
cessing my services makes you some kind of prima donna."

The tiny grin reappeared. "Too late for that. I'm a spoiled,
promiscuous bitch, didn't you know?"

Beneath the flip words he heard pain. "Does it bother you?
The constant scrutiny?"

Small white teeth worried her lower lip. "It shouldn't by
now. God knows I've had years to get used to it."

"But it stings."

Her gaze locked with his; her long-lashed eyes filled with
tears. "Understatement, Doc."

She visibly shook off her distress, wiping her eyes with the
back of one hand.

He offered her a box of tissues. "Sit down, Miss Dane.
Please."

"Call me Ariel." She sank into the chair once again, kicked
off her flat silver sandals, and tucked her feet beneath her.

Jacob tried not to notice the way her skirt rode up her toned,
shapely thighs. "It's a pretty name. And not very common."

She leaned forward, one elbow on the desk, head resting on
her hand. "*The Little Mermaid* was my mom's favorite movie
when I was born."

"But you're blonde. The real Ariel was a redhead." Even

as he said it, he scoffed at himself. Hair color in Hollywood changed with the tide and the seasons.

"Didn't matter. And yes," she said, seeming to read his thoughts. "I *am* a natural blonde, not that anyone cares. I've never dyed my hair for a part. Though I *have* worn wigs."

"Why draw the line there? I thought most actresses would do anything for a plum role."

"I always heard that blondes have more fun. I guess I'm still waiting to see if that's true."

He heard the self-derisive note in her voice. The wry cynicism made her appear far older than her years.

"Don't you enjoy what you do?"

"There's no such thing as a perfect job, Dr. Wolff. I'm surprised you don't know that."

"You've got me there." He inched back in his chair, her closeness making him re-evaluate his Hippocratic Oath. Becoming this woman's medical provider was not a realistic option. Not when he was already wondering if those soft pink lips tasted as good as they looked. "Are you ready to tell me why you've come to Wolff Mountain?" he asked, growing impatient and itchy to be done with this awkward though tantalizing interview.

"Tell me about this place," she demanded, clearly stalling. "I caught a glimpse of the main house through the trees. It looks like a castle."

"We call it that on occasion," he admitted. "But growing up, it was just home."

"Pretty amazing home. Acres and acres of wilderness. Tucked away in the Blue Ridge Mountains. Private drive a million miles long. Not bad at all."

"It was a prison growing up." He stopped short, nearly biting his tongue with the force of his about-face. Patients were patients. Not confidantes. "I think we need to get back to you, Ms. Dane." She shot him a warning glance, and he backpedaled. "Ariel. And you might as well call me Jacob."

"What if I prefer Dr. Wolff?"

He scowled, confused and aroused and frustrated with himself. "I thought that movie industry professionals preferred informality."

"I'd rather maintain a bit of distance with a man who might see me naked."

Naked? He gulped. "I think you've made a trip for nothing, Ariel. I can't help you."

She sat up, eyes narrowing. "I haven't told you what's wrong with me yet."

"Are you going to?" He sounded gruff, even to his own ears.

"Why are you angry?"

"I'm not angry," he corrected with pedantic exactitude. "I'm busy. I was in the midst of a project when you arrived."

"Most men make time for me."

He didn't doubt it for an instant. "I thought you wanted a doctor, not a man."

"Maybe I want both."

His jaw ached as he ground his teeth. "I think we're talking at cross purposes, Ariel. Do you or do you not want to tell me why you're here?"

Her pale skin flushed. It would be years before she needed plastic surgery to remain competitive in her line of work. She was the epitome of dewy youth, down to the faint smattering of freckles that lightly dusted the curves of her cheeks.

She hung her head, projecting defeat and resignation. Was it an act designed to make him rush to reassure her?

"Ariel?" He sighed inwardly. At eight years her senior, give or take a few months, he *should* be able to control the conversation better than this. And he damn sure should be able to withstand the effects of eyes designed by their creator to drive a man crazy. She was barely legal. "Talk to me," he coaxed. "Whatever you say will remain in this room, even if you don't become my patient. I swear."

The tip of her tongue came out to wet her lips. Her head

lifted, revealing an expression that was indecipherable. "I need to hire you for the next two months," she said, tossing it out there without ceremony.

He frowned, struggling to understand. "As your doctor?"

She winced, wriggling in her seat, exposing another three inches of thigh. "As my boyfriend."

Two

Ariel groaned inwardly. That could have gone better. She'd tipped her hand clumsily and far too soon. But there was something about Jacob Wolff that threw her off balance.

For one thing, he was nothing like she had imagined. She'd been expecting a fortysomething, lab-coat-clad father figure wearing gold-rimmed glasses. Someone she could pour her heart out to in comfort.

Jacob Wolff was young, seriously hot and made her nervous as hell. His gray-eyed gaze was X-ray-like, exposing her in ways that made auditioning for a part seem like a walk in the park.

His short-cropped black hair was styled in a no-nonsense fashion, as was the plain but expensive hand-tailored shirt he wore. Broad shoulders strained the seams of the garment. It was tucked into dark slacks that showcased his flat belly and hard thighs.

Ariel spent her days surrounded by handsome men. Men who made their living with the help of six-pack abs honed in a gym. But Jacob Wolff was real in a way unmatched by most males of her acquaintance. His calm confidence and unsmiling intensity were sexy and appealing.

At the moment, he could not have been less encouraging. His brows drew together in a fierce scowl, and his body language signaled his wish to end what was proving to be an embarrassing interlude.

He cleared his throat. "Forgive me if I don't understand. Your boyfriend?"

His incredulity made heat rise from her throat to her cheeks. "I realize that *boyfriend* is a fairly juvenile term. You're a mature man."

A trace of pique flittered across his face. "As in old? Trust me, Ariel. I'm well aware that I'm facing down thirty while you are a mere child."

"Don't patronize me," she snapped. "I'm no innocent. They eat babies for lunch in Hollywood. I had to grow up fast."

"You look about sixteen."

"Well, I'm not. No one would second-guess us as a couple. My mother says I'm an old soul."

"We're wandering away from the point. Again. Why do you need a boyfriend? Aren't you dating that rapper?"

"It was a publicity photo. I'm surprised you saw it." She was also intrigued.

"I may live like a hermit, but even decrepit men like me have moved beyond rotary phones and dial-up internet. You're in the news every other day. Haven't you noticed?"

His quick, wry smile made her stomach flip. "I don't read the entertainment news."

"Shocking, Ms. Dane. Shocking." He leaned back in his chair and clasped his hands over his trim waist. "It's a good thing I don't charge by the hour. You're not very good at this doctor/patient thing."

"Well, you suck at being a boyfriend."

He shrugged. "You're dumping me already?" A long, exaggerated sigh made his chest rise and fall. "Story of my life."

"Don't be ridiculous. I can't imagine any woman dumping you. Surely you've had your share of serious relationships?"

His face closed up, every nuance of expression wiped away. The quick but conspicuous glance at his watch was designed to put her in her place. "Either be honest with me, Ariel, or leave."

I have more important things to do. The unspoken subtext made her skin flame with color a second time. "I'm ill," she said quietly, knowing beyond a doubt that she had wasted a trip. Jacob Wolff was not the kind of man to be manipulated by feminine wiles.

He went still, his eyes narrowing with suspicion. "Is this a joke? I feel like we're in a play and you forgot to give me my lines."

She picked at a spot of lint on her skirt. "You're rather intimidating, you know. Aren't doctors supposed to have good bedside manners?"

Again, a flash of that sexy smile. Its rarity made it even more compelling. "We're not in bed, Ariel. Keep talking," he insisted. "You're on a roll."

"It's true," she whispered, her throat tight. The way he said the word *bed* made her all shivery inside. "I'm sick. That's why I need you to be my boyfriend."

Perhaps he realized how close she was to breaking down, because his voice gentled. "Start at the beginning. I won't judge and I won't interrupt. I promise. I want to help you, Ariel. You can trust me."

The room seemed far too silent suddenly. And annoyingly stuffy. Ariel wanted to throw open the windows and let in fresh air along with the sounds of the forest. But the room wasn't hers to command. So she resisted. Barely.

She lifted her shoulders in a careless shrug. If he wanted to begin with Act One, who was she to complain? "I took my mother to the Amazon a few months ago. She's been diagnosed with advanced breast cancer, and I wanted us to go on one last trip while she was still able to manage it."

Jacob's gaze was watchful. "I'm sorry to hear that."

Ariel waved a careless hand, feeling anew the pinch of grief. "She's made her peace with dying."

"And what about you?"

Her throat closed up painfully, making it impossible to speak for several long seconds. "I'm getting there. It's been just the two of us for most of my life, so you'll understand when I say that I can't imagine my world without her."

"I've read somewhere that she was responsible for putting you in commercials when you were little. Is that true?"

"Yes. Most people assume it was for the money…since my father walked out on us."

"But you disagree?"

"The money helped. I know that. But I think it was her way of giving me options. She had very few financial resources. But one of her cousins was a talent scout, and she asked him to help her get me started in the industry."

"Did you ever resent her for that?"

Ariel laughed, caught off guard by his assumption. "Oh, God no. I was a ham from the very beginning. I loved the lime-light, the applause, the crowds. Acting gave me validation."

"But you never went to college, right? You've worked straight through?"

Was that criticism she heard in his voice? Or was she being way too sensitive? "I've done two movies a year since I turned fourteen, sometimes three. So no, my education ended rather abruptly with a high school diploma. Besides, I wasn't that good a student anyway, so it was no great loss. And I make plenty of money as it is. Getting a degree would have been a waste of time."

"Are you trying to convince me or yourself?" he asked quietly.

Stunned at his perspicacity, she bit her lip. "Now *you're* wandering off topic," she said pointedly, ignoring his question.

He held up his hands. "Duly noted. Please continue."

"My mother loves to travel. So when I became successful, I started working on her bucket list during breaks in my schedule. We've been to Paris and Rome and Johannesburg and—well, lots of places."

"Was the trip to the Amazon a success? Did her strength hold out?"

"My mother was a rock. I'm the one who got sick."

His gaze sharpened. "What happened?"

"We'd been there almost five weeks. It was time to go home. I came down with malaria."

"You didn't take medication before you left?"

"I did, but apparently the particular strain I contracted was resistant. I honestly don't remember much of those three or four days. It was terrible. My mother was so scared. We had hired a guide through a travel service, and he was great. But we were in the middle of the jungle and I was too sick to move. Makimba found a tribal medicine man who treated me."

"Good Lord." Jacob sat up, expression aghast. "You could have died."

"Believe me, I know. But whatever combination of herbal remedies and witch doctor mumbo jumbo he used finally worked. I was weak as a kitten when it was over, but I turned the corner."

"What happened then?"

She shrugged. "We came home. I was slated to do voiceovers for a character in an animated film. Fortunately, that was studio work in L.A., so I could be in my own bed every night. And the schedule was not as arduous as if I had been in the midst of shooting a regular movie."

"You need blood tests," he said urgently. "To identify the exact parasite and to determine what schedule of medication is appropriate. Have you had any of that?"

She winced. "No."

"Why in the hell not? Jesus Christ, Ariel. This isn't something to fool around with." He was almost shouting.

"That's why I'm here," she said evenly, projecting as much dignity as she could muster in the face of his disapproval. "I had another flare-up three weeks ago. Not as bad as the first, but still pretty awful. I can't go to a regular doctor and risk any of this information getting out."

"Why? It's not as if you need rehab. You're ill. What's the big deal?" His genuine puzzlement was evident.

"In ten days I will start shooting a movie that could change my career forever. Everyone who has read the script agrees that it's the kind of picture that will generate Oscar buzz. I beat out five other A-list actresses to get the part. If word leaks out that I might become incapacitated in the midst of filming, they could take it away from me."

"And your career is more important than your health?" Now he blasted her with both criticism *and* sarcasm. Silvery gray eyes glittered, spearing her with his disgust.

"Back off," she said heatedly. She leaned toward him, furious with his imperious dismissal of her motives. "You don't know the slightest thing about my life or my circumstances. It's a good thing you don't see patients often, 'cause I gotta tell you, Doc. You're an arrogant pig."

They hovered there like that for half a minute, their faces almost touching, fury arcing between them like a renegade lightning bolt. She could see the rapid heartbeat in his tanned neck, could smell his expensive aftershave.

Amazingly, he was the first one to back down. "I'm sorry," he said stiffly. "I promised I would listen without judgment and without interrupting, and I managed neither. Please go on."

Ariel, primed for battle, was unwillingly disarmed. How rare was it to find a man who knew how to apologize? And yet somehow, he still managed to project an air of absolute superiority that set her teeth on edge. Forced to accept his regret at face value, she settled back into her seat.

"I love what I do," she said. "And I'd be lying if I said I didn't care about the possibilities. I've played so many blonde bimbo parts, I wonder sometimes if the character is taking over. But beyond the professional perks of this new role, I have to be honest. The money this movie will make is no small consideration. My mother has no health insurance. I'm paying for all her bills."

"Ouch."

"Exactly. But even more than that, I want this for my mother. She's had to read all the bad press about me. The stuff they invent, the disparaging remarks. For once, I want to make her proud. She cried when I told her I landed this part."

Jacob Wolff sat in silence, his sharp-featured masculine face giving away no hint of his thought process. Finally, he sighed. "I can't argue with your motives, but I have a hunch that your mother is already proud of you. It sounds like the two of you are very close."

"We are." The words whispered from a throat squeezed by the inescapable knowledge that sometime very soon, Ariel Dane was going to be all alone in the world. She shoved the melancholy thought aside. "So to continue... I *have* to make this movie. But another bout of malaria is the sword of Damocles hanging over my head. I'd like to hire you as my 'on location' physician for the duration of filming."

"Won't that make you look like a diva?"

"Focus, Dr. Wolff. This is where the boyfriend part comes in. No one can know I'm sick. As far as the director, cast and crew are concerned, you and I will be an item. If I have a flare-up, you'll cover for me, treat me and make sure the downtime is minimal. They'll know who you are, of course. No way to hide that you're a Wolff. And your profession doesn't have to be a secret. But they can't know I'm sick."

"Has anyone ever told you you're delusional?"

"My whole world is an illusion, Doc. I do my best work on the other side of reality."

He shook his head. "You make it sound so easy. I deal in facts, Ariel. Black and white. I doubt that I have a drop of dramatic talent anywhere in my body."

"Perhaps not," she drawled, feeling the urge to needle him, "but you do have a very fine body. That and your medical skills are all I need."

If she had hoped to embarrass him, she failed.

Jacob Wolff stared at her, almost visibly picking apart her artless words. "What makes you think I'd even consider such a proposition? I have my work, Ariel, my research. Why would I walk away from that?"

Ariel had learned at the tender age of sixteen that she could use her looks and sexuality to get what she wanted in life, particularly from men. Though her repertoire of ploys had been back-burnered as she matured, this might have been a good time to pull one out. But something about Jacob's invisible but palpable integrity made her loath to cheapen a budding relationship.

She shrugged, gambling wildly. "For the same reason that you became a doctor. You like being needed. And I need you, Jacob Wolff. You and no one else. Will you help me?"

Three

Jacob's poker skills were stretched to the limit. Keeping a professional mask of impassivity was damned near impossible. By God, the little wench had nailed him.

If Ariel died—a very real possibility if she had a serious relapse—he'd never forgive himself. He had sworn an oath not to do harm to anyone. If he let her walk out the door, he would be violating everything he held sacred about preserving human life.

It was more than any altruistic desire to play the hero. He'd seen death too many times. His mother. His fiancée. His childhood friend. Not to mention patients he had lost in med school—never due to any negligence on his part, but loss nevertheless.

In this instance, there was only one choice to be made, despite the upheaval it would cause in his life. But the danger in agreeing—the emotional and unpredictable side effect—would be his surprising hunger for the delicious Ariel Dane. And that admission raised all sorts of warning flags in his psyche.

"When would you need me?" he asked, mentally flipping through his calendar.

"Ten days from now, more or less."

"And where will we be staging our tryst? Please don't tell me that this Oscar-worthy movie is an action flick set in downtown Detroit."

His humor eased some of the tension from her narrow shoulders. "Lucky for you, no. We'll be heading to Antigua. Sun, sand, sangria."

"I'm not much of a drinker. Would that be a problem...in terms of image?"

"Not at all. I rarely drink, either."

His skepticism must have shown through.

Ariel bristled. "I've only been legal for a relatively short time. And in all those months, I've rarely had more than a single glass of wine at any party or event."

He worked to shrug off his preconceptions. She was an actress. A very good one. Playing the wronged innocent would be a piece of cake for her. And Jacob just one more dupe along the way.

But he wanted to believe her. He did believe her. "If I agreed, how long would we be gone?" The flicker of hope that bloomed in her eyes affected him in ways he didn't want to admit.

"The director hopes to wrap in ten weeks and head back to L.A. All the interior shots will be filmed on a sound stage. You'd be free to return to Wolff Mountain then."

"What happens if you get sick once you're back in California?"

She shrugged. "My mother will be around. And I have a couple of friends I trust. But the truth is, by that point, the director and producer couldn't afford to fire me. Not with that much of the movie in the can. Their only choice would be to wait for me to get better."

"You've given this a lot of thought."

She waved a hand at the wall behind his desk. "I may not

have your credentials, Doc, but I've got street smarts in spades. It's a dog-eat-dog world out there in Tinseltown. I should know. I've got the bite marks to prove it."

"I'm not committing to anything until we do a complete medical exam. Will you agree to that?"

"Do I have a choice?"

The atmosphere in the room was charged. Jacob felt the blood pumping in his veins. "No." He was blunt. Determined. In some areas he might be led around by his sex, but not this. Not when it came to a patient's health.

She paled, her hands twisting in distress. "I've already been diagnosed."

"Doesn't matter. I have to make my own assessment. What are you afraid I'll find?"

She stilled, her chin lifting and her expression haughty. "I'm not afraid of anything. I just don't like doctors."

"I'm distraught." He hadn't expected to find anything funny in their situation, but her sheer cussedness amused him. "This will be painless, I assure you."

"Says the man with the needles."

He lifted a brow. "Is that the problem? I'll have to draw blood, you know. But I have a light touch, I swear."

She rocked back and forth in her chair, arms clasped around her waist. "I've been known to pass out when donating during a Red Cross Drive. It's embarrassing."

"I'll take care of you." The words slipped from his lips easily, sounding more like a vow than a simple statement. He cursed inwardly, swallowing hard. "Seriously, Ariel. There's nothing to worry about."

"Will I have to take off my clothes?"

His entire body went on red alert. Ariel. Naked. Beneath his roof. Perhaps building a clinic in his house had been a stupid idea. Because it sure as hell had never occurred to him that he might one day want to walk a patient down the hall to his bedroom.

Or better yet, drag her into the hall and take her standing up because he didn't have the patience to wait.

Sweat dampened his forehead. His hands, his surgically trained hands, trembled. "No," he croaked. "That won't be necessary."

"Then let's get it over with," she muttered, rising gracefully to her feet with a little bounce that made her seem younger than at any moment so far. She reached for her designer purse.

"Leave it," Jacob said. "We won't be gone long and there's no one around to bother it."

As they stepped into the hallway that connected the clinic to the rest of the house, Jacob glanced toward the window that offered a view of the driveway. "Is someone waiting for you?" he asked. "A driver perhaps?"

Ariel yawned and stretched, her breasts straining the thin, soft fabric of her dress. "I drove myself. Flew coach. Wore a black wig and fake glasses. Rented a car. I was lucky. No one recognized me."

"Or if they did, they had the decency not to bother you."

She laughed. "Do you always assume such nice things about the world at large?"

"People are not all bad."

"I'm amazed you can have that attitude after what happened to your family. Isn't that why you're holed up here? To isolate yourselves from danger?"

Jacob sighed, ushering her into an exam room. "My father and uncle brought us to the mountain for that reason initially, but as adults, we've all chosen to live here for different motives. My brother Gareth likes the wild remoteness of the land. Kieran has discovered that despite his world travels, no place else feels like home."

"And you?"

"I like being nearby to care for my father and uncle. They're both getting up in years… Both started families late in life. I keep an eye on them. And the location is perfect for my patients who need privacy." Not to mention the fact that the world at large was a painful place. Jacob had begun his life as an introvert, and the experiences that had shaped him only served to reinforce that tendency.

"Who else lives here on the mountain?"

He fancied she was chattering to distract herself from the upcoming exam, but he indulged her. "I have two brand-new sisters-in-law. And three cousins who come and go."

She perched on the end of the exam table, swinging her legs, hands propped behind her. "You need a decorator," she said bluntly.

"Excuse me?" He frowned, opening a drawer and extracting supplies.

"Your color scheme," she complained, wrinkling her nose with disgust. "It's like a morgue in here. Black and white and stainless steel. And from what I saw of your house, more of the same. What's the deal?"

Jacob had never really thought about it, but what she said was true. Her petal-pink dress was the only spot of color in the room. He put a stethoscope around his neck. "Medical research requires extreme cleanliness. I suppose it's a habit."

Ariel rolled her eyes and sat up straight. "There's a difference between sanitary and institutional. You're rich. Spring for some throw pillows for Pete's sake."

He put his left hand on her shoulder and with his right, placed the cold metal disk over her heart, just at the slope of her breast. "This isn't Club Med. Breathe naturally."

Ariel froze.

He moved the stethoscope. "Don't hold your breath." Her heartbeat was steady, no sign of anything out of the ordinary. Moving around to her back, he said, "Breathe in and out."

She cooperated. Her skin was warm, even through the fabric of her dress. Inwardly, Jacob quaked, stunned by how much he wanted to lean down and trace the line of her spine with his tongue. His usual interactions with actual patients were impersonal. Professional. Businesslike.

But in Ariel's presence, his brain and his body rebelled. He'd had courses in medical ethics. Never in his life had he been tempted to test the limits of what was decent and right. She had come to him for help. The fact that he could imagine her naked was irrelevant.

He stepped back, out of her line of vision. "Heart and lungs sound fine," he said hoarsely. The feel of her soft resilient skin was burned into his palm. "The most important thing will be the blood work."

Ariel flinched visibly. Unable to help himself, he put a hand on her arm. "I'll be quick. Don't watch. Turn your head away."

She craned her neck to see him gathering several empty vials. "This is where a tasteful Monet might come in handy. Something for a focal point."

He chuckled. "You're not in labor. Close your eyes if you have to."

Her expression was morose. "That makes it worse."

Jacob readied the needle, keeping it out of sight. "Tell me about your trip to the Amazon," he coaxed. "And keep your eyes on the cabinet over there."

"Okay." Her voice hit a high squeak. She was more than jumpy, she was terrified. Shaking, even.

He stroked her arm. "Relax, Ariel. All you'll feel is a little sting. I need you to make a fist." With deft movements, he inserted the needle in a vein at the crook of her arm and started filling the first tube.

She made a funny muffled sound and her body went limp. It all happened so quickly, Jacob barely had time to react. He caught her as she fell, but the needle popped loose and blood spurted, spattering her dress and his clothes with modernistic flair.

"Damn it." He eased her back onto the table, determining that despite her extreme pallor she was in no immediate danger. It seemed prudent to grab another needle and get the blood samples before she came to. No point in torturing her.

When he had what he needed, he took a small towel, wet it and dabbed her face and throat. "Wake up, Ariel. Wake up. It's all over."

Finally, her long lashes lifted, eyes the color of gentians gazing at him with confused supplication. "What happened?"

"You fainted."

"Sorry," she muttered, struggling to sit up.

He held her down. "Take it easy. No need to rush."

She extended one arm, squeezing her eyes shut. "Go ahead," she said through gritted teeth. "Do it. I'll be okay this time."

He stroked her cheek, smiling in spite of his concern about her general health. "I'm finished."

One eye opened. "What do you mean?" she asked suspiciously. "I thought you had to fill several vials."

He slid an arm beneath her and slowly lifted her upright. She smelled like sunshine and sweet peas. He inhaled the scent and told himself it didn't go to his head. "I took the blood samples while you were out cold. It seemed like the thing to do."

"That's a little creepy." Ariel smoothed her hair with both hands and straightened her skirt, rubbing ineffectually at the blood spots.

He stared at her. "Creepy? I was trying to be helpful."

"Why are we both covered in blood?"

Her suspicious gaze ruffled him. "It's only a few spots. When you keeled over, the needle popped out."

"Hmm. Maybe you should hire a nurse. This doesn't seem to be your strong suit."

Jacob counted to ten. "Has anyone ever told you you're impertinent?"

Her grin weakened his knees. "Every day, Doc. Every day."

"Would you like to change clothes?" he asked abruptly, vastly afraid that he had no control over this situation at all.

"If you're offering a paper gown, the answer is no."

Ignoring her levity, he cleaned up the mess, replaced his instruments, and labeled the tubes of blood. "How many times a year do you give blood?" he asked.

"As often as they'll let me. Every few months."

"Why?" He was genuinely puzzled.

She nibbled her lower lip, glancing up at him through lowered lashes. "I have a rare blood type," she said simply. "It's important."

And just like that, any last qualms he had about his decision disappeared. Any woman who was tough enough to face down a daunting fear in order to do the right thing deserved his help. Her spunk and "spit-in-the-wind" courage disarmed him as completely as her stunning beauty unmanned him.

He would agree to her proposition. But his emotions wouldn't become involved. He wouldn't allow it. Ariel Dane was his patient. And she was far too young for him. Eight years might as well be twenty. Her delicate spirit needed protection, and he was the man to shield her from the world both physically and emotionally.

Only one other woman in his life had drawn from him such an urgent need to play the white knight. And though she had been the light of his world, Jacob had failed her. By the time Diane's diagnosis was confirmed, restoring her health had been impossible. All Jacob had been able to do for her was offer his love and support through weeks of painful treatments and then hold her hand when she breathed her last breath.

Never would he put himself in that position again. It was far too painful. This time, he was prepared for his role. Doctor, protector, friend. This time, the outcome would be different.

Four

Ariel watched Jacob Wolff carefully. Early in life she had learned to study people…their habits, their idiosyncrasies. The dishy doctor fascinated her. Power and control emanated from him with invisible but potent force. She wanted to fling herself against his calm and see if she could ruffle the waters. Flirting came naturally to her, and though it was perhaps unfair to Jacob, already she acknowledged in herself an urge to see if she could crack the invisible wall he erected to keep people at a distance.

Jacob finished his task and eyed her warily. "I was serious about changing clothes," he said. She slid off the table, but had to reach out a hand when the room spun in dizzying circles. Unfortunately, the closest unyielding surface was the doc's chest. It was broad and firm, with sleek muscles that flexed beneath his starched white shirt.

He put an arm around her, which only served to make her dizzier. His cheek lowered to hers. "Are you okay?"

They were close enough that she felt a brief brush from his

slightly stubbled chin. She made herself slide from his loose hold. "Never better," she croaked. "But yes, I'd love to put on some other clothes. This dress looks a little too much like one I wore in a slasher movie a few years back."

Jacob ushered her out into the hall. "Shall I get your bag out of the car?"

She nodded, her feet glued to the floor by an unnerving bout of shyness. "I would appreciate it. The suitcase is in the trunk. The doors aren't locked."

As he stepped outside, she ducked into his office and retrieved her purse. When he returned, she managed a cheery smile. "You're acting awfully nice for someone who has a reputation for being antisocial."

He hesitated, looking abashed. "Not really antisocial. Merely focused on my work."

"I see." Another challenge.

She followed him into the living room. Acres of onyx carpet cushioned their feet, not a single dust bunny or speck of lint evident anywhere. White leather furniture looked comfy, but cold. All in all, Jacob's decorating scheme was modern and sleek. With the careful addition of well-placed colorful accents here and there, it might even be considered charmingly sophisticated.

They crossed the room to a hallway on the far side. Bedrooms opened off a long corridor.

Jacob entered the nearest open door, placing her generic black suitcase on the floor beside the bed. "Feel free to use the bathroom," he said. "I'll wait for you in the living room."

"I don't have any hotel reservations," Ariel said bluntly.

He cocked his head. "I can't decide if you're disingenuous or calculating."

"Wow." She winced. "Can I pick answer number three?"

"And that would be?"

"Focused. On my work."

He actually laughed, and she felt as if she had won the lottery. "Touché." His expression changed. "Why do you want to stay here, Ariel?"

"My flight is not until tomorrow. The closest hotels are well over an hour away. I don't want to take a chance of people recognizing me and wondering why I'm in the area."

He nodded briefly as if validating her reasoning. "Get changed. We'll hash out a plan when you're ready." He closed the door behind him, leaving Ariel alone in a huge room decked out in shades of ivory and taupe. The furnishings were feminine, and she wondered if he entertained female guests here. If so, they probably slept in Jacob's bed.

The pinch of jealousy was foreign.

Though she would have loved a shower after the long flight and the subsequent drive, she wasted no time in stripping off the dress and rummaging in her case for comfy jeans and a light cotton pullover. Silver leather flats completed her Ariel-out-of-the-limelight ensemble.

She left the suitcase behind when she went to find Jacob, hoping he was going to let her stay. When she found him, he was sprawled on the sofa in front of the TV looking relaxed and masculine with his sock-clad feet propped up on a black lacquer coffee table.

He stood immediately when she entered. "That was fast." His gaze went to her bra-less breasts for a split second.

"I'm low maintenance."

"That remains to be seen."

The note of sarcasm in his voice flustered her. In defense, she trained her gaze on the television screen. "I guess you've got satellite way up here."

He waved at an adjacent sofa. "Do you really want to talk about my electronics? Sit down, Ariel."

The intimacy of the living room lent a different dynamic than she had experienced in the clinic. Now she and Jacob seemed more like man and woman than doctor and patient. She curled into the embrace of the soft leather with her feet beneath her. Leaning an arm on the side, she propped her head on her hand. "What do you do for fun?" she asked, really wanting to know.

"Fun?" His face was blank as he settled back into his original seat.

"Leisure...recreation...hobbies...relaxation."

"Oh." For a simple question, it seemed to flummox him. "I read medical journals. And I hike the mountain with my brothers."

"That's it?"

He frowned. "What did you expect? I'm not the party type. Which is why you might want to reconsider asking me to portray your love interest."

"Jeremy Vargas told me you made a perfect score on the SATs when you were fifteen. He said you have three completely different master's degrees and you're a medical doctor. Is all of that true?"

Her host, his arms outstretched, drummed his fingers on the back of the sofa. "Does it matter?" His gaze and his words were bland.

"You're freakishly intelligent, aren't you?" She stood up and deliberately joined him, leaving a mere three feet between them.

Jacob's eyes narrowed. "What is this about, Ariel?"

"I'm rethinking my proposition."

"Why?"

"I'm not sure what a guy like you will do all day long in Antigua."

"Would I be allowed on the set?"

"If I say so."

"You have that much clout?"

"For what it's worth, yes."

"I'm thinking you're pretty smart, as well."

His gentle smile did something odd to the pit of her stomach. "Not the same thing at all. You save lives."

"I do research that helps other people save lives. It's not glamorous. Repetition and record-keeping and hoping every day for a breakthrough."

"What are you working on right now?" She inched a little closer, waiting to see if he would stop her. Her behavior was outrageous, but she couldn't seem to help herself. He was gorgeous. And smart. And far more appealing than any man she'd met in years.

Jacob didn't bat an eye at her not-so-subtle move. Was she making any impact on him at all? Or was he really immune to her femininity?

His even tone gave nothing away. "I'm not the only one, but I'm working to develop what one day may become a cancer vaccine."

"Well, crap." She pulled her knees to her chest and glared at him. Whether he meant to or not, he had shut her down.

"That's a problem for you?"

"How am I supposed to lure you away when my selfishness could cost someone their life?"

"It's rarely that time sensitive, Ariel. We're talking research that takes months, years. And to get back to your original concern, you don't have to worry about me. I'm a big boy. I make my own decisions, and I can entertain myself."

"Do you work out?"

Again the flummoxed look. "Following your conversational gambits is like chasing a rabbit in the woods."

"Sorry. My mind jumps. Can you answer the question?"

His eyes narrowed. "I swim laps at Gareth's pool. I walk up and down the mountain when the mood hits me. I cut firewood for the winter. Have I passed?"

"Passed?"

"The test. I got the impression that you were looking for some specific answers."

If nothing else, she had annoyed him. "Don't be ridiculous. I'm merely trying to establish what kind of man you are."

"There are varieties?"

"Of course there are. I've nailed you as the selfless, driven, save-the-world type."

He stood up. And from her vantage point, he looked really big. "Come here, Ariel."

She obeyed, more out of curiosity than anything else. When they were standing toe to toe, he reached out and tucked her hair behind her ears. Shivering, she lifted her chin and met his gaze head-on. "What do you want?"

"I'm wondering how good an actress you are. If you want to make people believe that you and I are a couple, we'll have to kiss at least once or twice, right?"

Her throat dried as she tried to swallow a lump the size of Texas. "Does that mean you're considering my proposal?"

His gray eyes warmed to charcoal embers. "Answer my question first. Would we have to occasionally kiss?"

She nodded slowly, feeling completely out of her depth. Rarely did a man manage to throw her off kilter. But Jacob Wolff was giving it his best shot. "Yeeessss," she drawled. "I'd say that would be necessary and appropriate."

His quick, self-deprecating smile warmed her to her toes. "Well then, let's give it a shot."

Before she could agree or protest, or better yet shoot back with a smart-ass response, Jacob's mouth moved across hers.

Ariel had kissed lots of men. Some tasted like cigarettes or salami. A few were pleasant but unremarkable. The guys who had something to prove usually bent her neck backward at an awkward angle. And occasionally there were one or two who were genuinely good at locking lips.

Jacob's kiss defied description, mostly because she didn't have the mental sharpness to analyze it. Her synapses were firing like random paintball gun explosions, making her knees rubbery and her head muzzy. Jacob's arms encircled her firmly, bringing her close to his chest. He was determined and possessive, but not forceful. The caress of his lips on hers was toe-curlingly sensual, but with barely a hint of tongue.

For a first kiss, it was damned near perfect.

They broke apart in unison. Ariel stumbled backward, reaching behind her for a seat. Unfortunately, reaching for her habitual cheeky repartee was not so simple. She cleared her throat. "Not bad, Doc. Especially for a first take."

He folded his arms across his chest. Was he breathing hard? She'd like to think so.

When he remained silent, she squirmed. "What's going on in that computer brain of yours?"

"I'll do it," he said quietly.

"Because of the kiss?"

He shook his head. "No. Because as much as I hate to admit it, you have me pegged. I can't let you go off on your own knowing you could fall ill at any moment."

"You don't look too happy about it. Was kissing me so awful?"

"Let's get something straight, Ms. Ariel Dane. I'll kiss you when the occasion demands it. And God help me, I'll enjoy it. But that's as far as it goes. You're my patient."

"Who said I wanted it to go any farther?" she pouted. "Do you think you're irresistible?"

"I'm a man…and you're an incredibly beautiful woman. Things happen."

"What kind of things?" When he got on his high horse, it was fun to tease him.

"Lord, you're a brat." The words were exasperated, but his reluctant smile was laced with humor.

"You can keep telling yourself that I'm little more than a child, but it's not true. I grew up a long time ago. Eyes wide open. Ideals shattered. Illusions dissolved. I'm no ingénue. And I'm in charge of my life. So while I will be eternally grateful for your help in this specific situation, I don't need or want you to boss me around."

"When it comes to your health, I'll have the last word. Or the deal's off."

"I don't understand."

"If I tell you to nap, you nap. If I expect you to eat healthy meals, that's what will happen. You're hiring me to be your doctor. The boyfriend is only a front. *He* won't make any demands, but Dr. Jacob Wolff will have plenty."

Her heart fluttered in her chest. Jacob's dictatorial manner might have raised her hackles in another situation, but after that kiss, his masculine authority made her swoon inwardly with an entirely non-PC fit of feminine vapors.

"Then we have a deal?" At this point, she might cry if he backed out. And she never cried in real life.

He nodded once, his pewter gaze hooded. "I may be losing my mind, but yes, we have a deal."

She wanted to throw herself in his arms and try for kiss number two. But she restrained herself. If Jacob was impressed by decorum and common sense, she could reform. Probably. "Thank you, Doc," she said quietly. "And since you're in the mood to say yes, I'll ask you again. May I spend the night?"

Five

Jacob tried to take her words at face value. He really did. But he was fairly certain the little minx was baiting him. She was so accustomed to getting what she wanted, her boldness came across as a mix of innocence and unabashed confidence.

Kissing her had been a test—for him. He wanted to know what he was up against before he agreed. Given the way his body reacted to hers, the answer to her proposition *should* be an unequivocal no. But even knowing the danger she presented, he couldn't get past the fact that she needed him. And God help him, he couldn't turn her away.

He picked up the remote and turned off the TV. It had been playing quietly in the background while he and Ariel sparred. Keeping his back to her for a few seconds, he marshaled his thoughts. It was inevitable that she had picked up on his attraction to her. His erection had pulsed between them during that restrained but surprisingly steamy kiss.

But she needed to know from the beginning that he wouldn't be led around by his— Oh, hell. She was probably amused by his lust. He surely wasn't the first man to want Ariel Dane, and he wouldn't be the last.

Bending to put the remote inside the entertainment center, he at last straightened and faced her. "Sure," he said laconically. "I've got bedrooms to spare. But you're leaving tomorrow, right?"

She nodded. "I have lots to do at home to get ready for the trip. I'm guessing that you will, as well."

"Indeed. Starting with an edited but truthful explanation for my family as to why I'm jetting off to the Caribbean on a whim."

"Why does it have to be edited? Couldn't you just call it a vacation?"

"I want to protect your privacy. And I don't take vacations."

She flushed. "You'll think of something." While Jacob leaned a hip against the back of the sofa, she stood up to prowl, her nervous energy palpable. A Barbie doll peeking from beneath a chair caught her attention. She picked it up. "Is this for research purposes?"

"I have a brand-new niece…not an infant," he hastened to explain. "But Kieran recently found out he has a daughter. Cammie. She must have left it when they were here last."

Ariel's expression was wistful. "How old is she?"

"Five. Starting kindergarten. We've all fallen in love with her." He paused, struck by the naked longing he saw on her face. "Do you want to have children one day?"

She set the doll on the coffee table and shoved her hands in her back pockets. "It's tough to give kids a normal life in Hollywood."

"Some people manage."

"I don't think I'd be good at it. Motherhood, I mean. I have too many bad habits, too many faults. What kind of example would I be?"

He cocked his head, trying to decipher the words between the lines. "The idea of a perfect mother is a myth."

"You haven't met my mom."

"Perhaps I'll get to one day."

She shrugged. "Doubtful." With an almost visible effort, she slipped back into movie star mode. "I'm hungry," she said with a winsome smile. "Do you cook?"

"Only the basics. We can always go up to the main house and have dinner with the extended family. I can make up some excuse for why you're here."

Unease skittered across her face. "Let's not. I'm sure they are charming people, but they'll want to ask questions and talk movies, and I'm—" She stopped abruptly.

"You're…?"

"I don't know. Tired, I guess. I like your house. It's peaceful. Do you have a pantry?"

There she went again, dragging the conversation off on a tangent. "I do," he conceded. "But I'm not sure how well it's stocked."

She paused beside him during one circuit of the living room, her breast almost brushing his shoulder. "Let's go check it out. It will be fun."

Bemused, he stood up and directed her toward his large kitchen. His cousin, Annalise, had contributed to the design here. Top-of-the-line appliances and countertops in black granite speckled with gray adorned this room where he seldom spent time. It was easier to hop up the hill when he wanted more than a peanut butter sandwich.

Ariel paused, hands on hips, and scanned the area. "Nice," she said. "Nothing a few red dishcloths couldn't spruce up. Why do you have such a fancy kitchen if all of you eat together in the castle?"

"We don't always. I suppose it seems odd to outsiders, but my father and Uncle Vincent hold court every evening. Now that my two brothers are married, they're often tucked away in their own houses. But my cousins and I may or may not show up at the Wolff dinner table depending on our schedules. And

Gareth and Kieran are welcome with their new brides. It's sort of an open door policy."

"I feel sorry for the chef. Meal planning must be a nightmare."

Jacob had never really thought about it. "The kitchen staff is compensated well," he said, ruefully noting the defensiveness in his voice. Again, Ariel had put him at a disadvantage. Certainly she was surrounded by a host of people to do her bidding on any given day. And yet somehow she seemed more clued in than most about other perspectives than her own.

The copper-bottomed pots hanging overhead caught her attention. "Here's some color," she teased.

"I could probably dig up a blue pot holder if it would make you feel better."

She ignored him, flinging open the door to the roomy pantry. "Heads up, Doc." He nearly dropped the bag of flour she tossed in his direction. It was a good thing he was ready for the cans of peaches and blueberries. The fusillade continued until he was hard-pressed to juggle the assortment of groceries.

Finally she was satisfied.

Leaving him to carefully deposit the pile of supplies on the counter, she began flinging open cabinets willy-nilly. Watching Ariel bend over was not the smartest thing Jacob had ever done. Her heart-shaped ass was delineated beautifully in soft, faded denim. His hands itched to palm her butt.

Instead, he crossed his arms over his chest. "May I ask what you have in mind?"

She straightened, a shallow pan in her hand. "Fruit crepes à la Ariel. And bacon if you have any."

His mouth watered while his stomach, for an instant, took precedence over his baser instincts.

"You don't have to cook for me. We have thirty or forty employees on staff."

She twirled the pan, placed it on the stove, and reached in the fridge for butter and bacon. "I like being waited on as much as the next girl," she said, her voice muffled. "But it's kinda nice to be alone, don't you think?"

As her seemingly innocuous words sank into his brain, she straightened. "Sit on a stool and talk to me."

"This is my house," he muttered, the statement a complaint and a reminder to himself. Her loose ponytail exposed a swan-like neck.

"Well, so what. Get over it, Doc. How do you like your bacon?"

"Crisp," he sighed. They chatted while Ariel prepared the meal. On the surface, their conversation was completely ordinary. But something about Ariel's husky voice made the most banal comments sound like an invitation into her bed.

And at the moment, *her* bed was in Jacob's house.

"Do you have relationships with a lot of your leading men?" he asked bluntly.

Her hand stilled, spatula suspended over the thin egg mixture. "Define relationship." Her head was bent, only her profile visible.

"You know what I mean."

She flipped the second crepe onto a plate warming on the side of the stove and shot him a cool glance. "Are we going to share notes on our sex lives? I'm all agog. I hear that doctors are a hot ticket item in the dating pool. You must have plenty of notches in the old bedpost. Orange juice?"

The juxtaposition of her prosaic question with the flammable topic silenced him as he followed her to the small table in the breakfast nook. As she shook out her napkin and took a seat, he realized she wasn't going to answer him. He should be ashamed of his probing question, but he wasn't. He told himself the information might have implications about her general health, but the truth was, he was jealous as hell.

And angry, if he were honest. Ariel was hardly the first talented young actress to fall victim to immaturity. She wasn't exactly Lindsay Lohan or Britney Spears, but she had scored her own share of the tabloid pages.

She said she didn't drink, and Jacob had seen no evidence of drug use. But there had been plenty of men. Lots of men. One who was even old enough to be her father. Had her mother been unable to protect her from the predators who were lured by Ariel's fresh-faced innocence and joie de vivre?

Okay, so maybe *predator* was a harsh word. Thinking of the ways she might have been taken advantage of made his stomach hurt. But more than that, he was uncomfortably aware that he wanted her in the exact same fashion.

His only saving grace would be to resist temptation and to take care of her in every way possible. As he dug into his food, he watched her. Someone had been working overtime when she was conceived. Like an impressionist painting, if you examined every facet of her face and body, she was simply a woman. But put it all together, and Ariel Dane was a masterpiece.

The eyes alone would have made her attractive, but with her luminous skin, perfect bone structure and lithe body, she was the epitome of feminine grace and beauty. The only flaw he could spot anywhere—if you wanted to call it that—was that her ears were a tiny bit big for her head.

As if she had read his mind, she covered the side of her face and frowned. "Quit staring at me. I shouldn't have put my hair up this morning."

"What are you talking about? It's hard not to look. You're a stunning woman."

"On the set, when I was younger, every time I put my hair into a bun or a ponytail, some of the other kids would call me Dumbo."

Jacob frowned. The vulnerability and hurt in that one sentence staggered him. Ariel Dane was regarded as one of the most beautiful women in America. But she had no clue. Incredible.

He finished his last few bites and sat back. "That was fantastic. Thank you, Ariel."

She beamed. "Thank my mom. She started teaching me how to cook when I was ten."

When he saw that she had cleared her plate, he stood up. "If I'm going to be your pseudo boyfriend, let's get one thing straight."

Apprehension widened her eyes. "What?"

He bent down and first kissed the shell of one ear and then the other. "Your pretty little ears are perfect. And if anyone thinks differently, you send them to me and I'll straighten them out."

Ariel scooted away from him and stood to gather the plates. "I didn't know I was hiring Sir Galahad." The words were flip, but he saw her blink away tears, though she tried to hide her emotion.

Concern and empathy mingled in his heart. He knew what it was like to be the cynosure of all eyes, to be judged by a different standard. In his final year in med school, it had come out that he was one of *the* Wolffs. His classmates, many of whom had worked alongside him for years, suddenly regarded him with suspicion and, in a few cases, envy. One angry intern demanded to know why he was taking up a coveted spot in the program when Jacob had more than enough money for a lifetime.

In the blink of an eye, Jacob was standing on the outside looking in. The profession that had welcomed him into its ranks and made him feel as if he belonged was no longer an oasis of normalcy.

Everyone knew that Wolffs were a breed all their own. Some sympathized with him for surviving the long-ago tragedy. But for most, Jacob's connection to the clan meant he was now an alien presence in the world of the hospital.

With an inward sigh for the problems of the past, he followed Ariel into the kitchen and laid down the law. "Leave it," he said firmly as she began attacking the pile of dirty dishes.

Her jaw thrust mulishly. "I was taught to clean up my own mess."

"Don't push it, Ariel." He took the dishcloth out of her hand. "Someone will take care of it. I can see on your face that you're exhausted. Go take a bubble bath. Put your pajamas on. Read a book. Call your mom. You're done for today."

She didn't like being bossed around. That much was clear. But perhaps her reserves of strength were waning, because she finally conceded. "Thank you for your hospitality," she said stiffly. "Will you be here when I leave in the morning?"

"Yes." If he cancelled a meeting in Charlottesville at the university. "What time is your flight?"

"Midafternoon." The surprising intimacy that had bloomed so quickly between them had vanished, leaving behind the stilted conversation of strangers.

He followed her back to her assigned bedroom and hovered in the doorway. "Do you need anything?"

"No." She paused by the bed looking waifish and lost. "Good night, Doc." Her gamine grin was a shadow of its former glory.

"Good night, Ariel." Backing away from the door and shutting it firmly took a great deal of effort.

Six

Ariel wasn't sleepy. By her body clock it was only late afternoon. Jacob Wolff had been trying to get rid of her.

She brushed her teeth and changed into a silky nightie before climbing into bed and surfing the satellite channels. Two of them were showing her own movies. Flipping past them rapidly, she made a face. Watching herself onscreen was torture.

Nothing amid the vast and varied programming schedule seized her attention. And she didn't really have the patience to settle in for a movie.

She'd read the new script a dozen times already. And she had all of next week to prepare. After a long call to her mother, she was still wide awake.

Digging into her suitcase, she found her athletic sneakers and a pair of warm socks. Stripping off the sheer nightgown, she changed into her earlier jeans and top and added the shoes.

French doors on one side of her bedroom opened out onto a ground level patio. She wouldn't be bothering Jacob. No doubt he was sound asleep. Carefully opening the glass panels, which did *not* squeak, she slipped into the scented night.

Her sense of direction had stood her in good stead on many occasions. Tonight, it enabled her to explore. She wouldn't go near the castle—too much chance of discovery. Instead, she headed up and to the left, following higher and higher ground until she broke through the trees and gasped in fright.

Even in the gloom, she could tell that the ground fell away beneath her feet. She paused abruptly, clinging to a small tree to steady her knees. Her breathing was labored, pushed to the limit by the steep climb. Beyond where she stood, the sea of night gave way to a heavenly canopy. Her heart beat faster.

It was spectacular. All around her the forest chirped and whirred with a million night sounds. Unseen animals prowled the woods, but Ariel wasn't afraid. She was one of them. A silent, still creature paying homage to the wild and wonderful darkness.

Time ceased to have meaning. She inhaled the scent of pine, dragging in lungfuls of non-polluted air and feeling it fill her chest with a light, giddy pleasure. Badly, she wanted to see what was in front of her, but an atavistic sense of danger kept her feet rooted in place.

She rested her cheek against the tree trunk, feeling the rough bark press into her cheek almost painfully. This was real. Honest. Deeply spiritual. So much of her existence was make-believe, which she lived for. But sometimes it was nice to remember that the world was bigger than her corner of it.

She might have dozed, her arms wrapped around the tree like a lover. Tomorrow, in the daylight, she would return. The need to expose the mystery in front of her was urgent, exciting.

Jacob's mountain was a place of infinite possibility. Was it fair of her to ask him to leave?

As she pondered the difficult question, a rustle behind her and a disgruntled male voice shattered her calm. "Are you insane?" He loomed beside her, barely breathing hard, his big body radiating warmth and security.

"I didn't mean to wake you. I couldn't sleep."

"So you thought you would throw yourself off a cliff instead?"

Even without seeing his expression, she registered his disapproval. "I'm being careful."

"Ariel," he said, his voice deep and aggravated, "you're about four feet away from a seven-hundred-foot sheer drop."

Wow. Her stomach did a little flip. "I'm fine. Don't be such a worrywart."

She thought she heard him counting to ten. He took her arms, pulling her away from the tree. "Step carefully. Back up slowly."

Clinging more tightly to the trunk, she resisted him. "I like it here. I don't want to leave."

"This is your doctor speaking. Your skin is frozen and you're trembling. Come here."

"Or what?"

"Or the deal is off."

"That's blackmail."

"You signed on for it."

She was definitely tired and chilled, but it went against the grain to let him be so bossy. "Maybe the deal was a stupid idea." She felt him go still.

"Why?" he asked gruffly.

"Because I shouldn't be taking you away from this mountain. It's part of who you are."

"Let me worry about my life. You've got plenty of balls to juggle in yours." He ran his hands up and down her arms, warming them. "Take my hand."

Without thinking, she let go of her bulwark and linked the fingers of her right hand with his left. He tugged her backward insistently, but gently so she didn't stumble.

When they were safely away from the precipice, Jacob

strode back to the house, practically dragging her in his wake. Finally, she dug in her heels. "What's your hurry? I like it out here…with you."

He stopped so abruptly she bumped into him. Instinctively, her arms went around his waist and she burrowed into his warmth. The calendar said late summer, but here on the mountain the night was cold.

Jacob went rigid. "Don't play with me, Ariel," he warned. "I'm not one of your Hollywood pretty boys."

"What does that mean?"

"You may be used to screwing every guy you meet, but that's not my style."

She jerked away, almost tripping over an exposed root. "God, you're a pig. What makes you think I want you?"

"There's something between us," he said quietly. "I'm not imagining it. You're very sexy and you radiate an invitation that would be hard for most men to resist. But if I'm going to help you, I don't want to complicate things. Grow up, Ariel. You don't need to have every man in the universe worshipping at your feet."

"That's a terrible thing to say." She shoved him hard, making him stumble before he regained his balance. Appalled and confused and anxious and angry, she faced off with him, unable to see his expression, but terrified by his silence. Had she made him change his mind?

"I'm sorry," she cried out. "You provoke the hell out of me. Please don't be mad. I have a temper."

Though the mountain climb hadn't strained him, he was breathing heavily now. "So I see."

She flung her arms around him in an agony of remorse. "I'm sorry. I promised to follow doctor's orders. And I will, I swear." When he still didn't respond, she went up on her tiptoes and kissed him. His lips were firm and warm and unresponsive. She pulled back. "Am I forgiven?" She was banking on his good nature, but she didn't know him well enough to read his silence. The anticipation of his response was killing her. "Say something," she cried.

"Does anyone ever deny you anything?" He drew her into his embrace, his mouth covering hers with aching slowness. "One day," he muttered, the words muffled against her lips. "One damn day and already you've got me spinning in the wind."

His tongue slipped between her lips. "Open for me, Ariel."

She obeyed instantly, crying out when his teeth trapped her lower lip and tugged. Her body went liquid, boneless. All of her weight was supported by arms whose tensile strength was normally hidden beneath crisply starched shirts.

Jacob Wolff might look like a man of science, an academic whose computer-like brain dealt with tasks that went beyond the capacity of the normal human. But strip away the veneer, and he was an alpha male. Aroused. Hungry. Determined to teach her a lesson.

The kiss went on and on until her neck ached. Heat pooled between her thighs and made her squirm against him. "Jacob," she panted. "Oh, Jacob."

He was deaf to her tremulous homage. His hands cupped her ass, lifting her more closely against him. She felt the press of his belt buckle, heard the hitch in his breath when her tongue shyly dueled with his.

They were rapidly reaching a point of no return. And she realized in a haze of yearning that she would have to be the one to call a halt. As much as she wanted to see where this led, the memory of Jacob's scathing assessment of her character held her back.

She pushed at his chest. "You don't want this," she panted. "Stop. Now."

"The hell I don't." His arms were bands of steel.

Every instinct she possessed told her that becoming this man's lover would be an experience she would never forget. But he had rules. And she needed him in more ways than one. "Let me go, Jacob," she said gently. She put a hand to his cheek. "Let me go."

A mighty shudder shook his frame and he dropped her to her feet so suddenly, she stumbled. Though he steadied her automatically, he jerked his hand away afterward as if touching her was unbearable. "I don't know what to make of you, Ariel Dane." His voice was quiet, troubled. "Are you a spoiled princess or a recalcitrant child?"

She sucked in a breath, stunned to realize that this man she had just met could wound her. "What if I'm neither? The world is not as black and white as your house and clinic, Doc. Most of us live in shades of gray." Her throat was tight with emotion, making speech difficult. "Perhaps we can start over."

"It's too far gone for that. So we'll make the best of it. I made you a promise and I don't go back on my word."

"Even to a promiscuous party girl?"

"Is that what you are?"

"You seem to have me all figured out. Far be it from me to shatter your illusions." She wrapped her arms around herself and shivered. "It's late. I'm going back to the house. Please don't feel any obligation to see me off in the morning. I think it's best if we keep our distance."

"Is that what you want?"

"We can't always get what we want," she said flatly. "Good night, Doc."

Seven

Ten days later, Jacob stood on the tarmac, watching in bemusement as a young man loaded Ariel's array of baggage into the Wolff private jet. She had balked at the idea of traveling with him at first. Jacob fancied she didn't like the idea of being beholden.

But this way was clearly easier on her, both healthwise and in terms of avoiding her legions of fans. Even first class was no longer the luxury it once was.

He had offered to pick her up in L.A., but they had rendezvoused instead in D.C. Ariel was in full movie-star mode today: five-inch heels in hot pink and black, a chic ebony linen sheath, designer sunglasses and a straw hat trimmed with pink ostrich feathers.

Jacob couldn't remember the last time he had seen a woman wear a hat, with the exception of the queen. But Ariel pulled it off.

Once they were settled in the cabin, she pointedly ignored

him, all her attention on her iPhone as she texted. Her hat was now on the seat beside her.

He moved the frivolous piece of millinery, took the seat and belted in. Most people were impressed the first time they saw the luxurious interior of the Wolff jet. Ariel had barely spared a glance for the plush, armchair-like seats or the trolley of freshly prepared snacks and baked goods offered by the male flight attendant.

Nudging her arm, he demanded her attention. "It's good to see you, Ariel. How are you feeling?"

She paused and looked down her nose at him. "Very well, thank you."

If her voice had been any colder, it would have frozen him to the bone. He ran a hand down her arm, feeling both its fragility and its strength. Despite her illness, she had a body that was physically fit—a necessity in her line of work. Jacob knew enough to realize that the rigors of shooting on location were demanding in more ways than one.

"If people are going to believe I'm your boyfriend, you should probably work on that hostility."

"Couples fight. Big deal."

He rubbed his thumb over her wrist. "Talk to me," he said. "Tell me about the movie. What's it called?"

Finally, she shut off the phone and tucked it in her purse, withdrawing her arm from his loose hold. Her gaze was wary. "*A Rising Tide*. It's based on a true story from the time of the British presence in Antigua in the eighteenth century. My character, Viola, is the madam of a high-class brothel that caters to officers and wealthy plantation owners. She was raised a lady in England, but when her husband died, his heirs threw her out. She stole some money, hid out on an outbound ship and ended up in the Caribbean."

"So what's the rest of the story line?"

"Viola rounds up a dozen young, destitute local women, takes them under her wing and turns them into stylish prostitutes. But she never actually sells her own body. One of the high-ranking naval officers on the island lusts after her and threatens to shut down her operation unless she becomes his mistress. They fall in love with each other eventually, but neither one wants to admit what they see as weakness. So they are as much adversaries as lovers."

"What happens in the end?"

"Viola winds up pregnant, but the officer has been commanded to return to England for a promotion that will put him into administration rather than on the high seas. He begs her to go with him, but she can't face the thought of rejoining polite society, knowing that her sordid activities in Antigua will always shadow her. On the eve of his homeward voyage, Viola goes into labor, loses the baby and dies in his arms."

Jacob winced. "Wow. Not exactly a romantic comedy."

"No. But funny, upbeat pictures don't get nominated. To get a bid, it's the sadder the better. Usually. And if the movie is based on truth, it's even more likely to be noticed."

"So you think you have a shot?"

"No film is ever a sure thing, but this is my biggest chance so far to break out of the blonde bimbo mold."

He grimaced. "No one believes you're a bimbo." When Ariel didn't say anything, he took her hand. "I should have called you long before now."

Her gaze was wary. "Why?"

"To apologize. I'm sorry I intimated you sleep around," he said quietly. "It was a cheap shot."

She moved restlessly in her comfortable seat, again breaking his loose hold, as if she couldn't bear for him to touch her. "It's not anything I haven't heard before."

"That doesn't make my regret any less valid or sincere. I really am sorry."

She gave him a sideways glance before turning her attention to the window and lapsing into a remote silence.

Jacob sighed inwardly. He deserved her pique. It *had* been

a cheap shot, but that night in the woods, he'd been scrambling to regain his equilibrium after Ariel cuddled up against him, all warm and soft and sexy. It was a miracle he hadn't taken her there in the forest.

But he had come close. Damn close. Which was exactly why he had to keep his distance. She seemed so damned alone and vulnerable. But though Jacob was determined to help her, the situation was emotional quicksand.

With Ariel giving him the silent treatment, he decided he might as well get some work done. Once the pilot turned off the seat belt sign, Jacob retrieved his briefcase and pulled out an article he'd been meaning to read.

It was late afternoon when they prepared to land at the small airport outside of St. John's, the capital city. Jacob had visited the Caribbean a couple of times for various professional conferences, but never Antigua.

He leaned across Ariel to get a better view. Below them, the irregularly shaped island was a splash of green vegetation and white sand against the azure of the ocean. "Looks like a postcard," he said, noting the way Ariel shrank back in her seat. His arm had brushed her breast when he moved. Not on purpose. But her reaction was telling.

Ariel shoved him away. "Quit hogging the view."

Grinning, he sat back in his seat while she glued her nose to the Plexiglas. For someone who had traveled a great deal, Ariel surprised him with her almost palpable excitement.

She pointed at a pristine bay as they circled to touch down. "Look at how deserted the shore is. They say the island has a beach for every day of the year."

"Maybe in our free time we can explore."

She shot him a pitying look over her shoulder. "Free time? You've got a lot to learn."

The business of disembarking and heading through customs took less than an hour. Outside the modest terminal building a white SUV sat waiting. A slender, plain-featured woman hovered anxiously, and as soon as Ariel stepped foot into the sunlight, the female scurried forward.

"Welcome to Antigua," she said breathlessly. "I'm your P.A.—Harriet Logan. We'll head straight to the hotel if you're ready."

She ignored Jacob completely, all her focus trained on Ariel. As far as Jacob could tell, Harriet was in her mid to late thirties. Her attire fell somewhere between '60s hippy and shabby librarian. A single long braid hung to her waist in back, and she wore thick, horn-rimmed glasses.

Ariel held out her hand, a blinding smile on her face. "Hello, Harriet. Lovely to meet you."

Harriet blinked, perhaps stunned by the wattage of Ariel's beaming goodwill. Jacob sympathized. Ariel in "celebrity" persona was nothing short of mesmerizing. He felt a kick in his gut even ten feet away.

The assistant nibbled her bottom lip, clearly unsure of how to respond. "I've paid the boy who's taking care of your bags. Would you like something to drink in the car?"

"How far is it?" Ariel yawned, rubbing her eyes like a child.

"Twenty-nine minutes."

Ariel gaped, then grinned. "Not twenty-eight? Not thirty? You must be very good at your job."

Her teasing seemed to stymy the prim employee. "Is that a yes or a no?"

Ariel glanced at Jacob, eyebrows raised. "No, thank you," she said, her tone gentle. "I'll grab something at the hotel." She reached back and snagged Jacob's hand, dragging him closer. "Harriet, this is my boyfriend, Jacob."

Harriet blushed and stuttered. "I'm so sorry. I didn't realize anyone was traveling with you. That must not have been in my notes." She flipped frantically through a day planner. "Welcome, Mr. …"

"Wolff. Jacob Wolff." He bent down to pick up the rainbow of sticky notes that had apparently lost their adhesive in the muggy heat. "No problem, Harriet. Why don't I see if all the bags are accounted for?" While Ariel climbed into the back-seat, flashing a mouth-drying expanse of leg, Jacob watched the kid loading the bags, did a quick count and joined his pseudo girlfriend in the sweltering interior.

Harriet slid behind the wheel, put the car in gear, and ac-celerated with a jerk that plastered Ariel and Jacob to the seat back. "Sorry," she tossed over her shoulder. "AC should be working in a minute." She drove with both hands on the wheel at ten and two, her gaze fixed intently on the road ahead.

Ariel, still wearing her stylish hat, wiped sweat from her forehead. "Not one paparazzi. Hallelujah. Brad and Angelina must be doing something noteworthy this week. Remind me to send them a thank-you note." She leaned forward, her hand on Harriet's shoulder. "What's the schedule?"

Harriet never blinked. "Meet and greet cast and crew party at eight in the hotel dining room. You're due on set at five in the morning ready to go. Rod will give you the rundown."

Ariel wrinkled her nose, but didn't seem unduly concerned. Jacob noted her calm with a puzzled frown. God knows what time she would have to get up to be ready. But apparently she was accustomed to the brutal hours. "Rod?" he asked.

"Rod Brinkman, the director. He's a legend. I'll be scared spitless."

"Who's your leading man?"

"A kid you've never heard of... John England. It's his first major motion picture. He'll be a mess."

"What do you mean?"

"He's only ever done commercials and a few guest spots on an afternoon soap. He went in for a cold audition with this proj-ect and nailed it. The powers that be saw his face and knew he was what they wanted. Plus, they could pay him crap, which they like, because my salary is straining the budget."

Jacob was forced to do mental hoop jumping to adjust the current reality to his first impressions of Ariel Dane. On

Wolff Mountain she'd seemed frail, almost tentative…painfully young. Suddenly, in her natural environment, he saw boundless confidence, professional savvy and a maturity that told him he had most definitely underestimated his lovely diva.

As the car swung into the driveway of a luxury resort, Jacob looked around with interest. The place had seen better days, but it had the charm of an aging beauty. Only two stories high, the building arced in a crescent that swept around a jewel-like pool and bisected lush grounds crisscrossed with palm-shaded pathways.

Harriet shoved the gearshift into Park. "You're not staying in the main hotel, Ms. Dane. Mr. Brinkman reserved a waterfront villa for you." She stopped short, her skin flushing. "And for Mr. Wolff, of course."

Ariel threw her arms around Jacob's neck and gave him a big kiss square on the mouth, her breasts pressed against him. "Jacob and I can't wait to get settled in, right, sweetheart?"

Rigid with shock and a surge of lust, Jacob inhaled sharply, only to groan in disappointment when Ariel abandoned him and hopped out of the car. Reality smacked him in the face. *She's acting, Jacob. Get a grip.*

Feeling more foolish than he cared to admit, he exited the vehicle and inhaled the combined scents of coconut and hot sunshine.

Harriet smacked his hand lightly when he tried to pick up two of the bags. "No, no, no," she cried. "Leave those. I'll get you and Ms. Dane settled and someone will deliver your luggage shortly."

The short walk to the cabana was interrupted four times by star-struck hotel employees. In every instance, Ariel responded with charm and humor, signing autographs and chatting with her admirers.

Jacob became more and more confused. Who was the real Ariel Dane? This exotic creature who took adulation matter-of-factly as her due? The sexy, approachable woman who made his body tighten with deep, infinite hunger? Or the lost little girl who gave up her childhood to play make-believe?

There was no time to decide. Harriet ushered them into a pleasantly furnished apartment decorated in varying shades of sea-green and white. Through double louvered doors, Jacob could see a king-size bed. Opposite that was a huge bathroom with a granite shower enclosure and a Jacuzzi.

"You have a fully stocked kitchenette through this door," Harriet said. "The wireless internet works fairly well as long as it isn't raining. Maid service daily, of course, but if you need anything in the meantime, the manager asked me to give you his card. You have your usual personal staff for hair, makeup and wardrobe."

She looked up from her checklist, eyes big behind her lenses. "Am I forgetting anything?"

Ariel took off her hat and tossed it on a chair. "I think you have it covered, Harriet. Feel free to take some time off and lounge by the pool. Mr. Wolff and I are going to…rest."

Harriet was scandalized, whether by the first half of that speech or the last, Jacob couldn't tell.

Her hands fluttered aimlessly, stacking and restacking the pile of papers she carried. "Oh, no, ma'am. I have too much to do. I won't disturb you, but call me if you need anything at all."

The bags arrived on cue. Minutes later Harriet exited, preceded by a smiling bellhop who clutched the handful of bills Ariel had tucked in his palm.

In the subsequent silence, all Jacob could hear was the gentle whoosh of rattan ceiling fans and his own rapid heartbeat.

Ariel kicked off her shoes, let down her hair and flopped backward onto the mattress. Her gaze was mischievous as she smiled at him. "Which side of the bed do you want?"

Eight

Ariel was nervous as hell and trying not to show it. Jacob's inscrutable expression gave nothing away. Was he impressed with their accommodations? He'd wondered aloud if she was a spoiled princess. Maybe this confirmed it.

"Say something," she urged, pretending that they weren't all alone in a honeymoon-like suite.

He folded his arms across his chest. "You didn't tell them I was coming, did you?"

The room suddenly seemed much too small, Jacob's disapproval sapping all the oxygen from the air. His frown judged her and found her wanting.

"I didn't have to," she said evenly, trying not to let him intimidate her. "I can bring whomever I like. And it wouldn't have mattered anyway. All of the villas have king-size beds. They wouldn't put me in the hotel."

"Because you're the star?"

Was that derision she heard in his voice? She shrugged. "Yes."

Her cell phone rang, freeing her from his assessing stare. She answered it quickly and sat up, turning sideways on the bed in a futile attempt for privacy. "Hello, Mama. Yes. I'm here safe and sound. Yes, he's with me. How was your day? Is the new medicine working?" The conversation went on for a few more minutes, before Ariel said her goodbyes. She hung up and saw Jacob still staring at her.

He leaned a hip against the door frame. "How is she doing?" he asked quietly.

Ariel shrugged. "Okay, I guess. She never wants to worry me, so she puts on a brave face. The doctors aren't making us any promises."

Jacob's eyes were shadowed. "I know how hard it is to lose someone," he said.

"Your mother?"

"I was pretty young. Most of that is a blur. But…"

Shock flooded her stomach. He was reaching out to her, offering her, without delineating it, his strength and his understanding. "But what?" she whispered, her throat dry.

Jacob was looking at her, but she had the feeling that his gaze was really trained inward, seeing painful images that still tormented him. "There was someone in med school. A fellow intern who had cancer. She was—" He stopped abruptly. "Never mind. I shouldn't have brought it up. It didn't end well."

Ariel slid off the bed and padded across the room to stand beside him. "I'm sorry, Jacob."

She put her hand in his and he gripped it, his fingers strong and warm against hers. "Becoming a doctor can be both a blessing and a curse," he said, looking down at their linked hands. "You think in the beginning that you have the keys to saving the world, or at least the people who are important to you. But as time passes, you begin to understand that whatever skills you possess are sometimes little more than smoke and mirrors."

Her heart contracted. She sensed that the pain inside him

was rarely allowed to surface. Perhaps the only reason he had acknowledged it now was to assure her that he understood her fears. Or maybe he was warning her, obliquely, that he was still in love with some mystery woman from his past.

It was becoming clear to Ariel why Jacob had agreed to help her. He felt the burden of what he perceived to be repeated failures. The deaths of his friend, his mother and perhaps a lover?

Ariel didn't want to be another millstone around his neck. Nor could she bear to think she was nothing more to him than an obligation. She reached up on tiptoe to kiss his cheek, wanting to comfort him.

He went rigid at the touch of her lips. "Do you expect us to share that bed?" Color slashed his cheekbones and hunger glittered in his eyes. Deep emotion stripped away the veneer of conventionality.

A tiny smear of lip gloss marked his cheek. She smoothed it away with her finger. "It's a huge mattress. Would it be so terrible?"

Outside their windows she heard the crash of waves on the beach. Somewhere a woman laughed. The smells of cooking wafted pleasantly on the air, making her stomach rumble.

Jacob took her face in his hands, his breath warm on her face. "I'm a man, Ariel. What you ask is unfair, next to impossible," he said flatly. "I'll do it, because I'm well over six feet tall and I can't spend night after night pretzeled up on a love seat. But you have to promise me something."

"What?" His sheer masculinity made her heart flutter. In his firm grasp she felt the twin pulls of security and danger. Jacob Wolff would do whatever it took to keep her safe and well. But he was a seductive threat to her peace of mind and her heart.

His thumbs smoothed her cheekbones. "You have to behave. No prancing around in see-through nighties. No flirting. No physical contact other than what is necessary to protect your little cover story. Do you understand?"

She curled her hands over his. "You're touching me now," she pointed out, breathless and bold enough to move closer.

How had she not noticed the length of his eyelashes? His eyes were beautiful, sometimes pewter, at other moments the simple gray of a rainy afternoon. His jaw clenched. "It comes naturally to you, doesn't it?" The gruff, accusatory words put her on trial.

"No one's holding a gun to your head," she pointed out, desperately wanting to taste his kiss again. "You can let go anytime you want." Pushing him to the edge was becoming a habit, a yearning to see if she could break his control.

In her bare feet, she felt at a disadvantage, but one look into his stormy eyes told her that whatever leapt and quivered between them leveled the playing field in her favor.

His hands tightened. "Damn you," he groaned.

They surged together like the tide making love to the beach. He was big and broad, and she felt both cherished and ravished by his wild kiss.

Still waters ran deep. Who knew the reserved Jacob Wolff would be so ferociously, dominantly passionate? Taking what he wanted in a kiss without apology.

Time no longer registered. His hands covered her breasts, caressing them until she cried out. Her dress closed in the back. Had she been able, she would have stripped bare for nothing more than the drunken pleasure of feeling his hands on her bare skin.

A doctor's hands. With a sure touch and gentle mastery that melted her into a puddle of need with no more than the bold squeeze of his fingers against an aching nipple buried beneath a frustrating layer of cloth.

They were fire and tinder, stunningly quick to ignite, impossible to extinguish. And yet one of them was in control. Not Ariel. Not by a long shot. She would have done anything to coax him into getting her naked.

But Jacob was, at many levels, a man with phenomenal

strength of will. Slowly he gentled the kiss until they broke apart, chests heaving, lips swollen with passion. She felt the tiny burn where his late-day stubble had marked her chin.

She licked her lips, feeling light-headed and frustrated. "You can't blame that one on me," she said self-righteously.

"The hell I can't." His hooded gaze was derisive. "Go put your damned swimsuit on," he insisted. "Maybe water will cool us off."

She changed in the master bathroom while Jacob took his suitcase into the outer room. As she gazed into the mirror over the vanity, her naked body embarrassed her. Her breasts felt swollen and achy. Rosy nipples cried out for Jacob's touch.

No wonder he thought she'd had multiple lovers. She'd fallen into his arms like the proverbial ripe peach. Whatever connection they had forged might be new, but it was powerful.

She was sure that Jacob thought she was playing with him for sport. The truth was, she had never been more serious in her life. She needed the doctor. But she wanted the man. Her brain shied away from acknowledging a more disturbing truth. Jacob was like no one she had ever met. At times she wanted nothing more than to destroy his granite-clad control. But at others she craved his strength. He made her feel things that no man had ever made her feel…drawn from a secret place in her heart. An ache. An unanswered need.

For one long moment, she debated sending him home. He had turned his life upside down for her because of his honor, his integrity, his calling. But it was dangerous for both of them. He didn't want to be attracted to her. And she didn't want to be his charity case. What an impossible dilemma she had created.

After throwing a mesh cover-up over her one-piece navy maillot, she tossed a few things in a beach bag and knocked on the door that separated her from Jacob. "Are you decent?" she called out, her heart beating rapidly.

He flung it open. "I may be, but you're not." In her absence, he seemed to have returned from some dark, unsettling place.

He scanned her from head to toe, his eyes lingering on her legs. His chest heaved in an appreciative sigh. "Sunbathing with a movie star. Wait until I tweet this."

She snorted, walking past him to the front door with an inward sigh of relief. "Don't make me laugh. You're too brilliant and important to dabble in mindless social media."

He closed the door behind them and slung an arm around her shoulders. "Has it ever occurred to you that turnabout is fair play? You've made a lot of assumptions about *me*, princess. Do I seem so dull to you? I have been known to goof off on occasion."

"When? Back in 2009 on a Friday night in May? I'm not buying it. You probably hide out in your lab for fun. Admit it."

"Perhaps. When I get excited and results are headed in a direction I think will be meaningful. But maybe it's because I don't have any reason to do anything else. I'm not really a people person in case you hadn't noticed."

The walk to the beach was brief in reality. But tucked beneath Jacob's arm, Ariel had a hard time breathing during the seemingly interminable stroll. "I thought you said no touching," she whispered.

He stopped suddenly and picked a magenta bougainvillea blossom to tuck behind her ear. "We're in public," he said simply. "I'm working on my role as adoring boyfriend." His head lowered. "Exhibit A."

The kiss was fleeting. Definitely manufactured for anyone who might be watching. But its effect on Ariel was nonetheless potent. She stumbled when they resumed walking and had to grab Jacob's arm to keep from falling. "Sorry," she muttered, wincing as her ankle throbbed.

Jacob shook his head in disgust. "You couldn't settle for a nice pair of flip-flops?" As they reached their destination, he released her and began spreading out their beach blankets.

Her three-inch cork-soled wedges were meant more for show

than for practicality. "We live and die by fashion in this business, Doc. I can't wear just anything. It's all about the package."

He held out his hand. "Sit down before you break a leg. Your talent is what makes the movie. Why should they care what you wear when you're not working?"

"I play a role on this side of the camera as much as I do during shooting." She knelt beside him. "It's not the same, of course. I play myself, but it's a jacked-up version of me. Glam clothes, perfect hair, pricey accessories. When I'm the *movie star,* everyone wins. My films get more buzz, the tabloids snap pictures, and my fans get to believe that my life is perfect."

He registered her sarcasm, but the sympathy she saw in his steady gaze made her squirm. "Sounds like a lot of work for nothing. But you're looking better," he said, grabbing a few large shells to pin down the corners of their towels. "I think you've gained a few pounds. Have you taken the medicine every day?"

She nodded, whipping her cover-up over her head and stretching out on her back with a sigh of contentment. "Everything the doctor ordered," she murmured. Eyes closed, she tried to ignore the big, warm male body stretched out next to hers.

She had used the term *sunbathing* loosely. Rarely did she court the full sun. Too many older actresses she met had skin like leather, not to mention the health risks of UV exposure. So she and Jacob were tucked away in a patch of shade beneath a trio of palm trees.

The hotel had cordoned off this stretch of beach with a neon-orange plastic barrier and a sign that read *Cast Only.* She saw Jacob glance at the placard as they passed it, but he didn't comment. Did he really see her as a spoiled diva? She had tried her best not to fall into that stereotype. But for Ariel Dane, the current arrangement was the only way for her to have a modicum of privacy. Otherwise, she would be thronged by tourists and gawkers.

Thankfully, the hotel was small enough that movie personnel filled it to capacity. But that didn't preclude someone walking up along the beach or even invading the grounds without permission. She had learned to be very protective of her safety and her personal space.

She couldn't decide whether to be amused or miffed when she heard Jacob's gentle snore. Cracking open one eyelid, she studied him without fear of discovery. Even in his professional garb, there was no disguising the fact that he had a tough, masculine body. But stripped down to nothing more than a pair of black swim trunks, he was breathtaking.

An arrow of black hair bisected his chest. His skin was naturally darker than hers, and muscles corded his arms and sculpted his torso. Her hands fisted at her hips, fighting the urge to stroke from his shoulders to his waist.

She would undoubtedly stop there. The fabric of his shorts was thin, outlining the shape of his resting sex. The fact that he wanted her, even reluctantly, was amazing and unfathomable. Jacob possessed a keen intellect that far outstripped her own modest mental abilities. But then again, men could overlook a variety of sins when they wanted to get laid.

Despite the sizzling attraction that simmered between them at a slow burn, Jacob was no boy to be bent to Ariel's will. His confidence and resolve were things she envied. She feared that one day the public would realize that Ariel Dane was only ordinary. And her career would be over. What would she fall back on? She had no degrees, no skills. Just a knack for imitation and a gift for memorizing dialogue.

Brooding, she rolled to her side and put a hand on the blanket close to his hip. He was so still and relaxed she had to search for evidence that he was breathing. He must not be too enamored with her if he could be this close and yet forget she was around.

She was amazed, even now, that he had agreed to her proposition. Though she knew enough of her own appeal to realize he wanted her, that wasn't reason enough for his cooperation, given that he had made it very clear they weren't going to indulge in any bedroom gymnastics.

The only motivation he could possibly have was his instinctive, impossible-to-subdue urge to be healer and protector. She hoped she didn't have a relapse. She didn't want him to see her as a sick, helpless woman. Instead, she craved his admiration, his regard.

Such a simple thing. And perhaps naïve. Why on earth would Jacob Wolff think she was anything special? Her looks were nothing she could take credit for. And her acting was child's play compared to Jacob's profession.

Nevertheless, in some small corner of her heart, she wanted him to be proud of her.

Fat chance. After he watched the filming of the first sex scene, he might be turned on. He possibly could be offended. But he wasn't likely to be too happy about it. Men were territorial. And Ariel was pretty sure the Wolff had decided she was his to protect.

Nine

Jacob heaved a sigh of relief when Ariel stood up and walked down to the water's edge. He knew enough about relaxation techniques to simulate sleep, but he had been hyper-aware of Ariel's intense regard. It took everything he had not to get an erection.

From beneath eyelashes at half-mast, he watched her pace back and forth, her long legs flashing white against the dark blue water behind her. Though her swimsuit was modest, the body in it was anything but. She had the grace of a prima ballerina, and even on the thin side of perfect, she was femininity personified.

He wanted her. Jacob never lied, even to himself. And though he was pretty damn good at denying himself the pleasures of the flesh, a man had his limits.

Emotional involvement was out of the picture. If he decided to break his long run of celibacy with the delectable Ariel, it would be purely physical. She wouldn't think that strange. Their lives had no points of intersection. He was an introvert, a man of science, a loner who liked the company of his own thoughts.

Ariel was light and laughter and chaos in the best possible way. She tempted him to abandon his rigid control and drown himself in her softness, her open heart. Jacob hadn't fully worked out the ethics in his own mind. Without equivocation, he could convince himself that Ariel wasn't really his patient. No money had changed hands. They were not initiating anything that would extend beyond this one moment in time. He was helping out a friend.

Though the explanation sat uneasily in his mind, even more difficult to process was the conundrum of her age. In Jacob's estimation, people had taken advantage of Ariel. *Men* had taken advantage of her. No way in hell would he allow her to think that his aid came with a price tag.

She was young, too young. Standing on the cusp of adulthood. Having street smarts was one thing, but was she really mature enough to know her own mind when it came to a sexual relationship that had no future?

Troubled and at a loss for concrete answers, he sat up on his elbows, squinting against the glare of sunlight on the ocean. Ariel was standing now with her back to him, arms wrapped around her waist. She was still for the moment. Pensive perhaps. Or merely enjoying the beautiful view.

Lunging to his feet, he loped down to where she stood. Though their charade indicated he should put an arm around her waist, he did not. He stood by her side—close, but making no physical contact. "Do we dress for dinner?" he asked, trying to draw her attention from whatever painful thoughts had claimed her.

She half turned her head, her expression hidden by large sunglasses. "I will," she said. "The crew may be sloppy, but this initial soiree with the cast will be all about first impressions."

"Will there be dancing?"

Now she faced him fully, astonishment on her face. "Is that your way of saying you hope so?"

He shrugged. "I like to dance. Is that so strange? There you go with those preconceptions again."

Ariel laughed softly. "I'll give you this, Doc. You're never boring."

"I could say the same for you."

"I'm starving. Let's go in and grab something from the mini fridge."

"You told Harriet that we were going to 'rest.' What do you think she imagines we're doing?"

"Lord knows. She's a darling, but I'm afraid that if I look at her wrong, she'll have a coronary. Am I that scary?"

"You're Ariel Dane. And yes," he said, holding up a hand when she tried to protest. "You're pretty intimidating. But maybe when poor Harriet figures out that you don't bite, she'll calm down."

"I hope so." They walked back toward their towels. Ariel bent to pick hers up and shake it out.

Did she do it on purpose? To drive men insane? He dragged his gaze from her barely-clad bottom and grabbed up his own gear. "I call first shower."

Ariel chased him up the path. "No fair," she cried. "You can use the outdoor stall. No one's going to be peeking in on you."

"I think I've just been insulted."

They draped their sandy towels on the lanai before going inside. Ariel made a beeline for the bedroom. Still laughing, he rummaged in his case for clean boxers and his shave kit. The shower enclosure tucked away behind a wall of tropical foliage produced a torrent that was hot and hard, just the way he liked it. As the salt and sand winnowed from his skin, he raked his hands through his soapy hair, turning his face upward into the pelting spray. Imagining Ariel here with him, her naked skin wet and slick with bubbles, had predictable results. In moments, his boner was an iron spike, aching and full.

It was going to be a long evening. And when they returned to their villa, that damn huge bed was going to turn into a torture rack. Eyes closed, he imagined taking her, sliding between those supple thighs and plunging deep, feeling the fist-tight squeeze of her slick passage.

Ariel laughed at him, teasing, taunting. "Is that the best you can do, Doc? I've been waiting for you. Show me how much you want me."

His sex was on fire, burning with the drive toward release. He put his hands beneath her ass and lifted her, dragging her down onto his aching flesh with a force that made both of them gasp. "This much," he croaked, forcing the words from between numb lips.

His face pressed into the valley between her breasts. Lips with their own agenda found a pert nipple and suckled, making Ariel groan. "So beautiful," he crooned. "So incredibly beautiful."

Ariel tightened her legs round his waist, rubbing her body against him in such a way that with every thrust he stimulated her intimately. She kissed him lazily, catching his tongue between her teeth and tugging gently. "Come now," she gasped. "I'm so close."

He paused, breathless, holding back to prolong his release. "I'll want you again," he swore. "As soon as we're done."

"You'll have to catch me first." She bit his neck, sending sparks of pain into every nerve ending. The extra stimulation sent him over the edge.

Jacob turned his face into the crook of his arm, muffling a choked moan as he found release. Dropping to his knees, he felt the rough scrape of concrete against his skin. He was weak and dizzy. And as his fantasy self had predicted, he wanted her again.

The water cascaded over his bent shoulders. When it began to run cold, he dragged himself upright and turned off the taps. He was terrified suddenly to go back inside. What if he pounced on her? What if he saw her smile at him and found himself shoving her back on the bed and taking her like a wild man?

He had chosen celibacy by default, burying himself in his work to forget his first doomed love. Two massive tragedies in his life had stunted his ability to connect with women. Denying himself sex was preferable to loving and being destroyed a third time.

For a long time now, he had been the architect of his future, steering the course of his work and his personal life to fit rigid parameters. Suddenly, Ariel had redirected all of it. His body felt like a wounded animal with no place to hide.

Gathering himself by sheer force of will, he dried off and donned his underwear. In hindsight, he should have brought a pair of pants outside with him. But he had assumed that he'd be finished with his shower long before Ariel was.

She was waiting for him when he walked inside. Sitting in an overstuffed armchair, legs swung up over the side, she eyed him assessingly. "Guess you're not too concerned with saving water."

He felt his cheeks redden. "What are you? The shower police?"

Ignoring the fact that she was dressed and he was half naked, he went to his suitcase and extracted a pair of dark dress slacks. He stepped into them calmly, feeling her gaze like a caress. His hair was still dripping water. He tossed his shirt on the bed and grabbed the damp towel, rubbing it over his head.

Ariel studied his every move. "It will make you go blind."

"What in the hell are you talking about?"

"Manual stimulation."

The heat in his face increased. There was no way she could know for sure. Her naughty teasing was nothing but a shot in the dark. "Are you ready? Sorry to keep you waiting."

She cocked her head, swinging one foot clad in a lime-green

stiletto. "How many times are you going to have to do that before you can sleep with me?"

He buttoned up the shirt and sat on the end of the bed to slide his feet into socks and shoes. "You have a vivid imagination, Ariel. And a dirty mind. I took a shower. End of story." Apparently he could lie after all, especially when backed into a corner.

To his enormous relief, she gave up tormenting him. "I'm about to faint from hunger," she said, standing and straightening the fabric of her mauve taffeta skirt. The jersey tank she wore melded the two colors of her outfit in a blinding Rorschach pattern. "Let's go meet the others."

They meandered down the path lit with tiny ankle-high lanterns that did little to dispel the romantic, scented dark. He dared not touch her now. It would be difficult enough when he was called upon to play his part in public.

The restaurant sat on the opposite end of the property, built up on pilings that extended out over the water. Already, pulse-pounding music spilled out into the night. Strings of white lights outlined the palm-thatched, open-air building.

Far out over the water, the crescent moon painted a narrow path of light across an indigo sea. Jacob would have far preferred a moonlit walk on the beach to an evening with strangers. But Ariel had a job to do, and she and Jacob were about to perform Act One without a script or a rehearsal.

She never hesitated at the door. Wading into the melee, she dragged Jacob in her wake. It was an odd experience for him. He was accustomed to being the point man in his endeavors. But for Ariel, he would try to be compliant.

Harriet was ensconced in an out-of-the-way corner. She gave him a shy wave from across the room and returned her attention to her paperwork. In a chair near the center of the restaurant, the director held court. Rod Brinkman was balding, fiftyish, and possessed a Santa-type face and physique that was at odds with his clout in the industry. He had achieved success in the movie business by working from the ground up. Not only was he smart, but he had the contacts to make things happen.

TIME magazine had only last year named him one of the ten most influential directors in Hollywood. Ariel made a beeline for the man, giving Jacob only moments to get in character.

She paused, waiting for the cluster of people surrounding Rod to melt away. Curtsying with a gamine grin, she said, "Reporting for duty, sir."

Jacob watched the older man. Ariel claimed to be intimidated by her new boss, but from where Jacob was sitting, Rod Brinkman, despite his reputation for being a hard-ass, was enchanted with his leading lady. He jumped up and gave her a quick peck on each cheek before pulling a chair out beside his and urging her to sit.

Ariel stalled, pulling Jacob into the conversation. "Rod, I'd like you to meet Jacob Wolff. He'll be staying here with me." She put her hands on Jacob's shoulders and gave him an enthusiastic kiss.

Jacob's stomach hitched, but he managed an indulgent grin. "I couldn't keep away," he said, tucking Ariel into a chair and pulling his seat close so that their hips and thighs were in contact. He stretched his arm across the back of her chair, running his fingers along the nape of her neck. "A woman like Ariel makes a man want to drop whatever he's doing and come along for the ride. Hope you don't mind, sir."

Brinkman's eyes narrowed. "Jacob Wolff. As in *the* Wolffs?"

Jacob shrugged. "Guilty as charged."

Rod didn't miss a beat. "How would you like to invest in a few dozen movie projects?"

"My plate's full at the moment," Jacob said, laughing. "But I'll keep it in mind."

Ariel waved a hand between the two men. "Helloooo. Do we have to talk business right off the bat?"

Rod beckoned to the waitress and held up his glass, asking for another whiskey sour. "No business tonight," he said.

"Plenty of time for that tomorrow. So tell me, Jacob Wolff, how did you meet Ms. Dane? I've never seen you in Hollywood at any of our dozens of A-list functions."

Jacob ordered a seltzer water with lime and leaned back in his seat. "Ariel and I were introduced by mutual friends. It was pretty much love at first sight on my part."

Ariel's eyes narrowed. *Overkill,* she mouthed.

He nuzzled her neck. "I'm so proud of her. Word on the street is that your movie is garnering Oscar buzz."

Rod drained his drink and slammed the glass on the table. "It's true," he said, the words only the slightest bit slurred. "It's a lot of pressure, you know. Sometimes I wish I were a plumber."

People at the surrounding tables laughed along with Ariel and Jacob. Brinkman's reach was legendary, and everyone wanted to stay on his good side for future projects.

After polishing off a bowl of seafood chowder, Ariel tapped Rod's arm. "If you'll excuse me, I'm going to mingle." She stood up and kissed the top of Jacob's head. "Stay here, honey. Talk to Mr. Brinkman. I'll be back."

For the next hour and a half, Jacob watched her work the room. Her reputation as a party girl was well-deserved. Everywhere she stopped to chat, uproarious laughter soon erupted. She didn't distinguish between cast and crew. Ariel was just Ariel.

Rod shook his head. "She's an effin' miracle. None of that prima donna bullshit. I can't understand why nobody before me has given her the chance to spread her wings. The kid's awesome."

"I happen to think so."

Someone else stopped by to claim Rod's attention, giving Jacob the opportunity to study Ariel in her element. Table by table, she canvassed the crowd, introducing herself to the people she didn't know and hugging those she did. Not once did he see her drink anything other than water. And though weed was passed freely around the room, Ariel declined anything she was offered with a smile and a joke.

Men flirted with her, openly hoping for a chance to snag her attention. Women gossiped with her, their eyes wistful as she glowed. Without Ariel's presence, the social gathering would have been just another party. With her, it was an occasion.

At nine o'clock on the dot, she returned to their table. Perching on Jacob's lap with unself-conscious affection, she wrapped one arm around his neck and leaned forward to grab a handful of cocktail peanuts. "Time for bed, Mr. Wolff. I hear the new director's a bear when anyone's late for a shoot."

Rod, bleary-eyed, nodded. "Indeed." He got to his feet and yawned. "Half these pups won't go to bed at all, but I need my beauty sleep." He grinned wryly at Jacob. "I'm an old S.O.B."

Jacob shifted Ariel to her feet and stood, as well. He shook the older man's hand. "It's been a pleasure getting to know you, Mr. Brinkman. I'm looking forward to watching you in action."

The three of them exited the rowdy restaurant and stepped out into the humid night air. Brinkman pinched Ariel's cheek. "It's your big day tomorrow, Ariel. I don't like to toot my own horn, but after this movie, I doubt your life will ever be the same."

Ten

Ariel watched the director walk toward his villa as she and Jacob took a fork in the path that led to theirs. "I don't want to let him down," she said, feeling the inevitable onslaught of nerves. "I know he got an earful from people that harassed him for hiring me."

No one was around to see the fact that Jacob wasn't touching her. No hand-holding, no stolen kisses on a balmy night.

"He's a smart man, Ariel. He sees something in you that you may not see in yourself. Untapped potential." He held her elbow briefly in a dark patch and then released her. "I didn't get to meet your love interest... John? Was that his name?"

"His flights got messed up. He'll barely make it here in time for the morning shoot."

"Poor guy."

"Yeah. Talk about starting out on the wrong foot."

She wished they were a normal couple on vacation so she could justify lingering outside. Instead, she waited for Jacob to unlock their door and then moved past him to enter. "I hope

Rod knows what he's doing, hiring me and an unknown. Lord knows I don't want to be responsible for Brinkman's first flop." It was a dismal notion.

Kicking off her shoes, she padded to the minifridge for a bottle of water. The king-size bed still dominated the suite, practically shouting an invitation for sexual mayhem. But unless Jacob crumbled, and that wasn't likely, this room would see no action tonight.

She picked at the label on the water bottle, unable to meet his eyes. "You don't have to go with me in the morning. Rod wants to shoot a sunrise scene, so we'll be on set before daybreak. Stay here and sleep."

He kicked off his shoes, as well, along with his socks, and reclined on the sofa with his hands behind his head, his large, masculine feet propped on the glass-topped coffee table. "I came to Antigua to look after you," he said, his gaze intense and unnerving. "And I survived many a brutal shift as an intern. So don't worry about me."

She shrugged. "If you say so."

"I can't decide if you're an extrovert or an introvert."

Her conversational style must be rubbing off on him. The sudden jump in topic threw her. "Can't I be both?"

"Most people are one or the other."

The dimly lit room was giving her ideas…dangerous ideas. Reaching over to switch on a lamp, she curled into a chair opposite Jacob, wishing she had the right to snuggle down beside him instead. By all rights, she should be in the shower by now. The alarm was going to go off at an obscene hour. But she couldn't tear herself away.

"It depends on the situation," she said, taking another swallow of water. "I love people and I enjoy socializing. But sometimes I get really tired, and I have to shut down for a while."

"Makes sense."

She yawned. "Sorry."

"Go get ready for bed, Ariel. I'll take a turn in the bathroom when you're tucked away under the covers."

She stared at him, gnawing her lower lip, a habit she had kicked long ago. "Thank you for coming," she said. "And I want you to know that I understand your ground rules."

"And you plan to follow them?"

"That, too."

A tiny smile teased his lips and disappeared. "Scram, Ariel."

She departed reluctantly, closing the French doors behind her as she entered the bedroom. After rummaging in her suitcase, she extracted the least seductive piece of sleepwear she owned and headed for the shower.

Jacob was in trouble. Imagining him and Ariel in the dark, on opposite sides of a mattress, gave him heartburn. The only thing holding his hunger in check at the moment was the knowledge that tomorrow was a very important day. Ariel needed her sleep.

When he heard her call out, he opened the door and took a deep breath. "I'll be quick," he promised. "You can turn out the—" He stopped dead, his heart lodged in his throat.

Ariel was standing beside the bed, bending over to fiddle with the radio alarm clock. She was wearing a faded oversize T-shirt that was so big on her, the neckline had slipped off one soft, sloping shoulder. "This stupid thing won't work. I guess I'll use my phone instead."

He turned away, ruefully aware that the image was imprinted on his brain. Was she wearing any undies?

Damn. He grabbed what he needed and locked himself in the bathroom away from temptation. After an icy cold shower, he was no less agitated. But when he could no longer think of an excuse to stay away, he opened the door and saw that Ariel was sound asleep, the covers tucked to her chin.

He walked around the bed and quietly turned out her bedside lamp. Touching her was not an option, though his hand tingled with the urge to do so. This close he could smell the fragrance of strawberries.

She was a fascinating woman, one moment shy and vulnerable, the next mischievous and slyly seductive. If he had been in the market for a relationship, Ariel would fit the bill. But he liked his quiet clinic and the comforting routines of his work. And Ariel was nothing more than a shooting star lighting up his firmament for a brief, exhilarating moment.

Perhaps thirty was too young to settle for safety. But he had tasted the depths of despair twice in his life, and he wasn't eager to suffer again. Besides, Ariel needed someone in her life who could match her openness and exuberance. Jacob had to be strong enough to keep both of them from falling into a relationship that was doomed from the start.

Allowing himself one brief caress, smoothing her hair from her soft cheek, he reminded himself of all the reasons he couldn't have her. Then he returned to his side of the bed and crawled under the covers with a movie star.

Ariel slept soundly and woke before the alarm. Quietly turning it off, she slid out of bed. Years ago she had taught herself to wake at whatever time necessary to meet her schedule. Getting ready took no time at all. After splashing her face with water and brushing her teeth, she threw on black yoga pants and a thin fleece pullover.

Jacob stirred when she came out of the bathroom. "What time is it?"

"Still the middle of the night. Go back to sleep."

He scraped his hands though his hair and threw back the sheet, sitting up on the side of the bed. "Coffee?" he asked with a gravelly voice.

"Harriet will have it in the car. It's a short drive. We're shooting in the next cove. Are you sure you want to go?"

He stood up. His broad chest was bare. Thin cotton sleep pants, still with a crease from the package, hung low on his narrow hips. "Give me five," he growled, rubbing sleep from his eyes.

She put a hand over her heart when he was out of sight, amazed that it hadn't punched its way out of her chest. Bare-chested, Jacob Wolff looked more like a mercenary than a doctor of medicine.

The man was as good as his word. He joined her at the door just as the indomitable Harriet pulled up, driving the vehicle in which she had picked them up at the airport. Her subdued greeting baffled Ariel. Trying her best to be conciliatory, she smiled at her newly-minted P.A. "Good morning, Harriet. Thanks for being so prompt."

Harriet's expression was hard to read in the single porch light, but her body language was no more relaxed than it had been yesterday.

Ariel and Jacob climbed into the backseat. A small insulated carafe was lodged between them in a cardboard box. Jacob fell on it with a muttered *thank God*. He poured two cups and handed Ariel one. She drank it hot and black, wincing when it hit her empty stomach.

Grabbing a handful of granola from an open bag, she forced it down. Nerves curled in her belly, making her feel sick. She huddled into her corner and stared out into the dark.

She flinched when Jacob's warm hand landed on her thigh. "Relax, Ariel. Are you always this jumpy?"

Feeling his touch through a scant layer of cloth shocked her out of her intense introspection. She laughed shakily. "Sometimes worse. It won't last. By day three or four, we'll all be settled into a routine. But it's always rough in the beginning."

He rubbed her back, holding his coffee cup like a lifeline in his other hand. "Is this where I'm supposed to tell you to imagine all of your co-stars in their underwear?"

She giggled. "Please don't."

His hand linked with hers, offering her his quiet strength. It was nice having a companion. Though Jacob was a fake boyfriend, she suddenly understood why so many stars took their families on location. The comfort of a familiar face would go a long way toward easing stress.

Harriet rounded a curve in the road and pulled off to the right, bumping down a newly graded track that led to a roped-off area near the beach. The moon hung low on the horizon now, but there was plenty of artificial light as Ariel and Jacob exited the car.

Ariel took it all in, feeling the sizzle of excitement new projects always generated. Jacob stood beside her, downing his third cup of coffee. She pointed to a large tent. "You'll find food and anything else you need over there. If you want to catch a few more z's, the car won't be locked. I have to do hair and makeup. Will you be okay?"

He surprised her with a soft kiss that tasted of creamer and warm male. "I'm a big boy. Don't worry about me. Go do your thing."

She touched his cheek, loving his confidence, his inherent strength. "I'm glad you're here." Some men were threatened by Ariel's success, but that wasn't Jacob's style. For a moment, she envied the unfortunate woman who had known the security of Jacob's love and commitment.

He rolled his shoulders and stretched. "Me, too. Now quit stalling. You're going to be great."

She walked away smiling, a quick glance over her shoulder telling her that Jacob tracked her with his eyes. She felt the intensity of his regard and wondered what he was thinking. Moments later the frenzy of trying to get everyone ready to catch the fleeting morning light demanded her attention. But despite the confusion, she was conscious that Jacob Wolff stood guard.

Eleven

Jacob prowled the fringes of pandemonium, marveling at how dozens of individuals appeared to know exactly what to do in their own little corner of the production process. Rod barked out orders, his nicotine-roughened voice made worse by lack of sleep.

Ariel had disappeared into a row of tents that bulged at the seams with all manner of staff coming and going. The early hour had done nothing to dim her beauty. Even on five hours of sleep, she'd been clear-eyed and rosy-cheeked when he first saw her this morning.

After scouting the layout, he rounded up a camp chair and parked it in a spot where he could see what was going on, but wouldn't be in the way.

When Ariel appeared forty-five minutes later, he didn't recognize her at first. It was only when Rod threw up his hands and made a gesture of obeisance that Jacob understood who she was. Viola, the madam. The courtesan.

She was dressed in period clothing, her purple satin dress

the shade of ripe plums. Her hair was done up in a complicated chignon, with artfully curled tendrils at her nape and ears.

Upon closer inspection, Jacob saw that the bodice dipped dangerously low in front, exposing smooth breasts that had been plumped up to showcase a voluptuous figure.

His mouth dried. Ariel never even looked in his direction. She and Brinkman were deep in discussion, him leading her to a spot on the beach, Ariel posing with the wind ruffling her skirts and exposing a teasing glimpse of leg now and again.

John England was no kid. He was six-three, broad in the chest and as blond as Ariel. If he was nervous, he didn't show it. Quietly deferential to the director and to his leading lady, he followed instructions quickly and well.

The faint light of dawn tinted the horizon when Brinkman set the cameras rolling.

Ariel faced off with the naval officer, haughty pride in every line of her body.

"I won't be blackmailed," she said, fully in character. "I've told you. My body's not for sale."

Her tormentor radiated power and authority, along with a lustful hunger. His hands closed with bruising strength over her narrow shoulders. "I can shut down your little operation, Miss Viola. Turn all those pretty trollops back into serving wenches and laundresses. Is that what you want?"

Viola struggled to free herself.

The officer, Landon, yanked her back. "You've pranced around the shipyard in your fancy clothes with your teasing laugh. What did you think would happen? I've three ships of single men, sailors far from home and family. Most of them can't afford what you and your lightskirts are offering. But I can, Viola. And you'll meet my terms or suffer the consequences."

He dragged her against his chest, covering her mouth in a wild, dominant kiss. Viola beat at his shoulders with her fists. "I'm a lady," she cried. "You can't do this."

Releasing her slowly, he stepped back and wiped a hand across his mouth. John England did an impressive job of portraying a man shaken by the power of that embrace.

"I can and I will," he said quietly. "I'll come to you tonight. After dark. Be waiting."

He turned abruptly and strode down the beach, disappearing around an outcropping of rocks. Viola lifted her face to the sky, tears streaming down her face. Against the backdrop of the ocean, she looked small, defenseless.

"Cut."

Jacob jerked, coming back to reality with a jump at the sound of Rod Brinkman's voice. Jacob had been so caught up in the story that he'd lost all sense of time. The camera crew scurried to block another take before the light became too bright. John walked back. A wardrobe assistant adjusted Ariel's dress. And the scene commenced again.

Ariel was amazing. She had been standing ankle deep in foamy water, but she never once complained. Though she and John England had never met before today, the chemistry between them was electric. Jacob felt her fear, her frustration. And he empathized with Landon's hunger.

The naval officer was an honorable man, a hero. Ariel had let Jacob read part of the script, and the story line was appealing. A man torn between what he knew was right and the driving urge to possess the lovely Viola.

The irony wasn't lost on Jacob.

At eleven, the shoot wrapped. Ariel walked up to him, her hips swaying in the voluminous skirts of another era. She shivered, wet from the knees down. "What did you think?" she asked, her expression anxious.

For the benefit of their audience he pulled her close in a long, lazy kiss. His heart stumbled. His lungs gasped for air. Kissing Ariel was no innocent exercise. She was a siren, luring him into deep waters. He knew exactly how the fictional Landon felt.

"You were spectacular," he said simply. "Even with the distraction of cameras everywhere and all the hustle and bustle of the set, I can already see that Brinkman is right. This film will make you a star."

Her saucy grin belied the fatigue in her posture. "I'm *already* a star," she pointed out, deliciously adorable in her braggadocio.

"A superstar then, a nova."

"That's better."

Her smug smile made him laugh. "Can you leave now? Are you done for the moment?"

"Definitely. I'll change in a flash. You tell Harriet we're ready."

She fell asleep in the car on the way back, her head on his shoulder. Jacob was the only one who knew that Ariel had been so ill her stamina was not back up to par. He held her against his chest, concerned that she was pale.

Harriet met his gaze in the rearview mirror. "Shall I take you straight to your villa, or would you like to grab something at the restaurant first?"

He debated rapidly. "I think we'll do room service for today."

She nodded. "Okay, then."

When they pulled up in front of their lodging, Ariel didn't wake up. Concern gripped Jacob's belly, but he dared not let it show. "I don't think she slept much," he said lightly. "Nerves, I guess. I'll carry her in."

The P.A. didn't comment, but her eyes were round. Jacob hoped she wasn't a gossip. She held the door open for him and closed it as she left.

Housekeeping had already been in, so Jacob folded back the covers and deposited Ariel gently on her side of the bed. Her eyelashes fluttered. "Nap with me," she commanded drowsily.

Jacob hesitated. He was exhausted. They were both fully

dressed. "Don't you want some lunch?" he asked, stalling until he could make a decision.

She closed her eyes. "Too tired to eat." The muttered words were the last ones she spoke. Sleep claimed her. Curled up in a ball, clutching a down pillow in her arms, she looked younger than ever, her sunlit yellow hair tumbled around her face.

A giant fist squeezed his chest. He didn't want to feel anything for Ariel but concern and admiration. Those were safe emotions. He couldn't afford anything more. Not when his main concern was her well-being.

But the lure of holding her bested him. Toeing off his shoes, he climbed in beside her, pulling her against his chest and spooning their bodies. The last thing he remembered before sleep claimed him was looking up at the ceiling and watching the dizzying twirl of the fan.

Ariel inhaled, dreaming of something wonderful. But the image slipped away as she awakened. Hard on the heels of that nebulous memory was an even more delightful reality.

Jacob Wolff lay in bed with her, holding her tightly, her cheek pillowed on his arm. She stayed perfectly still, savoring the sensation. He surrounded her with warmth. His big body dwarfed hers, creating a feeling of utter safety and, paradoxically, delicious danger.

She was frankly stunned that he had capitulated to her sleepy request. Fatigue must have weakened all those pesky morals and ethics. His hand cupped one of her breasts, stealing the breath from her lungs and making both of her nipples bead in helpless yearning.

It felt so damned good....

Stealthily, she eased onto her back so she could see his face. He hadn't had time to shave that morning. Dark stubble covered his chin. Ridiculously long lashes lay in dark crescents on his tanned cheeks.

His profile was classic, but for the tiny bump at the bridge of his nose that suggested it had been broken sometime in the past. What caused it? A brawl with his brothers? A skiing accident? Daringly, she traced his lower lip with her finger.

"What do you think you're doing?" Eyes still shut, he grumbled.

Since he hadn't batted her hand away, she continued her exploration, touching the shell of his ear.

"God in heaven." He manacled her wrist, dragging it away from his face before letting go. Sleepy eyes glared at her. "What part of *behave* don't you understand?"

"I want you, Jacob Wolff," she said, stripped of any desire to dance around the subject. "I've never met anyone like you. Don't you think we'd be good together? In bed?" She clarified her question so there would be no misunderstandings. Did he realize he was kneading her breast?

She gasped when he tugged at her nipple. Heat streaked from the place where his fingers teased her, joining with the ache between her legs. If this simple contact turned her inside out, what would it be like if he actually made love to her in earnest?

"We have nothing in common," he said, his gaze sober.

She sat up and brushed the front of his trousers, not lingering, but making her point. "We have this."

This time he didn't bother to move her hand. Emboldened, she stroked him through a layer of denim. His sex flexed and hardened even more. He closed his eyes, jaw rigid, brow furrowed.

His silence worried her. "Shall I stop?" she asked, her voice shaking with nerves though she hoped he didn't notice.

He trapped her hand against his pelvis. "Don't move. Just hold me."

She obeyed, curling her fingers against his shaft and feeling the pulse of his hunger. One of his hands fisted in her hair, and his breath came in great gasps. "Why do you have to be so hardheaded?" He groaned when she squeezed gently.

Knowing that she could affect him in such a way humbled her. His iron control was one of the things she admired about him. So why was she testing its limits? Since the day they had met, she'd taunted and teased and chipped away at his boundaries, trying to force him to give her something…anything.

"I think you've been lying to me," she said, determined to bring her worst fears out into the open.

That got his attention despite his extreme state of arousal. "I don't lie."

His fierce glare should have cowed her, but over the years, she had faced down her share of ranting directors. Angry males were nothing new in her experience. "You've been making excuses for why we should avoid this thing between us."

One sardonic eyebrow lifted. "Do me a favor and don't call it a *thing*."

When she realized he was joking, her face flamed. "That's not what I meant and you know it. We want each other, Jacob. And there's no reason we shouldn't be together. Be honest. That stuff you said about me being too young or you being my doctor was just an excuse."

"You might consider the fact that we've known each other for all of five minutes."

"Details," she said, bending down to kiss him softly. "I want you to be honest. Are you holding out because you think I've slept around…and that disgusts you?"

He sat up, dislodging her hand from his pants. Sliding his fingers beneath her hair, he kissed her roughly. "Don't be ridiculous. Give me a little credit. Why would I expect you to be a nun? I don't believe in double standards."

They fell backward together, her legs tangling with his. "Then give us a chance." She mumbled the words against his throat, groaning as he nipped the side of her neck with his teeth. Her whole body shivered in reaction. There was so much goodness in him, such a deep vein of decency. It seduced her more than anything ever had.

Some women wanted bad boys. Ariel needed something entirely different.

When his hand moved between her thighs, she tensed. It was one thing to torment him, another entirely to be on the receiving end. Her thin, stretchy pants didn't stop him. Rubbing gently, he zeroed in on the spot that throbbed and ached.

Ariel cried out in shock as he stimulated her deliberately. The pleasure was liquid and electric. Clearly, Jacob Wolff had more than a working knowledge of a woman's anatomy. In mere minutes she was hovering on the edge of climax.

He nuzzled her collarbone, his breath hot and labored. "This is a really bad idea," he muttered. Without warning, he reversed direction and found his way inside her panties, touching bare flesh.

Ariel, already primed, came immediately, riding out the wave of intense pleasure as Jacob stroked her intimately. Afterward, she curled into his embrace, burying her face at his throat. "That's not what I meant," she whispered. "You're still…"

"Still what?" he asked, humor evident in his wry response.

"You know. I want to make you feel good."

"You did, princess. You do. But that's as far as we're going today. One of us has to have some sense."

She sighed, licking the underside of his chin. "I don't know why you have to be so stuffy. We're in a tropical paradise. You're pretending to be my boyfriend. And I'm not sick. What will it hurt to have a little fun along the way?"

"Are you really that naive?"

"Now you're being rude. And patronizing."

He played with her hair. "I think you're an amazing woman, Ariel. And you have an incredible future ahead of you. Why complicate matters with an old guy like me?"

"You're thirty," she snapped. "Hardly Methuselah's contemporary."

She felt the chuckle that rumbled through his chest. "Let's

slow this down. Give it some time. You're going to be too busy, anyway, to have a fling. Aren't I right?"

"Maybe," she said grudgingly. "But I still think you're bossy and overbearing."

"I can live with that," he said, kissing the top of her head. "But I couldn't forgive myself if I took advantage of you. And that's what it would feel like. So don't push me, please."

Tears burned her eyes, but she didn't let them fall. "I'll try," she whispered. "But I'm not making any more promises."

Twelve

Jacob made himself climb out of bed. Releasing Ariel and acting as if nothing momentous had happened required every bit of acting skill he could muster. His whole body was in agony. He needed her with a white-hot ache that infused every cell in his body with yearning.

Damning his conscience and his scruples, he reached for the phone. "I'm going to order lunch. You okay with that?"

She still looked mad, but mad was better than hurt. "Whatever."

He hid out in the living room while she showered, not trusting himself to be so close while she was naked. His hand still burned from touching her. She'd been warm, wet and willing. Every guy's fantasy.

Jacob Wolff was an idiot. He could almost hear his brothers jeering at him for his misplaced nobility. Of course, Gareth and Kieran were getting laid nightly now, each with a brand-new wife tucked in his bed. Jacob had felt the sting of envy at their weddings and been shamed by it.

He wanted what they had, but he was a damned coward. Even witnessing their complacent joy, he wasn't willing to go out on an emotional limb. The tree was flimsy and the fall a long one. He told himself he was satisfied to remain with his feet firmly planted on the ground.

Ariel was a challenge. One he would have to work hard to handle. She was impulsive and tempestuous and sensual. The kind of woman every mother warned her sons about. If Jacob let her into his soul, she had the potential to drag him to the heights and in the end watch him tumble into despair.

He could fall in love with her. Along with every man in her orbit. And in his case, it would be as much love as lust. Something about her tugged at his heartstrings and made him half believe that there was such a thing as happy endings.

But when all was said and done, Ariel dwelt in a world of fiction. Where the final scene was always emotionally satisfying. Even now, poised to take on the character of a tormented heroine, she would play her part so well that the audience would be convinced it was better to have loved and lost than never to have loved at all.

Jacob didn't buy it. Tennyson clearly hadn't watched a beloved fiancée waste away in pain and suffering, helpless to do a thing to save her. In retrospect, Jacob didn't really understand how he had finished his residency. The days had been a blur of nonstop work. Hour after hour of mind-numbing routines that managed to anesthetize the torment for brief periods.

And when his compatriots had discovered his true identity and had turned on him en masse, it had been the final straw. Jacob was done with humanity. He liked his hermit ways. Sex made a man stupid, and he was smarter than most. So he would handle Ariel. Somehow. No matter how many cold showers were required.

The location schedule became his friend. Up before dawn. Falling into bed at night, completely exhausted. In the afternoons, Ariel and John England rehearsed the following day's script. The grueling pace was hardest on Ariel, because she was in virtually every scene.

Her ability to memorize entire pages of lines stunned Jacob. She had a chip on her shoulder about her lack of formal education, but she was brilliant in ways Jacob could never manage. For someone at the height of her career, she was surprisingly insecure. He wished she could see herself as others saw her. People gravitated to her happiness, her energy.

He'd never experienced life on another movie set, but he had a hunch that not all stars hobnobbed with the crew the way Ariel did. She played poker with the old men and traded bawdy jokes with the young ones. She commiserated with women about the foibles of their mates, and was charmingly appreciative to everyone who made her life as leading lady flow more smoothly.

After their intimate nap, Ariel reformed. Though she still teased him verbally, there was a new line drawn in the sand. Other than the necessary PDAs, she never touched him. Even if it was a lie, she always feigned sleep by the time he got out of the shower at night.

Their uneasy truce ushered them through the first three weeks of shooting, but trouble loomed on the horizon. Rod drove them all relentlessly, taking advantage of an unprecedented string of postcard-worthy days. Ariel worked harder than anyone, pushing herself to the limit in order to make every scene perfect in as few takes as possible.

She and John established an immediate friendship, sharing a love of juvenile video games and a penchant for practical jokes. Jacob might have been jealous were it not for the fact that even a blind man could see they acted more like siblings than lovers.

Fortunately, John and Ariel's camaraderie enabled them to slip easily into character when the cameras rolled. Jacob watched the lovely Viola reluctantly falling in love with the man who had claimed her and tamed her. Though not politically correct by modern standards, the love story was compelling and deeply moving.

Jacob hoped that the death scene would be shot back in L.A. He didn't think he had the fortitude to watch Ariel perish in front of his eyes. She was such a convincing actress, he knew that her demise would wrench tears from even the most jaded movie-goers.

She seemed to live on coffee and yogurt. Whenever possible, he coaxed her to eat more, but the heat and the pressure of filming combined to decimate her appetite. He kept an eagle eye on her. Even when he saw her lose a pound or two, it was obvious she was not trying to watch her weight. She was simply worn out.

One afternoon when she was supposed to be sneaking in a cat nap, he found her sitting on the side of the bed signing a stack of head shots.

Jacob leaned in the doorway. "I thought you were sleeping."

She looked up guiltily. "Have you met Reggie, the assistant cameraman? His daughter is having a birthday party. I offered to send these autographed pictures to hand out to her friends. Middle school girls are ruthless. It never hurts to have a little bribe in hand."

"That's nice of you."

"It's no big deal."

Perhaps not. But most people wouldn't have been so generous with their time, or so thoughtful in the first place.

He sat down beside her and tugged at the end of her ponytail. "I have good news."

She rested her head for a brief moment on his shoulder. "Do tell."

"Rod is giving everyone the night off. He's pleased with how shooting has gone thus far, and he's showing his gratitude."

"Who knew that under that cranky, gruff exterior lurked a teddy bear?" She signed the last photo with a flourish and tucked the stack in an envelope.

"Well, I wouldn't exactly say that. But then again, you always see the best in people. It's one of the things I like about you."

Her cheeks reddened. "That's a sweet thing to say."

"I can be nice if I set my mind to it." He put his arm around her. "How about celebrating? I'll steal the car from Harriet and take you up to Shirley Heights to watch the sunset. I'm told you can see all the way to Montserrat. Live reggae music. Dancing. Great seafood. What do you think?"

"What are we celebrating?"

"Oh, I don't know. Life in general. I'm glad I came with you, Ariel. Seeing part of your world has been eye-opening."

"Everyone in the cast and crew loves you."

It was his turn to flush. "Everyone?" He caught her earlobe between his teeth and tugged.

She inhaled sharply, and he saw her hands curl into fists as her eyelashes lowered. "I'm not allowed to love you," she said primly. "I'm not even permitted to get near you. Sort of like a kid in a china shop. *Look, but don't touch.*"

"You're a sassy brat." He kissed the skin just below her ear, tasting warm woman and coconut oil. "You've been on your best behavior, haven't you?"

Her head lolled on her shoulders, a dreamy smile on her face. "You have no idea."

"Then you deserve a treat. We both do."

She curled an arm around his neck and surprised him with a quick kiss. "Define treat."

Damn it. He'd thought he could keep this light and fun. But already, his body betrayed him. His sex was hard and ready. And Ariel was soft and warm in his embrace. She was wearing a white gauze skirt with a lemon-yellow bikini top that barely covered her nipples.

His fingers ached to tug it aside, but he was on a hair trigger, and he knew he couldn't chance it. Not yet.

"How about if we start with some very public hand-holding and go from there?"

She released him and pouted. "Doesn't sound like much of a treat. I'm guessing you do your best work in private. We could always stay here. In this room."

He was tempted. God, he was tempted. His decision to keep his distance from Ariel, both emotionally and physically, had been tested on a daily basis…sometimes hourly.

"We're going out," he said firmly. "Put on your fanciest dress. I'll be back for you in an hour."

Ariel's heart soared. A date with Jacob Wolff…an honest to God date. She was giddy with excitement. She jumped in the shower, washing from head to toe with some of the expensive gel provided by the hotel management. After shampooing her hair and shaving her legs, she got out and dried off, all the while pondering what to wear.

Though she hoped she wasn't being vain, she sensed Jacob's desire deepening. He was affectionate with her, almost indulgent at times. But that was not what she wanted. Despite his reservations, she was a grown woman with needs that only he could fulfill.

She was falling in love with him. And though she knew it was stupid and self-destructive, she couldn't seem to help herself. Jacob Wolff was a Renaissance man. Confidence came as naturally to him as breathing. Whether he was playing a rowdy game of beach football with the guys or discussing politics with Rod, or helping out when one of the young actresses suffered a migraine, he was completely comfortable in his own skin.

For a guy who professed to be happy with his solitary lifestyle, locked away in his research lab, he seemed remarkably content to fit into her world. And that was dangerous. Because Ariel began to weave dreams that included a leading man who was as real as it gets.

Physically, Jacob could have been an actor. He had the good

looks. His body was overtly masculine, sculpted with muscle and sinew, and his rakish grin, when he forgot to be serious, was so sexy it literally stole her breath.

She knew everyone thought they were having sex night after night. The teasing had been subtle but persistent. Her only response was a bland smile. What happened between her and Jacob was not information for public consumption. And besides, if word leaked out that her roommate was resorting to cold showers rather than making love to her, no one would believe it.

After dithering in front of the closet for ten minutes, she finally chose a silver, knee-length dress made of fabric so thin it was almost like cobwebs. Lined in matching satin, it caught the light when she moved. The neckline was simple with spaghetti straps and a bodice that dipped modestly in front and back. Fitted at the waist, it twirled out in a froth of layered crinolines.

It was a party dress, a look-at-me-I'm-pretty frock that made her feel feminine and daring. And it wasn't so sleek and fancy that she would feel out of place in the casual atmosphere of Antigua's nightlife.

Three-inch silver heels and a tiny matching clutch completed the outfit. She wore her favorite diamond studs, ones that had belonged to her grandmother, along with a single diamond bangle bracelet.

Staring in the mirror as she put up her hair, she wondered if Jacob would find her sexy…or if he would see a little girl playing dress-up. His refusal to acknowledge her maturity and their mutual attraction frustrated her. Perhaps tonight was her opportunity to change things.

She was pacing the floor, waiting on him, when the door opened. Holy Hannah. The man gazing at her with such heat was heartthrob material. He had dressed up, as well, though she suspected he had patronized one of the upscale menswear shops in town.

Dark gray linen slacks molded to his long, lanky thighs.

He wore leather deck shoes with no socks. Broad shoulders strained the seams of a heather-gray linen blazer layered over a cream silk crew-neck shirt. Except for the very dark hair, he had the look of a young Kennedy, classy, rich, oozing charisma.

She gulped inwardly. "I'm ready if you are."

He walked toward her, and to her deep chagrin, she backed up, bumping into the wall.

His rakish grin said he knew exactly how he affected her. "Tonight you really are a princess," he muttered, putting his hands on her shoulders and stroking down her arms until he gripped her wrists. Holding her hands away from her body, he gazed his fill.

Her heart racketed away in her chest. Straightening her spine, she tilted her chin to meet him eye to eye. "You don't look half bad yourself. Sort of a Greek god out on the town. I see you've been shopping."

He shrugged. "A necessary evil. I didn't want you to be ashamed of me." He reached in his pocket and pulled out a navy velvet box. "But I bought something for you, as well."

"I'm always up for receiving gifts, but why? We aren't done with the movie."

He shook his head, smiling wryly. "It's your birthday, Ariel."

"Oh." So it was. Her mom usually made a big fuss, but they were hundreds of miles apart. "I never know what day it is when we're on island time."

"Unbelievable." He shook his head.

"How did you find out?"

"I looked at your passport one day. Presumptuous of me, I know. But I was curious about all those stamps you've collected. Pretty impressive. Go ahead," he said. "Open it."

She slowly flipped the lid, crying out in surprise and delight. Nestled in a cushion was a small pin, a crown no larger than a nickel. The base of the piece was covered in tiny diamonds, and the top was studded with even smaller rubies, emeralds and sapphires.

Any larger, and it would have been gaudy. But sized as it was, it was perfect. "This must have cost a fortune," she said. "I'm not sure it's appropriate for me to accept it. You're the one doing me a favor."

He frowned. "It's rude to talk about price. Put the damn thing on and let's go."

"What did I say to make you angry?" She was genuinely puzzled. "It's a lovely gift, Jacob." She pinned it at the spot where one strap met the bodice of her dress. The little tiara glittered with sassy charm. It was a rare man who could select a gift so incredibly perfect. Jacob knew her well.

She leaned up to kiss him softly. "I love it. I really do. I didn't mean to seem ungrateful."

His lips moved reluctantly beneath hers before he stepped back. "I'm not doing you a favor," he said bluntly. "I'm a doctor fulfilling my responsibilities."

"I thought you were my friend." It was true that in the beginning she had sought him out because of his reputation as a physician. But now she wanted something entirely different from him.

He stared at her, his eyes hot with barely concealed hunger. "I don't know what we are, Ariel. That's the problem."

It heartened her to know that he was struggling. That surely meant he cared. But Jacob Wolff was not a man to be manipulated or maneuvered into doing something he thought was wrong.

Perhaps it was up to her to show him how right they could be.

Thirteen

Jacob cursed the impulse that had led him to buy her a gift. The damp sheen in her eyes and her dumbfounded expression told him she was reading things into his offering that he hadn't intended.

It was just a damn pin, albeit an expensive one.

The truth was, he'd wanted to buy her something pretty and fun. The birthday had been his excuse. She was so easy to please, it made a man want to indulge her. Doubtless, he wasn't the first *boyfriend* eager to see her smile, and he wouldn't be the last.

He escorted her out to the car. Ariel had trouble negotiating the high seat of the SUV in her nonsensical footwear, so Jacob took her by the waist and lifted her up into the passenger seat.

"Thank you," she said softly, her face aglow with happiness.

He touched the tip of her nose with a finger. "Anything for the princess."

Harriet had delivered the vehicle washed and waxed and with a tank full of gas. Jacob had thanked Ariel's P.A. with a light peck on the cheek, which seemed to both please her and mystify her. She was an odd creature, but clearly devoted to her job.

Fortunately for Jacob, she had been willing to entrust the keys to someone other than herself.

The drive up to the high point of the island was curvy but doable, even in a large vehicle. Ariel, unusually quiet, sat with her hands tucked around her small purse as she took in the sights and sounds.

Jacob pulled into a parking area and squeezed between a VW bug and a Lexus. After helping Ariel out, he took her hand. "Watch out," he said. "The pavement isn't smooth."

He led her to the front door of a two-story structure that looked as if it had been there since the First World War. Windows dotted all sides of both stories. Colorful awnings provided protection from the sun while letting in the stiff ocean breezes. From somewhere inside, a steel drum beat out the rhythm of a Jimmy Buffett song.

Ariel urged him forward. "Come on," she said. "Let's get a seat before things get too crowded."

He stalled. "Don't you want to watch the sunset?" A quick glance at his watch said they had arrived earlier than he intended.

Ariel pushed past him, the toes of her sexy shoes practically tapping in impatience. "Since we're only *friends*," she said pointedly, "no thanks. I'm ready to dance."

He reached beyond her and flung open the door. The interior was dim and cool. His eyes struggled to adjust.

Suddenly, light flooded the room, and about six dozen voices shouted in unison. "Surprise!"

Ariel stopped dead, reaching for his hand in an unconscious gesture of nerves. "Jacob?" she said urgently.

All around them cast and crew beamed out a greeting. Several of them were more boisterous than others, obviously getting a head start on the bar tab. Rod Brinkman—irascible, cantankerous Rod—smiled. "Happy birthday, Ariel."

Jacob watched as she blushed from her throat to her forehead. She covered her cheeks with both hands. "I don't know what to say."

One of the gaffers, well on his way to being sloshed, shouted from a far corner. "Play the damn music and let's party."

Everyone broke into laughter and returned to their seats, leaving Jacob and Ariel to find their way to a table hosted by the director. The drums picked up pace again, and soon the small dance floor was filled. Brinkman patted Ariel's hand. "Hope you don't mind. The wardrobe staff came up with the idea. They happen to think you hung the moon."

Seeing the usually irrepressible Ariel momentarily speechless was worth the price of admission as far as Jacob was concerned. For the next half hour she was uncharacteristically quiet as they dug into the food Rod had ordered. Oysters on the half shell, shrimp cocktail, and at last, a fresh coconut pie. When Jacob was satisfied that she had eaten enough, he leaned closer to be heard over the ruckus. "You still hungry? Or do you want to dance?"

She laid her purse on the table and took his hand. "I thought you'd never ask."

As if on cue, the band segued into a tropical version of Elton John's "Can You Feel the Love Tonight." Jacob clasped Ariel's fingers with his and pulled her into his arms. His free hand found a place on her back, lightly stroking her spine as they moved to the music.

She rested her cheek on his shoulder. "I thought it was going to be just us tonight."

"Do you mind terribly? They were all so keen to surprise you."

"Of course I don't mind. I'm touched. I'm a very lucky woman."

The hint of melancholy in her voice troubled him. "Are you okay, Ariel? Have you had bad news about your mother?"

"No. I talked to her this afternoon and things are about the same."

"Then what is it?"

"The crew," she said slowly. "And the cast. When I'm shooting a movie, I get so close to many of these people. It seems like a family at times, but it's not the same, not really."

He was silent, trying to decipher the words she wasn't saying. "It's not a bad thing to love the way you do, Ariel. You give of yourself without reservation. And people respond to you. There are many kinds of families."

"I envy you yours. I guess you think that's strange or insensitive given your past, but you have siblings and cousins. When my mom is gone, I won't have anyone at all."

"You don't have aunts and uncles tucked away somewhere?"

"I asked years ago... My mother wasn't very forthcoming. She was an only child like I am, and I assume my father's family didn't want anything to do with us."

"Why don't you ask her again?"

"I can't. Not now. She would realize I'm asking because I know she's dying."

He kissed her temple. "I'll share mine with you. The family, I mean. Believe me, there are times I'd gladly give them away."

"You're lying," she said with a choked laugh.

But he had accomplished his mission. She was smiling again.

Ariel felt amazing in his arms, perfectly made to fit against his chest. Their legs brushed as they danced. He wished they were alone, but this was better for her sake. Jacob was surrounded by dozens of built-in chaperones. He could do nothing about his arousal that pulsed between them.

Ariel had to notice. They were close enough to be making love if the setting had been different.

One song ended, and another began. As if by design, the band had given up its earlier, fast-paced play list and was now reminding the audience that a fabulous moon hung above, illuminating the view of English Harbor below.

Jacob steered Ariel out onto the terrace and into a patch of shadows. "You deserve a birthday kiss," he murmured, dragging her flush up against him, his hands at her hips.

She tipped back her head, her hair glossy even in the gloom. "I would have thought a spanking was more in order according to you."

"Don't tempt me." He started at her forehead with chaste, light brushes of his lips. Her familiar perfume, light and evocative, teased his nostrils. "Happy birthday, Ariel."

She dragged his head lower, finding his mouth with hers. "I'm a year older now," she whispered. "And twenty-three is only seven years younger than thirty. If you round the numeral seven down, it's only five. That's nothing at all."

"I'm still your doctor."

"I've never felt healthier."

Her arms curled around his neck, forcing him to support her weight as she balanced on those totally impractical shoes. His mouth moved over hers lazily, his tongue rubbing her lips, sliding inside when she moaned.

"We have to talk," he said hoarsely. He was no longer able to pretend that he could resist her. With several weeks of shooting still to go, it was painfully apparent, at least to him, that he was going to succumb to Ariel's sexual invitation…and soon.

But first there were things she needed to know.

She reached beneath his knit shirt and ran her small palm over his chest. Ariel touching him made a mockery of all his resolutions and high ideals. He wanted her. He needed her. Whether he called it gratification or disaster, the end result would be the same. Ariel…beneath him, calling out his name as he made love to her.

When her fingernail scraped lightly over his nipple, he jerked.

Ariel laughed, the sexy, knowing laugh of a woman who

acknowledged her own power. "I can't wait to hear what you have to say," she said, that husky voice raking his nerve endings almost physically. She kissed him again, and her tongue mated with his. "But I believe that sometimes, actions speak louder than words."

Their kisses grew wilder, hotter. Sweat rolled down his back, courtesy of the tropical night. Ariel's skin was moist, lush. "If we don't stop," he gasped, fingers digging into her hips, "I'm going to take you right here, God help me."

He was out of control. His analytical mind assessed the situation at some subconscious level and cursed the public venue.

Ariel drew back, tugging until he released her. "Thirty minutes," she gasped, her eyes unreadable in the dark. "We have to go back inside. I can't leave my own party. It would be rude."

Jacob's curse was vicious and heartfelt. "You go. I can't let them see me like this."

Ariel hesitated, her fingertips touching his lightly as though any more direct contact would cause them to combust. "Are you okay?"

Scarcely able to breathe, he leaned back against the stone building, his body near doubling over from the ache of wanting her. "Go," he ground out, beyond polite conversation. "Go."

Finally, she melted away into the night, her hair and limbs a glimmer of light in the shadows.

Jacob sucked in air, his heartbeat deafening in his ears. Appalled at how close he had come to entering her standing up, he closed his eyes and reached for sanity.

But he came up empty. Ariel had shattered the one thing above all others that he could count on. His control. If he was this completely torn asunder emotionally and physically by the prospect of screwing her, how much worse would it be if he committed the ultimate sin of falling in love?

Like an exhausted swimmer trying to cross the English Channel, he was left without options. He had come so far into deep waters that turning back was impossible. But going forward promised to be dangerous and potentially deadly.

Finally, he returned to the party, citing an important phone call as the reason for his delay. Ariel was out on the dance floor, working her way through a bevy of admirers who were taking advantage of a rare opportunity to bask in the star's undivided attention.

Jacob's expression must have given him away, because the taciturn Brinkman tossed back a finger of Scotch and said, "What's eating you?"

He shrugged. "I'm not much of a party animal."

"Then you've hooked up with the wrong girl. Ariel lives to socialize. I don't mean that in a derogatory way," he said quickly. "She's the least vain star I've ever worked with. No demands. No enormous ego to be stroked. Simply a hardworking, incredibly beautiful and talented woman. People gravitate toward her."

"I see that," Jacob said quietly, his gaze following her around the room as she moved to the music. "In fact, I've witnessed it since the first day I walked onto the set." He barely refrained from grinding his teeth as a surge of possessiveness overwhelmed him. Seeing other men as the recipients of her sunny smile was almost more than he could bear in his present mood. "Tell me, Rod. Do you believe the stories they write about her in the tabloids?"

Brinkman snorted. "We call that fiction."

"But the men. Do they take advantage of her good nature?"

The older man narrowed his eyes, his gaze also on Ariel as they spoke. "They may try. But don't underestimate Ariel. She's survived in this business and kept not only her head but her sweet nature. No artifice at all. What you see is what you get. That's a rare thing in a woman and even more unusual in a profession that breeds narcissism."

"I'm not jealous."

"Never thought you were. A man likes to gauge the cost before he takes a risk."

"What risk?"

"Don't play dumb with me, Wolff. You've been hit hard with tragedy…twice. I know your background. Had you investigated as soon as she showed up with you in tow. I couldn't afford any surprises with my moneymaker."

"Is that how you see her?"

"It's part of my job to calculate everything in dollars and cents. If you're asking a personal question, then no. Personally, I like her. If I'd ever been dumb enough to have kids, I hope one of them would have turned out like her."

"Not likely. You're a hard-ass." Jacob delivered the jab with a wry smile.

Brinkman was actually flattered. "I am. And don't you forget it."

One song ended, and the band signaled a break. Jacob counted the seconds until Ariel made her way back to the table. He stood as she approached, handing her a glass of water. "You look hot," he said mildly.

She took the glass and tilted her head as she drained it dry. Twirling spontaneously, making her skirts fluff out in a circle, she grinned. "I *am* hot, big boy. And aren't you lucky to be taking me home."

Brinkman chortled, clearly enjoying Jacob's not-so-subtle hunger. "You tell him, Ariel."

Ariel leaned down and kissed the top of her boss's head. "Don't wait up. Wolff man and I are going to find a deserted beach and howl at the moon."

Fourteen

Ariel took Jacob's hand and dragged him toward the exit. At least three people tried to stop them. She forged on, desperate to leave. The promised thirty minutes had turned into forty-five.

Outside, she stopped short, trying to remember where they had parked the car. Darkness had fallen, and the exterior lighting was almost nonexistent. The moon hung low in the sky, blocked from view by the building.

"Over there." Jacob was in charge now, his arm around her waist as they dodged another set of would-be conversationalists.

Ariel paused beside the vehicle, waiting for Jacob to help her in. Instead of opening her door, he forced her to back up, his hips pinning hers to the side of the car. He was aroused and hard. The feel of his rigid flesh nudging urgently at her belly made her heart thud with uneven beats.

She licked her lips. "I gave up fooling around in parking lots when I left high school."

His head lowered, his arms bracketing her shoulders, hands braced on the car. With lips hovering over hers, he whispered, "No fooling, princess. I'm dead serious."

Over his shoulder, she saw a million stars begin to cartwheel drunkenly. Her senses were enhanced by the notion that she and Jacob stood not only at the apex of the island, but also at a precipice in their relationship.

Faint music drifted from the restaurant. As she flattened her hands behind her, resting them on the cold metal of the SUV, his scent teased her nostrils, a mix of hot male flesh and expensive aftershave.

Slowly, his mouth settled against hers. She tasted the coconut dessert they had shared. Jacob had banked his hunger in the interim since their earlier embrace, this time giving her exquisite tenderness.

"Oh, Jacob," she sighed. "Please don't tease me unless you mean business."

His laugh was a physical caress as he abandoned her lips and nibbled his way down her neck. "I was thinking more of pleasure."

The way he said the word *pleasure* took the starch out of her knees. "Not that I'm complaining about your technique," she muttered, "but I think a little more privacy might be in order."

He rested his forehead against hers. "You sure we can't just climb in the backseat?"

She cupped his face in her hands. "I like it when you forget to be all buttoned up."

His entire body tensed, and she cursed her stupidly impulsive words. When would she learn to censor her speech?

"We need to talk," he said quietly, pulling away, leaving her cold and bereft. "There are things you should know. Get in the car."

The mood changed so rapidly, she suffered mental whiplash. His chameleon-like shift from passionate lover to brooding loner scared her. "I'm all in favor of less talk and more action," she said, slamming the door and leaning into the comfy leather seat.

Her attempt at levity failed miserably. Jacob put the car in gear, his profile somber. "Do you mind if we take a drive?"

"Of course not."

Conversation languished after that. Jacob drove the way he did everything else, with calm competence. Despite the winding road and the black of night, she felt safe with him.

When her patience was about at an end, he turned off onto a sandy lane that led to the ocean. Much like the cove where they had done most of the shooting for the film, this section of beach was protected on both sides by arms of land that jutted out into the sea. But the area was much smaller, and there were no hotels in sight.

Jacob steered to a halt beneath a large coconut palm and shut off the engine. Without speaking, he got out and went to the back of the car. She heard him rustling about, and when he came around to open her door, he held a heavy cotton blanket in his hand.

"C'mon," he said. "Let's walk." While she was still seated, he lifted her feet one at a time and removed her shoes, tucking them in the pocket of his jacket. Then he eased her down to stand beside him and kissed her. A restrained kiss that promised something wonderful. When they broke apart, she rested her forehead against his chest for a moment, her legs weak.

The sand was warm beneath her bare feet, still hoarding the heat of the sun. The tide had reached its highest point and was beginning to slowly recede. Jacob steered their route with purpose, helping her clamber up and over the loose stones at one end of the cove. There in front of them lay another pristine beach, this one tiny and inaccessible by road.

"This will do," he said, spreading the blanket just above the damp demarcation that delineated the high water mark. "Have a seat, princess."

Hearing the nickname eased the tightness in her chest. Jacob

Wolff was an intimidating man, not physically scary, but so hard to read that she often felt as if she were tiptoeing on egg-shells in his presence.

They sat side by side. Jacob leaned back on his hands, his long legs stretched out in front of him. Ariel pulled her knees to her chest and clasped her arms around them, shivering slightly. Jacob noticed, of course, and removed his linen jacket, wrapping it protectively around her shoulders.

"Thank you."

He didn't acknowledge her quiet words. The lines of his face were austere. How could she ever really know him?

Timidly, she put her hand on his arm. "What do you want to talk about?"

He half turned, his slight smile self-mocking. "Here I am, on a secluded beach in the tropics with America's sweetheart. How did this happen?"

She shrugged. "I bludgeoned you into it. And I apologize for that, by the way. I haven't been sick at all. You could have stayed on Wolff Mountain with your beakers and your Bunsen burners."

That coaxed a chuckle from him. "Did you ever actually take a science class in high school?" he asked.

"I tried biology, but I couldn't bring myself to touch dead animals. So I transferred into anatomy. The first day I showed up, they were studying the reproductive system. I made some wisecrack about the birds and the bees and got kicked out."

"What then?"

"Rocks. Geology. And I was good at memorization, so chemistry worked, too. I can still recite the periodic table. You wanna hear it?"

Jacob held up a hand. "I'll pass." He sighed, his expression troubled. "I don't want there to be secrets between us," he said. "If we become lovers, you deserve my honesty, at the very least."

"Please don't tell me the castle has a dungeon full of dead bodies."

He covered her mouth with his hand. "Shh. Don't be afraid. It's nothing too terrible."

She wriggled away, turning to face him, her legs curled beneath her. "Start talking."

He eased down onto his back, hands tucked behind his head, eyes trained on the heavens. "I was a prisoner growing up. After my mother and my aunt died, my dad and my uncle hid us all away from the world. I had a plethora of tutors, did my first long-distance, university-level coursework before I grew facial hair. One day I looked in the mirror and realized that I was eighteen years old and had never been on a date."

She was silent, afraid to interrupt his monologue. It was difficult to reconcile the picture he was painting with the vital, masculine man who lay beside her.

He went on. "The only way we could persuade our fathers to allow us to go to college was to assume aliases. Dad and Uncle Vincent were afraid, even then, that we would be kidnapping targets."

"Did your friends know the truth?"

"No one knew. I mostly stayed to myself as a freshman. Even though I was a typical horny adolescent, the girls I met were so damned silly I couldn't bring myself to overlook their giggly behavior long enough to get laid."

"Somehow that doesn't surprise me. I'm betting you were born serious."

He ignored her jibe. "Then I met Diane."

Her stomach plunged. "Diane?"

"The intern I told you about. The one who died. She was my fiancée. She was at university on a full scholarship, pre-med, the same as me. We hit it off immediately. Pretty soon, we were deeply involved, but even having sex all hours of the day and night, we were focused on our goals. We decided we would do everything we could to get accepted into the same med school.

And it worked. By that time we had been together long enough to know that what we felt for each other was the real deal. I proposed to her and gave her a ring. She and her mother began planning a wedding for the month after graduation."

Ariel didn't want to hear any more, but the silent Jacob Wolff had opened up and now the words spilled from him in a torrent of remembered grief. She gripped her knees and dropped her head, not wanting to see the anguish on his face.

"When she died," he said slowly, "I lost my mind for a time. If I'd had a normal childhood and adolescence, I might have had the tools to cope. But I felt as if everything had been stolen from me. First my mother, then my best friend, and now Diane. Practicing medicine was the only thing that kept me going. Though even that was a mechanical exercise for a long while."

"How long ago did she die?"

"Five years, three months and twenty-six days. I agreed to help you, because I never want to feel that helpless again. I needed to know that I could make a difference in your life, even if I had failed Diane."

Her chest hurt. "Why are you telling me this?"

"Diane was my first and last love," he said. He turned on his side abruptly, head propped on his hand. "My first and last lover." His eyes were dark, unreadable. "I don't have it in me to relate to a woman that way ever again. So I've chosen to be celibate. I took an oath to do no harm. Breaking a woman's heart falls into that category."

"You think if we have sex I'll fall in love with you?"

"I hope not. I'm asking you not to take that chance. If I sound arrogant, I apologize. I know you have a great deal of experience, so I suppose it's conceivable that I'll be the one taking the risk."

There was a good chance that Jacob was still in love with his dead fiancée. And that would explain why he had been so vehement about not making love to Ariel. But even so, she wanted him. And she would take what little he was able to give her, even if it was only a sliver of his heart. Maybe, just maybe, she could seduce him into falling in love with her.

With her pulse pounding, she uncurled her body and eased down beside him. "I stand forewarned. Kiss me, Jacob Wolff."

Their faces were mere inches apart. When he didn't move, she closed the gap. "You're a handsome, strong, sexy man. I'm willing to take what you have to offer. Fair enough?"

The groan that ripped from his chest was tormented and raw. He rolled on top of her, his thigh wedging her legs apart. Her skirt bunched between them. The layers of fabric rustled against his pants legs.

"I care about you, Ariel."

The words hurt. Damn him for his integrity. Doggedly, she shoved them aside. "Then show me."

He fumbled with one strap of her dress, long fingers tearing it loose in his impatience. "I love your breasts." Without warning, he dragged the tight bodice down past her bosom, shoving her flesh toward his eager mouth.

She cried out, stunned at how quickly things were moving. In her head, this beach encounter was destined to be measured and slow. The reality was far different. He rolled her to one side to reach the zipper. Cool air wafted down her spine.

Lifting her like a doll, he dispensed with the dress, leaving her clad in nothing but a thong panty. She clasped her arms over her chest. "Stop, Jacob. I want to see you, too."

He froze, like a wild animal scenting danger. When she had the temerity to yank at his shirt, he shrugged out of it and sat up to drag it over his head. In a fumble of arms and legs and muttered apologies, they managed to strip him.

The sight of her naked Wolff was at once breathtaking and terrifying. He was beautiful in the way of classic statuary, hard-chested, broad-shouldered, sleekly muscled. Ariel's confidence waned in direct proportion to the size of Jacob's fully aroused shaft.

Did a man who hadn't had sex in five years have it in him to be gentle?

He reached out both of his hands and cupped her breasts, bouncing them lightly. The thin, watery moonlight bathed them in an ethereal glow. But Jacob was no mirage.

They were kneeling, facing each other. The soft breeze cooled the perspiration on the back of her neck. When he pinched her nipples, ever so gently, dual jolts of fire streaked toward her pelvis. Anyone could conceivably have stumbled upon them, but the feeling of isolation calmed her nerves.

He smoothed the hair from her face, his lips curved in a tender smile. "You look like a mermaid," he said. "It's hard to believe you're real."

For one bleak instant, memories of the poor, doomed Diane threatened to intrude, but Ariel pushed them away. Jacob was here. With Ariel. That was all that mattered.

Feeling both foolishly timid and shiveringly brave, she cupped his erection in both hands, stroking lightly up and down. The result was electric. Jacob's head fell backward, his hands fisting at his hips. His entire body went rigid, as though being tortured on a rack.

"Ariel…"

The word was broken, aching, pleading.

She used one hand to keep up the gentle rhythm on his shaft. With the other, she gathered his warm sac into her curled fingers. Crooning his name, she loved him with her caress.

He cried out suddenly. She felt moisture dribble over her hands as he came violently, doubling over, his forehead on her shoulder. "Ariel. Oh, God, Ariel." He was hoarse.

Not knowing exactly what to do, she wrapped her arms around him and leaned into his embrace.

To see such a powerful and masculine man shaking—at her mercy—troubled her. Would he be angry with her in the cold light of day? Would he resent her for destroying his control?

Her body ached for his possession, but she no longer wanted

to take the lead. Something had shifted between them. Something immense and immeasurable. It frightened and humbled her.

He stroked her hair, his breathing gradually returning to normal. "Forgive me, princess. It will get better from here on out, I swear." He managed a choked chuckle. "But in truth, that was probably for the best. I want to take my time with you."

One short sentence sent her stomach tumbling. "Promises, promises," she dared to tease.

Jacob straightened. In one quick glance she discerned that despite his release, he was primed and ready to go again. *Oh my...*

His hands bracketed her face and he dragged her close for a hungry kiss. "You've bewitched me," he said roughly. "I don't even know myself anymore."

She rested her hands on his, tilting her face to the moonlight so he could read her sincerity. "I need you to make love to me, Jacob, more than I need my next breath. No post mortems. No regrets. Only pleasure. You promised."

Fifteen

You promised. Jacob struggled to round up remnants of his usual self, but it was no easy task. Ariel Dane, virtually naked, her skin luminous in the glow of the moon, shivered in his arms. Soothing her automatically, he nuzzled her hair, his eyes damp.

His chest ached with emotion. She was temptation personified. The answer to all his unspoken pleas, the reward for a life he had done his best to make count for something.

All he wanted to do was please her, but he didn't know how. She was generous and open and loving. Jacob was shut off, emotionally sterile.

But at least he could give her this. Pleasure.

He lowered his hands to her curvy ass, pulling her against his hips.

"Put your arms around my neck," he commanded. Carefully, he stood, staggering slightly as Ariel's slim legs wrapped around his waist.

She rested her cheek on his shoulder, silent. Unusually silent.

Jacob walked toward the water. The waves in the tiny shel-tered cay were nothing more than ripples on the surface. He strode out into the ocean, wincing at the chill on his warm skin. In moments, as he adjusted, the sea felt like bathwater.

Ariel, still mute, clung to him like seaweed.

When he stopped, waist deep, she finally spoke. "Are you going to drown me?" she asked in a pleasantly conversational tone.

Her weight was barely a strain, though keeping his footing in the shifting sand was a challenge. "Should I?" he asked.

Her breasts pressed warmly at his chest. "I wouldn't advise it. Rod would be pissed."

Jacob stroked the crease of her buttocks, barely concealed by wet silk. "Do you trust me?"

"Always."

A simple, heartfelt word. Trust he perhaps did not deserve. With one hand, he reached up and began pulling the pins from her elaborate chignon, tossing them one at a time out into the dark water. Ariel's hair spilled like liquid gold, glimmering as it covered her shoulders.

Her familiar mischievous grin flashed in the dark. "Are you adding hairdresser to your resume?"

"I want you to float," he said. "I'll keep a hand beneath you, but you'll have to let me hold you." Easing her into a horizon-tal position, he supported her hips as she aligned her body, arms outstretched overhead. "Close your eyes," he murmured.

She obeyed, her compliance arousing. "Now what?" A smile still lingered at her lips.

"Nothing. Just feel."

With his spare hand, he combed through her hair, separat-ing each strand until the undulating tresses floated freely. Now she really did look like a mermaid.

He stroked her forehead, her nose, her cheeks and her col-larbones. Ariel's posture was lax, her breathing barely percep-tible. White breasts, tipped in dark raspberry, broke the surface of the water. Playing with each responsive crest aroused him even more.

Skating down toward her flat belly, he found the only item of clothing she wore. Wet black silk that outlined the shape of her sex. Jacob probed gently with a finger, his muscles clenching in hunger when Ariel gasped and lifted her hips into his touch.

As she did, she began to sink. He put both hands beneath her. "Stop," he commanded. "No matter what I do to you, I need you to relax. Do you understand?"

Her floating hair swirled as she nodded her head. "Yes," she whispered.

"Are you cold?"

"No."

He touched her again. This time, a choked groan was her only response. Pushing aside the panties, he bared her femininity. A tiny fluff of pale blond hair, neatly trimmed, led the way to plump, slick folds of flesh. He shivered at the sight, though his skin was hot.

Finding the little nub that was her pleasure center, he ran the tip of his finger across it, barely making contact. The keening sound from Ariel's throat made the hair stand up on his arms. He inserted a finger into her passage, just barely, and used his thumb on her sweet spot.

She was tight and slick. Imagining his sex delving into that warm welcome hardened his shaft to stone. "I want more access," he said quietly, moving her gently. "Lock your ankles behind my back. Keep your hands over your head."

Now she was fully open to him. So beautiful. So trusting. A slender sea nymph, begging to be loved.

Jacob used both thumbs to part her sex. Dragging the silk back and forth across her center, he tormented her. Ariel's whimper spurred him on. With a quick snap of his wrist, he ripped the cloth, never noticing when the silk floated away.

Now she was completely bare, utterly vulnerable. He stepped deeper into the water until he could move her legs around his neck. Her thighs, now spread wide by his shoulders, glistened wet in the moonlight. He put his mouth at her center and suckled her.

Ariel's shocked cry ricocheted over the surface of the water. She tasted of salt and secrets. With his tongue, he probed. Once. And again.

She writhed in his grasp, no longer able to obey his instruction to be still. He licked and nibbled and thrust until she went rigid for half a second and cried out his name as she came.

Barely waiting for the last tremors to fade from her limbs, he scooped her into his arms and strode toward the beach. Ariel's body was dead weight, her lips parted, her eyes still closed. When he reached the blanket, he laid her down gently and reached for his shirt to dry her.

As though she were helpless, he carefully ran the soft, warm cloth over every inch of her body. "Look at me," he said, tossing the damp shirt aside. "I'm going to make love to you now. Ariel?"

Her lashes fluttered. Her eyes, glazed with the dregs of physical pleasure, gazed at him in mute supplication. "I didn't know it could feel like that," she said, the words barely audible. "More. I want more."

The imperious demand dragged a laugh from his tight throat, though he would have sworn he was beyond amusement. "Whatever the princess desires."

He paused. "I have condoms in my pants pocket," he said. "Don't move."

She grasped his wrist. "I'm on the pill."

Surely she wasn't that naive. "There are other considerations, Ariel. Have you been to a doctor recently? Been tested?"

Lifting up onto her elbows, she looked him straight in the eye. "On my mother's life, I swear. You have nothing to fear from me."

A doctor never gambled on human life. But Jacob had never known Ariel to lie. And God knew, he wanted to feel her without any barriers between them. "You're sure?" His own past was no issue.

"Positive."

On his knees, he scooped her bottom into his hands and pulled her thighs over his. He looked his fill, laughing when Ariel squirmed in embarrassment.

"Quit staring," she said. "Let's get on with it."

"Haven't you ever heard about savoring the anticipation?"

"I've savored quite enough, thank you. I want you, Jacob Wolff."

He leaned forward, positioning the head of his shaft at her entrance. The skin covering his penis was so tight it was painful to touch. Shifting his weight onto his arms, he pressed into her.

Ariel tensed beneath him. "Slowly, please."

He understood her desire to drag out the pleasure, but what she asked for was going to be difficult. He wanted all of her. Now.

"I'll do my best, but you're squeezing me so damn beautifully, my eyes may bug out."

He shoved again, gaining maybe an inch, and met resistance. Considerable resistance. Cursing the darkness for making her expression hard to decipher, he stilled, his body trembling. *What the hell?* "Ariel?" he questioned hoarsely.

She bit her lip. He could see that much. "This is a first for me, Doc," she said flippantly, "so take it easy." Her tone didn't match her words. Ariel's husky voice shook with emotion.

Jacob's brain couldn't wrap itself around the obvious conclusion. "You're a virgin?" The tabloid princess, the ultimate party girl was a virgin? It didn't compute.

"Do you really want to discuss this now, or do you want to finish what you've started?"

The tart bite in her words reminded him that Ariel Dane was no shrinking flower. His body throbbed in agony, the interruption interminable. In some small corner of his brain, he acknowledged that she had outwitted him. Had he known the truth, this moment would never have come to pass.

"Damn you," he groaned, surging forward until the barrier was breached. Her cry of discomfort and the tear that trickled down her cheek lashed him with a thousand arrows of guilt.

Words thick with sobs, Ariel pleaded. "Don't be angry, Jacob. I want this. I want you. Please don't ruin it."

At that moment, his heart tore in his chest. A wave of tenderness far greater than any he had battled out in the water crashed over him. Using his thumb to wipe away the moisture on her cheeks, he thrust with shallow strokes until her untried body accepted him fully.

When he was seated inside her, touching her womb, he bowed his head to hers. "Relax, little princess. Breathe. I won't move until you're ready." He kissed her, aching to show her how much this meant to him. They lay in the traditional missionary position now, but nothing about how he felt was ordinary.

Ariel wriggled beneath him. "I'm okay. It's really kind of nice."

Nice? He withdrew all the way and eased back in quickly, but not so forcefully that she couldn't accept him. "Tell me if it's painful," he insisted, though in all honesty, stopping at this point would leave him writhing on the ground.

She wrapped her legs around his waist, deepening his possession. "It's a good kind of hurt," she insisted. "I like knowing you're my first. I've waited for a man like you. Smart and noble and kind."

Her declaration made him want to run. He was no one's hero. The responsibility attached to such an appellation was more than he could bear. But he wanted her still, no matter what. At the end of his rope, he began to thrust in earnest, hips hammering, eyes stinging from the salt of sweat.

"Don't talk," he pleaded. "Just feel."

Their bodies found a rhythm. Though she was inexperienced, she made up for it with enthusiasm and boldness. Her fingernails raked his ass. The pain was lost to the fire building in his loins. No longer able to process reasonable thought, Jacob made love to her blindly, searching for his own release, his own slice of heaven.

The end, when it came, dragged both of them to a place that was both ecstasy and pain. He felt pummeled, bruised. In some tiny corner of his brain he acknowledged the need to spare Ariel his considerable weight. But the muscles in his arms were boneless, much like the rest of him.

When he could breathe and feel his limbs, he rolled to his side, taking her with him. She curled into his embrace as naturally as if they had been lovers forever.

The moon had set, leaving the small beach wrapped in darkness. Overhead, stars glittered. He stroked her back, feeling the delicacy of her spine. "I'm not stupid," he said, the words slurred. "You didn't tell me you were a virgin, because you knew if you did, I would never touch you."

She turned away from him, spooning their bodies. "You got me, Doc."

He heard the tears she was trying so desperately not to shed. That she was upset made him feel like a bastard, a soulless son of a bitch. Without stopping to analyze, to guard his words, the truth tumbled from his lips in atonement. "I don't regret it, Ariel. I don't regret this. God help me, but it's true. Tonight was a miracle. *You* are a miracle."

He played with her breasts, drunk on the knowledge that no man had ever seen her like this. Didn't she know he wasn't worthy of her gift? He was flawed, broken. Ariel deserved so much more.

Her faint sigh was his only answer.

He shifted on top of her, moving between her legs again, sliding home with no difficulty. "Look into my eyes," he demanded. Their bodies were joined completely, plastered together by sweat and lust and urgency. "You've awakened the beast," he said, shuddering as her passage tugged at his tumescent flesh. "I don't know if I'll ever get enough of you."

Ariel moved with him, lifting into his thrusts, curling her arms around his neck and dragging his head down to kiss him repeatedly. Her lips were sweet, eager, addictive.

He thought they reached a climax together again, but he couldn't be sure. He didn't know yet how to read her body. Before he could figure it out, exhaustion claimed him, rolling over him like a rogue wave, dragging him under.

Sixteen

Ariel awoke to the feel of a small crab exploring her toes. She shooed it away with a lazy kick and yawned. Night still clung to the beach, but out on the horizon faint light struggled to gain a toehold.

She catalogued her circumstances, hardly daring to acknowledge what had happened. Jacob's left arm curled tightly beneath her breasts. They were both naked, but he had covered her with his jacket. Her feet and legs were chilled, but wherever his skin touched hers, she was toasty warm.

Her body ached pleasantly, bringing back vivid memories of how he had coaxed passion from her, the arrogant manner in which he'd exposed her sensuality and met it with masculine demand. For a first time, it had been darned near perfect.

But her chest ached with sorrow. The truth could not be denied, nor could it be spun, Hollywood fashion, into a happy ending. She was in love with a man who had no heart, a man who had buried that troublesome organ with his dead fiancée. He was kind and honest to a fault, but the walls he had built to protect himself were as fortified and impregnable as the mountain on which he lived.

Things would be far worse now. Before, she had only dreamed of what it would be like to belong to Jacob Wolff. She had spun childish fantasies of winning his trust, his admiration, his love. Now that his body had claimed hers, she knew the exhilaration of mating with him, of hearing his choked gasp as he called her name in climax.

Jacob had never wanted to be intimate with her. He'd made that clear from the beginning. It was Ariel's fault that they now lay in a tangle of arms and legs on a deserted beach.

She ran a hand down his flank, measuring its breadth, the tautly muscled strength. Some visceral instinct told her this might be the last time he held her this way. He was the kind of man who did not tolerate mistakes, either in himself or others. Though in the midst of passion he professed not to regret their coupling, in the cold light of day saner thoughts might prevail.

And if that were so, surely she was entitled to one last memory. Carefully, she nudged him onto his back. He grumbled in his sleep, but settled as she had intended, one arm slung over his face.

Tentatively, she caressed him, noting in awe and flushed excitement the way he grew beneath her touch. Already semierect when she began, now he flexed and hardened, his shaft thrusting upward against his flat belly. He was beautiful and warm and alive.

Bravely, she shed his jacket. Scooting carefully, so as not to awaken him, she straddled his hips and guided him into position. Wincing from the sting of their earlier romp, she lowered herself onto his shaft.

Jacob groaned, his hands coming up to grip her ass in a bruising hold. His lashes fluttered and his eyes opened. With a groggy voice, he whispered. "Ariel?"

She leaned down to kiss him, her damp, tangled hair cloaking their faces. "I hope you don't mind," she teased.

"God, no." His hips flexed, driving himself deeper. "Give me a second to catch up."

It was clearly a rhetorical request. Though Ariel was in the dominant position, there was no question in her mind who took control.

He forced her upright. "I want to feel you." He sat up, his hands bracing her back, and kissed her breasts, alternating in random sequences until she was panting and shivering, though her skin was burning up. His lips and teeth tugged at her nipples, initiating an ache that echoed between her thighs where their bodies were joined.

He reached between them and found that place, probing gently. The added stimulation sent Ariel careening into a stunning orgasm. Without the anxiety and discomfort of the first time, she flew higher, hit harder, fell longer.

Barely aware of anything around her, she felt Jacob jerk and shudder in his own release, his powerful loins pounding into her until she swayed like a rag doll.

Collapsing in exhaustion, she buried her face in his neck. "God in heaven, Doc," she whispered. "You're one hell of a man." She doubted he heard her, because he was already asleep again.

The blanket on which they lay was damp and clammy. During the night, moisture had wicked up through the fabric. Her legs chilled rapidly where they rested against the cloth.

Suddenly, reality intruded. "Jacob," she said urgently. "Wake up. I have to get back for shooting. Oh, Lordy. I'm never late. C'mon."

"What…" He sat up, his arms encircling her protectively. One glance at his watch prompted a groaned curse. "It's my fault. I should have set the alarm."

Ariel shivered as she scrambled away to don her dress and try to finger comb her hair. "It may be okay. They're filming at the dockyard. Perhaps he'll rearrange and shoot the exterior ship scenes with the sailors first. Maybe he won't mind too much that I'm missing."

She doubted it, but Jacob's face was grim, and she didn't want him to feel responsible.

When they were more or less clothed, they dashed for the car. Jacob actually turned on the heat for a few minutes. In her small clutch purse, Ariel found the basics: a comb, a compact and lip gloss. Flipping down the visor mirror, she did her best to groom away a night's worth of messy hair and makeup.

He put his hand on her wrist, halting her frantic movements. "Thank you," he said quietly. "I won't ever forget this night."

She stared at him across the small space. He was so ruggedly handsome, so dear. "Neither will I."

No declarations of eternal love. No promises of a repeat. Her eyes burned and her throat closed up. She would not cry. Not in front of him, at least. She tugged her wrist free of his grasp and returned to her task.

As Jacob sent the SUV hurtling up the rough path to the main road, she moaned.

He shot her an alarmed look. "What?"

"I can't show up in what I was wearing last night. Everyone will know exactly what we've been up to."

"Then we'll stop by the hotel first."

"It's in the complete opposite direction."

Jaw clenched, gaze trained straight ahead, he bit out the words. "Then what do you want me to do, Ariel?"

She debated rapidly. Slowly, her heartbeat steadied. Exhaling a cleansing breath, she scooted toward him and put a hand on his thigh. "I don't care. They already think we're lovers. What does it matter? As soon as I walk into wardrobe, I'll be changing anyway."

"Are you sure?"

"Yes."

"Ariel…" He stopped, still looking forward and not at her.

"What is it?"

"We need to talk about what happened."

Her stomach flipped and dropped. Here was her chance to let him off the hook. "It was wonderful, Jacob. Every bit of it. Except maybe for the fact that I'm going commando under this dress." She forced a chuckle. "But honestly, I'm fine."

He was silent for so long, her skin began to crawl with anxiety. "I owe you an apology. I could have stopped once I knew." The scowl darkening his classically handsome features depressed her.

"I didn't want you to," she said flatly. "I thought we settled this before. No regrets, remember?"

He swung out onto the so-called highway and hung a right. "A woman's first time deserves romance, soft lighting, a comfy bed."

She smiled, feeling a guilty little frisson of pleasure deep in her belly at the recollection of what they had shared. "The setting *was* romantic. We had moonlight soft as smoke, and clearly the blanket on the sand was comfy, because we slept for hours."

"You know what I mean."

"Real life isn't like the movies. I know that more than anyone. But honestly, Jacob. Nothing could have made last night any more amazing." *Unless, of course, you had professed your undying love for me.* "So let's drop it."

He was silent for the remainder of the thirty-minute trip. When they arrived at English Harbor and parked, Ariel jumped out and made a beeline for the wardrobe tent, only to pull up short in dismay when she saw Rod Brinkman pacing back and forth in front of the door.

His face was red. "Where in the hell have you been?" He held up both hands, palms out. "Sorry, sorry. None of my business."

Stumbling to a halt almost toe to toe with him, her heart quivered. "What's the matter?" His manner was far too agitated to blame on the tardy arrival of his leading lady. It dawned on her with guilty consternation that she and Jacob had left their cell phones in the car all night.

He put his hands on her bare shoulders, petting her gently. "Your mother is in ICU."

Ariel crumpled, her knees giving out as terror engulfed her.

Jacob grabbed her from behind, supporting her in his arms. "I can have the jet here pretty quickly."

Brinkman shook his head. "No need. We've already got you two on the next flight to L.A. It leaves in thirty minutes. Airport officials are waiting and will hold the plane if necessary. I threw my weight around a little," he confessed with a grimace. "Harriet has brought your bags. There's no time to change. She's put clean clothes for each of you in your carry-on. And she'll drive you. Go," he said, his florid face filled with sympathy. "Go see your mother, Ariel. We'll be here when you get back."

She scarcely knew what happened in the next eight hours. Possibly, Jacob gave her something in a drink to make her sleep. There was a plane change in Houston—a transfer to the Wolff jet—that much she remembered. But the rest of it was a blur.

On the flight from Antigua to Houston, passengers recognized her. Everyone knew the film was being shot on the island. In other circumstances, Ariel would have been embarrassed for people to see her looking so disheveled, but given the current situation, she neither noticed, nor cared.

The flight crew had been apprised of the situation, and the attendants were both solicitous and understanding. Through it all, Jacob was a bulwark, shielding her from unnecessary conversation and surrounding her with an almost visible cloak of caring and concern.

On the Wolff jet, Ariel and Jacob changed clothes, he into khakis and his habitual white dress shirt, Ariel into a comfy knit skirt and top.

At long last, they arrived at their destination. The hospital in L.A. was like hospitals everywhere. Sterile. Frightening. Smelling of antiseptic and worry. They located Ariel's mother without difficulty. Jacob offered to wait down the hall. Ariel, unashamed, begged him to come with her. Whatever emotional strength she possessed had been sorely tested in the last twenty-four hours.

She needed him.

When they entered the cubicle, a thin, gray-faced woman lay resting, eyes closed. Ariel blinked back tears. When she left L.A., her mother had been doing fairly well, her humor and spirit intact. "Mama," she said softly, "it's me."

Seventeen

Jacob studied the two women as they embraced. Ariel had to sit on the side of the bed and lean forward. Her mother was too weak to sit up even a little bit.

The resemblance, even with Mrs. Dane deathly ill, was striking. He couldn't remember Ariel stating her mother's age, but she couldn't have been much more than forty-five. Her blond hair, unlike Ariel's, was cropped short around her face, but she possessed the same classic bone structure.

Ariel patted her mother's hand. "What's wrong, Mama? Why are you here?"

"Pneumonia." The one word answer sparked a fit of coughing. When she could speak again, she continued. "The doctor says my immune system is weakened from the chemo. But I'm fine, baby. You shouldn't have come."

"Don't be ridiculous," Ariel replied, her voice stout. "Where else would I be?"

"Shooting a movie?" Mrs. Dane's droll answer held a hint of her daughter's mischievous charm.

"Don't you worry about that. Mr. Brinkman is happy with my work. We may even be a little ahead of schedule."

"I saw the news yesterday. Tropical Storm Karrie is brewing off the coast of Africa. I know the window is closing. You have to go back, honey. We discussed this. I swear I won't kick the bucket until you return."

Ariel blinked rapidly. "Not funny."

Her mom squeezed her hand. "I'm so proud of you, my love. You're talented and smart and sweet. The best daughter a mother could have."

"Careful," Ariel cautioned, wiping her nose with the back of her hand. "I really will think you're dying if you go overboard. I'm the kid who set the drapes on fire and tried to cook Barbie's legs in the toaster."

"You were spirited."

"I was incorrigible."

The two women hugged again, and for a fleeting moment, Jacob caught a brief flash of his own mother tucking him into bed. It was a good memory. Warm. Happy.

But short-lived. His heart bled for Ariel. The woman lying in that bed was on borrowed time. As a doctor he recognized that truth. Maybe not tomorrow or next week. But soon. And there was nothing he could do to ease the coming hurt.

Mrs. Dane glanced up at Jacob, lowering her voice. "Is this the doctor?"

Ariel nodded. "Better known on the set as my boyfriend. No one suspects a thing. Thankfully, I've been healthy as a horse."

Her mother nodded, her gaze trained on Jacob as though she suspected him of doing something he shouldn't have. He fought the urge to squirm.

Mrs. Dane patted her daughter's arm. "Will you run down to the gift shop and get me a copy of this week's *People* magazine? One of the nurses says there are several pictures of you in it. Jacob and I will chat and get acquainted."

Jacob saw Ariel hesitate. Her mother barely had enough strength to speak, much less hold a magazine. "But I…"

A parent's voice anywhere in the world holds the same authority. "Go, Ariel. I promise not to tell him any of your embarrassing secrets."

Jacob chuckled. "I know a few already."

Ariel stood reluctantly and brushed past him on her way out. Unobtrusively, he stroked her arm. He sensed she was barely holding it together. "We'll be fine," he murmured.

She didn't answer. The grief in her unguarded gaze drenched the pure blue and darkened it. "I'll be back."

When she exited the room, Jacob picked up a chair and positioned it beside the bed. "Don't tax yourself," he said quietly, compassion in his voice. "Tell me what's on your mind." Her ploy had been painfully transparent.

"Is she telling me the truth? The malaria is gone?"

"Not gone," Jacob corrected. "She could potentially have attacks for up to a year or more. But since we've been in Antigua, she's been feeling very well."

"I'm dying."

"Yes, ma'am. She told me."

"But you would know that anyway, because you're a doctor."

He chose his words carefully. "Outcomes aren't always as cut and dried as the medical profession expects. A patient's will to fight, the ferocity of the disease, the ways in which various medications are used… All of those variables make a difference."

"You're a wise man. But my time is almost up. Are you the person who can take care of my sweetheart when I'm gone?"

She cut to the chase with the swift slash of a knife, leaving Jacob's uncertainties exposed. Somewhere deep in his gut he knew the truth, but perhaps if he didn't give voice to it, he could maintain the status quo. "Ariel is a very strong young woman. She doesn't need a man to care for her. But I will be her friend, yes."

"Do you love her?"

Wolff men were known for their arrogance, their refusal to be manipulated. Jacob could shut down this painful conversation with one cutting barb. But he didn't. Because the struggle inside him had increased, choking him. "I respect and admire her enormously. She's a breath of fresh air."

"You didn't answer my question. Yes or no?"

Years of trauma knocked the wind out of him, leaving his chest cavity empty, a gaping hole where his heart had been. "No," he said steadily, believing he was speaking the truth. "I don't love her. But I swear to you that I will make sure she is okay. No matter what. You have my word."

Ariel stood frozen outside the curtained cubicle. She'd made it only a few steps down the hall before she remembered that Jacob needed shaving cream. The inestimable Harriet had slipped up on that one point. Turning around to go back and ask what brand to get, Ariel overheard part of a very private conversation.

Her mother's blunt question flashed on a neon mental marquis.

Do you love her?

No.

Desolation flowed like a sluggish river in Ariel's veins, quick-freezing every cell in her body. *No. I don't love her.*

Her fingers were so numb, it was a wonder she didn't drop her billfold on the white tile floor. Limbs paralyzed, she sobbed inwardly. Behind that cloth barrier were the two people she loved most in the world, and sooner rather than later, they would be leaving her.

At the nurses' station, curious eyes stared at her. She bit her lip, intent on nothing but escape.

No. I don't love her.

Forcing herself to move, Ariel backed away slowly. "I was going to ask about flowers, but I see the sign now," she said to the head nurse. "I'll be back shortly."

Eighteen

Something was wrong. Ariel was in shock as far as Jacob could tell. Earlier, healthy tears had flowed in dull acceptance of her mother's condition. But since Ariel's return from the gift shop, she was dry-eyed, her expressive face wiped clean.

A quiet authoritative word reminded them they had overstayed their welcome. Jacob bent to shake Mrs. Dane's hand. "Rest. Eat. Do what they tell you."

"I will. You can count on it." She accepted Ariel's hug stoically, but over Ariel's shoulder, as her eyes met Jacob's, he saw grief.

Ariel led the way out of the hospital, her rapid steps betraying her tumult. Jacob had been curious to see her house, but with their time so limited, it made sense to stay close by in order to visit Mrs. Dane as often as possible.

The adjacent hotel was unimaginative, but adequate. As soon as they checked in and arrived at their room, Ariel fell asleep again. Jacob watched the TV with the sound on mute.

He checked email on his phone and sent texts to his brothers and father.

Ariel awoke to an inner alarm just before six. "Time to go back," she said, scraping her hair back from her face.

"You need to eat some dinner."

"I'm not hungry."

"Just some soup," he coaxed, worried by her deepening pallor.

"I can't. Let's go. I don't want to miss the visiting hours."

This time, since their car was parked in the hotel garage, they elected to walk across to the hospital. The sun was shining, the sky a cloudless blue. Ariel had brushed her hair and tucked it up into a ponytail. The style emphasized her youth and vulnerability.

Just outside of ICU, she stopped him. "Will you examine her? See if you think the doctors are on the right track?"

He shrugged. "I'm not her physician. And I have no privileges at this hospital. It wouldn't be appropriate."

"But if she requests it… Sort of a second opinion? Please, Jacob."

He could never resist that beseeching gaze. "Only if your mother wants me to."

"She will."

"I'll wait out here to give you some privacy to discuss it." Cooling his heels in the hall, he paced. Ariel was expecting him to produce a miracle. But he didn't dispense those. Never had.

When he was summoned to the room, Mrs. Dane's eyes were closed, her breathing harsh and labored.

Ariel nodded. "She says yes. A nurse is on the way with a few forms for you to sign."

"I'll need to look at her chart, as well."

"I know."

"So do you want to be here for this?"

Ariel knelt beside the bed, brushing her mother's hair with her hand. "Mama? Should I stay?"

The older woman opened her eyes. "Let Jacob do this, baby girl. Go outside. Look up at the sky. Feel the sun on your face. We'll call you when we're done." She glanced at Jacob. "Is that okay with you, Dr. Wolff?"

"Of course."

The cubicle was silent in her absence. Jacob had a small medical bag with him that he carried everywhere. As carefully as he could, he examined his patient, frowning at what he heard in the stethoscope. The pneumonia was significant.

By the time he had finished his exam, Ariel's mother was in considerable discomfort. Fortunately, a nurse showed up with a pain pill. Jacob leaned a hip again the wall and flipped through the pages of Mrs. Dane's lengthy chart.

Test results from her latest blood work were alarming. But the cocktail of medications her oncologist had prescribed were in line with what Jacob knew to be the latest protocols.

He honestly could not spot a single decision that he would second-guess. Which was both comforting and depressing. Ariel was looking to him for hope, and there was little to be had. Not in this case.

When he sent Ariel a text, she showed up in seconds. Clearly, she had been hovering in the hall. She wrung her hands unconsciously. "Well, what's the verdict, Doc?"

"Shall we step outside?"

Mrs. Dane opened her eyes, shaking her head. "No secrets. I believe in straight shooting."

Jacob nodded. "I understand." He touched Ariel's shoulder. "Why don't you sit down?"

She perched on her mom's bed. The two women held hands, looking at him as if he were an executioner. Ariel took a deep breath. "Tell us what you think."

He had to smile despite the gravity of the moment. "Your mom is very sick, but you knew that."

Ariel nodded. "But the pneumonia?"

"It's responding to the antibiotic, albeit slowly, but perceptibly. The good news, Mrs. Dane, is that once the infection is gone, you'll be no worse off than you were before. This was a crisis, definitely, but you won't have any lasting effects."

"And the cancer?" Ariel spoke for her mother.

"It is what it is. You've both had frank conversations with the doctor about the prognosis. The physical exam and the records I've studied don't give me any cause to think you've been misled. All the treatments so far have done exactly what they were designed to do."

Ariel's expression was a puzzle.

He cocked his head. "Have I disappointed you, or are you encouraged?"

Ariel's teeth mutilated her lower lip. "Both, I guess. So there's nothing you would do differently as far as treatment?"

"No. The doctors you've been using are spot on."

"I see."

He felt a stab of guilt. "I'm sorry," he said stiffly. "I wish I had better news."

Ariel's mother spoke up, her eyes troubled as she stared at her daughter. "This is good news, Ariel. I'll be back to normal in no time. I'm determined to be sitting at the Oscars when they call your name."

"That's a long, long time from now, Mama. We don't even have a firm release date yet. And who knows if I'll get nominated. The Academy is capricious. They may think I'm too young or maybe they'll hate my performance."

"Impossible," Jacob said. "I've seen your daughter in action, Mrs. Dane. That nomination's in the bag."

A nurse came in to shoo them out for the night. Ariel hugged her mom. "We'll be back in the morning."

"If they move me to a regular room tomorrow, I want you to go back to Antigua."

The two women faced off, Mrs. Dane adamant, Ariel upset. "I'm not leaving you."

"Ariel," her mother said firmly. "You may need to take time off later."

Jacob winced inwardly. He'd had no warning when he lost his mother. One morning she was at breakfast with him, laughing, hugging. That evening she was gone.

Was it better or worse to see the end coming?

Ariel ignored her mother's comment. "We can discuss it when I see you. Sleep well, Mama."

Outside, he took Ariel's arm. "You have to eat dinner," he said.

She looked for a moment as if she would protest. Then her shoulders lifted and fell. "Fine. You pick somewhere. I don't care."

They walked a couple of blocks until they found a little Italian place tucked away on a side street. The smell alone was enough to coax them inside.

Dim lighting and snowy linen tablecloths contrasted with old scarred wooden furniture. On each table a single red candle burned, stuck in the mouth of a Chianti bottle. The room was filled with locals, not tourists, which meant that the food was delicious.

Though Ariel maintained a distracted air and was mostly silent, he managed to get her to eat half a salad and most of a plate of lasagna. Because he thought it might relax her, he ordered a simple red wine and poured her a glass.

When the meal was done, the table cleared, and they had consumed two small servings of spumoni, he leaned back in his chair. "Talk to me, Ariel. I'm not used to you being silent."

Her expression was difficult to read. "Sorry if I'm not entertaining you."

The bite of sarcasm shocked him. Ariel was never cynical, and she went out of her way to spare people's feelings. "You know that's not what I meant," he said quietly. "I understand you're worried about your mother."

"I think you should go home," Ariel said, her eyes the

stormy blue of a winter lake. "I dragged you away from your clinic and your lab under false pretenses. I'm not sick. And besides, we've filmed enough now to make my presence necessary. You're free to go."

Not for anything would he admit to her that the curt words stung. "You're doing it again," he complained.

"Doing what?"

"Having a weird conversation with missing pieces. Makes it hard for a guy to keep up. Is this because you're angry with me for not being able to help your mother?"

She shoved at a melting blob of ice cream, her gaze moody. "I haven't put you on a pedestal, Jacob. Don't worry."

He touched her hand. "I'm here because I want to be here, and you're not out of the woods yet. What's wrong, Ariel?"

I'm sick in love with you, and you don't feel the same way. What would he do if she flung the words in his face? She hated him in that moment. Hated his concern, his masculine strength, his integrity. She should never have gone to Wolff Mountain, should never have involved Jacob Wolff in her life.

But her bitchiness made her ashamed. It wasn't Jacob's fault that Ariel was in love with him. He'd made his position crystal clear. She cleared her throat. "I'm sorry. Chalk it up to jet lag and worry."

"You're entitled to be cranky, princess. No one expects you to be Suzy Sunshine all the time."

"Still," she said. "I shouldn't take it out on you. You've been wonderful through all of this."

While Jacob settled the check, she fretted. Would he expect her to have sex with him tonight? The local time was only eight o'clock, but Ariel was exhausted. And quite honestly, sore. Though it seemed emotionally manipulative, perhaps she could use her mother's illness as an excuse to create some much needed distance.

Her heart was broken. Her mother was dying. And soon,

Jacob would go back to his mountain. *No. I don't love her.* Would she ever be able to forget she had heard those words?

In their hotel room, he kicked off his shoes, and with a complete lack of self-consciousness, lay down on the bed, rubbing the heels of his hands against his eyes. "You take first shower," he said, voice groggy.

Without comment, she gathered her things and locked herself in the bathroom. When she came out, Jacob was asleep.

"Jacob?" She said his name quietly. He didn't move. "Jacob?"

She couldn't touch him. If she did, the walls she had erected around her emotions to keep from having a mental meltdown would collapse. The craving for his embrace was a physical pain. It seemed like days, not hours, since he had entered her so gently and taught her body about ultimate pleasure.

Thinking about their tryst on the beach was a mistake. Doggedly, she shut her mind to the memories. Quietly flipping off all the lights, she went to her side of the king-size bed, turned back the covers and crawled in between the cold sheets.

Nineteen

Jacob awoke in the dark completely disoriented. Something had dragged him out of a deep sleep. His heart beating rapidly, he lay still, cataloguing his situation.

Gradually, it came back to him. He was on top of the covers, fully dressed. Evidently, he had conked out while Ariel was showering. He rubbed the crick in his neck and turned his head gingerly to glance at the illuminated dial of the iPod dock on the bedside table. 3:30 a.m.. Which meant his body clock said it was time to get up, since he was three time zones from home.

Suddenly, he realized what had awakened him. Ariel was crying. He scooted across the mattress, cursing the comforter that bunched beneath him. "Ariel? Hush, princess. I'm here." With some one-handed gyrations, he burrowed to the level where she was curled into a fetal position, her feet cold as ice.

He pulled her close, trying to warm her with his body. "Shh, honey. It's okay. It's going to be okay." It took him a few moments to realize that she was crying in her sleep. For some reason, that made it worse. He wanted so badly to comfort her. But there wasn't a damned thing he could do to help her.

He couldn't let her continue to struggle in the midst of whatever terrible dream was tormenting her. Shaking her carefully, he whispered, "Wake up, princess. Wake up, Ariel."

At last, he felt her jerk and stir. He wanted to turn on the light so he could see her face, but the sudden shift from sleep to a brightly lit room might be too much for her. He brushed the hair from her cheeks. "Are you awake?" He stroked his hands down her arms, feeling gooseflesh.

She burrowed into his chest, a shaky affirmative muffled in the starched cotton of his shirt. Holding her this way had a predictable effect on his body. He couldn't hold her without wanting her—especially now that he knew what it was like to be inside her, to stroke deep and hard into her tight warmth.

His breathing accelerated. This wasn't the time for lust. She needed a friend, not a lover.

Ariel apparently had other ideas. He sucked in a sharp breath when one of her small hands closed around his hard flesh. "Make love to me, Jacob," she whispered. "So I can forget."

Understanding her plea wasn't enough to make him feel okay with it. "Just let me just hold you. It's been a tough twenty-four hours." He gently tugged her hand away from his aroused shaft.

Ariel tensed, her entire body rigid. "Sorry," she said abruptly. "I shouldn't have assumed…"

What cockamamie notion was she running with now? Frustrated and aroused, he reached across her to turn on the lamp. "What in the hell does that mean?"

She sat up, legs crossed, facing him with arms wrapped around her waist. Dark smudges beneath her eyes painted a picture of a woman at the end of her tether. The huge T-shirt she wore was as erotic to him as a transparent lace nightie. If she thought it made her less appealing, she was clueless.

"I asked you a question," he said, his irritation at her, at him, at the whole situation making his voice harsher than he had intended.

Big blue eyes stared at him. "I'm new to this man/woman/ sex thing. I shouldn't have assumed you meant for us to keep on having...well, you know...intercourse "

"Intercourse?" His eyebrows rose in direct proportion to his incredulous response.

"Isn't that what you call it in the medical profession?"

"Hell, Ariel. We were lovers last night. I'd say that gives you some pretty damned clear rights."

"Like what?"

The simple query stopped him cold. She watched him carefully, and he realized suddenly that this was some kind of a test. "Well, I..."

"We're not in a relationship. We had a booty call, right? And now it's over."

He ground his teeth. "Are you trying to make me lose my temper?"

She shrugged. "I wasn't aware that a man with your IQ stooped to such human emotion."

"If you want to pick a fight, Ariel, why don't you say so? I'm up for anything that will make you feel better."

"Don't patronize me," she snapped. "And don't lie."

His temper neared the boiling point. "I've been called many things in my life, but seldom a liar. Would you like to elucidate?"

"Quit using fifty-dollar words," she yelled, now up on her knees. "I only went to high school, you know."

"Oh, for God's sake..." He slid off the foot of the bed and started stripping off his clothes.

Ariel's eyes widened. "What are you doing?"

"I'm going to have sex with you."

"No, you're not. I won't be your charity case."

Naked, he climbed back into bed and tumbled her onto her back. "Does this look like I'm doing you a favor?" He moved between her legs and used his erection to stroke the crotch of her simple cotton bikinis. They were white, like the T-shirt.

Ariel's hands fisted at her hips, grasping the sheet. "A minute ago you didn't want me." Her youthful vulnerability twisted something in his chest.

"Of course I did, princess. But I was trying to take care of you."

"Try harder."

That she could make him laugh in this emotionally fraught situation sobered him. He outstripped her in so many ways—years, experience, formal education. But somehow, this childlike, beautiful, spirited woman held her own.

"I live to please you," he said wryly, testing her readiness by sliding two fingers under her panties and into her passage. She was wet and hot. Gently, he dragged her underwear down her legs and tossed it aside. His hand shook, and his brain—his much-vaunted, highly regarded brain—shut down.

Ariel watched him, big-eyed, as he positioned himself at her entrance. "You can touch me," he said, groaning in shock as he pushed his way in. Every cell in his body leapt to attention and started dancing in crazy circles that made him dizzy and weak.

Ariel's hands settled circumspectly at the small of his back.

"Am I hurting you?" he gasped, remembering her newly non-virginal state.

Her eyes closed, a dreamy smile curving those perfect lips. "I don't know. I'm too busy swooning."

Again, he laughed. The combination of physical stimulation and mental euphoria was a new experience. "Watch us," he commanded, suddenly feeling a few caveman impulses despite his evolved intellect.

She turned her head toward the dresser where a large mirror reflected their images faithfully. Ariel squeezed his ass. "I like your butt," she said. "See how nice it looks when you—"

He clapped a hand over her mouth. "Most people do this without talking."

Her eyes danced with amusement as her legs wrapped around his waist and tightened. Ariel worked with a personal trainer two hours every day. She was strong and limber. He shook his head, gasping and falling forward onto both hands. "Fine," he muttered. "Feel free to chatter away."

"I did a sex scene once where the director asked us to say dirty words to each other."

Imagining the mischievous Ariel mouthing sexual demands hardened his cock to the point of pain. "How did you do?"

She wrinkled her nose. "I kept laughing. After twenty-five takes, they rewrote the dialogue."

"Thank the Lord." He didn't want Ariel talking smut to another man. But his possessiveness was irrational. After he went home, the chances of seeing her again were slim. Shying away from that certainty, he pumped his hips more slowly, leaning up on one arm and using his free hand to play with her breasts.

Ariel's fair skin flushed pink, darker still at her throat where his chin stubble had marked her. It was his turn to look in the mirror now. Ariel's eyes were closed, her fingernails digging into his flanks. Her breath came in choppy pants.

Evidently, she had lost her urge to converse. He hovered, his body joined with hers, as he absorbed the picture they made. To an onlooker, they seemed a perfect match, Jacob dark and dominant, Ariel pale and lovely.

But that pairing was a lie. They were not meant for each other. Jacob walked alone, and Ariel was destined for bigger things.

She was still wearing her T-shirt, though it was bunched up beneath her armpits. He'd been in such a hurry to get inside her he hadn't bothered to remove it. But now he wanted her naked.

"Sit up," he said hoarsely. He reared back and helped her wriggle out of the offending garment. The operation buried him even deeper, all the way to the hilt.

Falling forward onto her chest, he cursed. "Sorry. I don't want to crush you."

Ariel held him tightly, nibbling his earlobe. "I like it," she said. "Makes my stomach feel all shivery. You Tarzan, me Jane."

Again, amusement caught him off guard. And how dangerous it was. A woman who could do this to a man was as fascinating and deadly as an unseen reef. For a captain at the helm of a smooth journey, the resultant collision could spell disaster.

He shifted, sparing her some of his weight. "Nevertheless."

"Whatever happened to slam-bam-thank-you-ma'am?"

"Excuse me?" God knows, he was not in the least interested in talking, but his little Ariel showed a regrettable propensity for coital conversation. Withdrawing almost completely, he took her chin in one hand. "I have no idea what you're talking about, but could we discuss it later?" He throbbed inside her, his balls on fire.

She shrugged, once again twining her legs around his back. "Sure. Do you think I can do that multi-orgasmic thing, or does it take more rehearsal?"

Everything conspired against him. Years without a woman in his bed. Lying atop perhaps the most beautiful female he had ever seen. Knowing that he was her first lover.

Fire jolted through his body. "Hell, Ariel…" He moaned her name as he climaxed violently, shooting his seed inside her, thrusting rapidly and with little finesse until every last nuance of his release faded away into stunned immobility.

She rubbed his back. "It makes me feel good to know you want me so much."

He knew she hadn't come. How could she? He'd been too damn caught up in his own hunger and need. "Sorry," he mumbled, his limbs the consistency of noodles.

"For what?"

"For being selfish."

She chuckled. "You're the least selfish man I know. You can't help it if I drive you crazy with unbridled lust."

The smug note of satisfaction in her words charmed him.

"I do seem to remember several moments of insanity on my part," he said, breathing hard. "But I am now in my right mind. Prepare to be wowed."

He shifted to his side and zeroed in on the little area of curls at the apex of her thighs. Pale as winter sunshine, wavy as the sea, it concealed what he was eager to pay homage to.

Ariel's small white teeth dug into her bottom lip. "Oh, Lordy."

Those were the last words she spoke. At last he had silenced her. Wanting badly to make sure she experienced the shattering release he had received, he devoted himself to learning each tiny breath that signaled her response. With his thumb and forefinger, he plucked delicately at the small bud.

Ariel's hips came off the bed. She strained into his touch.

"Easy, honey." He changed tactics, wanting to build her need until she was as crazed by desire as he had been. Starting with her head and neck, he massaged her tenderly. Moving to her breasts, he caressed them in circles, deliberately avoiding her nipples.

She trembled beneath his touch. He stroked her flat belly, ran a hand down the length of first one leg then the other. Switching positions, he licked her toes, pulling one perfectly manicured digit into his mouth and sucking hard.

Ariel cried out, writhing, thrashing, trying to coax him to where she wanted to be touched.

When she was red-faced and incoherent, he shoved two fingers into her sex and simultaneously gave a firm, gliding pass to her little bundle of nerves. It was enough to push her over.

Her body went rigid. "Jacob?" The single word was little more than a raw groan as she bore down on his hand and crested with a whimper and a sigh.

After she had time to recover, he pulled the covers over them. "Sleep, baby. It's still early in L.A. We've got all the time in the world."

Twenty

We've got all the time in the world. Ariel awoke with Jacob's words ringing in her head. They were lovely words, words that made her desperately want to believe. But he had gone off script, and the dialogue wasn't in character, not for Jacob Wolff.

She glanced at the clock. Still time for lingering. The experience of literally sleeping with a man was novel and exciting. Jacob's warm, hard, hairy legs tangled with hers. He held her tightly against his chest, one of her thighs resting on his.

It was an odd feeling, but she liked it. Far too much.

He stirred beside her, yawning and stretching. "Time to go to the hospital?"

"Not yet. Go back to sleep."

He turned his face to kiss her. "I'd rather talk."

Oops. He'd turned the tables, and she couldn't stave off what was coming. "You first," she said, trying for sassy, but coming up weak.

His hand found hers and clasped their fingers. "How and why are you still a virgin? I really want to understand. Not that I ever believed all that stuff in the press, but Ariel, you're nothing like the way they've portrayed you. Is part of that on purpose? To sell movie tickets?"

She was glad it was dark. "That's a lot of questions."

"Pick one."

He dragged her back against his chest, spooning her. She felt his erection nudge her buttocks. Her cheek rested on his arm. "My mother is and was very protective. When you're thirteen years old and making more money a week than some families earn in a year, life can be confusing. Mama kept me on the straight and narrow."

"You didn't ever try to rebel?" His warm breath stirred the hair at her nape.

"I probably would have, but something happened the year I turned fifteen."

He tensed. "What?"

"One of my directors tried to force himself on me…in my trailer on the set."

"Jesus." He sounded appalled and angry.

"Mama came back in time. She kicked him in the nuts and swore she'd report him to the police if he ever came near me again. He couldn't afford to protest. I was making piles of money for him."

"And how did you react?"

"It scared me," she said flatly, not wanting to remember that awful afternoon. "I had bought into all the romantic hype about first kisses and romantic love, and what he did to me was neither sweet nor tender. It's possible that the experience might really have screwed me up for a long time, but Mama made me go to counseling."

"Smart woman."

"I came out on the other side more or less unscathed, but I built walls after that. Fortunately, Mama made a point of entertaining at our house with kids my own age. I didn't think anyone would ever come because we didn't serve alcohol and there were no drugs allowed."

"But they did come?" He caressed her hair with a soothing rhythm.

"Yes. I think the other teenagers—actors and actresses like me—were relieved to have a place where they didn't have to put on a show. We had the opportunity to be young and silly like adolescents everywhere."

"My admiration for your mother's parenting skills is growing by leaps and bounds. But what about when you turned eighteen or twenty-one? Did you not want to move out?"

"I could have. There was plenty of money for Mama and me to maintain separate residences. In fact, she even suggested it at one point. I think she worried that I would never have a normal relationship with a guy because of what had happened."

"Were you dating by that time?"

"Oh, yes, of course. I went out all the time. And had fun doing it. But I knew my own boundaries, and I wasn't willing to settle for what Hollywood said was the norm. Mama still calls me an old soul, and it's true. I took self-defense lessons, and I was vigilant about things like date rape drugs. Pitfalls abound in my line of work. But Mama and the good Lord protected me."

He fell silent, probably processing her recounting, weighing it to see if all the parts meshed together. Her virginity he had proved himself, but even so, all those stories over the years would be hard for an outsider to discount.

She wished she were able to say that she was so smart and serious that she finished college along the way. Lots of kids did, even while working steadily. But Ariel could never seem to focus on boring textbooks, not when the world outside the classroom awaited her.

"Why me?" he said bluntly. "Why now?"

No. I don't love her. Damn. This was the moment she had been dreading. She couldn't let him know that she loved him.

His rigid code of honor might persuade him that he had to stay with her because he had taken her innocence. And that would destroy her.

Ariel swallowed her tears, called upon now for the most critical performance of her life. "It was time," she said simply. "I didn't want to be a freak. You were convenient. I mean that in a good way," she said hastily. "And I knew I could trust you. So I made my choice. You didn't disappoint me."

"Well, that's something, I guess." He sounded disgruntled.

She slid from his grasp and climbed out of bed. "Do you mind ordering us some breakfast from room service? I'm going to get ready. I don't want to miss visiting hours in ICU."

Jacob went through the motions for the next few hours, but his emotions were in turmoil. Mrs. Dane was indeed transferred to a regular room. She insisted that Ariel go back to the set, and her daughter was finally persuaded. Jacob summoned the jet. He and Ariel were back in Antigua before dinner.

He couldn't quite put his finger on it, but she was acting strangely. Still upbeat and smiling, but with a layer of darkness he'd not noticed before. Perhaps it was nothing more than well-justified concern about her mother. But Jacob worried that she regretted the step into intimacy they had taken.

As soon as the jet touched down in Antigua, Ariel and Jacob were dragged back into the whirlwind of filming. Time was more of an issue now with bad weather brewing.

Over the next week, Ariel held up well, hitting her marks and nailing her lines every time. She seemed more relaxed now that her mother had been released from the hospital and was resting comfortably at home. Ariel's performance amazed him, particularly one afternoon. At English Harbor—the only such example of a Georgian shipyard in the world—Rod directed a scene between Ariel and a drunken sailor. The heavy-set, brutish man accosted her in broad daylight and dragged her into an alley.

The scene called for Ariel to struggle and to finally be rescued by the naval officer who was her lover. As rehearsals rolled, Jacob watched carefully and with some consternation to see if Ariel's performance would be compromised by what had happened in her past.

Witnessing the action unfold had him on a hair trigger, his instinctive need to protect Ariel at odds with the knowledge that this was make-believe.

Again and again, the ruffian grabbed Viola by the hair....

"Come quietly, whoring wench. Or I'll shut you up for good." Even weaving on his feet, the man had vicious strength, and Ariel was a fragile wisp in his arms.

Jacob's pulse was pounding out of control, his chest heaving from the effort of not grabbing the poor actor by the neck and ripping out his throat. Seeing Ariel so abused, even in costume, was agonizing.

Suddenly, her lover appeared, a gun in his hand. He shot at the man's feet, catching a toe, perhaps. Ariel's attacker howled. The other man clubbed him on the back of the head with the barrel of the pistol. Slowly, the bear of a sailor collapsed in a heap on the ground.

"Cut." Rod was jubilant. "Fabulous, people. That's a wrap. Go catch some rays before the sun goes down."

Ariel crossed to where Jacob stood. Her hair clung to her face and neck in sweaty tendrils. Dirt streaked her cheek. "I'm beat," she said, her face pale, her eyes shadowed. "Do you mind if we have dinner in our room?"

"Of course not." The costume she was wearing bared most of her breasts. Men in audiences everywhere would love it. Jacob made the unpleasant discovery that his documented intellect was no match for sheer male possessiveness.

He put his arm around her waist as they climbed into the rear of the SUV. Harriet waited patiently in the front seat.

Ariel and Harriet normally chatted on the way back to the

hotel. But not today. Ariel's head rested on his shoulder, and he was forced to support her weight.

Harriet's eyes met his in the rearview mirror, their gaze filled with concern. Everyone on the set knew about Ariel's mother. Two things had happened since their return. An almost palpable empathy surrounded Ariel, and the cast and crew's respect and admiration for this young woman was evident.

She worked harder than anyone. And though she enjoyed playing the diva/movie star for the benefit of tourists and fans, in her work environment, she was anything but.

At the hotel, he would have carried her inside, but Ariel insisted on walking under her own power. Her skin was the color of milk, and she weaved on her feet. Jacob knew she had underestimated the physical and emotional toll of their quick trip to L.A.

Inside, she grimaced. "While I'm in the shower, would you mind ordering us some dinner? My stomach can't handle much. Maybe some soup?"

"Of course." He ran his hands down her arms. "Do you want me to help you?"

A faint ghost of her usual mischievous grin lifted the corners of her lips. "Naughty, Doc."

He kissed her cheek. "I was speaking strictly in my capacity as your physician. Can't have you passing out in the shower."

She rubbed her eyes like a little child. "I'll be fine. All I need is clean clothes, a light meal, and some sleep."

Despite her confidence, he opened the bathroom door a crack after he heard the water in the shower start up. Ariel was managing on little more than grit and adrenaline, and he was worried about her.

When she finally appeared, she was wearing a spaghetti-strap tank top and cotton sleep pants. Her skin was flushed from the warm water.

"Better?" he asked.

She nodded. "Almost human."

But he noticed that she was shivering even though the room was plenty warm. "Let me dry your hair for you," he insisted.

That Ariel didn't protest was a sign of how rotten she was feeling. They sat together, him in a chair, Ariel perched on the matching ottoman. With a wide-toothed comb, he removed each and every tangle in her damp, sun-kissed hair. The strands were like golden silk in his hands.

As he aimed the stream of hot air up and down the back of her head, Ariel tilted her face toward the ceiling with a blissful smile. "I goofed," she said softly. "I think your skills as a hairstylist far outweigh your value as a doctor."

"I'm strictly an amateur," he chuckled. He winnowed his fingers through the lush mass again and again until it was smooth and dry. Setting the dryer aside, he kissed the skin behind her ear. He was hard. No surprise there. But for now he was content to look after her. That alone gave him pleasure, though he hated seeing his irrepressible princess so delicate and fragile.

"All done," he croaked, his hands trembling with a hard-hitting lust. In a way, his reaction to her was a disease, an affliction of the heart and loins for which there was no immediate cure.

Ariel leaned back into him, her cheek turned to his chest. "Thank you." Two simple words, but they reminded him suddenly of the promise he had made to her mother. God willing, Mrs. Dane would hang on for many more months. But imagining Ariel all alone in the future with no one to care for her made his chest hurt.

When the doorbell rang, Jacob answered and ushered in the hotel employee who delivered their meal. Ariel disappeared momentarily, coming back in a moment wrapped up in the thin cashmere shawl she carried with her on flights to combat chilly cabin temperatures.

After a sweet smile and an autograph for the mesmerized kid who worked for the hotel, Ariel sat down when he exited and began to eat one-handed. After three bites she pushed the bowl away. "I'm sorry, Jacob," she said. "I can't stomach food right now. Maybe later. I'm going to stretch out on the sofa. The TV won't bother me. I'm just so tired."

She collapsed on the cushions and curled into a ball, her whole body shivering. Jacob started to get a bad feeling. Watching her the entire time, he wolfed down his meal and set the tray of covered dishes outside their door for pickup.

When he went over and crouched beside her, she was dead asleep. The shivering had worsened. Jacob fetched a blanket from their bed and covered her. "Ariel," he said quietly. "Can you hear me?"

Her eyelashes fluttered and lifted. "Is it the malaria?"

"Yes." She had been taking the medication he prescribed the entire time, but now came the worst. Ever since he saw the results of the blood smears he had collected back on Wolff Mountain, he had feared this day would come. "How do you feel?"

Her teeth chattered. Her small body quaked with tremors. "I'm so cold," she moaned.

He gathered her up, blankets and all, and carried her into the bedroom. Kicking off his shoes, he climbed into bed with her and pulled the covers over both of them. Even the strength and heat of his body was not enough to comfort her.

"Why does it k-k-keep c-c-coming back?" Her lips were blue.

"You have dormant parasites in your liver. They'll kick up now and again for a while." He'd established the particular strain, and she should be in the clear after a total of twelve months or so, but there was still the specter of kidney damage.

He imagined her like this in some God-forsaken jungle, her mother frightened and ill herself. It broke his heart and terrified him. Ariel could so easily have died, and he would never have known her.

She roused, her expression strained. "You'll have to t-t-tell Rod I can't work tomorrow."

"The truth?"

"Tell him…virus. No one w-will bother us." Her eyes closed, tears leaking from beneath her lashes. "Three more d-d-days," she whispered. "That's all we n-n-needed."

He held her more tightly, trying to ward off the waves of shudders that threatened to tear her asunder. "Don't worry about it. They'll do what they can to work around you. You'll get better quickly, I hope. The shooting will be done when it's done."

She lapsed into a semiconscious state after that. He left her only long enough to exchange a hurried conversation with Brinkman, who seemed genuinely more worried about Ariel than about his movie.

"Take care of our girl," the older man said gruffly.

"I will."

"Don't let her rush the recovery. I've got some scenery shots we can fill the schedule with. No one will mind a breather. It's been hot as hell. Tell Ariel not to worry."

It was a long night, and a sleepless one for Jacob. It took every bit of his patience and ingenuity to get fluids and medication down her throat. She fought him at times. The experience brought back unpleasant memories of Diane's long illness.

Around 1:00 a.m. they entered phase two. Ariel clutched her head, moaning at the ferocity of the headache that Jacob knew was tormenting her. She spiked an alarming fever. He alternated cold towels with a hastily manufactured ice pack, stripping her to her underwear and sponging her body from head to toe.

That he could do nothing to truly ease her suffering made him angry as hell. Malaria was a bitch, forcing Jacob to witness in impotent silence the misery and pain of a woman who deserved neither.

It was after five, just before dawn, when the fever broke. Ariel began to sweat profusely. She moaned every time he lifted her head to hold a cup of water to her lips. In one rare moment of lucidity, she clutched his wrist. "Don't leave me."

The piteous request pierced his heart. Is that what she thought of him? Or did she mean something more? Her eyes were as blue as ever, but their brilliance was muted, dull and cloudy.

"I'm right here," he said, soothing her with a low voice and a gentle hand.

But for how long? The gut-wrenching truth hit him like a two-by-four to the stomach. If he lingered in Antigua, he would be in danger of breaking every one of the hard and fast rules that had rigidly governed his life for half a decade.

He couldn't afford to care about Ariel Dane. The risk was too great. Allowing himself to love her was out of the question. He had already lost two women in his life who had been everything to him. To toss himself out there a third time was unthinkable.

He had done what she asked. Her job was secure. He should return to Wolff Mountain immediately. But as much as it hurt, he'd sworn to protect her. So he would stay until the end of the shoot. But not a day longer.

Twenty-One

Ariel opened her eyes slowly, wrapped in a lassitude that was as encompassing as the ocean. Her body ached in every joint, her bones feeling as if they had been beaten repeatedly.

Gingerly, she turned her head. After a moment, she recognized her surroundings. The hotel bedroom was comforting in its familiarity. But she had no idea of time. Her brain was fuzzy.

The clock near the bed said 7:00 p.m. Maybe she had simply napped after the day's shooting. But she had hazy memories of Jacob being here with her in this bed.

She called his name in a slight panic. "Jacob?"

He appeared in the doorway immediately, his feet bare, his longer-than-usual hair tousled. "What is it? Are you okay?"

"What happened?" She tried to swallow, and winced. The inside of her mouth was like the Sahara.

"You had a bout of malaria," he said, his voice calm as he came to sit beside her on the bed. "But the worst is over. Can you eat anything, do you think? I have some warm chicken broth in the other room."

"Is that clock right?"

"Yes. You checked out for a little more than twenty-four hours."

Holy cow. Her stomach still pitched and rolled, but she sensed that Jacob wanted her to eat, so she nodded. "Soup sounds good." Something was different about him, but it took her befuddled brain several moments to figure it out.

Then it hit her. Jacob was acting like a doctor. *Her* doctor. A job she had begged him to undertake. Though his manner was kind, he had erected a wall, an impersonal demeanor that separated the two of them.

When she tried to stand, her legs wouldn't support her. Jacob caught her with an arm around her waist and eased her back onto the bed. "I'll bring the food. Baby steps, Ariel."

He sat in a chair beside the bed and watched with a hooded gaze as she forced herself to swallow spoonful after spoonful. Fortunately, after an initial moment of uncertainty, her stomach decided to accept the warm, flavorful broth.

"I talked to Rod," he said abruptly. "Told him you're over the worst of your 'virus,' but will probably be too wiped out to work tomorrow. They've got you on the shooting schedule for the day after."

She nodded. "Okay." Cocking her head to study him, she wrinkled her nose. "You look terrible."

He shrugged. "Nothing a little sleep won't cure."

"I feel weak as a kitten, and you're exhausted from taking care of me. Why don't we call it a day and go to bed early?"

She saw him hesitate. Her heart contracted.

He shrugged, his face wiped clean of all expression. "I'm going to sleep on the sofa tonight so I won't disturb you."

"It's a king-size bed." *No. I don't love her.* Ariel had hoped she had more time. Had prayed that Jacob would want her enough physically to stay.

He stood up—a dark, godlike creature, far above the petty

foibles of mortals. A man with no soul, no weaknesses. "Rest, Ariel. I'll be in the other room if you need me."

It was as if they had never made love, as if they were the people who met for the first time in his office on Wolff Mountain. He was brooding, remote, totally devoid of any tender emotion.

Her protective response was to retreat behind a wall of indifference.

The next day, Jacob made himself scarce during the daylight hours. She didn't know where he went, and she didn't ask.

Taking a shower taxed her limited stamina, but she felt a hundred times better afterward. Several naps, an assortment of magazines and her iPad helped pass the time. Though it was not an appealing prospect, she knew she would be well enough to do what was required of her tomorrow as Jacob had promised.

For the next few days they shared the now-claustrophobic villa like strangers, much of the time sleeping in separate rooms. Shooting wrapped at last. The cast party was to take place on Friday night before everyone flew out on Saturday.

Friday afternoon Ariel walked down to the edge of the ocean and gazed out at the horizon. Despite her illness and the demands of a tight shooting schedule, this time with Jacob in Antigua had been idyllic. She wanted to hold on to the memories tightly, so they would never fade.

As if she had conjured him with her thoughts, he appeared, walking toward her, dressed in dark slacks and a crisply ironed shirt. Ariel frowned. The party was not due to start for several hours.

"You're ready early."

He focused his gaze on the horizon, his mouth set in a grim line. "I have to go home, Ariel. I'm driving myself to the airport. Harriet will pick up the car later."

"You're leaving?" Her brain had gotten hung up on his first words. "I don't understand. What's the rush?"

"No rush." His profile gave nothing away. "I've been gone a long time. I need to get back to work."

"But I…" Her pride stopped her. Her smile was bleak. "I thought you'd at least stay until the end."

He turned to face her, jerking her into his arms for one hard, punishing kiss. "This *is* the end," he muttered. "Goodbye, princess."

Twenty-Two

Jacob found no solace in his lab. And no absolution in the familiar sights and smells of the forest that surrounded his home and clinic. Everywhere he turned, something reminded him of Ariel.

He hadn't expected her to be so *present* when they were a couple of thousand miles apart. When Diane died, his life had ceased for months. He'd been an automaton. In many ways, this was far worse. He was alive. Every painful memory of his time with Ariel was played out on a giant movie screen in his head. The way she laughed. Her impish sense of humor. The manner in which her youthful naiveté mixed with wry pragmatism.

And her beauty. God, her unadorned, fresh-out-of-bed, luminous beauty. At night when he tossed and turned, his sex hard and aching, he felt as if he could reach out and touch her hair, stroke her cheek.

Leaving her had been an exercise in futility. She was lodged in his head, in his heart, in his gut. His brothers knew something was wrong, but in the way of men, they didn't press, at least not at first. Gareth enlisted him to chop wood. Kieran took him fishing. Though he enjoyed the change of pace, nothing helped.

On a rainy afternoon, two months after he'd left Ariel standing on the beach, he found himself gazing down at his mother's headstone. It and the one for his aunt occupied a place of honor in a small garden on the flank of the mountain.

He remembered Laura Wolff dimly. Mostly an image of laughter, of hugs.

Suddenly, out of the mist, Gareth and Kieran appeared.

Jacob frowned. "I get the feeling that you two are on suicide watch. Don't worry. I have no plans to blow my brains out... even if I have screwed my life royally."

Gareth shrugged. "I hope that's a joke. We know you too well to think that. You're strong, Jacob. You've had to be to survive what life has thrown at you."

"But this time it's entirely my fault."

Kieran kicked at a stone, his face sober. "I'll be the first to tell you it's never too late."

"It might be. I acted like a complete jerk, and I think I may have broken the heart of America's sweetheart. How do I recover from that?"

Gareth squatted and removed a weed that had sprung up in the neatly groomed plot. "I devoted a huge part of my life to being alone, we all did. Hell, we practically made an art of it. But it's wrong, Jacob. It's wrong." He paused, his eyes on the headstone. "Do you love her?"

The thick, wet, frigid air was a far cry from Antigua's warm breezes. But the current weather mirrored the state of Jacob's soul. He'd denied it for so long, had done his best to convince himself it wasn't true. "Yes," he said, his throat tight. "I love her."

Kieran's gaze was a mix of sympathy and challenge. "Then go. Do whatever it takes. But don't wait anymore."

His brothers abandoned him to his vigil, and he sighed as

he acknowledged what a fool he had been. The walls he had built for his ivory tower were as insubstantial now as the clouds that scudded over the mountaintop. There was no armor in the world strong enough to protect him from Ariel.

She had offered him her innocence, her trust, her joyous outlook on life. And he might as well have ground it under his heel. He knew she loved him, but he had been too scared to let her tell him so. And even worse, he had abandoned her, allowing her to believe that she was no more to him than another roll in the hay.

The man who looked back at him from the mirror this morning was not someone he admired. Not anymore.

For one more day, he pondered the mess he had made of his life. Fate had dealt him dreadful blows. Losing a beloved parent *and* an adored fiancée. Jacob had thought of himself as strong and invincible because he had survived. But the truth was less palatable. Maybe the hermit-like existence he had cultivated was nothing more than cowardice in disguise.

His life to date had been marked unfairly by tragedy. But the present debacle was *his* fault, and his alone.

Ariel likely hated him. At the very least, she must think him a user like so many people in her life, men in particular. But even knowing that he had committed unforgiveable sins, he had to tell her how he felt. She deserved to understand that what had happened on the beach in Antigua was as pivotal a moment in his life as it had been in hers.

He had packed for an indefinite trip and was preparing to fly out on the family jet when his cell phone rang. The area code was southern California.

Heart pumping, he answered. "Hello?"

"Wolff? This is Rod Brinkman."

Jacob's knees turned to water. He sat down hard. "Is it Ariel? What's wrong?"

"She needs you, Wolff. Her mother died early yesterday morning."

His poor princess. Throat tight, he demanded details.

"It caught everyone off guard. A heart attack. The chemo took its toll."

"Email me the specifics, please."

"Will do. Just get here as fast as you can. She's handling the details all alone."

Even flying in one's own family jet didn't lessen the mileage between the Blue Ridge Mountains of Virginia and the West Coast. Jacob tried to sleep and couldn't. All he could think about was Ariel—young, lionhearted, heartbreakingly vulnerable Ariel.

He landed at LAX and wasted no time. The private limo service had a car waiting. The address he gave the driver led them to a pleasant, though not opulent neighborhood north of town. It was a gated community with a guardhouse.

Jacob rolled down the window. "I'm Jacob Wolff here to see Ariel Dane. She's not expecting me. But her director, Rod Brinkman, sent me." Jacob was hoping the name-dropping would get him in.

The seventy-something Barney Fife lookalike leaned down to peer into the car. "Jacob Wolff? Well, hell, man. Brinkman's a household name here in Hollywood, but you're a Wolff. Everybody knows who you are, or your family anyway. Welcome to California."

Jacob concealed his impatience. "Thank you. I'm here to help Ariel with the funeral."

The guard removed his cap and scratched his head. "Yep. It's a damned shame about Mrs. Dane. She was a real nice lady." Finally, he stepped back and pressed a button. "Tell Miss Ariel I'm thinking about her. She always gives me chocolate chip cookies and a five-hundred-dollar bill at Christmas. I love that little gal."

The massive gates slid aside, and two minutes later, Jacob

was knocking at the door of an attractively landscaped, stucco
and terra-cotta tile, two-story condo.

The door swung wide. Framed in the opening was the
woman who had turned his life upside down. Her eyes were
red and puffy from crying. The sloppy ponytail, sweats and
bare feet were the dress of a woman not expecting company.

To Jacob, she had never looked more beautiful. He kept
his hands shoved in his pockets to keep from grabbing her.
"Hello, Ariel."

Her blue eyes stared at him warily. "Go home," she said
bluntly. "I know about the promise you made to my mother.
She told me. But I don't need you. You're off the hook."

She started to close the door. He stuck his foot in the gap,
his temper rising. "I've come a damned long way to see you."

"And I'm supposed to be grateful?"

Her cold expression made him wince. He was responsible
for her antipathy. "Let me come in." He softened his voice.
"Let me in, Ariel. Please."

Ariel felt brittle as glass, as if one wrong move would shatter her into sharp-edged pieces. Seeing Jacob in the flesh was
agony. She had dreamed about him for weeks. Though she
tried every way she knew to eradicate them, the memories of
making love with Jacob were as poignant and beautiful and
immediate as if they had happened only yesterday.

Now, here he stood. Imposing. Handsome. Broodingly masculine.

She was defeated by her own yearning. "Fine. Come in if
you must. I'm not very good company at the moment."

She turned her back on him and sought the protection of a
small armchair, thinking he would sit across the room on the
sofa. But Jacob had other ideas. He took her wrists and pulled
her to her feet, wrapping his big arms around her and tucking
her face into his shoulder. "God, I'm sorry Ariel. I'm so sorry."

He smelled of soap and starch, a fragrance she had come

to identify as uniquely Jacob. Without words he was offering her a good cry, the opportunity to lean on a big strong man for comfort.

That was a risk she couldn't take. She'd shed buckets of tears in the last thirty-six hours. Her chest was hollow with grief. But she would not allow herself to be lulled into the fiction that Jacob cared.

Oh, sure, he had a physician's compassion. He knew all about offering support to the bereaved. But that wasn't what Ariel wanted or needed. She could handle her mother's death. They had talked it through many times, and with brave honesty.

Ariel was as prepared as a person could be to lose a loved one.

She shoved her hands against his chest. "I'm fine, Jacob. We knew this was coming." More than anything she wanted him to hold her and never let go, which was why she had to be strong.

He released her reluctantly. "That doesn't make it any easier."

"Mama had made her peace with life and with God. She was ready to go. I'm honoring her by choosing to celebrate the life she lived."

Jacob folded his arms across his chest, staring at her with that X-ray gaze that reminded her of the first day they met. "You don't have to put on a brave front with me."

She shrugged. "We're having visitation and a small memorial service tonight. You're welcome to come."

"And then?"

"Then nothing. You go home."

"I didn't make a hotel reservation."

"You can sleep on the jet."

"I thought I would stay with you for a few days."

"No." She stiffened her spine, wrapping her arms around her waist. "I don't need your pity or your charity. I'm fine."

"You don't look fine."

"How charming. Anything else about me you'd like to insult?"

He glared at her. "You are the most provoking and contrary woman I've ever had the misfortune to meet."

"Sorry I don't live up to the memory of your sainted Diane," she retorted. "Most of us are mere mortals."

He took three steps in her direction and stopped dead, his face contorting with anger and something she couldn't decipher. "I can't remember what she looks like," he said in a low, tormented voice. "I destroyed all her pictures, because I couldn't bear to look at them."

A thousand knives pierced Ariel's heart, drawing a choked gasp of pain from her numb lips. "Not my problem, Doc. Would you mind leaving now? I have things to do." The tears she had thought were momentarily dried up clogged her throat.

Jacob stared at her, his dark eyes filled with secrets she couldn't decipher. "I don't have a single picture of you," he said hoarsely. "And yet every day you were there, driving me insane. I didn't want to remember you. But I had no choice. Awake or asleep, working or staring out the window in a blank stupor, it was you, always you."

"What do you want from me, Doc? Is this some weird man-of-honor thing about *deflowering* me? I assure you, it was no big deal."

Jacob stumbled forward, dropping his head on her shoulder, his hands caressing her arms. "It was to me," he said in a broken whisper. "I love you, Ariel."

Her fingers stroked the soft short hair at the nape of his neck, before she jerked her hands away, hardening her resolve. "Like I said before, you suck at this boyfriend thing. My mother just died and you pick now for your dramatic speech?" She shoved him away and strode to the other side of the room. "It's your guilt talking, Doc. I know your kind. But you'll get over it. Don't worry."

He stalked her, determination in every muscle of his body.

"My timing sucks. I'm a jerk. I get that. And yes, this damn sure isn't anyone's version of a Hollywood happy ending. But you have to believe me, Ariel. I love you. For better or for worse. Most couples start with the better. I'm sorry, but you're stuck with me for the worst. I won't leave you. Not today."

Everything inside her ached for him. She wanted to fling herself into his embrace and sob out her grief and desolation. But she was all alone in the world now. She had to protect herself. "It's your choice. We head out for the funeral home at five o'clock. I'll be in my room resting."

Jacob had expected some resistance from Ariel. But not outright hostility and the cold shoulder. He had hurt her terribly. And now her mother was gone. For once in his life there was no clear path, no road to follow. All he knew was that Ariel was his heart, his soul, his only reason for being. And as long as he had breath in his body, he would protect her.

She emerged from her room at ten before five, perfectly turned out in a Chanel-style black suit and heels. Her hair was caught up in a smooth chignon. Sheer black hosiery showcased her fabulous legs. A small, stylish hat in black linen perched at the back of her head.

In her hands she held a black leather clutch and enormous black sunglasses. She was beautiful and remote.

Skillful makeup had erased evidence of her tears. Movie star Ariel Dane was ready.

He grabbed his suit jacket and followed her outside. The studio had sent a limo in addition to the enormous bouquet of flowers that took up half of Ariel's dining room table.

She slid into the car and ignored him for forty-five minutes as they drove. He kept his silence, unwilling to do anything to upset her at this moment.

The parlor at the funeral home was filled with friends and acquaintances of Ariel and her mother. Ariel seemed taken aback at the turnout. She really had no clue how many people genuinely cared about her.

The two hours of visitation seemed endless. Jacob stayed at Ariel's elbow through it all, abandoning her only now and then to bring her a glass of water. Never once did she introduce him to anyone. He might as well have been invisible. Though some people stared at him curiously, he smiled as necessary and kept his vigil.

Seeing Ariel so proud, so young, so dignified in her grief brought more than one person to tears. But Ariel had shed her tears in private. Now she performed her role with touching grace.

When the funeral home staff signaled the need to adjourn to the chapel, Jacob felt Ariel inhale a sharp breath. He put a hand at the small of her back. "You can do this, princess. I'm proud of you."

Together they walked to the family pew and were seated. No casket or urn graced the front of the room. Mrs. Dane had been clear in her wishes.

Moments later, the service began. A world-renowned female recording artist sang a beautiful song with lyrics about partings and hope for the future. An unassuming minister spoke kind words about a woman who had faced hardship in her life but rose above it to be a good mother to her only child.

At last, only one song remained. The room was hushed, hundreds of mourners lining the aisles and spilling out into the hallway at the rear. The soloist completed her final verse, and sat down. The lights dimmed. As a screen lowered from the ceiling, Mrs. Dane's smiling face appeared.

Jacob felt Ariel's hand reach for his. He gripped it tightly, sliding an arm around her narrow shoulders and pulling her close.

Mrs. Dane spoke to the crowd.

"Many of you in this room live in a world of make-believe. You weave stories and tell tales and entertain us all. Sadly, real life is not so easily manipulated. All of us face moments of pain and loss.

"I have never asked the question 'why me?' My life has been graced with so many blessings, not the least of which is my dearest daughter, Ariel. I love you, my angel.

"To all of you I leave this one great lesson I have learned. Family is everything. And though families come in different shapes and sizes, the important thing is that we cling to those we love. Life's measure is never certain. Don't let bitterness and envy and past hurts define who you are. Live. Be free. Love.

"Don't grieve for me today. But instead, hold those who are important to you close to your heart and be glad."

The screen went blank.

Ariel got to her feet. Perhaps only Jacob was close enough to witness her unsteadiness. "Thank you for coming," she said, her usual sunny smile dimmed but functional. "It means a lot to me. Good night."

Leaning her head toward Jacob's, she whispered urgently, "Get me out of here…please."

At the front of the chapel, a doorway led to a private hall. As they walked rapidly, Jacob sent a quick text to the driver who met them at the back entrance.

One of the funeral home employees intercepted them, his sober face worried. "Everything okay?"

Ariel lifted her head like a wilted flower struggling to stay erect on a broken stem. "I appreciate all you did. The service was wonderful. Thank you."

She swayed on her feet, her face ashen. Jacob hurriedly tucked her into the car and instructed the driver. With the privacy shield in place, Jacob gathered her into his arms. "It's over, princess. You did well."

The tears came then, great choking sobs that seemed almost to tear her slight frame asunder. Jacob held her tightly, his own eyes damp. For a third time in his life, he was helpless to protect someone he loved. The inability to do so was humbling for a man who had been known to work miracles in the lab.

He smoothed his hand over her back repeatedly, murmuring words to comfort her. At long last, the storm abated. One of her hands curled against his lapel.

"I got snot on your Italian wool suit," she said, her voice shaky.

Stunned laughter burst from his throat. "Good Lord, Ariel. That's the least of our worries." He paused, unsure of how to please her. "Do you want to go to bed when you get home? Would you rather eat something? Tell me what you need."

She wiped a hand across her cheek, smearing mascara. "Take me to the beach. In my car. I want to see the ocean."

When the driver dropped them off in front of Ariel's door, Jacob helped her out of the vehicle. "You should go in and change," he said. "It will be cold."

Shaking her head, she pulled keys from her purse and handed them to him. "Just drive."

The car in the garage shouldn't have surprised him. It was a VW Beetle, sunshine yellow with a vanity tag that read *Mermaid*. He folded his lanky frame behind the wheel and backed out. "Tell me where to go."

They weren't far from the shore. Ariel directed him in a quiet voice. When they parked in the driveway of a darkened house, Ariel got out. "This cottage belongs to a friend of mine. He's traveling in Europe, so I've been checking on things for him."

Jacob thought she meant for them to go inside, but instead, she headed down the path to the beach, cutting between houses that were no more than darkened hulks in the night. There was no moon at all.

She kicked off her heels. Jacob bent to pick them up and tucked them in his jacket pockets. "Where are you going?"

His only answer was the screech of a gull. Ariel made a bee-line for the water, her feet still clad in nylons. She was a tiny, solitary figure framed by the immensity of the sea.

For one heart-stopping moment he thought she intended to

walk straight into the waves. And then he knew better. Ariel Dane was no coward.

She stopped when her toes were at the very edge of the surf. The water had to be icy, but she didn't flinch when rivulets of phosphorescent foam danced around her ankles.

Kicking off his own shoes and socks, he joined her. They stood, shoulder to shoulder, staring out at the horizon, a barely perceptible line where the steel gray of the ocean met the inky dark of the sky.

Ariel sighed. "Do you know why I like to come here?"

"No. Tell me."

"It reminds me that I'm insignificant in the grand scheme of things. The world would spin with or without me. That is comforting in an odd sort of way."

He took her shoulders, forcing her to face him. "You're wrong," he said hoarsely. "Without you, my world would stop."

"Is that a line from some low-budget movie? You're no actor, Doc. Leave the drama to the professionals."

That he was responsible for her sarcasm made him ashamed. "I'm sorry I left you in Antigua. I was scared."

She sniffed, huddling into her jacket. "You're a Wolff. You scare other people, not the other way around."

"You terrify me," he said bluntly.

"How?"

"I've searched for happiness my whole life and only been able to catch glimpses of it here and there. In you, I see the whole picture. Beginning and end. Eternity. But the knowledge that you can walk away is unbearable."

Twenty-Three

Ariel threw her pain in his face. "I heard you tell my mother you don't love me. So it's a little tough to buy into this whole devoted suitor business." Hurt, long since stuffed into a dark little box, escaped and spread through her body, reminding her that she was vulnerable to the Wolff.

"Oh my God."

"Exactly." She twisted away, almost stumbling in the damp sand. Humiliation scored her skin, leaving her raw and exposed.

Jacob stood, silent and strong, his face unreadable. "I was fighting my demons at that point," he said slowly. "And lying to myself in the process."

"Because you were still in love with Diane."

"No. Not that. I adored her. I can't deny it. But it was a young man's infatuation."

"And you're so ancient now?"

He caught a wisp of her hair and tucked it behind her ear. The brush of his fingers was fleeting. "I love you, Ariel. It took me too long to realize it, and I hurt you in the process. I'm sorry."

Her fingers itched with the need to reach out to him. Her emotions were all over the map. And she was afraid to be wrong. If he was coming to her out of some misguided sense of responsibility, she wouldn't be able to bear it.

"You were right before," she said slowly. "Our worlds don't intersect."

"I've thought about that," he said. "I'll move here. Where your work is. And I can travel with you."

Her heartbeat sped up in lurching thuds. "What are you saying?"

He went down on one knee, no doubt finishing off the damage to his suit. "Marry me, princess. I can't live without you. I don't want to."

In his hand was a small jewelry box. He flipped open the lid, and fire shot from the contents—an obscenely large solitaire set in a platinum band.

She inhaled a shocked breath. "Holy cow, Doc. Please tell me that's cubic zirconia."

Lifting the ring free, he took her hand. "Ariel Dane, will you be my wife?"

Her heart contracted painfully. The Wolff had humbled himself completely, offering to give up his home, his way of life, his pride. To win her.

She thrust out her left hand, joy zinging wildly throughout her body. "Keep talking. And stand up, damn it."

For a large man, he was graceful, with the sleek power of his namesake. He took her cold fingers in his warm grasp and slid the ring onto her fourth finger. "Wolves mate for life, Ariel. You know that, right?"

She blinked rapidly. She wasn't going to cry. Not about this. "I've heard that, yes. Are you sure you really want me, Jacob? I won't let you change your mind. It will be in the prenup somewhere. You're stuck with me forever."

He lowered his head and brushed a kiss across her lips. "I adore you, Ariel. Is that an acceptance speech?"

"Take me home to bed. Quick."

They ran like children, Ariel's muffled laughter the sweetest thing Jacob had ever heard. In the car, they held hands. The trip was too long for his liking, but his patience was limitless now that she wore his ring.

In Ariel's foyer, they faced each other. "I don't want sand all over the house," she said with a small, familiar grin. "We should undress here."

Jacob encountered his first real test as a husband-to-be. "Um, well… You go first and get in the shower." If he saw her naked, all bets were off.

She took his hand, her dear face earnest. "I need you tonight, Jacob. And not in some platonic, asexual way. Show me what you feel." The ragged edge in her low, coaxing voice slid down his spine and under his skin.

"You're not thinking straight," he said. "I can't take advantage of you at a time like this. Consider my proposal. We'll talk in the morning."

Her chin lifted, quivering only slightly. "I'm sad," she said quietly. "And I'll be sad for a long time. But when you're with me, I feel hopeful, I feel alive. Don't make me sleep alone."

When a woman strips naked, a man has two choices. He can run from temptation, or he can take what is offered. Jacob was tired of running.

Unable to touch her just yet, he shed his clothes rapidly. His shaft, thick and heavy, rose hard against his belly. When he was completely undressed, he picked her up in his arms and carried her to her bedroom and on into the bathroom beyond.

With one hand, he adjusted the water carefully and deposited her, standing, on the cold marble floor. Ariel reached to remove the pins from her hair. "Let me," he said, his hands shaking.

The sunlit gold darkened to honey as water soaked the

strands that tumbled over his hands. Drops of liquid clung to her raspberry-colored nipples. The steam warmed her skin to a healthy pink.

Ariel stood docile beneath his touch, eyes open, watching him with an azure gaze that still held remnants of uncertainty.

He took the soap and washed her, holding his own need at bay. His hands soaped her slim arms, narrow waist, long legs that went on forever. His princess, his mermaid, his Ariel.

When she touched him, it shocked him out of his reverie.

She laughed. "I love the gentle side of you, my Wolff. But I won't break. Make love to me."

Her firm caress on his sex blurred his vision. His hips flexed of their own volition, pressing into her hand eagerly.

"Whatever my mermaid wants."

Shutting off the water, he nudged her out of the shower enclosure and dried them both. Ariel nestled against his chest. "I love you, Jacob Wolff."

The words struck deep at a wound he'd thought would never heal. Both pain and penance slid into his heart and staked a claim, mending years of raw suffering. "And?"

"And yes, I will marry you."

Exultant, he carried her again, this time to the king-size bed through the doorway. The covers were tumbled from her earlier nap. Laying her down gently, he came down beside her.

Ariel rolled on top of him, dragging his wrists over his head and trapping them with hers. "You're mine now, Wolff."

She straddled his waist and lowered herself onto his erection with a downward thrust that made them both cry out. He gripped her hips, shuddering as her sinuous ride unmanned him. "Always," he groaned. "God, Ariel…"

Reaching between her legs, he stroked her intimately.

They reached the peak together, her passage squeezing him with little flutters that made the top of his head explode.

The end lasted forever, radiating endlessly in ripples of release.

Ariel kissed him, her hands braced on his shoulders. "I want to live with you on your mountain," she said, her gaze watchful. "I can do one movie a year, but I think I want to earn my degree. What do you think about that?"

Still half erect inside her, he struggled for coherence. "I won't stand in the way of your success. It wouldn't be fair to you or to the world."

"I'm a great multi-tasker, Doc. You wait and see. And what about babies?"

"Babies?"

"You know. Those little things that scream and poop?"

He grinned, bone-deep contentment wrapping him in a haze of wonderment. "I could be persuaded."

Ariel sighed. "This will be my best role ever—mate to the Wolff."

He flipped them with a neat maneuver that put Ariel right where he wanted her. "I like the sound of that, my darling diva. Now hush and let's rehearse that last scene. I think we can do better."

Eighteen months later...

Jacob Wolff stood on the red carpet, rigged out in an Armani tux, surrounded by photographers. At his side stood his wife, luminous in a backless ball gown of cotton-candy pink. The skirts poofed out in true princess-worthy fashion.

During a brief lull, he whispered in her ear. "Are you nervous?"

She tucked her hand into his, reaching up to kiss him square on the mouth despite the crowd of onlookers. "About the award?"

The best actress nomination had been no surprise to anyone but Ariel.

"Yeah," he said, shaking his head in bemusement. She was the belle of the ball, and she was his.

"It's an honor to be nominated, Doc," she said with her trademark sass.

Snorting at her exaggerated theatrical accent, he led her a few steps down the runway. "You're a brat."

"You're a bully."

They exchanged smiles, in perfect accord.

And for once, the following morning, the tabloids printed the unadorned truth—*Hollywood Princess Finds Her Happily Ever After.*

* * * * *

MILLS & BOON

MODERN

Power and Passion

Prepare to be swept off your feet by sophisticated, sexy and seductive heroes, in some of the world's most glamourous and romantic locations, where power and passion collide.

MILLS & BOON

Desire

Indulge in secrets and scandal, intense drama and plenty of sizzling hot action with powerful and passionate heroes who have it all: wealth, status, good looks… everything but the right woman.

JOIN US ON SOCIAL MEDIA!

Stay up to date with our latest releases, author
news and gossip, special offers and discounts, and
all the behind-the-scenes action
from Mills & Boon...

 millsandboon

 millsandboonuk

 millsandboon

It might just be true love...